HIDDEN IN LIES

ALSO BY VIVECA STEN

Still Waters

Closed Circles

Guiltless

Tonight You're Dead

In the Heat of the Moment

In Harm's Way

In the Shadow of Power

In the Name of Truth

In Bad Company

Buried in Secret

The Åre Murders

Hidden in Snow

Hidden in Shadows

Hidden in Memories

HIDDEN IN LIES

TRANSLATED BY MARLAINE DELARGY

VIVECA STEN

This is a work of fiction. Names, characters, organizations, places, events, and incidents are either products of the author's imagination or are used fictitiously. Any resemblance to actual persons, living or dead, or actual events is purely coincidental.

Previously published as *Vilseledaren* by Bokförlaget Forum in Sweden in 2023. Translated from Swedish by Marlaine Delargy. First published in English by Amazon Crossing in 2026.

Published by Amazon Crossing, Seattle

www.apub.com

EU product safety contact:
Amazon Media EU S. à r.l.
38, avenue John F. Kennedy, L-1855 Luxembourg
amazonpublishing-gpsr@amazon.com

ISBN-13: 9781662529832 (paperback)
ISBN-13: 9781662529849 (digital)

Cover design by Ploy Siripant
Cover image: © Maridav / Shutterstock; © Travelpix / Stocksy

Printed in the United States of America

To Lennart
For better or worse

PROLOGUE

The Åre valley is trapped in the depths of the winter chill.

It is so cold that the air is crackling, and the temperature has dropped to minus twenty-five degrees Celsius. The wide slopes are empty and deserted, even the flashing yellow lights of the snow groomers have disappeared. They have completed their work for today.

Everyone is sleeping in the January night.

The body is lying outside the luxurious timber house, high up in the area known as Sadeln.

One cheek is resting on the snow; the eyes are closed against eternity.

Thick clouds hide the stars. The sky is black. The building seems to melt into the darkness, and the faint illumination from the external lighting spreads a ghostly glow over the outside area.

Enough to see, but not be seen.

A few snowflakes drift down from the sky and settle on the frozen face.

Everything is still.

FRIDAY

1

The atmosphere at the station in Uppsala is buzzing as Filippa Smedsås hurries through the crowds to catch the night train to Åre. Her best friend, Olivia Hallin, is right behind her. Filippa's light-brown hair falls forward as she groans, thanks to the bulky ski bag she is carrying over her shoulder. Both she and Olivia are each burdened with a heavy suitcase as well. The amount of stuff needed for a week in the mountains is ridiculous, although Filippa has tried to pack as little as possible.

It is after eleven; the train is due to leave in only five minutes. Olivia was late, which is typical of her, but Filippa is used to that by this stage. She rarely gets mad at her best friend.

"The guys are over there," Olivia informs her breathlessly.

Filippa looks up. Farther down the platform she sees Olivia's four fellow students from the economics program, who are also on the trip.

At the front is William Löwengren. As always he is standing with his legs apart, gesticulating eagerly and convincingly. Nothing affects William's self-confidence, which is something Filippa envies about him. That's probably why he and Olivia are drawn to each other. There is a special aura about both of them, they invariably end up in the center of things and are used to attention.

Next to William, Amir is moving his feet up and down impatiently. He runs his fingers through his dark-brown hair, grins when William says something the girls can't hear above the general noise. There is no mistaking the admiration in Amir's gaze.

Filippa wishes that Amir would look at *her* like that. Something happens to her body when she sees his smile. She can't stop staring at his intense brown eyes.

She has been trying to capture Amir's interest for months, often when she has been in a bar with Olivia, but he barely seems to be aware of her existence. She hopes that will change in Åre.

Anticipation bubbles up inside her as she tightens her grip on her suitcase. She is studying political science and doesn't know the boys as well as Olivia does. She should really be working this week, but she couldn't resist it when Olivia kept talking about all the fun they would have. Plus they have free accommodation in William's parents' house.

And Amir will be there.

She glances at him again, feels a tingle in her breasts. He is *so* good looking. Maybe a week together in the mountains will make him realize how she feels about him?

Pontus spots them and waves.

"Hi—we were starting to wonder if you were going to miss the train," he says in his broad Skåne accent. A bottle is sticking up out of his jacket pocket. Pontus seems to have started partying already, even though they haven't left Uppsala yet.

"This is going to be amazing!" Olivia shouts, flinging her arms around William's neck just as the Åre train arrives from Stockholm. Filippa greets the others—including Emil, who is standing a few yards away talking on his phone. He is from Umeå in the north, and is the only one who doesn't think Uppsala is cold in the winter. He ends his call and puts the phone away as the doors open with a hiss.

Filippa finds herself at the back of the people pushing to embark. She tries to locate Olivia, but her friend seems to have boarded already, so Filippa joins the crush, smiling broadly.

They have booked their own sleeping compartment with six beds. In just over nine hours, they will be in Åre.

2

The world spread below the aircraft is white and flat as Detective Inspector Hanna Ahlander peers out of the window. In the distance she can make out dots of light, suggesting that they are approaching a town, but she can't work out which one. It is almost seven o'clock in the evening, and they are heading north.

"Where are we going?" she asks for the third time, turning to Henry Sylvester, who is sitting opposite her in the cream leather armchair.

He shakes his head, managing to look both mysterious and pleased with himself.

"I've told you—it's a surprise."

He raises his champagne glass in a toast as the flight attendant comes over to offer a refill.

Hanna doesn't know what to think. When Henry said he wanted to come up with a fun way of celebrating her thirty-seventh birthday, she had imagined a night of luxury at one of Åre's hotels, as he had told her to pack an overnight bag. The fact that they drove to Moland airfield outside Järpen, where a plane was waiting for them, left her speechless. She usually tries not to think about the fact that Henry is an extremely successful financier, since his immense fortune stresses her out. Today however, traveling by private plane for the first time in her life, she can't ignore it.

She tells herself to stop brooding, enjoy the moment.

She raises her crystal glass and toasts her companion. In the soft glow of the cabin lighting, he is strikingly attractive. Intelligence shines from his deep-set eyes; his sharp profile conveys strength and inspires trust.

She feels a tingle deep in her belly, then leans back and takes another sip, allowing the bubbles to roll slowly over her tongue. She tries to relax, let go for once, simply allow Henry to take command. The fact that he is so secure in himself is one of the things she really likes about him. He doesn't appear to be in the least bit threatened by having a detective inspector as his girlfriend.

This is the first time she has experienced a relationship like this, and she is enjoying not having to tone down either herself or her professional role. Which is something she has had to do many times with other guys.

A voice comes over the loudspeaker system.

"We are approaching our destination and expect to land in Kiruna in fifteen minutes."

Hanna looks up. *Kiruna?*

She glances at Henry, who is still wearing his secretive expression. What has he come up with? Could they be on the way to the Ice Hotel in Jukkasjärvi? Hanna has only heard about the famous venue, which is rebuilt every year with ice from the River Törne. A stay there is out of reach for someone on a police salary.

"Are we going to the Ice Hotel?" she ventures in an attempt to wheedle information out of him.

"Nope."

"Oh, come on—give me a clue!"

Henry shakes his head, and Hanna can see how much he is enjoying keeping her on tenterhooks.

"You're like a curious child," he says. "Have you never been told that patience is a virtue?"

Hanna wrinkles her nose. “It’s not my style.”

Henry spreads his hands wide, pretending to give up on her. “I ought to know that by now.”

When Hanna looks at Henry, it still surprises her that they have gotten together. He is a billionaire who mingles comfortably with the elite in both Stockholm and Saint-Tropez. She is an ordinary cop who works in a rural community, with a salary that has usually been spent by the time the next paycheck arrives.

Technically they have been dating for around eight months, although Hanna hasn’t told anyone. Not even her sister, Lydia, who is ten years older and the person Hanna relies on most in the entire world.

Henry wants to show her off, but she is doing her best to keep the relationship secret.

Nor has Hanna said a single word to Daniel, her closest colleague. He has really struggled over the past year, since separating from his partner, Ida. His new life is anything but straightforward, as Hanna has learned from their frequent chats as they travel between Åre and Östersund, where the Serious Crimes Unit to which they are both attached is located.

Informing Daniel that she was seeing someone new would have been tactless—at least that’s what she tells herself.

Nor does Daniel know how she felt about him before she started going out with Henry.

Hanna rests her forehead on the cool glass of the window to chase her complicated thoughts away. Why is she thinking about this when they’re off on a dream vacation? She ought to focus on Henry, who has gone to all this trouble, instead of getting entangled in old crap like her unrequited feelings for a colleague.

Henry’s voice brings her back to reality.

“Okay, one little clue,” he says, emptying his glass. “When we land in Kiruna, a helicopter will be waiting for us.”

Hanna frowns.

A helicopter?

As far as she knows, it isn't very far from Kiruna to Jukkasjärvi, it would hardly be worth flying there by helicopter from the airport, bearing in mind what it would cost. And in any case surely you're not allowed to fly in the dark without special permission?

Then again, with Henry you never know. Nothing is impossible for him.

The rich are different, she once read. Indeed they are. She has definitely learned that since they started seeing each other. It's not that Henry is trying to impress her. He's not the kind of person who throws his money around or behaves arrogantly just because he is phenomenally rich.

In fact he has already made it clear that most of his fortune will go to a foundation when he dies, rather than to his three sons.

But there is something else that comes with having unlimited resources—as if it gives him a kind of armor. No one can get to him, and he has unlimited freedom to do whatever he wants.

How does it affect a person when they never have to think about what things cost? It is a position that separates Henry from ninety-nine percent of humanity, and Hanna has often wondered whether she should envy him or loathe him for it.

Purely on principle she doesn't believe that anyone should have that kind of income; it is neither healthy nor fair. The thought of what she and her colleagues earn also drives her crazy, given that they risk their lives in the line of duty.

However, it's hardly Henry's fault that society doesn't reward its police officers according to what they deserve.

He leans forward, gently caresses her cheek. The smell of his fragrance fills her nostrils, a seductive blend of cedarwood and bergamot with a base note of vetiver, which has an immediate effect on her.

"You're going to love it," he says softly. "But you need to relax. Trust me."

Trust is not her strong point, especially as her former partner cheated on her for months before dumping her, but Hanna decides that Henry is right.

For once she is going to give herself permission to be taken care of.

Tomorrow is her birthday.

3

Detective Inspector Daniel Lindskog is wandering around the apartment, picking up Alice's brightly colored toys. Yesterday he collected his daughter from Ida after work, and she will be spending the weekend with him. Then Ida will have her for two days before it is his turn again.

It's called the two-two-three system.

Two days with Mom, two days with Dad, then Friday, Saturday, Sunday with Mom. Then they swap. Next weekend it will be Ida's turn to have Alice, as Daniel has her this time.

It was Ida who suggested the arrangement, because Alice is so little, about two and a half. It felt too difficult to change over every other week, she argued. She couldn't bear the thought of not seeing her daughter for such a long time.

Daniel didn't have the strength to protest, even though deep down he finds it awkward. Alice gets used to being with him, and then she has to go back to Ida. In addition, Ida often wants to make a change at the last minute or keep Alice for an extra day. Everyday life is less stable, and things are trickier for Daniel to plan at work.

The agreement with his boss, Chief Inspector Birgitta Grip, who is head of the Serious Crimes Unit in Östersund, is that he must work from there at least a couple of days a week, even though he lives in Åre.

He creeps into Alice's room and places the last of the toys in the blue plastic crate by the wall. She is fast asleep, lying on her back, cuddling her favorite soft toy. It is a pale-brown reindeer with kind eyes and soft horns, and its name is, not surprisingly, Reindeer.

He stands by her bed for a moment, inhaling the scent of baby shampoo, a faint hint of freshly picked green apples that makes him think of sunny days and outings to swim in Lake Ottsjön, with its wonderful sandy shore.

Alice's cheeks are rosy, her little hands outstretched, those tiny, perfect fingers. He would really like to pick her up and carry her to his bed just to be close to her, but he doesn't want to disturb her when she is so peaceful.

His daughter is almost the same age as he was when his own father abandoned him and his mother, Francesca. When Alice was born he promised himself that she would have a completely different childhood, secure and full of love, with a daddy who was present and who would always be there for her.

Daniel has dreamed of a family of his own throughout his whole life, and yet he couldn't make things work with Ida, despite his good intentions.

Alice was just twenty months old when his partner left him.

I don't know if I'm still in love with you.

He remembers the exact words as Ida delivered the fatal blow to their relationship, her voice thick with tears.

It was Easter Monday last year. They were sitting at the kitchen table, and he had just finished an unusually taxing investigation that had begun with a fatal stabbing at Copperhill Mountain Lodge, the famous designer hotel in Förberget, to the east of Åre.

Her timing couldn't have been worse. Daniel was completely exhausted, and had found it difficult to make sense of what she was saying. He had simply stared at Ida's tear-filled eyes, couldn't work out what she meant, even though her words left no room for doubt.

The very next day she went to stay with her mother in Järpen, and never came back. After only a few months she had moved in with Gustav, her new boyfriend, who is a skiing guide and an old friend from the days when she worked for SkiStar.

Even though almost ten months have passed since then, Daniel is still having problems coming to terms with Ida's decision. From a purely intellectual point of view, he knows they're over, yet he still lies awake at night, brooding over the situation.

Why she chose to leave him.

Why it hadn't worked between them, when this was what he had longed for through so many years.

He was prepared to do anything to avoid a separation. He had been seeing a counselor for over a year in order to become a better father and partner, so he had suggested couples therapy.

It took a while for him to realize that Ida simply . . . didn't want to.

She didn't want to be with him anymore.

Sometimes that feels like the greatest betrayal—the fact that Ida wasn't prepared to fight for their family, that she was ready to throw away everything they had built up together.

That it meant nothing to her.

Alice's coverlet has slipped down. Daniel gently pulls up the duvet adorned with teddy bears, watching her little chest rise and fall with her steady breathing.

He is still living in the same apartment within walking distance of the police station, having bought out Ida at a generous price to avoid any argument. It was a solution that suited both of them, because she made it very clear that she wanted to make a fresh start and find somewhere else to live.

With Gustav.

Daniel sighs wearily and leaves Alice's room. Life was turned upside down less than a year ago, and he still can't really explain what happened.

4

Filippa tries to swallow the feeling of nausea. The air in the compartment is warm and stuffy, and the corner of the sofa where she is sitting by the window smells quite unpleasant. She has drunk considerably more than she should have done, and feels dizzy.

Amir has barely glanced in her direction since they left Uppsala. All his attention is fixed on William, who, in turn, is mainly focused on Olivia.

They have just passed through Gävle, and there are already two empty vodka bottles in the trash can. They are all clutching plastic glasses, the noise level is high, and Ed Sheeran is belting out his latest hit from a speaker Amir brought with him.

A while ago someone banged on the wall; then the conductor came and asked them to turn it down. However, as soon as he had gone, Amir turned up the volume again.

Filippa looks out through the dirty window.

The winter cold has settled over the whole country. According to the forecast it is supposed to be well below zero all week in Åre. The dark landscape whizzes by, snow-covered fir trees and white fields following on from one another.

Sweden is sleeping.

William leans forward and holds up a little plastic bag of white powder.

"Want some?"

Filippa shakes her head, tries to smile at the same time. She doesn't like drugs; she's afraid of losing control. And she's tired; it's been a very stressful week, with a complicated assignment on political theory.

She would really like to lie down in the hope that the nausea will pass, but no one else seems particularly keen on breaking things up, and she doesn't want to come across as a party pooper. She will also need help to unfold the top bunk if she is going to lie down.

Opposite her, Olivia is leaning on William's shoulder as she gulps her pink concoction, which is made up of equal parts vodka and lingonberry juice. It goes down the wrong way, and she splutters, spraying the drink in all directions.

"For fuck's sake!" shouts Amir—most of it went in his face.

Olivia simply rolls her eyes and laughs at his pink-spattered cheeks. She is in top form; it doesn't look as if she turned down William's offer of coke, and she tosses her black shoulder-length hair before taking another slug.

As usual Olivia has no problem keeping going all night. In that way she and Filippa are very different, even though they have been best friends since high school and went to Uppsala together, where they live in the same student corridor.

Olivia staggers off to the toilet. Filippa would really like to lie down for a while. She yawns, and out of the corner of her eye, she sees Pontus react.

"Are we so fucking boring?" he says loudly. The comment is clearly aimed at Filippa.

He could have kept his tone lighthearted, but the question suggests that he is annoyed. As if he is taking it personally that she isn't partying as hard as everyone else.

It was Pontus who sorted the booze; he made that very clear as soon as they boarded the train. By this stage he is pretty drunk, they all are, but Pontus is slurring his words a lot more than anyone else. Plus his gaze is unfocused, his forehead is beaded with sweat, and there are big damp patches under the arms of his shirt.

He rummages around in his bag and produces a fresh bottle of Explorer, which he holds out to Filippa, almost like a trophy.

She shakes her head; she can't face one more sip.

"Fussy, aren't you?" Pontus says, loud enough for everyone to hear. "Not happy with the selection on offer?"

"I just don't want any."

She swallows, gives Pontus a hard stare. Surely they don't need to fall out over this. But Pontus won't give in. He stands up, still clutching the bottle, and leans over Filippa. He is way too close; she can smell his sweaty armpits.

"Give me your glass, and I'll fill it up."

It sounds like an order.

"I don't want any."

Suddenly she feels as if everyone is staring at her, which makes her go red. Fucking Pontus. Which part of "I don't want any" doesn't he get?

"Of course you do," he slurs.

He reaches out and tries to take her glass, but she refuses to let go.

"Leave me alone!"

Amir, who has been absorbed in his phone, glances in their direction. Filippa wishes he would put down the phone and tell Pontus to stop.

Why doesn't he do something?

Pontus keeps tugging at her glass until Emil intervenes.

"Leave her alone. She told you she doesn't want any."

Emil tugs at Pontus's sweater, almost making him overbalance, but at least he sits down again. He mumbles something unintelligible, opens the new bottle, and takes such a huge swig that the clear liquid runs down his cheeks.

Filippa tries to give Emil a grateful smile, but it ends up as more of a grimace. She would like to say something about Pontus's behavior, point out what an idiot he is, but she is afraid that he will hear and kick off again.

"If you want to go to bed, I can help you with the top bunk," Emil offers.

Filippa nods, and Emil unfolds the bunk with a few skillful movements. He pulls down the ladder and helps her to climb up so that she can stretch out. When she is settled with a blanket over her, he remains standing on the ladder just by her pillow.

Emil is so nice, Filippa thinks tipsily. It's only Pontus who is hard work.

Their faces are just inches apart; she can feel Emil's breath on her cheek.

"Sleep well," he says, disappearing from view as he jumps down onto the floor.

Amir laughs at a comment from William. Filippa feels a stab of pain; he hasn't really spoken to her since they left Uppsala. She rolls over onto her other side, facing the wall, and consoles herself with the thought that she has a whole week to capture his interest.

In Åre.

5

The sky is filled with billowing waves of intense green and violet shades that almost take Hanna's breath away. The helicopter is flying between steep snow-covered mountains, surrounded by the northern lights.

It looks as if God himself has used a broad brush to color the pitch-black polar night.

Aurora borealis.

It is indescribably beautiful, with thick emerald stripes moving back and forth across the sky.

"Wow," Hanna says into the microphone. They were given headsets to enable them to communicate in spite of the engine noise. "I've never seen anything like it."

"Amazing, isn't it?" Henry reaches out to squeeze her hand. He is in the back seat, wanted her to sit beside the pilot so she could enjoy the best view. It is the first time she has been in a helicopter for pleasure; previous outings have all been work related, and on those occasions she didn't really have time to admire her surroundings.

"We're almost there," the pilot informs them.

Hanna doesn't want it to be over. She could sit here for hours, continue into eternity in this world of snow and ice.

Everything is close by and far away at the same time.

She has the urge to open the thick side window, stretch out her hand, and touch the bright colors. If she looks down for just a second, new extraordinary patterns immediately form in a never-ending, glowing dance.

They have been flying for approximately forty minutes and must be close to the Norwegian border. It is impossible to imagine that there could be a hotel out here in the wilderness.

At that moment the pilot swings to the left.

"There," Henry says, pointing ahead.

Dots of light quickly grow in size. As the helicopter comes in to land, Hanna sees burning torches and glowing firepits. A brown wooden building, surrounded by a semicircular stone wall, emerges from the shadows. There are several smaller buildings gathered behind the large one, as if they have huddled together for protection against the polar chill.

No one can survive out here without warmth and company.

"Where are we?" she asks as the helicopter gradually drops down in front of the main building. They land with a small thud, and the intense sound of the rotors fades to a quiet whisper.

"Welcome to Niehku Mountain Villa," Henry says with a smile. "This is where we're going to celebrate your birthday."

6

It is dark and quiet in the compartment when Filippa wakes. She is groggy, no doubt still drunk, and can't see a thing in the dense gloom. All she can hear is heavy breathing from her sleeping companions, and the regular clunk of the metal rails as the train races through the night.

Something is wrong.

She is lying on her back and doesn't have room to move. The back of her head is touching the wall, and she feels trapped.

Why is it so cramped?

The realization hits her in a second, and her whole body goes ice cold. She is not alone in the bunk. An unfamiliar smell reaches her nostrils, a mixture of alcohol and sweat.

It is way too close.

It is suffocating her.

Then she becomes aware of the hands groping their way around her body. Fingers fumble over her collarbone and breasts, try to find their way beneath the T-shirt she sleeps in.

One hand finds the zip of her jeans and slips inside the fabric. Someone is breathing heavily in her ear, pressing their body against her chest with such force that she can hardly breathe.

Filippa tries to orient herself, but everything is spinning around. Her arms are under the blanket, and she can't free them in order to defend herself. She knows she ought to scream, but the fear is paralyzing. She can't remember how to do it; she simply lies there hating herself for being so passive.

When she eventually manages to open her mouth, not a sound emerges. It is as if her tongue is refusing to cooperate.

Is she going to be raped here, among her friends, on the way to Åre?

Is this even happening?

The dizziness takes over, and she closes her eyes.

A sound comes from one of the bottom bunks. There is a rustling noise, and a deep voice mumbles sleepily, "What are you doing?"

The weight instantly disappears. Filippa can move again. Everything is back to normal.

There is a thud, as if the person has jumped down and landed on the floor. Filippa stares into the darkness.

Was there really someone there, or was she just dreaming?

The only sound is the rhythmic clunk of the metal rails.

And Filippa drops off to sleep again.

SATURDAY

7

When the cab pulls up outside William's parents' house in Sadeln, Filippa catches her breath. A huge pink timber structure looms in front of her. It takes up almost the entire plot of land, and the front, with a wide balcony, is supported by sturdy wooden poles above a steep slope.

It is not exactly a little mountain cottage, which was how Olivia described it when she asked if Filippa would like to come along. The view over the Åre valley is like something out of a movie, as if Disney had shown up with a whole bunch of amazing winter backdrops.

The sun is so bright that Filippa has to shade her eyes with her hand, but the beautiful weather does nothing to dispel the unpleasant sensation left by the train journey.

When she woke up this morning, just over half an hour before they arrived in Åre, she started shaking before she even realized why she felt so uncomfortable.

Then she remembered the night, those fingers groping their way around her body.

Had it actually happened, or was it just a bad dream?

Filippa isn't sure, and that makes her both anxious and nervous. She glances over her shoulder; if someone really did try it on with her, then she doesn't want to stay. But what if it was all in her mind? A fantasy that her brain came up with when the vodka fog took over?

She can't accuse the others if nothing happened, plus she doesn't know who was touching her in the darkness.

The more she thinks about it, the less certain she is. The whole situation is so difficult. She is ashamed, both of her suspicions and the fact that she got drunk. She can't even bring herself to talk to Olivia about it, even though they are such close friends.

"Come and get your stuff," Emil shouts from behind the cab.

They unload their luggage and drag their suitcases down the short slope leading to the front door. Before they left the train station, they stopped by the ICA grocery store, so they are also weighed down with large bags of food.

One of Pontus's suitcases makes a clinking noise as he picks it up, suggesting that it is full of bottles. Yesterday evening he was boasting about how much he had bought for the trip.

He lets out a little grunt as he hauls the heavy case toward the door. Filippa glances at him out of the corner of her eye. He looks seriously hungover; his eyes are bloodshot, his lips flaky. Hardly surprising, given how much he drank on the train. No doubt that was why he was so persistent and rude.

Could he have been the one who clambered up to her bunk in the middle of the night?

If anyone did?

"How are you?" she can't help asking, in spite of his behavior the previous day.

"None of your fucking business," Pontus replies without looking at her.

Filippa stops dead. What the hell is wrong with him? She turns her back on Pontus and hurries over to join Olivia, who is standing by the entrance with William. The keypad beeps as he enters the numbers, and the door swings open.

"So," he says. "This is where we're staying."

Filippa can tell from his voice that he is enjoying the situation, showing off his fine house for the admiration of his friends.

William's parents are rolling in money, and he makes no secret of it—quite the reverse. He comes from Östermalm in Stockholm, the most expensive area in the capital, and therefore in the whole country. Just like Olivia, Filippa grew up in Västerås, to the northwest of Stockholm. Admittedly her father is a doctor and her mother is a nurse, but their lifestyle is nowhere near what William is used to.

"Wow, this is amazing!" Olivia exclaims, nudging Filippa in the side. "What a place! Have you had it for long?"

William grins. "It's not too bad," he admits. "My parents had it built a few years ago. Before that we had another place farther down the valley, but they wanted to be higher up. They like being able to look out over the mountain—you can see Renfjället from here. It's sunny up here even when the village is in shadow during the winter months."

"I could stay in this house for a very long time." Olivia laughs. "Is it okay if we don't go back until Easter?"

She gives Filippa an excited hug and pulls her into a spacious hallway that is about the same size as the rooms in their student corridor. It leads to a large living room with a double-height ceiling and huge south-facing windows.

"This is so cool," Olivia says, wide eyed.

Filippa can't stop staring. Lake Åre is spread before them, and the panoramic view stretches across the entire valley, all the way to the mountains in the west. A short distance away she sees the lift known as Sadelexpressen, which enables them to join the ski system. The track runs below the property, so all they have to do is put on their skis and set off in the morning.

Ski-in, ski-out, as William called it.

Filippa finds it all a bit much. Pontus slams the front door shut as the toilet in the guest bathroom flushes, and Emil emerges. He joins them by the window.

"Were you in there chatting on your phone?" Pontus asks with a grin, as if he had caught him doing something wrong.

Emil ignores him and turns to William. "Fantastic view."

William is beaming, as if the fact that they are standing here in front of the perfect ad for a mountain vacation is entirely down to him.

"Unbelievable," Olivia agrees.

"So there are five bedrooms and four bathrooms in the house," William explains. "So either two of us will have to share or you girls can have the guest cabin to yourselves." He points to another building about ten yards away. "It has two bedrooms, separate bathrooms, and a kitchen."

"Nice." Olivia smiles and tucks her arm through Filippa's. "A place of our own—this is like a luxury hotel!"

"Okay, come with me," William says.

The girls grab their luggage and follow him to the cabin. It is built in the same style as the main house, with wood-paneled walls and tall south-facing windows. Filippa feels a little happier once they are inside. This is much better than sharing the house with the boys.

Especially Pontus.

If only she could remember what actually happened last night . . .

8

Daniel's doorbell rings at just after nine in the morning. He isn't expecting anyone, but goes into the hallway and opens the door.

Gustav is standing there beaming, holding a plastic bag. As usual he looks fit and fresh; he is wearing black activewear, which suggests that he is off to the gym.

Daniel has never needed to doubt that Ida was searching for a completely different life from the one they shared together—he only has to look at Gustav. He is ten years younger than Daniel, works as a ski guide, and loves the outdoor life and all kinds of outdoor activities.

Daniel has never seen him look remotely stressed or tired.

Alice comes running and breaks into a big smile when she sees who it is.

"Gustav!" She holds out her arms for him to pick her up.

Daniel instinctively takes a step forward to stop her, then realizes what he is doing. Instead he stays where he is while Gustav swings Alice around and around in the air, reducing her to helpless laughter.

He puts her down and hands the bag to Daniel.

"Ida asked me to drop this off on the way to the gym. It's Alice's favorite dress. She's worn it almost every day this week."

Daniel manages a stiff little smile and takes the bag.

It was nice of Ida to send the dress; Alice has already asked about it this morning, but as always Gustav's presence puts him in a bad mood.

Why does he get to be an important person to Alice, someone she smiles at, when Daniel has to miss out on half of his daughter's life?

Gustav should have his own kids if he wants to play Daddy.

"Thanks," he says, desperate for Gustav to leave.

He honestly wishes he could be happy that Ida has met someone who is nice and cares about Alice, but it feels like a stab in the heart whenever he sees Ida and Gustav pushing Alice along in her stroller.

She's my daughter, he wants to yell at Gustav. *Stay away from her!*

Instead he just turns away and heads in a different direction.

It is equally painful every single time.

9

The air is filled with steam as Olivia steps into the generous sauna on the lower floor, with only a small hand towel wrapped around her.

William, Emil, and Pontus are already sitting on the top bench, and their eyes are immediately drawn to her breasts.

Let them look. Olivia smiles to herself. She isn't especially shy, and has nothing against skinny-dipping in the summer. She knows she has an attractive body.

William leans forward and hands her a beer; the bottle is cold and covered in condensation.

"Make some room," Olivia says, giving Amir a push. He does as he is told, and Olivia settles down. She rests her head against the wall, reveling in the heat.

Outside the wide window, the Åre valley is resting in shadow. The sun sets shortly before four, and the lifts close at three. They managed only a few hours' skiing today because they spent the morning unpacking. It was also bitterly cold, minus seventeen on the slopes and all the way down to minus twenty-three by the VM8 lift, which is one of Åre's most notorious cold spots.

It was nice to get back to the warmth of the house. Olivia has been looking forward to the sauna; she has always enjoyed allowing herself to be wrapped in the intense heat.

Maybe she has some Finnish blood in her?

The door opens again, and Filippa appears. She is wearing a red-and-white striped swimsuit and a tense expression, as if she isn't entirely comfortable with being here. Olivia gives her friend an encouraging smile and beckons her in. Filippa doesn't know the boys as well as she does, and she can be a little reserved. She has seemed kind of subdued all day, and Olivia hopes she isn't regretting her decision to come along. The idea is to have a fun week together, after all.

"Shut the door," Pontus grunts. "There's a draft."

Olivia frowns at him. Why does he have to sound so bad tempered?

"Sorry," Filippa says, quickly closing the door.

Olivia shuffles along the bench, and Filippa sinks down beside her.

"Here," Amir says, handing Filippa a beer.

"Thanks." She takes a small sip, then starts picking at the blue nail polish on her toes.

"*Skål,*" Olivia says, clinking her bottle against Filippa's with a big smile. "Don't you just love a sauna!"

She has almost finished her beer, and notices that the towel has slipped down, exposing one breast. But so what? It's not as if the others haven't seen a naked girl before.

Out of the corner of her eye, she sees Pontus react; there is something sticking up beneath the towel he has placed over his crotch. Olivia is both amused and slightly disgusted at the same time. She wouldn't let Pontus anywhere near her—no chance.

He isn't in her league—not by a long way.

"Time to roll in the snow!" William announces enthusiastically.

He leaves the sauna and opens the patio door, which leads directly outside. Then he hurls himself into the deep drifts.

"Fuck, that feels good," he shouts, challenging the other guys. "Come on, you cowards!"

Olivia follows and throws herself down beside him, gasping with shock as the snow envelops her. It is so cold it makes her teeth tingle, and the adrenaline surges through her body. In a second any hint of tiredness is gone.

William smiles appreciatively as she lies naked beside him. Pontus and Amir are racing around shrieking and laughing, without a stitch on.

Filippa is standing just inside the door, frowning as she watches the others.

"Come on, Filippa—it's amazing!" Olivia yells.

But Filippa shakes her head.

10

The sight of the naked youngsters rolling around in the snow makes Åke Carlsson scowl.

He is standing in the kitchen, staring at the spectacle that is playing out before his eyes. There is only about twenty yards between the two properties, yet they are behaving as if they were completely alone—running in and out, yelling and shrieking with no thought for anyone else.

And none of them have the sense to cover themselves up, like decent people do.

Badly brought up brats.

It is only five thirty, barely evening, yet judging by their behavior, their sense has diminished in direct proportion to the amount of alcohol they have consumed.

He feared the worst this morning when the big cab dropped them off, talking at the tops of their voices. He didn't bother going out to say hello, even though he recognized the son of the family who are his next-door neighbors.

The less he has to do with the Löwengrens the better.

Åke finishes off his drink and reaches for the gin. Irritation fizzes through his veins, and he slams the bottle down so hard on the granite countertop that a shard of glass breaks off.

He didn't move to Åre on his retirement in order to watch drunken kids. He and Karin came here because they wanted peace and quiet; they wanted to enjoy the fresh air and the magnificent scenery. After many years working in Linköping for the organization that supplies materials and services to the Swedish military, he wanted to get away from the city. When the opportunity arose thanks to government cutbacks and a generous redundancy package, he jumped at the chance.

At that time, just over fifteen years ago, few of the plots in Sadeln were occupied. He and Karin had plenty of choice among those that were for sale. They soon found somewhere in a quiet location with a fantastic view. Then one plot after another was sold, and before long there were new houses everywhere.

Only the neighboring plot remained empty, presumably because it was unusually large and expensive.

Åke actually tried to buy it on more than one occasion, mainly because he wanted to avoid having a neighbor who would block the wonderful view of the mountain known as Åreskutan, but things never quite worked out.

The owner was a greedy Norwegian. He had bought on spec, and as the market improved, he raised the price every time Åke was ready to swallow his annoyance and make an offer.

Then suddenly he had sold to some guy from Stockholm who was rolling in money, and whose architect, judging by the result, must have been blind.

Åke pours himself a generous measure of gin, then adds tonic before taking a gulp. How he has regretted not buying the plot all those years ago, even though it was overpriced at the time.

But who could have predicted the exceptional increase in the value of land in Åre? These days the price of property is approaching Stockholm levels. The pandemic made people desperate to buy a second home in the mountains.

Through the window he sees a young woman hurl herself into the snow, yelling and screaming. Her bare breasts are bouncing, admittedly it is dark outside by now, but the external lighting is bright enough for him to see her naked flesh.

There is no denying that she has a fine body, but Åke can't help feeling irritated. How can she behave so shamelessly?

Their eldest son, Peter, is visiting for a few days with the grandchildren, who are only three and five years old. Åke doesn't want them to witness this kind of drunken exhibitionism.

The girl isn't even wearing panties!

She sends the snow whirling as she rolls around on the ground. When she has finished waving her arms about, she shrieks again, then runs back inside. The boys soon follow, and silence reigns once more.

Åke snorts as he often does when he contemplates his neighbor's house. It is the ugliest in Sadeln—no competition. It has gotten on his nerves ever since the first sod was turned over.

Or to be more accurate, since the moment he saw the architect's drawings that were sent over so that he could make any comments, if he wished to do so.

"There is actually a design program that sets out the guidelines for the area," he mutters to himself. The houses are supposed to adhere to a certain style. Åke was on the board of the joint housing association during the early years, and made a point of ensuring compliance.

But what the Löwengren family built goes against every recommendation.

The color alone sends Åke's blood pressure soaring. Unlike the rest of the local buildings, which are in muted colors or treated with iron vitriol to preserve the wood, this house is . . . pink.

Who the hell comes up with the idea of building a *pink* house in the mountains?

It also diverges from the prevalent architectural style in a way that defies belief. It bears a strong resemblance to a giant cuckoo clock, something that might possibly belong in the Swiss Alps, but absolutely not in Åre.

And the cherry on top: The house is completely out of proportion, since they have made maximum use of the surface area while ignoring the appearance of the plot as a whole. Åke can't understand how they got planning permission for this eyesore. The planning officer must have suffered brain cramp when he approved the drawings—or maybe the Löwengrens have influence on the council. With the right contacts you can push anything through—Åke has been around long enough to have seen most things.

Construction began three years ago, and that was the end of his uninterrupted view of Åreskutan.

And the end of his peace of mind.

In addition, the neighboring property is so close to the boundary that they can see straight into his kitchen and living room. And vice versa.

Now the Löwengrens' son has brought his insufferable friends up here to party and carry on.

The next week is going to be unbearable.

11

Hanna leans back in the armchair and smiles at Henry. Dinner was fantastic, there is no other word for it. It consisted of a mixture of Norwegian and Swedish ingredients, fish to start and then fillet of reindeer, all prepared with mountain delicacies and a Norrland touch.

The taste of lingonberries and fir cones lingers on her tongue as she looks over toward the other end of the room, where the chef is busy preparing something on a wide kitchen island that also acts as a room divider. Shining copper lamps are suspended above the island, and a dark stone wall looms up behind the chef. It is almost as if the restaurant has been hewn straight out of the granite.

Hanna sighs with pleasure.

Only now does it strike her that they are alone in the restaurant. It is eight thirty in the evening, so surely other guests should be hungry by now?

"Where's everyone else?" she asks Henry. He has just finished mopping up the last of the delicate sauce with a piece of bread. "I haven't seen a single person since we arrived, apart from the staff," Hanna adds.

Henry's mouth is full. He didn't bother to shave this morning, and his cheeks are covered in gray stubble. On many men that would be aging, but in Henry's case it simply makes him more attractive. Hanna rarely thinks about the twenty-year gap between them, although it did occasionally cross her mind in the early days of their relationship.

"There's only us here this weekend," Henry replies, as if this were obvious.

Hanna puts down her glass of red wine, tries to get her head around what he has just said.

"What do you mean?"

"There are no other guests."

Hanna still doesn't understand. Surely they can't be all alone in the hotel? She has secretly googled Niehku, realized that it is a much-sought-after destination and that it is hard to get a room. They have been open for only a few years, but they have already won several international awards.

Niehku means "dream" in the Northern Sámi language, and being here does indeed feel kind of dreamlike.

"They're actually closed in January and February because it's too dark and cold to run the hotel at this time of year," Henry explains. "They don't usually open until the first weekend in March."

"But we got rooms?"

"It took a little persuasion," Henry says with a smile. "But isn't it wonderful, having the place to ourselves?"

Hanna stares at him as the realization slowly dawns.

"You got the hotel to open over a month early just for us? Seriously?"

Henry raises his glass in a toast. The wine is a Bordeaux, Hanna dare not even guess at the price, but it is unlikely to be less than three thousand kronor a bottle. She has a pretty good idea from her time as a bartender in Barcelona.

Henry is a real connoisseur. He always says that life is too short to deny oneself good food and wine.

He waves a dismissive hand.

"You make it sound so dramatic. It's not as if I got the hotel owner in an armlock. I simply asked if it would be possible to book us in for this weekend, even though the place is closed to the general public."

"So you called and said, 'Hi, please could you open the whole place just for me and my girlfriend?'"

"It wasn't quite like that." He winks at her. Hanna can imagine what happened. No doubt he had one of his assistants take care of the matter—he has several. Highly driven young men and women with master's degrees from the Stockholm School of Economics who fight to work for him, because the position is regarded as a prestigious springboard for a career in finance.

She sinks back in her chair again.

Being with a man like Henry is like visiting a land of make-believe, a kingdom she didn't even know existed. Everything is possible as long as you're prepared to pay for it.

Their conversation is interrupted as the chef approaches their table. He is carrying an elegant cake, topped with perfect chocolate roses and lit sparklers.

Suddenly they are surrounded by the staff, who burst into song. The Swedish version of "Happy Birthday to You" echoes around the room. Then a sommelier appears with a bottle of Dom Pérignon in one hand and two champagne flutes in the other.

"Wow," Hanna says when the champagne has been poured and they have each been served with a slice of cake. "You're spoiling me. This isn't quite what I imagined when you said the two of us should go away together."

Henry puts down his fork.

"I wanted to surprise you with something special. You're always working. Now that I've got you to myself for a few days at long last, I couldn't afford to waste the opportunity."

This is one of the things they can't agree on—Hanna's working hours. Or rather, her ability to become completely absorbed by her job.

They have a long-distance relationship, and Henry thinks she should visit him in Stockholm more often, but Hanna doesn't like traveling to the capital, and often uses work as an excuse.

Which means that more often than not, he comes to her.

In a way it is easier to spend time with Henry on her home turf. In Stockholm she is constantly reminded of his status, and the circles in which he moves.

How well known he is.

In Åre she can think of him as an ordinary person, and she can also avoid having anything to do with his upper-class friends and acquaintances. She has yet to meet his three grown-up sons—this is something she has actively tried to steer clear of, maybe because she doesn't want to admit to either Henry or herself that they are a couple.

Or that she is only five years older than his firstborn son.

Suddenly she notices a square, flat package in front of her on the table.

"Happy birthday."

The thick, shiny gift wrap and the pretty ribbon tied in a perfect bow suggest that the contents are high end to say the least.

"Aren't you going to open it?"

Henry sounds like an expectant child; she can't help smiling at his infectious enthusiasm.

"Absolutely."

She pulls the package toward her and fumbles with the ribbon. A red velvet box reveals itself, engraved with the characteristic *C. C* for Cartier. It must have cost a fortune, whatever it is.

She places her fingers on the box, can't quite bring herself to open it yet. It's too much, everything is too much. She doesn't know how to react to this kind of excess. They have had a wonderful day together, flown over the mountains in a private helicopter until the pilot gently set them down on a mountaintop amid virgin snow. After a few hours of superb skiing, which beat most of Hanna's experiences so far, their guide was ready with a gourmet meal, complete with champagne, on a sun-drenched plateau with a view of the Norwegian peaks that went on for miles.

And now an extravagant gift.

Whatever it is, no doubt the price tag represents several months' salary for Hanna and her colleagues.

Daniel would never give her something by Cartier. He can't afford it; plus he doesn't even like jewelry.

The thought pops up and immediately disappears.

Don't think about Daniel.

Inside the box she finds a slender bracelet in rose gold, resting on a velvet cushion. Next to it is a tiny screwdriver in the same color.

"It's called a Love bracelet," Henry explains, picking up the screwdriver. "Let me show you how it works."

He opens the little lock and gently slides the bracelet over Hanna's right hand. Then he clicks it shut.

"Don't lose the tool," he says, feigning gravity. "Because then you will never be able to take my present off again—you will have to wear it forever."

The soft-rose-colored bracelet shimmers in the glow of the candles on the table. It is a perfectly designed circle, decorated with smaller circles with a narrow line in the center. Tiny diamonds complete the effect.

Hanna has never been given anything so beautiful.

Or so expensive.

"Do you like it?"

Hanna gives Henry a big smile.

"It's fantastic. It's just . . ."

She stares at the shiny piece of jewelry, trying to understand what it actually means. What he is trying to say with such a magnificent gesture.

And how is she ever going to be able to give him an equivalent gift?

"Too much?" Henry wonders, adjusting the bracelet on her wrist.

Say what you like about Henry, but he is never tone deaf or insensitive. He is probably one of the most intelligent people Hanna has ever met. It is partly why she enjoys his company so much. He is excellent when it comes to understanding people; he hears what they are saying, picks up nuances and the slightest shift in the atmosphere around him. He also has a big heart. He has devoted a great deal of time to his godson, Filip, over the past year, after the tragic events last Easter when Filip's mother was brutally murdered.

This evening it is clear that Henry has made a huge effort, and the last thing Hanna wants to do is appear ungrateful.

"A little too much, maybe," she admits. "It's so beautiful. But you do realize that when it's your turn, it'll be dinner at the local restaurant if you're lucky, and possibly something from the craft store in Åre. Whatever I come up with, it's never going to match the way you've treated me this weekend."

"If you're happy, that's enough for me."

Henry leans back and sips his champagne. "Besides, it is more blessed to give than to receive, according to the Bible."

"Since when did you become a believer?"

Hanna laughs at her own riposte, and the atmosphere lightens. Then something changes in Henry's face; he looks almost shy. He reaches for Hanna's right hand and presses her palm to his lips.

"I have a question for you. We've been dating for nearly nine months now. And we're both old enough to know what we want."

Hanna smiles uncertainly. She doesn't know where the past year has gone. She hasn't given it much consideration, just taken each day as it came. Enjoyed Henry's company, but rarely thought beyond their next meeting.

To be honest, she has enjoyed allowing herself this kind of escape from reality. She hasn't wanted to think about where their relationship might be going. As soon as her mind has drifted in that direction she has ignored it, well aware of how complicated everything would get if she started planning for the future.

"Hanna," Henry says, his gaze so intense that she can't look away. "How about moving in with me?"

12

There is an amazing aroma coming from the pan of pasta sauce on the table in front of Filippa.

Emil has cooked; he enjoys experimenting in the kitchen, and has worked in a restaurant for several years. He is the group's self-appointed chef, and has made pasta pomodoro with freshly baked bread, a round, golden-brown focaccia.

"Fucking delicious," Pontus grunts in Filippa's ear.

He is already well on the way to getting drunk. She doesn't want that idiot anywhere near her. She steals a glance at Amir, who is standing at the end of the table. This evening he is wearing a lovely moss-green shirt with the sleeves rolled up; it suits his complexion perfectly.

Filippa wishes he would come and sit beside her so that she doesn't have to sit with Pontus. At that moment Amir turns his head in her direction. He smiles, and her wish comes true—he takes a few steps and pulls out the chair next to her.

Her whole body tingles. She wants to say something witty and clever, make him think she's funny and exciting, but instead she is lost for words. Then she blushes, making things so much worse. She reaches for her glass and takes a big gulp of wine to hide her confusion.

"Can we start?" Olivia asks, grabbing the spaghetti server.

"Help yourselves," Emil says, bringing over a bowl of grated Parmesan.

William, who is crouching by the open fire, brushes off his hands. His cheeks are still glowing from the sauna. Filippa can't understand how Olivia had the nerve to show herself completely naked in front of everyone. First of all outdoors, when they were messing around in the snow, then back in the sauna. She didn't seem bothered at all, and William couldn't take his eyes off her. It was as if he wanted to eat her up right there and then.

Pontus too—he was virtually drooling when Olivia sat down on the bench without her towel. He is so disgusting.

If only Amir would look at Filippa that way—but she was too shy to take off her swimsuit. She wishes she could be as cool as Olivia. Just roll in the snow, or start chatting to Amir. Charm him, knowing that she is the most attractive girl in the room, and that he should be grateful she's interested in him.

It's not that she's envious of her best friend. Quite the reverse, she loves Olivia; she would just like to be . . . the same. Everything is always so easy for her. Olivia is unafraid and beautiful and cool to be with, and clever enough never to have needed to study particularly hard.

While Filippa struggles with her work, and has to battle for every decent grade. If she is going to complete the program, that's what she has to do. Anything else is unthinkable; she couldn't possibly return home as a dropout. It's bad enough that she didn't get into medical school as her parents had hoped; now she has to prove that she can at least gain a good degree. Maybe even apply to the foreign office after she graduates?

She knows how proud that would make her mom and dad—but also how disappointed they would be if she failed, and she couldn't bear that. Filippa is their only child. Everything depends on her; it always has done. It's not her fault that Mom had several miscarriages after Filippa was born, but she still feels responsible for fulfilling their hopes and dreams.

"This is so good," Amir says as he tucks in. He doesn't seem to have noticed that Filippa lost the ability to speak as soon as he joined her. She reaches for her glass, takes a few more gulps. The warmth spreads through her chest, making it easier to talk to Amir, so she drinks some more and asks him about skiing, whether he's been to Åre before. The full-bodied red wine comes courtesy of William's parents, who have said they can help themselves from the large wine store.

As long as it doesn't cost any more than four hundred kronor a bottle.

Filippa giggles at the thought. She has never tasted such an expensive wine before; she has no idea what the difference might be.

But it's free, and free is good.

She empties her glass, refills it so that she can carry on chatting to Amir. She wants to find out as much as possible, what his taste in music might be, what games he likes, his favorite sport.

Suddenly a strange voice comes from the hallway.

"Hello? Anyone home?"

When Filippa looks up, she sees a man in his mid-forties standing just inside the front door. He has gray stubble, and is wearing heavy boots and a dark-green padded jacket. A few white snowflakes have stuck to his black woolen hat.

William waves to him. "Hi, Staffan." He stands up and shakes the man's hand. "Say hello to Staffan, everyone. He's the one who made sure the heating was on and the drive had been cleared when we arrived."

Filippa mumbles hi, as do the others.

William chats to Staffan for a few minutes, then sees him out before rejoining his friends.

"Staffan just wanted to check things out," he explains. "See if we needed anything. Without him nothing would work in this place. He takes care of the house when we're not here. All we have to do is call him if there's a problem."

"I wish we had someone like him at home." Olivia laughs. "A fixer to take care of any problems. Can I have his phone number?"

An hour later everyone has finished eating and settled down on the sofas. Amir is shuffling a pack of cards. Filippa is sitting next to him, idly surfing on her phone. Olivia and William are in the kitchen, clearing up after dinner.

They had intended to head down into the village and to go to Bygget, the best nightclub in Åre. However, they are all tired after the journey. They have decided to leave it until tomorrow—they've got the whole week, after all.

Dinner was a hit. Filippa has never talked to Amir so much. She is excited and full of good food. Emil made a lush chocolate mousse for dessert—Filippa had two helpings.

"Shall we make things a little more fun?" Amir whispers in her ear. He takes a clear plastic bag containing white powder out of his pocket. The same kind William was waving around on the train. Filippa immediately realizes what it is.

"Want some?" Amir adds with a wink.

She responds with an uncertain smile; she has seen what drugs have done to other friends who have lost it completely.

The white powder sparkles, almost like snow crystals.

The gateway to another world.

"Come on," Amir says, his eyes sparkling like the coke. "It'll be cool."

Filippa loves the way he is looking at her tonight, as if she belongs, as if she really is part of the gang.

Someone he could fall in love with.

He takes out a key ring with a tiny scoop on it. He dips it into the bag, then inhales the powder. Dips in again, holds out the scoop to Filippa.

"You're going to love it," he assures her with an encouraging wink.

Filippa hesitates; then she leans forward and breathes in. At first she feels as if she's going to sneeze, but soon everything is just . . . wonderful.

Colors are brighter. Amir is so good looking. Life is . . . shimmering.

She has never felt so amazing.

Amir puts away the scoop and the powder, then calls out to William and Olivia.

"How much longer are you going to be? It's time to play!"

"We're nearly done!" Olivia replies. Five minutes later she flops down on the sofa next to Filippa, followed by William.

"So what are we going to do?" Olivia asks.

Amir smiles, with a cunning glint in his eyes.

"How about a game of Truth or Consequences?"

"Okay," Olivia says immediately. Her gaze is less than focused; she is slightly drunk. "I'm in."

Filippa stares at Amir in fascination. Truth or Consequences?

If she is asked a question, she has to tell the truth, however difficult it is, or take the consequences and receive a punishment. Maybe knock back the contents of her glass, or do something dumb like kiss Olivia on the lips. But it can go further, like stripping to the waist or even running around the house stark naked. Sometimes it turns nasty; you might have to say which of the people in the room you dislike most, or which one you wouldn't want to invite to a party.

Filippa usually avoids games like this, but tonight she is giggly and intoxicated by the wine, the coke, and Amir's attention. At dinner she made him laugh more than once. Surely over the next seven days, she will manage to capture his interest for real. She reaches for her glass and empties it, relishes the taste of the strong red wine and the courage spreading through her body.

"Me too!" she says with a flirtatious smile. "Let's go!"

13

The bass notes of the loud music coming from next door infuriate Åke Carlsson, seated in his favorite armchair in the living room.

It is well after eleven, and he can barely hear the TV show he is watching. The kids have opened the windows on the side of the house facing his, and the pumping racket is driving him crazy.

They don't seem to understand that some people actually live here all the time.

Not everyone in Åre wants to party.

"Aren't you coming to bed? You got up so early."

Åke turns his head and sees his wife, Karin, gazing at him with concern. He picked up Peter and the grandchildren from the airport this morning; they landed at nine fifteen, so he had to leave home at seven.

He glances crossly in the direction of the neighbors' house.

"As if I'd be able to sleep with that racket going on."

Karin waves a dismissive hand, but Åke ignores her.

"They think they can behave however they like, with no regard for anyone else."

"Are you maybe overreacting a little?"

"I saw them when they arrived. Spoiled brats from Stockholm who believe they can have whatever they want."

"They're students—they don't realize how loud it sounds."

"Are you trying to defend them?" Åke glares at his wife.

"Calm down," Karin says. "If Peter can sleep through it, I'm sure you can."

They have been married for over thirty-five years, and she ought to know better than to correct him. The fact that Peter went to bed early is irrelevant, but there's no point in saying so.

His wife pulls her robe more tightly around her body. "I'm only thinking of what's best for you."

Åke lets out a snort. "I've got a good mind to go over there and unplug their speakers. That might teach them to behave like decent folk!"

Karin rolls her eyes as she tucks a strand of gray hair behind her ear.

"Wouldn't it be better if we just went to bed?" she ventures. "Your bedroom is on the other side of the house; I'm sure it won't be as loud there."

"You go up," Åke says. "I won't be long."

14

The pleasant but loud hum of conversation at Boqueria means that Inspector Anton Lundgren can hardly hear what the waiter is saying as he pours the full-bodied Rioja they have just ordered. The restaurant is full, and behind the wide counter, the bartender is mixing colorful cocktails just as fast as she can.

Carl, Anton's boyfriend of nine months, is sitting opposite him. Over the past year he has allowed his blond hair to grow out. When they first met it was cropped short, but the new style suits him better.

They have spent a wonderful day on the slopes, skiing off-piste at the back of Skutan. It is one of their main shared interests; they are both experienced skiers with season passes.

"*Skål,*" Anton says, raising his glass. "Here's to a wonderful evening."

The waiter returns with a generous sharing platter of olives, charcuterie, Manchego cheese, and fresh bread.

"Here's to us," Carl responds, reaching over to cover Anton's hand with his. The tender gesture makes Anton freeze immediately. He simply can't help it, but he forces himself not to pull away as Carl squeezes his fingers. He really doesn't want to worry about them being spotted, about someone noticing the evidence that they are more than friends, but he finds it incredibly difficult to relax.

What if someone he knows sees them?

Not even his parents, his sister, or his closest colleagues—Daniel, Hanna, and Raffe—know about Carl.

At the same time, he doesn't want Carl to pick up on how uncomfortable he is.

"This looks delicious," Anton says. "I'm starving!"

He frees his hand and pushes the platter toward his boyfriend. "You'd better help yourself before I eat the lot!" he says with an awkward smile, hating himself. Carl is the most important person in his life. They love each other.

"Take the best bit," he adds, pointing to the Serrano ham as if that might compensate for his cowardice. He hopes that Carl isn't aware of what he is doing, but he can see that little frown between the blond eyebrows. The same frown that appears whenever Anton refuses to hold hands with Carl in the street, or pulls away when Carl hugs him in public.

The last thing Anton wants to do is ruin their evening.

And yet it is so hard to stand up for who he is.

15

The temperature and the atmosphere are as high as the music pumping from the portable speaker Amir has brought with him. Olivia has just opened another window because the heat from the fire is making the house feel like a sauna.

"Your go," Pontus slurs.

He is very drunk again. Olivia knows what he's like, but she can't understand why he always has to get into this state. It's as if Pontus only has two settings: Either he's sober and barely speaks, or he's drunk and very hard work.

"Shut up," she says.

Pontus scowls at her, but she knows he won't dare start a quarrel. He is no match for her.

They are interrupted by an aggressive banging on the front door. Olivia looks enquiringly at William, who goes into the hallway. The knocking comes again, even harder this time. William opens the door, and they hear a loud voice.

"You need to turn that damned music down! Have you any idea what time it is?"

From her seat Olivia can see a tall man with thinning hair standing in the doorway. He looks ancient, at least seventy, and he is waving his hands around as he shouts at William.

This must be the next-door neighbor. Olivia seems to remember seeing him earlier, when they got back from skiing.

"It's gone midnight, for God's sake—people are trying to sleep!"

William mumbles a barely audible apology. The man takes a few steps into the hallway and spots the rest of the group. He registers the bottles on the table and the clothes strewn across the floor because of the game. There is no mistaking the disapproval in his eyes.

"What the hell are you doing?" he yells. "Is this some kind of orgy?"

William opens his mouth, but then Filippa gets to her feet. She is wearing only her bra, panties, and a camisole. The game hasn't gone particularly well for her, she kept choosing consequences, but she seems excited rather than embarrassed. She really has gone for it tonight, almost as if she is trying to prove something.

"Don't be cross, Granddad," she chirrups, dancing over to the old man. "Come on in and play with us!"

He ignores her.

"I'm calling the police if you don't turn the music down," he informs William. "I'm serious!"

Filippa is so close now that she is almost rubbing up against the visitor. Then she suddenly pulls up her camisole and bra, exposing both breasts.

Olivia's jaw drops.

"Is this what you wanted?" Filippa's tone is teasing. "Is that why you came?"

The man recoils with an expression of disgust. Filippa must be even more drunk than Olivia thought.

"We're playing Truth or Consequences, come and join us," Filippa continues, thrusting her breasts forward until they are practically touching the old man.

"Stop that!" he says.

"Stop that!" Filippa imitates him.

Olivia doesn't know what to do. She has never seen her friend behaving like this; it's as if she's turned into a completely different person.

How much has she had to drink? Or has she tried out William's coke?

The neighbor's face is getting redder and redder. He looks as if he is about to explode.

Filippa pouts coquettishly at him; then suddenly she reaches out and pinches his cheek, so hard that her fingers leave a red mark on his skin.

"What an old misery you are!"

Then she directs her attention to his crotch.

"Although you do seem to be a little bit interested . . ."

Then everything happens fast.

Filippa's hand is on its way toward the old man's cock, but before she gets that far, he gives her a hard shove, and she loses her balance and crashes to the floor.

"What are you doing?" she shrieks, wide eyed with shock. "Are you crazy? You hit me!"

Everyone is staring at the man.

The silence is broken by a howl from Filippa: "Fucking pervert!"

The old man's mouth is half-open; he quickly backs away. Before anyone has the chance to speak, they hear the sound of the front door slamming behind him.

Olivia is dumbstruck. She doesn't know what to say; the situation is completely ridiculous. Then Filippa starts giggling—she is still lying on the floor.

"I mean, did you see his face? What a loser!"

"What a fucking loser," Amir agrees.

He is laughing too. Pontus joins in. Emil is smiling. Only William seems slightly concerned—maybe he is worried in case the neighbor calls his parents?

Filippa is on all fours now. She tries to get up, but it proves impossible. Eventually she grabs hold of Amir, who hauls her back onto the sofa.

Olivia notices him stroking Filippa's breasts as he helps her. He's a disgusting creep too, taking advantage of Filippa when she's drunk. She has to get her friend out of here—she's never seen her like this. Poor, poor Filippa—she's going to feel terrible tomorrow when she remembers this.

If she's trying to impress Amir, she's going about it the wrong way.

"Shall we call it a night?" she says to Filippa. "I think we should go to bed—we're going skiing tomorrow."

She looks around for support, and Emil obligingly yawns. But Filippa ignores her and shuffles closer to Amir, who smiles smugly. Almost as if it's a competition, and he has just beaten Olivia.

She is so fucking tired of him. Why can't he help out instead of making things worse? Surely he can see the state that Filippa is in. He can try his luck with her some other time—right now it's obvious that she doesn't know what she wants.

Olivia glares at him, but he simply presses closer to Filippa.

"Let's go!" Olivia says to Filippa, holding out her hand.

But Filippa shakes her head and waves a dismissive hand. "You can't tell me what to do! I'm staying here."

16

There is only a faint glow left in the open fire when Filippa looks around. It is almost one o'clock in the morning; everyone is pretty drunk. The coffee table is sticky with the residue of spilled drinks, and the floor is littered with empty chips packets and dropped cheesy puffs.

Only Emil has gone to bed.

Filippa reaches for her pink cocktail and finishes it off. She has certainly proved that she can party tonight.

She smiles at Amir, who is looking appreciatively at her.

"You're really going for it," he says, pointing to her empty glass.

"That's the kind of girl I am!"

Filippa spreads both hands wide, and the movement almost makes her lose her balance. She thinks about that stupid old man again, and starts laughing. He looked like such an idiot, standing there red in the face and yelling at William.

"That old fucker from next door," she half gulps, setting Amir off too. Filippa can't stop laughing. She laughs and laughs until her mascara is running, and she almost throws up. In the end she flings her arms around Amir in a spontaneous hug.

"I think I might be a little bit drunk," she gasps, wiping her eyes. "Very drunk, actually."

Then she gives him a wet kiss on the lips. She would never have dared to do that before dinner, but now it feels perfectly natural. When she pulls back she sees that Olivia is looking disapprovingly at her. Almost as if she is trying to tell her to slow down.

But Filippa doesn't care. There is no need for Olivia to get involved when Filippa is having so much fun. She's already suggested they should go back to the guest cabin, but that sounds very, very boring.

Filippa giggles. For once she is the fun party girl, the one who is keeping things going.

She picks up her glass and looks around.

"I need another drink!"

"Maybe we should go to bed?" Olivia says again.

Jesus, what's wrong with her? It was Olivia who wanted them to have a good time and relax—why is she trying to spoil things now?

Filippa turns to Amir. "Would you like to go to bed?" she asks, deliberately imitating Olivia.

It is hard to get the words out; she stumbles over them a bit, but she thinks it sounds okay.

"That depends . . . ," Amir replies with a grin.

There is no mistaking the invitation. Somehow his arm has found its way around her shoulders, and they are sitting very close together. He is bare-chested; she can feel his warm skin against hers, the hairs on his chest tickling slightly.

Amir's bedroom is in the loft, one floor up.

Filippa feels a flush of heat; this is what she has wanted all along. She parts her lips, smiles seductively at him, only for Olivia to pipe up yet again.

"It's late—shouldn't we head back to the cabin?"

That's the last thing Filippa wants to do. She pushes away her friend's arm. Olivia is not her mother; Filippa has the situation under control.

She waves her glass in the air again. "Is the bar closed, guys?"

Pontus picks up a bottle and pours her a generous measure. He's okay tonight. Filippa can't understand why she thought he was so useless yesterday, or why she got annoyed on the train.

Life is amazing.

"You're so nice!" she tells Pontus. She can hear that she is slurring her words, but she doesn't care. "Unlike *her*!" She points to Olivia. "She's a pain in the ass. She wants me to go to bed."

Olivia shrugs. "Fine. Do what you want. I'm going to the cabin right now."

SUNDAY

17

When Olivia opens her eyes in the morning, her mouth is dry and she doesn't feel great. She drank way too much yesterday. She hadn't intended to have more than a couple of glasses of wine; she wants to make the most of the skiing now that they're here, but somehow she ended up knocking back God knows how many cocktails.

She looks around, listens. There isn't a sound from the other bedroom, and Olivia has a strong feeling that she is alone in the cabin. She fell asleep as soon as her head touched the pillow.

Did Filippa sleep here last night? She has no idea.

What the hell came over Filippa yesterday?

Olivia groans and rolls over in bed. Filippa was crazy after dinner; it was as if she wanted to prove that she could party harder than any of them.

Presumably she's still in the main house with Amir.

Olivia wishes her friend would be more careful with her heart.

Okay, so Amir is very good looking, with his dark hair and those warm, charming brown eyes. But he is shallow, and way too conscious of his appearance. The only thing Amir really cares about is what William thinks—whenever William clicks his fingers, Amir comes running. He will do anything to be allowed to hang out with William and his rich childhood friends.

If only Filippa could see that. Realize that she will always come second as far as Amir is concerned.

Not that Olivia has a problem with William and his wealthy pals. She likes his style, and they've had a kind of on-off relationship for a while. However, she is well aware that William is very spoiled, and mainly interested in himself. She won't stand for any of his nonsense, and she has no intention of falling for a guy who gets bored as soon as he has what he wants. If Olivia fell in love with him, he would run a mile.

A glance at her phone tells her that it's time to get up if she wants to hit the slopes. She pulls on yesterday's thermal underwear in merino wool, and looks into Filippa's room.

It is empty, as expected. That means Filippa didn't come back to the cabin last night—but if she thinks she and Amir are going to be a couple just because they slept together when they were drunk, she is going to get hurt.

Olivia shouldn't feel guilty—she did her best to persuade Filippa to leave with her more than once. She can't help worrying, though; she already feels sorry for her best friend, waking up with a hangover and a sense of anxiety as the memories of the previous evening come flooding back.

When Olivia walks into the main house, she is struck by the overwhelming smell of stale beer. She stamps the snow off her boots, slips them off, and heads for the living room, where Emil is busy clearing up the mess.

A red-eyed Pontus is standing by the coffee machine, spooning powder into the paper filter. He is a lot quieter this morning.

There is no sign of Filippa, Amir, or William.

"Okay?" Olivia says, gathering up the empty bottles from the coffee table.

Emil gives her a wry smile. He was the one who drank the least, and looks fresh and wide awake. "I'm fine. How about you and Filippa?"

Olivia pushes back her hair and yawns. The aroma of freshly brewed coffee begins to spread from the kitchen, which immediately makes her feel better.

"I'm good. But apparently Filippa spent last night somewhere else."

The door of the master bedroom, where William is sleeping in his parents' double bed, opens with a crash. William emerges, wearing a dark-blue robe with the Ralph Lauren logo.

"Morning everyone!" he shouts with exaggerated enthusiasm. "Time to hit those slopes!"

Olivia's attention is drawn to the window. The weather isn't great—it's overcast and misty. A thick layer of fog has settled over Lake Åre, and half the valley appears to be wrapped in grayish-white cotton wool. The thermometer is showing minus seventeen, and if the wind gets up, it will feel even colder.

But that doesn't matter. She can't wait to be out in the fresh air, moving her body.

She goes over to the refrigerator and starts to take out what they need for breakfast: ham, jelly, salami. "Anyone want eggs?" she calls over her shoulder.

Sounds come from the loft, where Amir's bedroom is located. Olivia looks up to see him making his way down the stairs. He is barefoot and looks very much the worse for wear, with tired eyes and dark stubble. Bearing in mind that he's probably just had a fuck, Olivia thinks he ought to look happier.

"Is Filippa awake?" she asks as he comes over to the kitchen island.

He raises an eyebrow. "How should I know?"

"What do you mean?"

"Why should I know anything about Filippa? I'm not her mother."

Olivia puts down a carton of milk. "Didn't she spend the night with you?"

Amir shakes his head. "Nope."

Olivia doesn't understand. "But she stayed here when I went back to the cabin. I thought she was with you."

Amir runs his fingers through his hair. He is starting to get annoyed. "I just told you she didn't stay," he snaps.

A little flame of anxiety springs to life in Olivia's chest. She tries to quash it, focuses on Amir instead. "So where is she? She wasn't in the cabin when I woke up."

"She probably went to bed in one of the other rooms. How the fuck should I know? There are plenty of bedrooms in this house."

His breath smells unpleasant. He clearly didn't bother to brush his teeth before coming down to breakfast.

Olivia thinks for a moment. There are five bedrooms—the one in the loft, where Amir is sleeping, and the luxurious master on the ground floor. Downstairs there is a study and three more bedrooms. When all the boys had chosen, there was one spare. Olivia sighs with relief—of course, that's where Filippa must have slept.

"Okay," she says, closing the refrigerator. "I'll go and check. Can you make a start on breakfast?"

Before Amir can object she hands him a carton of butter and leaves him to it. She hurries down the stairs. The first room is a complete mess, with crumpled sheets and clothes all over the floor, but she recognizes Pontus's suitcase. The next room must be Emil's—it is much tidier, and the bed has been made.

So Filippa must have taken the last room, the one on the other side of the sauna and the chill-out area.

Olivia walks toward the closed door. In a way she is relieved that Filippa doesn't seem to have spent the night with Amir—he can be a total shit. She might have gotten irritated yesterday evening, but she doesn't want anything bad to happen to her friend.

She doesn't want Filippa to have her heart broken.

"Time to get up!" she calls cheerfully as she flings the door open.

Then she stands there, frozen to the spot. The bed is empty and untouched.

Filippa isn't there.

18

It is bitterly cold, almost to the point where Daniel doesn't want to take Alice out, but they both need fresh air. She woke at twenty past five, so he didn't get much sleep last night.

He pushes the stroller in front of him as he turns into the square. There is mist in the air, but the pretty Christmas decorations are still hanging in the trees, creating a warm and welcoming atmosphere. Thousands of tiny lights twinkle among the branches, which are covered in fluffy winter-white rime frost.

The plan is to grab a coffee at the café in the middle of the square. No one can beat them when it comes to a really good cappuccino. Daniel knows his coffee—with an Italian mother, it's part of his DNA.

"Would you like a bun?" he asks Alice, whose face immediately lights up.

"Bun!" she repeats, beaming at him. "Bun, bun, bun!"

She loves vanilla buns; they're the best thing in the world.

Just as they arrive, Daniel sees Gustav approaching, dressed in his full ski kit and with his skis over his shoulder. He seems to be heading for the lift. Ida is with him, also in her skiing gear. They have obviously planned a day on the slopes, maybe with lunch at Kastrullen or Hummelstugan, as they have a child-free weekend.

Daniel bends his head, pretending to be doing something with the stroller. He hopes they won't notice him; he doesn't want to speak to Ida or Gustav.

Especially Gustav.

Alice is facing the opposite direction, so she doesn't see them.

Ida is talking, and it is clear that she is full of enthusiasm; she gesticulates with her free hand, then laughs out loud.

When she and Daniel met just over three years ago at Bygget, she laughed just like that. He still remembers how he fell for her like a ton of bricks. The attraction was immediate. He had never been so in love; he wanted to touch her all the time.

Somewhere along the way, that laugh disappeared.

Somewhere along the way, they stopped touching each other.

Alice's birth was life's greatest gift, but their lives quickly became an endless round of planning and logistics; it was all about Alice and how they could make their everyday existence work.

Ida became quieter, more introverted. Anxious.

She started to loathe his job; she worried constantly that he would be injured in the line of duty. She hated the fact that he was away so much during major investigations, accusing him of prioritizing his work over his family.

And then she left him.

Ida smiles at Gustav; her whole face is lit up as they continue toward the ski lift.

Daniel is glad she didn't see him. He finds it difficult to keep the mask in place when Gustav is there. It was tricky enough when he called by the apartment yesterday. The sense of sorrow and loss tears at his heart as he picks up Alice and goes into the café.

19

Olivia races up the stairs. Everyone is sitting around the table, helping themselves to breakfast.

"Filippa's gone!"

The room falls silent.

"What do you mean?" Emil asks.

"She's disappeared!"

Olivia can hear the panic in her voice. She doesn't mean to sound hysterical, but where can Filippa be?

"Calm down," Emil says. "What's happened?"

Olivia tries to explain, but the words come out all wrong.

"Are her boots and her jacket still here?" William goes into the hallway. "Doesn't look like it," he calls out. "There are only your moon boots here."

Olivia takes out her phone to check again. She has already tried several times, but her calls go straight to voicemail. The map on Snapchat that enables a user to see where their friends are is turned off, so she can't find Filippa that way.

She hasn't been in touch via text, WhatsApp, or Messenger.

"Who saw her last?" Emil wonders.

Olivia looks at Amir. When she left, he was sitting on the sofa with his arm around Filippa's shoulders. He gave the impression that he was about to eat her up.

Would he have lost interest, just like that?

"Amir?" she says slowly. "Wasn't Filippa with you last night?"

He shakes his head. "I've already told you—no. Anyway, I went to bed soon after you left."

"Really?"

"Do you think I'm lying?"

Olivia backs down. "But where did she go?"

"How the hell should I know?"

"I went to bed too," William says.

Olivia turns to Pontus. "In that case you must have been the only one left in the living room with Filippa. What happened?"

"I can't really remember."

"Try!"

Pontus's cheeks flush.

"I fell asleep. When I woke up, everyone else had gone."

Olivia isn't giving up. "So where can she be? She can't have simply vanished!"

"Is her stuff still in the cabin?" Emil asks.

Olivia tries to think. Filippa's bed was untouched, but was her stuff there? Yes, definitely. Her suitcase was in the corner, and yesterday's ski clothes were draped over a chair.

"In that case she's probably gone for a walk," William concludes. "Or she's gone skiing without us. There's nothing to worry about."

Olivia is still clutching her phone. She has sent several new messages, but there has been no response.

"Maybe she wants to be on her own for a while?" William goes on. "She might have been embarrassed about last night."

"Embarrassed?" Olivia can't believe her ears.

"I mean, she got very drunk. It wasn't exactly a pretty sight . . ."

Olivia stares at William in astonishment, but he just leans back on his chair, totally at ease. What a fucking hypocrite he is. Pontus and the others were drunk too, but nobody is suggesting that they should be embarrassed.

Emil seems to notice that Olivia is on the edge.

"I think we should search both houses again, just to be on the safe side," he suggests. "I can take this floor. William, can you check Amir's room and the sauna area."

Olivia is grateful for Emil's calm and sensible approach. She can't think straight; she is becoming more and more anxious. When Emil sets off, she follows him. Everything seems perfectly normal. It feels kind of stupid to be searching inside closets and looking under the beds, but they do it anyway.

Fifteen minutes later they are all back around the table. There is no sign of Filippa, but William informs them that her skis and poles are still in the outdoor storage area.

"Okay, let's check the cabin again," Emil says. "If she did go for a walk, she might be back now."

During the short walk to the other building, Olivia almost manages to convince herself that Filippa is there. That she just went out, like William suggested, and came back without telling anyone.

By the time they open the door and step into the small hallway, she already feels better.

Everything is going to be okay, Olivia has been worrying for no reason.

"Filippa!" she calls out immediately. "Where are you?"

But no one answers. Filippa's room is still empty.

"She's not here either."

Emil starts opening closet doors. He peers under the double bed; then he does the same in Olivia's room before glancing into the bathroom.

"What if she went out last night when she was so drunk?" Olivia whispers. "She could have frozen to death."

Emil shakes his head. "There's no need to think the worst. Let's go back to the others—she might be there by now."

"Did you find her?" William calls out as soon as Olivia and Emil walk in.

"I'm afraid not," Emil replies.

They go into the kitchen, and Pontus stares blankly at them from the end of the table. Olivia clamps her lips tight shut to stop herself from yelling at him. He's no help at all; he doesn't even seem to care.

Just like Amir, who is munching away on a cheese sandwich.

"Should we call her parents?" William asks.

Olivia isn't sure. It sounds dramatic—but what if there has been an accident? Then again, she is reluctant to contact Aron and Jenny. They have been so kind to her since her mother died almost three years ago, let her live with them for long periods.

She doesn't want to scare them for no reason.

"I'm sure she'll show up soon," Amir says. With his sandwich in his hand he goes over to the panorama window facing the slopes. The mist is dispersing, and the sun has risen. It is much lighter than it was only an hour ago. "So what are we going to do?" He gestures toward the view. "The lifts are open—shall we go? If we don't make a move soon, we'll lose a whole day's skiing."

At this time of year, the system is open only from nine thirty until three. Through the window they can just see Sadelexpressen, its chairs slowly moving up the mountain.

Olivia doesn't get how Amir can stand there talking about skiing.

Something is wrong; she can feel it.

"I think we should go," Pontus says.

William looks undecided. At least he seems worried. But then he pushes back his chair and joins Amir to check the thermometer outside the window.

"What's that?" he says suddenly, resting his forehead on the glass. His eyes are fixed on a point outside, down the yard.

Olivia immediately reacts to his tone of voice. "What is it?"

William's face has lost all its color. Olivia hurries over to him, her mouth has gone dry. On the ground below the window lies a bundle that almost looks like part of the snow.

A long, narrow bundle.

A bare foot is sticking out among the whiteness, its toes painted with blue nail polish.

And Olivia begins to scream.

20

The call comes at nine forty-two.

When Daniel's phone rings he is in his pajamas in the kitchen, clearing up after breakfast while Alice runs back and forth, happily fetching one toy after another from her room. Everything he gathered up the previous evening is rapidly being spread across the living room floor.

He sees from the display that it's his boss, Birgitta Grip. His muscles automatically tense. A call from Grip on a Sunday morning when he is not on duty is unlikely to involve good news.

"Morning," he says. "Has something happened?"

"We have a situation in Sadeln." Lengthy greetings are not Grip's thing. "A young woman aged about twenty has died. She was found outdoors at one of the second homes—already dead, according to the person who called."

Daniel clutches the edge of the sink with his free hand. Cases involving young people are more difficult to deal with; they make his skin crawl in a particular way.

He glances toward Alice.

He constantly worries about his daughter's safety. That is the consequence of having seen too much evil, too many repulsive crimes. He is permanently aware that life can be turned upside down at any moment, with no warning.

"Are we looking at a homicide?" Daniel keeps his tone neutral, not wanting his boss to hear how her words are affecting him.

"Too early to say. It could be an accident. Can you drive over and take a look?"

What is he going to do with Alice?

He can hardly take a two-year-old to a possible crime scene, nor can he tell Grip that he doesn't have a babysitter. He already has his hands full dealing with the shared custody scenario; he doesn't want it to impact his work situation or how his colleagues regard him.

He sighs quietly. There is only one solution. He will have to ask Ida's mom if she can watch Alice for a few hours, although this is unlikely to win him any bonus points with his ex if she finds out.

But right now he has no choice.

"I'm on my way."

"Good. See if you can get a hold of Hanna too."

Daniel seems to remember that Hanna said she was going away this weekend, and that she isn't working tomorrow either. When they were driving back from Östersund on Thursday, he had asked how she was going to celebrate her birthday. He had been on the verge of suggesting dinner at Broken, one of their favorite restaurants, if she didn't have other plans.

But Hanna had mumbled something about not being around, without offering any further details. He had found it strange that she was so vague, as if she didn't want to share her plans with him.

"I think she's away," Daniel says. "It was her thirty-seventh birthday yesterday."

"Okay, see if Anton can go with you."

Anton, who used to be based in Åre as a general investigator, is now attached to the Serious Crimes Unit in Östersund. He took up the post back in the fall.

"Call me as soon as you've assessed the situation."

Grip's tone is challenging, and Daniel understands why. Over the past few years a number of harrowing murders have occurred in the area, and the police have had to cope with limited resources. Both the local population and local industry have begun to worry about Åre's reputation.

Every year hundreds of thousands of visitors come to Scandinavia's largest ski resort, and everything depends on retaining a good name. Many articles have appeared in the press, highlighting the police's lack of capacity and declining clear-up rate, and complaining about their inability to create a sense of security for both residents and visitors.

The council has also applied pressure, demanding clear improvements.

A young woman found dead in the snow is the last thing they need.

This winter has been relatively calm, and Daniel had hoped it would stay that way. They still haven't gotten on top of the staffing situation; they haven't managed to find enough investigators who want to work on violent crime in Jämtland and Härjedalen.

He goes into the bedroom and starts to get changed as he ends the call with Grip.

"I'll be in touch as soon as possible."

21

Several patrol cars are already on-site when Daniel arrives at Nedre Svedjevägen 7, the address where the deceased was found. He recognizes Anton's red Toyota, parked a short distance away.

It took just under an hour to contact Ida's mother and hand over Alice, so Daniel is both late and stressed as he hurries toward the enormous wooden house. It reminds him to a certain extent of Hanna's sister's lodge. Hanna lived there when she first came to Åre, before she found a place of her own in Solbringen. This is almost as impressive, with oversize windows and a magnificent view. It must be three times as big as the average Swedish terraced house, even though it is meant to be used only for vacations.

However, the color is astonishingly ugly—a lurid fleshy pink. It doesn't fit in with its surroundings at all.

According to Grip, the body is at the front of the house, down at the bottom of the plot. The slope is steep; the snow must be three feet deep, so it is no easy task getting to the scene. It helps that he can follow his colleagues' footprints, but the snow still manages to find its way inside his boots, chilling his ankles.

He spots Anton as soon as he rounds the corner of the house. The younger detective is standing with uniformed colleagues who are busy cordoning off the area. The distinctive blue-and-white tape signals that this could be a crime scene, and that the general public must stay away.

"Good to see you," Anton says. "There she is."

He points to the body of a young woman lying just a few feet away, with one cheek resting on the ground, facing the slope.

Daniel remains where he is for a moment, forcing himself to take in what he is seeing: the naked skin covered in ice crystals, the limbs that have stiffened in the cold.

The bare feet and the toes with their blue nail polish form a heartrending contrast to the whiteness surrounding the body.

"Where are her clothes? She doesn't even have shoes on her feet."

The deceased is wearing only a bra, panties, and camisole. It is horribly reminiscent of Daniel's first homicide case in Åre a couple of years ago, when a half-naked body was found on one of Åre's best-known ski lifts, the VM6.

It was a tragedy that shook the entire community. Daniel shudders at the thought of having to deal with a similar situation.

"No idea," Anton says, waving a hand in the general direction of the property. "I haven't seen anything nearby."

Daniel looks around. The plot is large; he estimates that the area in front of the house alone must measure some four or five hundred square yards. Outside a door leading into the lower floor, presumably where the sauna is located, he sees a wooden hot tub with a green plastic cover. The ski run is immediately below the property.

Three warmly dressed skiers, their scarves pulled up to protect their faces from the cold, pass by and disappear toward Hermelinbacken, unaware of the tragedy playing out above their heads.

What is the significance of the fact that the deceased is hardly wearing any clothes and is outside with no shoes?

"Would she have come out into the snow of her own free will, barefoot, then simply lain down and gone to sleep?" he says.

It seems unlikely.

"There were high winds all night," Anton points out. "The snow has drifted, and any possible tracks will have been obliterated by now."

"But we should be able to spot the contours," Daniel objects, gazing around once more.

Everything looks perfectly normal. There don't seem to be any formations suggesting that clothes might be hidden beneath the snow cover. Nor footprints from anyone else who could have been there during the night.

When Daniel turns his head, he sees the neighboring house. For a second he thinks someone is peeping from behind a curtain; then the feeling disappears.

He focuses on the body again, moves closer to see if there is any indication of the cause of death. He is very conscious of the need to proceed with caution. CSI Carina Grankvist, who lives in Mattmar, is on her way. Daniel knows exactly what she thinks of careless police officers who stomp all over the scene of a crime before she and her team have had the chance to carry out a thorough examination.

Is this the scene of a crime?

When he crouches down and gazes at the young woman, he can't see any sign of external force. Nothing to explain why she is lying dead outdoors on an overcast Sunday in January.

There don't appear to be any bruises on the body, nothing to suggest strangulation, or that someone has gripped her arms or upper body.

No visible scratch marks.

"What do you think?" he says to Anton. "Was she murdered, or was this an accident?"

"There are no immediate signs of violence," Anton replies pensively. "But why is she lying here? Who goes out in the middle of the night wearing next to nothing, when the temperature is minus twenty-five?"

Exactly.

The temperature was very low last night; it is still bitterly cold even though it is almost eleven o'clock in the morning. Daniel's feet are already starting to go numb, despite the fact that he is warmly dressed.

Logically, it seems unbelievable that the dead woman would have voluntarily gone out into the darkness and frozen to death, but there is nothing in sight to suggest any other explanation.

Unless of course she was under the influence.

When people are very drunk, they do crazy things. Or if they've taken drugs.

"So what do we know about her?"

"Her name is Filippa Smedsås, and she's nineteen years old," Anton replies. "She arrived here yesterday with a group of friends—students from Uppsala. The house belongs to the parents of one of the boys, and they were planning to stay for a week."

"Are they in there?"

"Yes."

"Okay, let's start by talking to each of them, see if we can form a picture of what happened."

Daniel turns to face the house, which is surrounded by a wide balcony.

The subdued winter light is reflected in the windowpanes.

It is impossible to see through the glass from where he is standing, but he can almost feel the fear seeping through the walls.

Six friends arrived here yesterday.

Now there are only five of them.

22

The sunlight is dazzling when Hanna takes off her sunglasses to wipe away a few tears caused by the high speed of their descent. She and Henry have just stopped on a sunny ledge after an unusually long and intense downhill run.

Just like before, the helicopter set them down on a high peak so that they could enjoy virgin terrain. Yesterday they landed on a massif called Bossosčohkka, and today they are on a mountain known as Drakryggen. After a couple of hours' skiing, it is time for an outdoor lunch, which their ski guide is currently producing as if by magic from his well-filled rucksack.

"Good snow," Henry puffs, sitting down next to Hanna on a reindeer skin. "Excellent."

Once again she is impressed by his physique and fitness. They have really pushed themselves; they have hardly stopped to rest since leaving the hotel. There is nothing to suggest that he is approaching sixty.

Henry has taken good care of himself, and he is probably better at it than she is. He is much more aware of the importance of food and sleep. He avoids red meat and processed foods as far as possible, while Hanna often wolfs down a hot dog or burger, as most police officers do when they are working.

"Fantastic," she agrees with a smile as she continues to admire the view.

She can't get enough of it.

They are enjoying a fairy-tale landscape where human beings are only temporary guests. They are surrounded by snow-covered formations that look like billowing waves. The Norwegian peaks are visible on the horizon, and even farther away, invisible to the eye, are the cold, rolling depths of the North Atlantic.

Hanna has often skied in the Alps, but the sight before her bears no resemblance to either Switzerland or Austria, where the mountains are sharp and pointed, reaching up to the sky in jagged ranks.

Here everything is . . . rounder. More inviting and friendly. The mountains, which are sometimes called sleeping giants, simply go on and on into the distance. Far away she can just see a few fluffy clouds in the dips, but otherwise the sky is completely clear.

And there are no hordes of tourists like in the Alps. They are completely alone among the powerful peaks.

Even the reindeer don't come this high up in the winter.

Hanna knows that the world is round, yet it feels as if the world below them is a plateau of ice, snow, and ancient mountains.

It is like sitting on a throne at the top of the universe.

"Top of the world," Henry says, as if he has read her mind.

"It's amazing. So beautiful. Thank you for bringing me here."

Henry leans back on his elbows and smiles, completely relaxed. Hanna admires his ability to lose himself in the moment, to focus wholeheartedly on what is going on right now.

She is still brooding over what he said last night.

His suggestion that they should move in together.

It was the last thing she had expected him to come out with. In her confusion she tried to brush it off with a joke—she hasn't yet given him a proper answer.

Move in with Henry?

That would mean taking their relationship to a whole new level. She hasn't even told her family and friends about him, and now he wants them to live together. They would officially become a couple. And where would they live? In Stockholm, in an inner-city apartment? Or in Jämtland, where she has worked so hard to build a new life for herself?

Her job and her cat are in Åre.

And so is Daniel.

Once again she has that strange sense of disloyalty, the feeling that she is betraying him by being with Henry.

She leans forward and loosens the straps on her ski suit in order to increase her circulation.

They are only colleagues, she tells herself as so many times before. Even though she has cared about Daniel for a long time in a way that definitely oversteps how you should feel about a coworker, she has taken great care to hide her emotions. There is no chance that he suspects anything; she is absolutely sure of it.

While he was with Ida, it was of course unthinkable to give any hint of her inner turmoil. Hanna herself has been the victim of infidelity. It hit her hard, much harder than she could have imagined, when she found out that Christian had been cheating on her for months.

It didn't exactly help when he dumped her the same day she was fired from her job with the City Police in Stockholm.

The fact that he chose to stay with the other woman, Valérie, left a bitter taste that still lingers. After that ordeal she would never contemplate subjecting another woman to the same thing.

Much later, when it became clear that Daniel and Ida had decided to split up, she still couldn't bring herself to tell him how she felt. Especially as he was in the middle of a painful separation.

It was around that time when Henry started courting her, in a way that Hanna had never experienced before. So she made up her mind to stop pining for the unattainable and to be with someone who actually wanted her.

She glances at Henry, who is enjoying the sunshine with his eyes closed. He has made such an effort to celebrate her birthday—she must stop thinking about Daniel.

Their guide comes over with two steaming mugs containing something red.

"There you go," he says with a smile. "Hot lingonberry juice flavored with cinnamon. The food is almost ready."

When Hanna turns her head, she notices that he has lit a small spirit stove in the snow. A pan is bubbling away, giving out a seductive aroma of sautéed reindeer. In another pan she can see fluffy mashed potatoes.

She suddenly realizes how hungry she is. She leans over and gives Henry a kiss on the cheek.

"Can't we just stay here forever?"

Then out of sheer habit she reaches into her pocket to check her phone. The letters on the screen seem to scream at her.

Another murder in Åre!

23

When Daniel and Anton walk into the spacious hallway, the floor is littered with winter shoes in various sizes. Several jackets have been dumped on a bench that is covered with a gray sheepskin.

The five friends have gathered in the living room.

A faint smell of beer and spirits reaches Daniel's nostrils as he goes over to them. The rug bears traces of chips trampled underfoot, and the coffee table is covered in sticky rings. It seems as if they had quite a party last night.

After ten years as a police officer, Daniel is well aware that anything can happen when people get drunk.

He stands by the coffee table, trying to form an impression of the young students.

The group is made up of four boys and one girl. She is curled up in the corner of one of the sofas, with her face hidden in her hands. A boy with dark hair, wearing a gray T-shirt, has his arm around her shoulders. Daniel can see shock and bewilderment on his face. It looks as if he is trying to comfort the girl, yet at the same time he can't take his eyes off the two police officers who are still outside.

They are guarding the body until the CSIs arrive. Daniel glances at his watch; Carina should be here soon.

On the opposite sofa is a blond boy who is slightly shorter. He is staring at his phone as if he is trying to escape reality. The other two friends are seated at the dining table, among the remains of what was presumably breakfast. In the middle is a large, sweaty cheese that really needs to go back in the refrigerator.

"So we're from the police," Daniel begins. He introduces himself and Anton as officers from the Serious Crimes Unit; then they sit down, and Daniel takes out his notebook.

"If we could start with your names?"

The young woman looks up, her eyes blank. Her name is Olivia, she is almost nineteen and was best friends with Filippa. The boy with his arm around her is William, and it is his parents who own the house. He talks fast and is clearly stressed. His words tumble over one another as he tries to clarify the situation.

The two at the table are Emil and Amir, while the boy on the other sofa is Pontus.

They confirm that they know one another from university in Uppsala, as Anton said. They are all studying economics, except for Filippa. They started together back in the fall, and are now in their second semester.

"We're going to need to ask each of you some questions about Filippa's death," Anton explains. "Is there a room we could use?"

William nods in the direction of the staircase.

"There's a study down there," he says unsteadily. "Otherwise there are only bedrooms on that floor, plus a TV room."

"And there's a guest cabin," Emil volunteers. He points through the window to a smaller building a few yards away. He is strikingly tall, around six foot five, Daniel guesses.

Broad-shouldered too.

Strong enough to carry a young woman out into the snow and leave her there in the middle of the night.

"That's where Filippa and Olivia were staying," Emil adds.

Olivia lets out a faint whimper.

"Okay, we'll take a look in there before we leave," Daniel says. "But we'll start with a chat."

"I want to go home," Olivia bursts out.

"I understand that, but I'm afraid you'll have to wait a while."

"Do we have to stay in Åre?"

Anton speaks up. "We'd like you all to stick around for the time being—at least until we've had the chance to look more closely into Filippa's death. We might need to interview you again."

Daniel looks at the group. They are all noticeably shocked, yet they give an impression of being quite composed. They are neatly dressed, polite, and articulate.

However, the question must be answered: Was this an accident, or is one of the group behind Filippa's tragic death?

24

Olivia can't get up from the sofa; she can barely raise her head. It's as if someone else has taken over her body and robbed her of every scrap of strength and the ability to act.

Fifteen minutes have passed since the two detectives left. Through the window she can see new people standing around Filippa's body on the ground. A stretcher has appeared, and it seems as if they are about to take her away.

Less than a year ago they graduated from high school together. Celebrated the start of their adult lives with a champagne breakfast in the park. The whole class was there, and she and Filippa had bought identical dresses. They danced all night, and when one of Olivia's high-heeled sandals fell apart, she carried on barefoot.

She wants to scream at the police, tell them they can't take her best friend. Filippa needs to stay here, with Olivia, forever. Instead she sinks back against the cushions, shaking with cold. There is a blanket over the arm of the sofa, but she can't summon up the energy to pull it over her.

Filippa is dead. She is never coming back. And the last thing Olivia said to her was those harsh words: *Do what you want.*

If only she'd known . . .

She wraps her arms around her chest and rocks back and forth.

William comes in from the kitchen with a mug of tea, which he tentatively offers her.

"You might feel better if you drink this."

Olivia doesn't understand how a cup of Earl Grey is going to make her feel any different, but she can't bring herself to protest. She accepts the cup and takes a sip. William has added plenty of milk and honey, and she actually stops shivering as the warmth spreads through her body.

William isn't usually this thoughtful if they're not alone. In fact she has seen this aspect of him on only a few occasions, when they've been studying in the library together with no one else around, or strolling in the botanical gardens. When William is with his friends, the need to play the alpha male takes over. He has to be in charge, dominate the group. Showing his softer side could be interpreted as a weakness, and he can't handle that.

She gives him a grateful look and takes another sip, but her hands are still trembling, and she spills some of the tea.

Amir and Emil come over to join them.

"So what did those cops want to know when they interviewed you on your own?" Amir asks after a while.

Olivia looks up. "What do you mean?"

"Like I said—what did they want to know?"

"They asked me when I last saw Filippa alive. And I told them."

She doesn't mention that she kept quiet about their disagreement, about the fact that Filippa was very drunk and Olivia lost her patience and left her to it. It was too hard to tell the detective with the beard what had really gone on. She didn't want him to think badly of her, to see her as the kind of person who turned her back on her best friend.

She can't really explain why that seems important; her emotions are all over the place.

A sob rises in her throat. If only she'd insisted that Filippa come back to the guest cabin with her instead of walking out. Then maybe none of this would have happened.

Amir looks around, focuses on Emil. "So what did they ask you?"

"The same thing. What did we do last night, what the atmosphere was like, what time I last saw Filippa."

Olivia can hardly breathe when he says those words.

What time I last saw Filippa.

It sounds completely unreal.

Through the window she sees that Filippa is no longer on the ground, but there is a black plastic bag on top of the stretcher, which two police officers are wheeling away.

They are taking her.

A wave of dizziness comes over Olivia; she feels as if she is going to faint. She leans forward and clutches the armrest to stop herself from losing consciousness.

Amir has also noticed the activity outside. "I hope no one told the cops we were using?" he says, sounding stressed.

Olivia inhales sharply. "Did you give Filippa coke?"

Amir looks even more agitated.

"I didn't exactly force her! I asked her if she wanted to give it a try, and she was up for it. Then she was the one asking for more. Several times."

That was why Filippa behaved as she did last night, why she was so different from her normal self. Not only had she drunk a lot more than usual, she was high as well.

And that is Amir's fault.

"Are you out of your mind?"

William places his hand on hers, but Olivia can't control the anger that flares up.

“Filippa wasn’t used to drugs, she hardly ever drinks! How the fuck could you do that?”

Amir doesn’t like her tone. His eyes darken; he is just about to respond when William steps in.

“None of us needs to tell the cops that we took coke yesterday—we can keep that to ourselves.” He turns to Emil and Pontus. “All agreed?”

No one objects, and William seems to interpret this as a yes.

“I’ve flushed everything we brought with us down the toilet,” he adds, as if that is going to make things better.

Olivia can hardly bring herself to look at Amir.

William turns to Pontus. “What did they ask you?”

“Same. What happened during the evening, what time I last saw Filippa.”

There is something in Pontus’s tone that catches Olivia’s attention.

“This morning you said you fell asleep on the sofa, and no one was there when you woke up. So what time was that?”

Pontus blinks repeatedly. “I don’t really know. Maybe three or four, but I haven’t a clue. All I remember is that I was on my own, and the fire had gone out. I assumed the rest of you had gone to bed, so I went downstairs to my room.”

“So Filippa wasn’t here then?” Olivia pushes him.

“No.”

Olivia tries to think, although her head is scrambled. She’s pretty sure she went back to the guest cabin at about one, and Emil had already gone to bed by then.

“So who saw Filippa last?”

No response.

“William?”

“She was still sitting on the sofa with Amir when I went to bed. Pontus had already fallen asleep in the armchair.”

None of this makes any sense to Olivia. One minute everyone except Emil was in the living room. Then she left, then William. And Amir claims he also went to bed, even though they all saw him making out with Filippa on the sofa.

Which means only Filippa and Pontus remained in the living room—but he was so drunk that he'd fallen asleep.

What happened next?

Why would Filippa, wearing so few clothes, lie down in the snow in the middle of the night, when she could simply have gone back to the guest cabin? If she wasn't spending the night with Amir.

Another question pops into Olivia's mind. Where are the rest of Filippa's clothes, including her padded jacket and boots, which should still have been in the hallway?

Olivia forgot to mention that to the police. She looks at the boys.

"I left at one o'clock. Filippa was here, and everything was okay. But when Pontus woke up, she was gone. Don't you understand? Something must have happened in the meantime. Did you have an argument after I'd gone?"

No one answers.

No one meets her gaze.

"Why do you think she went out into the snow without getting dressed? Why would she do that?"

Then Olivia remembers something else. When she came over from the cabin to the main house this morning, she only had to push down the handle to open the front door.

It wasn't locked.

Which means that anyone, a stranger, could have come in under the cover of darkness.

And done something to Filippa.

25

Back at the station, Daniel and Anton go straight to the conference room to the left of the entrance, where video equipment makes it easy to link up with colleagues in Östersund, Umeå, or other places within the northern region.

Grip is at her desk when she appears on-screen. "So where are we?"

Daniel exchanges a glance with Anton. They spent a couple of hours interviewing the five friends individually. When they had finished they took a look in the guest cabin, but didn't find anything of note—just lots of clothes, and the signs of two girls putting on their makeup and brushing their teeth in the bathroom.

"It's hard to say," he begins. "It seems as if no one really knows what happened last night."

He briefly summarizes what the young people said, which he and Anton had discussed before leaving. They had both gained roughly the same impression of what had gone on during Saturday evening. There had been a lot of partying, and it sounded as if no one was particularly sober when they went off to bed after several hours of drinking games.

They all said that Filippa had drunk a lot more than usual, and that she had been unusually wild and extroverted. One of the boys—William—had mentioned that Filippa and Olivia had almost fallen out over her behavior.

The meeting is drawing to a close when the door opens and Carina Grankvist appears. Daniel gives her a welcoming nod and beckons her in. Carina's input will be critical in assessing whether they are investigating a serious crime or not.

She sits down next to Anton and slips off her jacket as she greets Birgitta Grip.

"Okay," Grip says. "What's your impression, Carina? Are we looking at a homicide?"

"It's not that straightforward," Carina replies, unzipping her thick cardigan. "There are no obvious signs of violence or any other kind of assault. However, with all the snow that drifted overnight, it's hard to tell if there was another person in the picture. We can't find any possible shoe or footprints. It is also impossible to say whether the deceased went out in the middle of the night of her own volition, or whether someone placed her there. She was frozen stiff when she was found."

Carina unwinds her long knitted scarf and places it on the chair beside her.

"I would really like to see what the autopsy shows before I make a definitive statement. At the same time, there's something about the situation that bothers me, but you'll have to take it for what it is, a feeling more than anything . . ."

Daniel leans forward a fraction. Carina rarely expresses herself like this. She prefers to base her judgment on hard facts, and is often cautious in her conclusions.

If she's getting bad vibes, she should be taken seriously.

"Can you expand on that?" he says.

"Put simply . . . I don't understand how she ended up in the place where she was found dead."

This is exactly the same issue that has been bothering Daniel ever since he arrived at Nedre Svedjevägen.

He pictures the house and the yard. From the front door to the spot where Filippa was found must be at least fifty steps. It took him a couple of minutes to get there in the deep snow.

Plenty of time to come to your senses, even if your blood alcohol levels are through the roof.

"If she'd been wearing shoes, I might be able to buy the idea that she was so drunk that she stumbled outside and happened to fall asleep there . . . ," Carina continues.

"But who goes out barefoot when it's that cold?" Anton asks the question on all their minds.

"You would have expected her to go back to the warmth of the house when the cold hit her," Grip agrees.

From the kitchenette they hear the sound of the coffee machine starting up. Daniel could do with another cup; he hasn't stopped for the past few hours.

"Like I said, we need to wait for the forensic pathologist before we can determine the cause of death," Carina says. "But personally I'm not convinced it was an accident."

Daniel nods. "The cause of death will be key. Did she die of hypothermia, or was she already dead when she ended up in the snow?"

"We need to ask for priority with the National Forensic Center in Umeå," Grip says. "Make sure the body is sent up there this evening."

"Already done," Carina says. "I think she's on the way now."

Daniel makes a note.

"What about the parents—have they been informed?" Grip asks.

"Filippa Smedsås was registered in Västerås," Anton says. "I was going to ask our colleagues in the central region to contact her relatives."

"As soon as possible, please."

"What do we do with the other students?" Daniel wonders. "Several of them were talking about going home this afternoon, but we told them to wait. Personally I would prefer to see the results of the autopsy before we let them go. If they disappear back to Uppsala, it will be a lot more difficult to find out what might have happened."

From a formal perspective they have no authority to force the group of friends to remain in Åre. However, this can be solved by arranging interviews that they will be required to attend over the next few days. In which case it would be pointless for them to leave.

If you don't show up for a formal interview, a police car is sent to fetch you.

Daniel knows they will need to speak to the five of them again. If Filippa's death was not accidental, then the situation will change. Suspicions will fall on those who last saw her alive.

Her friends.

Grip runs a hand over her short, steel-gray hair, looking troubled.

"If they disperse, that could make things very tricky for us. Bearing in mind how Filippa was found, half-naked and barefoot, in my opinion there is reason enough to suspect that a crime has been committed."

Grip looks straight at Carina.

"I trust your instinct. Something isn't right. We instigate a preliminary investigation into homicide, manslaughter, causing the death of another person. That gives us access to the whole toolbox."

"House search?" Daniel asks, and receives a nod in response. Carina is going to have her hands full.

Anton clears his throat. "There's one more thing." He tells the group about the angry neighbor who went over to the house the previous evening.

"There's also a property manager called Staffan Berg who called by while the friends were having dinner," Daniel adds. "We need to speak to both of them."

He catches himself wishing Hanna were there. She is a good interviewer, and has a special talent when it comes to talking to young people.

His phone vibrates in his pocket. He glances at the display and smiles to himself.

It's her, of course.

26

Hanna is sitting in a quiet corner of the restaurant when she calls Daniel. She doesn't want Henry to overhear her conversation; she made an excuse to go off on her own. He is in their room, having an afternoon nap. He wasn't exactly pleased when she suggested they should go back to the hotel earlier than planned, even though he did give in quite quickly.

It is almost two o'clock, and Hanna tells herself that the sun will be going down in half an hour. It's not as if they've lost a whole day on the mountain, just a few hours.

She has to find out what is going on in Åre.

When Daniel answers on the second ring, relief floods her body. And another feeling, warm and familiar, that she can't put into words.

"Hi, it's me. I saw the news flash about another murder in Åre. What's going on?"

"We don't know yet if it's a murder."

Daniel explains the circumstances around the young woman's death: the lack of clothing when she was found, the group of friends who had come to the mountains for a week's skiing, the wild partying that seems to have taken place the previous evening.

"There are no signs of external violence," he says in conclusion.

"So she was just lying there dead in the snow when they found her? Surely it can't be anything but murder, even if the body doesn't have any visible injuries."

"People do strange things when they're drunk," Daniel points out.

"Who gets so drunk that they walk out barefoot when it's minus twenty and simply lie down in the snow?"

"That's what Carina said," Daniel concedes.

Hanna's gut instinct tells her that this is no accident.

"Do we know if she'd taken drugs?" she asks. "It's easier to imagine her wandering off in the middle of the night if she was under the influence of ecstasy or something similar, something that messes with the brain."

"None of her friends mentioned drugs, but of course they could have agreed among themselves to keep quiet about it. We'll see what the autopsy shows—Grip has asked for priority."

Hanna leans back in the leather armchair, crossing her legs as she thinks. An inviting fire is burning at the other end of the room, sparks shooting up above the logs that are slowly being consumed by the flames.

The icy temperature should have sobered the girl up, however much alcohol she had consumed. And she wasn't far away from a source of warmth. If Hanna has understood Daniel correctly, she was found only about thirty yards from the main house, and even closer to the guest cabin. There must have been doors on the lower level too, maybe access in and out for skiing as well.

"Have you done a background check on the friends?" she asks. "Are any of them in our databases, or with a tendency to violence? Could there be a jealous boyfriend in the picture?"

Hanna spent many years working in the Domestic Violence Unit with the City Police in Stockholm. She has no illusions about the violence men can perpetrate against women, even those as young as this particular group.

"We've opened a preliminary investigation, but like I said, it could have been an accidental death."

Hanna glances over at the window, where the sun is going down. The sky has been transformed into a mosaic of pink and orange shades. The mountaintops to the west look as if they are on fire.

The decision is obvious.

"I'm coming in."

She can't possibly stay here if they are facing a brutal murder. The only thing she will be able to think about is the case.

"But you're supposed to be off until Tuesday," Daniel protests. "You don't need to interrupt your break for this."

"It's no problem. I can take some time off later. There will be plenty of other opportunities."

There is a brief pause, as if Daniel is wondering whether he ought to try to persuade her to stay.

"Where are you, by the way?"

The question puts Hanna in a difficult position. She can't possibly tell Daniel where she is, because he would immediately realize that she is with a man.

A man who can afford to stay in a place like this.

A man like Henry Sylvester.

Daniel met Henry during the investigation into the murder at Copperhill last Easter. Hanna recalls the case with a shudder. Right from the start, Daniel had seemed suspicious of Henry. Hanna could never bring herself to ask whether it was because of Henry's wealth or because he initially kept crucial information to himself.

She finds it difficult to imagine what Daniel would say if he knew that she and Henry were a couple, but it probably wouldn't be positive.

"I'll tell you when I see you," she says to avoid giving him an answer. "I have to go—I'll be in touch as soon as I'm back."

Henry won't be pleased that she is interrupting the break that he had planned so carefully, but it can't be helped. Under these circumstances she cannot stay in a luxury hotel to go skiing with her secret lover.

Her intuition is telling her one thing and one thing only.

There has been another murder in Åre.

27

Olivia is lying in bed with the covers pulled over her head. She has just spoken to her dad, but as usual he just made vague noises, as if he didn't really know what to say.

She is so lost without her mom, completely helpless. She almost regrets calling her dad to tell him about Filippa. She doesn't want to worry him even more, and he can't really do anything anyway.

Just like three years ago.

Olivia has never longed for her mother as much as she does right now. *Fuck cancer,* it says on the little bracelet with plastic letters that she always wears on her left wrist.

Her thoughts turn to Aron and Jenny, Filippa's parents. They must be devastated. She ought to call them, but she can't do it, can't find the strength to cope with their grief when she herself is so bereft.

There is a gentle tap on the door of the cabin.

Reluctantly Olivia gets up, wraps the quilt around her, and shuffles into the hallway. Emil is standing there—he isn't wearing a jacket, and is shivering after walking the short distance from the house.

"Can I come in?"

He is so tall compared with Olivia, especially when she is barefoot.

"Of course." She leads the way to the seating area by the window and sinks down in one corner of the leather sofa, still with the quilt wrapped around her.

"How are you feeling?" Emil asks, taking the armchair opposite.

He is three years older than Olivia, and one of her best male friends in Uppsala. He is calm and thoughtful, whereas she is quick and spontaneous. She has often thought that he is a good listener—for a guy. When they started the economics program back in the fall, they ended up in the same team, the recce group as it is known, along with Pontus, Amir, and William. That was how they became friends.

"Two police officers just called by," Emil goes on. "They repeated that we have to stay here for a few more days. We're not allowed to go home until the forensic examination has taken place."

He is clearly upset, speaking more quickly than usual, his voice slightly more shrill. Olivia sees her own despair reflected in his eyes.

"You mean the autopsy?" she asks, wanting to make sure she understands.

The thought of them cutting open Filippa's body makes her shudder. Not long ago Filippa was standing in the bathroom, brushing her hair. Soon she will be lying naked on a slab, sliced open while strangers' hands examine her.

"Can they do that?" she whispers. "Force us to stay?"

Emil runs his fingers through his hair, making it stand on end. "I think so."

Olivia has no idea about the law, she doesn't know what the police can and can't do. "I want to get away from here." She hates the thought of having to remain in Åre.

"Me too, but I guess we have to do as they say."

There are lines of tension around Emil's mouth, as if he too is struggling not to cry. Twilight is falling outside, Olivia can see that the chairlift has closed for the day. Over by the Hermelinen lift, a long line has formed as people wait to make their way home.

"What do you think happened to Filippa?" she says hesitantly. "Could she have been so out of it that she went outside and fell asleep in the snow?"

Emil clasps his fingers together; they are long and slender like the rest of his body.

"I don't know," he replies, his expression troubled. "I'd gone to bed."

Olivia has the feeling that Emil doesn't want to talk about it. Maybe that's his way of dealing with this terrible thing. She, on the other hand, can't let it go; it's like picking at a scab you know you shouldn't touch.

She will go crazy if she can't talk about Filippa, why she is no longer alive.

"What if she had an argument with someone and it all went wrong?"

Emil gives her a searching look. "Like who?"

Olivia has been wondering all afternoon. Pontus claims he fell asleep in the living room while Filippa was there, but after William had gone to his room. Amir claims that Filippa was still sitting on the sofa when he went to bed.

But what if that isn't true?

What if Amir and Filippa started to quarrel, and he's lying about it?

Olivia remembers waking up alone in the cabin. She assumed Filippa had spent the night with Amir, because he'd been stuck to her like a leech all evening.

Would he have lost interest, just like that?

Olivia finds it hard to believe. She doesn't trust Amir. He's a social climber who doesn't hesitate to use others in order to get where he wants to be. That's why he likes hanging out with William and his rich friends. He has big plans for his life, and he thinks his networking will give him access to the high-flying career he wants—access that his own background cannot offer.

Who else could be behind Filippa's death?

William would never be interested in her, and Emil was already in bed. Pontus was drunk and had fallen asleep.

"What do you think about Amir?" she says quietly. "Could he have done something to Filippa?"

28

After the conversation with Hanna, Daniel sits down in his office in front of the computer with yet another cup of coffee. His eyes are stinging with tiredness—or maybe it's the weight of a young life that has been snuffed out too early.

He never gets used to it, in spite of all his years as a police officer.

Alice is with Ida now; it is Ida's turn to have their daughter for two days, so he's not in a hurry to get home to the empty apartment. It feels kind of desolate without Alice's chattering, so he might as well stay at work and carry out the background checks on the five friends.

The interviews have provided a pretty cohesive picture of the course of events yesterday evening. Filippa had gotten very drunk. They all said there was a lot of alcohol. Maybe drugs too, although none of them mentioned that. Daniel is well aware that drug use is very common among today's students.

No one saw Filippa leave the house and go outside in the middle of the night. No one can provide a reasonable explanation as to why she was found dead in the snow the following morning.

So how did she end up there?

He reads through his interview notes and makes a list of the five students. He also adds the name of Staffan Berg, the property manager who looks after the house when the family are in Stockholm. And Åke Carlsson, the neighbor who came over on Saturday evening.

Both men must be contacted and questioned as soon as possible, but first he wants to revisit the interviews.

Olivia was the first person he spoke to. He accompanied her to the cabin, and took the opportunity to check out Filippa's room. Olivia was clearly devastated, but she made a good impression on Daniel. She came across as clever, made an effort to give clear, well-thought-out answers. According to Olivia, she and Filippa were best friends, and the four boys have confirmed this. At first glance Daniel finds it hard to believe she had anything to do with Filippa's death. Olivia's grief seemed completely genuine.

He finishes his coffee and turns to the next interview.

William Löwengren grew up in Östermalm in Stockholm, and it became clear that he had attended prestigious schools in the city center and is used to a high standard of living. Apart from the showy house in Åre, the family also owns a summer cottage in the Stockholm archipelago, and they often holiday abroad. His father has a high-ranking position with one of Sweden's largest merchant banks, and his mother works for an investment company. William is the oldest of three brothers.

Daniel chews the end of his pen as he thinks about William Löwengren. Judging by his own description, he saw himself as the informal leader of the group. It seemed to Daniel that William enjoyed the role and was keen to maintain that position. He had accompanied the two detectives to the door when they were leaving, and had loudly requested that the police should keep them informed of any developments in the case, as if he were automatically acting as the group's spokesman.

What would happen if anyone challenged his authority? How would he react?

And what if that someone happened to be a girl?

However, no one has suggested that Filippa was the kind of person who wanted to be the center of attention. Quite the reverse, in fact—according to Olivia, she could be shy and reserved. Yesterday evening had been an exception, when Filippa had had way too much to drink and acted out of character.

What does that mean?

Daniel has no idea.

His third interview was with Amir Ghazemi, who described himself as William's best friend in Uppsala. Amir's parents come from Iran. Both are highly educated; his father is a dentist, and his mother works in HR in one of the larger clothing chains. Amir has a younger sister.

Daniel reaches for the mouse and brings up a picture of Amir Ghazemi on Instagram. The photo seems to have been taken outdoors; he is half lying on a lawn in the sunshine, smiling at the camera. There is no denying that he looks good, with his dark, longish hair, a charming smile, and brown eyes with a hint of green.

Not the kind of guy who would find it difficult to get the girls.

Olivia had hinted that Amir and Filippa had been making out on the sofa, but she wasn't sure how it had gone after she left.

Daniel makes a note to follow this up. Hanna's comment about a jealous boyfriend lingers in the back of his mind.

Although he hadn't gotten the impression from Amir that Filippa was a particularly important person in his life. Even though the interview was about her, Amir seemed to want to focus on his friendship with William. He was clearly impressed by his friend and the Löwengren family, their lifestyle, their houses, their luxury vacations, how cool it was to live like that.

Daniel removes the image of Amir's face from the screen and types "Pontus Englund" in the search box. The picture matches the young man he met earlier: Pontus looks a little lost and awkward, as if the camera has perfectly captured his lack of self-esteem.

He doesn't seem to belong in the group, somehow. He is a lot less confident than the others. According to the notes, he comes from a small village in Skåne, and grew up on a farm run by his parents—the fourth generation to do so.

Anton, who conducted the interview, described Pontus as nervous and sweaty during their conversation. However, he couldn't be sure whether this was because Pontus was hungover or simply stressed by the situation.

He got the impression that Pontus was embarrassed to admit that he'd gotten so drunk he'd fallen asleep on the sofa. Pontus couldn't remember what time he'd last seen Filippa.

Daniel moves on to the last name on the list: Emil Sandström. Born and brought up outside Umeå, with two younger sisters. Both parents are teachers. Daniel thinks back to the tall, fair-haired twenty-two-year-old he met this morning. A young man from Norrland who had moved south to study. Emil had a calm, measured way of speaking. Daniel has heard this same tone many times north of Sundsvall, where he himself was born and raised. Emil is the oldest in the group, because he worked for a few years before going to university. He said he was used to the outdoor life and enjoyed sporting activities. According to Anton, he came across very well.

Daniel leans back and links his hands behind his head. Thinks for a few seconds.

All the facts on the table give a cohesive picture of a group of students who are generally decent individuals. There is a clear reason why they know one another, although some seem to be closer friends than others. They had just completed the final assignment of the semester, and they had a few days free before the beginning of the spring semester. So they came to the mountains, where one of the group had access to a large, luxurious house where they could stay for free.

They seem to have partied hard since they arrived in Åre, but Daniel can't really criticize them for that. Who didn't do the same at their age?

Nothing that emerged during the interviews comes across as suspicious or unreasonable, but if Hanna's instinct is correct—and unfortunately he has to admit that this has often been the case in the past—then a crime has been committed.

If Filippa's death wasn't accidental, then he must assume that one of the five friends he met this morning must have been involved.

It is difficult to find another explanation.

But which one of them?

29

The light is on in Daniel's office when Anton walks into the station at four thirty in the afternoon. He was halfway to Duved when he decided to turn around. He couldn't stop thinking about the young woman who had died; he can spend a couple more hours on the case before dinner.

He stamps the snow off his boots and knocks on Daniel's door. His colleague is absorbed in his notes, pen in hand as he looks up.

"Haven't you got anything better to do on a Sunday?"

"Apparently not," Anton replies, sitting down in one of the visitors' chairs.

All the offices in the station are more or less identical. They are equipped with a height-adjustable desk, a bookcase, and two armchairs upholstered in blue with a small table between them. Functional, but not very exciting.

On Daniel's desk there is a photograph of Alice as a newborn.

Anton's phone buzzes, and he glances at the display. It's Carl—they are having dinner at his place tonight to celebrate their nine-month anniversary.

The thought of his boyfriend makes him smile.

"What was that?" Daniel asks.

Anton quickly slips his phone in his pocket; he doesn't want to have to explain who Carl is.

"Nothing." He points to the open notebook in front of Daniel. "Anything interesting?"

Daniel shrugs. "I'm trying to form a picture of the five friends. The group dynamic. If there's something that doesn't sound right. You know how it is—we have to look for things that don't quite fit."

He stretches his arms out in front of him, turns his head from side to side a few times until the tension in his neck eases.

"By the way, Hanna called. After we'd talked for a while, she seemed pretty convinced that we're looking at a crime here."

That sounds like Hanna in a nutshell. Anton knows what she's like—always quick when it comes to both thinking and acting, even if she can be a little too quick sometimes. He likes Hanna. He was the one who suggested they should offer her a post in Åre when she arrived just over two years ago. At the time she was at a low ebb, damaged by her experiences in Stockholm. Now she is a key member of the team.

And her instinct as a police officer has never been wrong.

"Have you had time to carry out any searches?" Anton asks. "Has anyone appeared as a past suspect, or with a conviction?"

Daniel points to the screen. "That's what I was just doing. So far there's nothing on William, Olivia, or Amir, although it's too soon to write them off at this stage."

"How about Emil and Pontus?"

"I'll take a look now."

He types in a few numbers, then waits.

"Nothing on Pontus Englund either. I did a multiple search, and he's as pure as the driven snow."

Which leaves just one person.

"How about Emil?"

"It's probably a long shot, but here goes."

Anton leans back in the armchair as he waits. Then he sees Daniel's expression change. "What is it?"

"Emil isn't as innocent as he seems."

Daniel turns the screen so that Anton can see.

"He has a conviction from the county court in Umeå—assault during his final year at high school."

Anton lets out a low whistle. He'd gained a very positive impression when he interviewed Emil, but you can't judge a book by its cover. "So what happened?"

Daniel skims through the text.

"The assault happened four years ago, shortly before Emil turned nineteen. It started with a quarrel at a restaurant in Umeå and ended with him headbutting one of the other customers."

Not a minor scuffle, in other words.

"What was the sentence?" Anton asks.

"Let's see . . . He received a suspended sentence and a fine, because he was so young and it was his first offense. Plus his family background was solid, which no doubt helped."

Emil was lucky, Anton thinks. Assault usually carries a sentence of up to two years in jail. Headbutting someone is not regarded as a minor offense, but in this case presumably the reduced sentence for a young person kicked in. Sweden still has generous laws when it comes to young perpetrators, even if a growing number of voices are demanding more stringent punishments.

"He didn't mention this when I spoke to him," Anton says.

"No. Although surely he must have realized we'd find out. He can't be dumb enough to think we'd miss it."

Anton isn't so sure. Sometimes people keep on hoping until the very last minute.

"The question is, what does it mean?" Daniel adds.

"Surely it's very clear—Emil has a tendency toward violence. Or at least he's proved himself capable of violence in previous situations,"

Anton says. Then he softens his stance—he doesn't want to jump to conclusions.

"I'm not saying we should accuse him of being behind Filippa's death just because of a past conviction, but the likelihood of his being involved has definitely increased."

30

Olivia would have preferred to stay in bed for the rest of the day to grieve in peace, but hunger drives her up to the main house. She needs something to eat.

She finds Amir and Pontus in the living room, while Emil is in the kitchen, preparing dinner. She can hardly bring herself to look at Amir. She doesn't believe him when he says he left Filippa on the sofa and went to bed alone.

Something happened between them.

But what?

When Olivia and Emil talked about it earlier, he came up with a new theory. Maybe Filippa willingly had sex with Amir, then tried to stagger back to the cabin, but collapsed in the snow because she was so drunk.

It sounds like a reasonable hypothesis, except if it's true, Amir is keeping quiet about parts of the evening.

Why?

If he can lie about that, maybe he's lying about other things too?

Every question throws up a new one, and Olivia can't control the thoughts spinning around in her head. She would really like to sneak upstairs and take a look in Amir's room to see if there is any trace of Filippa or her clothes, but she doesn't have the nerve.

At least not while he's sitting there on the sofa.

Olivia pulls off her moon boots. She is wearing sweatpants with a loose top, and has pulled her hair into a messy ponytail. She can't be bothered to make an effort.

Another, more frightening thought is that Amir had sex with Filippa against her will, that he forced himself on her and she fled out into the snow, where she collapsed for some reason.

Olivia didn't dare voice her fears when she and Emil were talking in the cabin. She doesn't want him to think she's gone crazy.

Although right now, looking at Amir relaxing and surfing on his phone, she wonders what he is capable of. He seems totally unconcerned, not remotely upset by Filippa's death. Olivia has cried and cried, her nose is swollen and her eyes are red, but Amir looks exactly the same as usual.

Has he even called his parents to tell them about the tragedy?

She feels an overwhelming need to be with someone she likes, someone who is kind, so she joins Emil at the stove. He is making a thick soup, and her tummy rumbles.

Is she letting Filippa down by thinking about food?

"Won't be long," Emil says. "Lentil soup with homemade wholemeal bread with sunflower seeds."

Olivia flings her arms around him and rests her head on his broad chest, which is where she comes up to.

"You're so good," she says. "I don't know how you can do all this after what's happened."

Emil gently kisses her on the forehead. "We have to eat." He hands her some tomatoes and a chopping board. "There you go—you can make a salad."

Olivia gratefully accepts the task. It's nice to occupy her hands; it's easier to escape all those terrible thoughts. She has actually wondered if she is going mad.

If only she had insisted that Filippa go with her last night. If only she had gone back herself, instead of going to bed. If only she had stayed in the living room as long as Filippa was there.

Then maybe she would be alive now.

Olivia swallows hard and tries to concentrate on slicing tomatoes.

William's bedroom door opens, and he comes over to the kitchen island, where she and Emil are working.

"I've just spoken to my dad. He and Mom are in New York this week, but they're going to try and get an earlier flight home and come up here. Dad says the police have no right to tell us what we can and can't do."

As usual, William sounds completely sure of himself. Olivia wishes she had parents like that, making it clear to other people what is going to happen. But her dad is a service technician. It would never occur to him to tell the police how to do their job.

William puts his arm around Olivia's shoulders and pulls her close. Out of the corner of her eye, she sees Emil's reaction—his expression darkens.

"Everything will be fine," William says gently. "I promise."

But Olivia doesn't believe him.

Nothing will ever be fine again.

31

While Karin clears away after dinner—game stew with lingonberry sauce and mashed potatoes—Åke sits down in front of the TV to watch the evening news.

He is alone in the living room—Peter is downstairs, putting the boys to bed.

Next door has been a hive of activity all day—police cars all over the place. Information about what had happened was posted online later.

Åke has followed every report, all the speculation, read every word he could find.

At last it is time for the local news from SVT Jämtland.

He immediately recognizes the view on-screen. It is Sadeln, seen from Lake Åre. The Löwengrens' ugly house is clearly visible as the camera pans across the area.

Karin comes over and stands beside Åke's armchair with a tea towel in her hand.

"Can you turn it up?" she says, her eyes glued to the TV.

The reporter gives a detailed account of the police presence during the morning, how the body of a young woman was found outside one of the biggest houses in Sadeln. Then she interviews a gray-haired female police chief in her sixties, who refuses to say whether or not this is a homicide.

"But do you think she froze to death, or was she killed?" the reporter presses the police officer. "Surely you must have a theory?"

"Unfortunately I can't comment at this stage."

The reporter continues to push, but she gets nowhere.

"Terrible business," Åke says when the piece is over.

Karin sinks down on the sofa as if she has no words. She looks pale and tired; she seems to have been deeply affected by the events next door. Åke has always known that his wife has a bigger heart than he does—especially when it comes to children and young people.

"I'm not surprised it ended so badly," he continues. "You should have seen how drunk they were last night."

"They treated you terribly," Karin says. "So disrespectful!"

Åke agrees. He told Karin what happened when he went over there; he still shudders at the memory of their behavior. He remembers the surge of anger he felt, the rage he could barely control when that girl tried to touch his penis.

Someone had to put their foot down.

She needed to be taught a lesson.

"It was only a matter of time before an accident happened in that house," he says, drumming his fingers on the arm of the chair. "No doubt about it."

"In a way they have only themselves to blame," Karin says quietly, as if she doesn't want to speak ill of the dead. "No one forced them to drink so much."

"It was their choice," Åke agrees.

"Still, it's a tragedy that she's dead," his wife adds. "Her poor parents—it won't be easy for them."

Åke sees that Karin has tears in her eyes. She wipes them away discreetly with the blue-and-white striped tea towel.

"Like you said—tragic," he agrees, mainly to soothe his wife's feelings.

They hear footsteps on the stairs, and Peter joins them. He sits down on the sofa beside his mom. Åke notices that the hair at the back of his neck his way too long—he really needs to go to the barber.

Åke sighs. Things are difficult for his eldest son right now. His whole life fell apart when his wife, Anna, left him a year ago. Åke will never understand how she could ask for a divorce, with no warning whatsoever—especially when the boys were so little.

On top of everything, she had the nerve to argue over custody. First of all she demanded sole custody; then eventually she agreed that Peter could have the boys every other weekend and during some of the school breaks.

But Peter doesn't want to talk about it. As soon as Åke or Karin tries to bring up the subject, wondering why the marriage collapsed, their son simply shuts down.

"Are they asleep?" Karin says, patting Peter's arm.

She worries about him all the time. The fact that he lives in Gothenburg while they are in Åre doesn't exactly help now he's a single dad. Karin often talks about how difficult things are for him, and goes down as often as she can to help out.

Peter adjusts his glasses, which are greasy and covered in fingerprints.

"They were both worn out. I didn't even finish reading them a story before they fell asleep."

Peter seems tired too, Åke thinks. But of course it's hard work looking after two little ones on your own, even if it only involves visiting Grandma and Grandpa for a few days.

Anna should be ashamed of herself.

He would like to teach his former daughter-in-law a lesson. Sometimes he wishes she were standing in front of him so that he could tell her exactly what he thinks of her behavior.

The local news is coming to an end, and is followed by the weather forecast for the next three days—the low temperatures are set to continue.

"Hell of a business with the neighbors," Peter says, gazing at the screen. "Terrible." He yawns without covering his mouth.

"Accidents happen," Åke says. "That's just the way it is."

"You think it was an accident?" Karin says, with sadness in her eyes.

Åke does his best to answer calmly and with conviction—he knows how sensitive his wife can be.

"Of course. What else could it be?"

32

Anton is sitting at the round table in Carl's kitchen, and they have more or less finished dinner. A meal he knows Carl has been planning for days—whitefish roe on toast to start, and beef fillet Provençale for the main course. Two panna cottas with cloudberries are waiting in the refrigerator.

Carl hasn't said much during dinner, and Anton can't help wondering if he has something on his mind. Maybe he noticed that Anton was uncomfortable at Boqueria yesterday, when Carl squeezed his hand in public.

"How about a trip to Vita Renen on Saturday?" he suggests, hoping to cheer Carl up. They both enjoy a visit to the cozy waffle house—they can ski there and back.

"I can't on Saturday, I've promised to help my brother move some stuff. Sunday's okay, though."

Anton shuffles uncomfortably. It's his sister Karro's birthday on Sunday, and she has invited both Anton and his parents over for tea and cake. He had hoped to avoid mentioning it to Carl.

"I can't do Sunday."

"Why not?"

Carl's expression is challenging, as if he senses that Anton is hiding something from him. Playing for time, Anton pops the last piece of beef in his mouth and chews away, hoping that Carl will drop the subject.

"This is delicious," he says. "You're a real master chef!"

Carl gives him a searching look. "What are you doing on Sunday that's so important?"

Anton doesn't want to lie to him, but he doesn't know how to explain. He searches for the right words, hoping to avoid making the situation worse, but his mind is blank.

His tongue feels stiff as he decides to tell the truth.

"It's my sister's birthday, and she's invited the family over to celebrate."

As soon as he says the word *family*, he regrets it, but it's too late. He doesn't mention that Hanna will be there too, because she and Karro are good friends.

"And that doesn't include me?" Carl says. "Or is there another reason why I'm not allowed to come? Are you ashamed of me?"

"Of course not—don't be stupid! We're together."

"In that case I would really like to know why you haven't told me that there's a family gathering to which I am not invited."

"We're only talking about a couple of hours," Anton mumbles. "And Karro's kids will be racing around like lunatics as soon as they've had a sugar hit. It will be messy and noisy. And my parents are pretty boring."

"Surely I'm going to have to meet your family at some point?" Carl says, folding his arms across his chest. "We've been together for nine months—that's quite a long time."

"Of course you'll meet them . . ."

"We can't go on pretending forever, can we?"

Carl is rarely sarcastic, but he asks the question in such an acidic tone that Anton is taken aback. He fiddles with his knife and fork, puts them down on his plate without meeting Carl's gaze. He has tried to avoid this issue, he has never wanted to admit to Carl that he still hasn't come out to anyone even though he is over thirty. Even though Carl must have wondered why Anton never wants them to hang out with his family and friends, why he only wants them to spend time alone together, Anton has done his best to pull the wool over Carl's eyes.

"I didn't think you'd be interested." He can hear how lame it sounds. His pathetic efforts to explain simply make the situation worse.

"You don't think I can decide for myself whether I want to go or not? Or don't you trust me to behave properly when I meet your parents for the first time?"

There is no warmth in Carl's voice. His dark eyes have narrowed, and deep inside, Anton can read both sadness and disappointment.

Feelings that are a lot harder to deal with than pure anger.

"How long are you intending to keep our relationship a secret?" Carl goes on. "Or do you think I don't realize what you're doing?"

It hurts when Anton hears Carl's bitter words. He is more than angry and upset. It sounds as if Carl is having doubts about their relationship.

Don't do this, Anton wants to cry out. *You're the most important person in my life. I love you!*

Of course he wants to introduce Carl to his parents, let him meet Karro and her wonderful, wild kids. But Anton can imagine how shocked his mother would be—she is desperate for him to meet a girl and have children before it's too late. Not to mention how his father would react—the retired lieutenant colonel who is a real man's man and likes to boast about his military achievements and macho behavior.

He knows how awkward and embarrassing it would be if he took Carl along on Sunday; he can picture the disaster playing out. It is more than likely that his father would say something unforgivable that would make Carl walk out in a fury.

Then his mother would start crying, and Karro would think Anton had ruined her birthday.

"It's not about that," he says.

"Okay, so what is it about? Go on."

Carl starts tearing the paper napkin into tiny, tiny pieces as he waits for Anton's explanation. He is fully committed, and has even hinted that maybe they should move in together. He really wants to introduce Anton to his family and friends, and to be a proper couple.

Anton is the one who resists and keeps coming up with excuses and objections.

Carl's beautiful eyes are shining with unshed tears; his expression is stiff and distant. There is nothing Anton would like to do more than erase the last fifteen minutes, explain how important Carl is to him, see that loving smile again.

But he can't bring himself to say the right words. Instead he sits there in silence.

Eventually Carl tosses the remains of the napkin in the direction of his plate. The movement is so violent that he misses the table, and the fragments float down and spread over the floorboards like sad confetti.

"I can't do this anymore," he says, getting to his feet.

The gap between them is as deep as an abyss. Anton is too ashamed even to look up.

"I'm going to bed."

Seconds later the bedroom door slams behind Carl's implacable back.

And Anton remains seated at the table, among the pathetic leftovers of what was supposed to be a romantic meal to celebrate their nine months together.

33

The lights of the landing strip outside Järpen appear before Hanna's eyes just as her ears become blocked. She swallows several times to even out the pressure.

"Nearly there," she says to Henry.

He is sitting opposite her in the cream-colored leather armchair with his eyes closed. He has been unusually quiet during the journey home.

Hanna wouldn't exactly describe the atmosphere as oppressive, but she knows he is disappointed in her decision to put her job before his carefully-thought-out plans for her birthday.

She touches the beautiful bracelet he gave her, and thinks that she must remember to take it off before she goes into the station tomorrow morning. She can hardly show up to work with an exclusive piece of jewelry worth hundreds of thousands of kronor. She mustn't lose that little screwdriver from Cartier.

Henry gives himself a shake and yawns.

"I'm going to stay on the plane and carry on to Stockholm," he says. "I might as well go into the office tomorrow."

His comment takes Hanna by surprise. Somehow his words make her feel rejected, even though she is the one who has broken off their trip. But of course it makes sense for him to return to the capital. What would Henry do in Åre if Hanna is about to throw herself into an investigation? Sit in her little cottage stroking Morris the cat?

She has no right to be upset.

"Listen," she says, taking his hand. "It's been a fantastic weekend, and I appreciate it enormously. I just have to . . ."

What is it that she has to do?

Why is she behaving like this?

No one is forcing her to cut short her leave. Daniel expressly told her that there was no need for her to rush back. However, the compulsion to go in and find out exactly what has happened is overwhelming. She has googled every search term she could think of in order to learn more about the case. Her brain is already busy formulating various theories, and the image of the young woman's body in the snow is already etched on her retinas.

Henry squeezes her hand and gives her an enigmatic smile.

"You don't have to explain. You're committed to your job, just like I am. I understand completely." Then his expression grows serious. "But it would be good if we could talk about the future—about us. Next time we meet, I'd like to do that."

34

Olivia is standing in the doorway of the cabin; she can't decide whether it feels safe or unsafe to sleep here alone after what happened to Filippa. However, she couldn't face staying in the main house with the guys. Being there was no consolation; the atmosphere was weird.

She steps inside and makes sure she locks the door behind her.

She didn't bother yesterday, because she thought Filippa might stagger in during the night. Right now it feels vital to make sure that no one can get in, although she can't explain why.

To be on the safe side, she goes around and checks that all the windows are closed and secured; then she crawls into bed without brushing her teeth. She makes a little nest under the covers and curls up in the fetal position.

If only Filippa were here.

The room is pitch black when Olivia wakes up. How long has she been asleep? She doesn't know.

She fumbles for her phone to check the time, but before she finds it, she hears a faint squeaking, a sound that doesn't belong in a cabin where she is the only occupant.

That must have been what woke her.

Someone is trying to get in.

Olivia sits up, listens hard. She is pretty certain that the sound is coming from the front door, as if someone is slowly pushing down the handle.

Her heart starts racing, her mouth goes dry. She is too scared to switch on the bedside lamp, but she slips out of bed and creeps over to the window.

She cautiously peeps out, and at first she can't see anything. It takes a little while for her eyes to get used to the darkness. Then she becomes aware of a shadow that shouldn't be there. She is at an odd angle from her position by the window frame, and the light is too poor to make out anything other than vague contours, but there is definitely someone by the door.

Olivia can't take her eyes off the unknown figure. Time is passing both slowly and quickly.

The person turns around. She can't distinguish the facial features, yet she has a strong sense of something familiar.

And then the shadow melts into the night and disappears.

MONDAY

35

It is early in the morning when Anton opens his eyes. He had lain awake for a long time, didn't fall asleep until about two, then was plagued by weird, incomprehensible dreams about the body in the snow.

Carl is sleeping by his side, still turned away, exactly as he has been all night.

This is the first time they have had a serious quarrel, and the first time they have gone to bed without sorting a problem.

Anton props himself up on one elbow so that he can see Carl better.

In sleep he looks completely relaxed. His fair eyelashes are resting on his winter-pale skin, his hair on the pillow. His mouth, which spoke such harsh words last night, is once again soft and tempting.

They both grew up in Duved, around ten minutes' drive from Åre, and went to the same elementary school. But because Anton is a couple of years older, they never hung out back then.

Until they bumped into each other at Bygget two years ago.

Anton loves the memory of that evening. The attraction was immediate, a bolt of lightning, and they spent a few fantastic days together.

Until he threw everything away.

Carl was an important witness in an ongoing homicide case, and Anton, who was right in the middle of the investigation, didn't dare to show how much Carl meant to him. Whatever they had simply disappeared.

Against all the odds, he got another chance a year later.

At the time he found it hard to believe that he could be so lucky, and he was prepared to do anything to win Carl back.

Until reality caught up with him.

Is he in the process of destroying their relationship for the second time?

Before Carl came into his life, Anton had almost given up hope of meeting anyone. He had more or less resigned himself to living alone, and hid behind the cliché of the "eternal bachelor." It was easier to pretend that he had never met the right person than to explain what his sexual orientation actually was.

Is Carl growing tired of the fact that Anton is still playing that role, refusing to stand up and acknowledge that they are a couple?

Every time Carl tries to raise the issue, Anton ducks and dives and changes the subject. However, the longer they are together, the more he worries that Carl will grow tired of the secrecy and deliver an ultimatum.

Anton groans to himself.

This is his fault; he has only himself to blame.

He buries his head in the pillow and curses his behavior, hating himself for his cowardice. He doesn't want to be a person who hides behind half truths and evasion. Carl is worth more than that. He deserves a partner who is proud to be seen with him.

And yet it is still too difficult.

Through the gap between the roller blind and the window ledge, he can just see an ice-cold Duved. Under normal circumstances he would have rolled over, close to Carl's body, maybe woken him with a kiss and explained that he had to leave early because of the new case.

But right now Anton doesn't know if he dare touch him.

He is afraid of being rejected, afraid of seeing the disappointment in Carl's eyes as the memory of yesterday evening returns.

Maybe Carl will ask him to get out?

Or even worse, finish with him?

Anton slips out of bed and gathers up his clothes. It's probably better to leave Carl in peace for a while. Give him some space.

Carl probably won't want to see him when he wakes up.

Anton gets dressed and lingers in the hallway, hesitates. Should he leave a note? He grabs a pen and a piece of paper and scribbles down the words.

Sorry. I love you.

But then his courage fails. He screws up the note and shoves it into his pocket before quietly leaving the apartment.

36

From her seat at the kitchen table, Hanna can see that the thermometer on the window is showing minus seventeen. It is time to go to work. She hasn't collected Morris yet; it was too late to disturb the neighbors when she got back to Åre last night. They had promised to look after him until Tuesday anyway, so he might as well stay there today, even though she longs to cuddle her big, fluffy cat.

She has just finished breakfast when her phone buzzes. It is seven fifteen, and she needs to leave soon in order to get to the morning briefing. It is a message from Lydia, her older sister.

Have you seen the online edition of *Expressen*?

Hanna frowns. The newspaper is one of Sweden's biggest dailies, and has written a great deal about the death in Åre, but it isn't like Lydia to concern herself with the tabloid press. She is a successful lawyer who is well aware of the media's tendency to wallow in murder inquiries. She rarely bothers with that kind of publicity, unless it specifically involves one of her clients.

Hanna doesn't really have time right now, so she sends a quick reply.

Is it urgent?

Lydia comes straight back to her.

Take a look for yourself.

The phone buzzes again after only a few seconds.

Why didn't you say anything?

Hanna is completely bewildered. Surely this must be about the young woman who died in Sadeln? So far the media haven't gone to town like they did with the murder at Copperhill last Easter, but as long as her death might still be an accident and hasn't been confirmed as a crime, it probably isn't as tasty to write about.

She opens the app and brings up the newspaper's website. The first headlines cover another gang shooting and a major road accident in Gothenburg. Then there are a few shorter articles, one of which is about the death in Åre, but that's it.

Why did Lydia want her to see this?

She scrolls down, just to be on the safe side. And physically recoils, as if someone has pushed her hard.

Shit.

Billionaire's new love! yells the headline. The bold letters are positively glowing at her. They are followed by a picture of her and Henry, walking toward the helicopter that was waiting for them in Kiruna. Hanna looks happy and excited; Henry has a protective arm around her shoulders.

There is no mistaking the warmth in his expression.

The article is unbearably detailed, and is all about the exclusive romantic break the well-known financier arranged for his new, significantly younger lover. The reporter also makes much of the fact that Hanna is a detective with the police in Åre, so their relationship means two different worlds have come together.

Hanna feels a cold sweat break out on the back of her neck. The whole of Sweden has just found out about her relationship with Henry.

And who she is.

She buries her face in her hands and lets out a groan.

This is the last thing she wanted.

37

There is a weird buzzing sound inside Olivia's head as she sits down at the breakfast table in the main house. She feels like a wreck, and her hair is all over the place. It took her hours to get to sleep last night. Horrible thoughts about Filippa's death and the creepy figure outside the door kept swirling around in her mind.

As if by an unspoken agreement, they all got up around nine and gathered in the kitchen. Olivia is spooning lingonberry jelly over a large bowl of porridge. William is sitting next to her; he reaches out and squeezes her thigh. No doubt it is meant as an encouraging gesture, but somehow it feels kind of crude in the morning light.

"Did you get any sleep?" Emil asks. He is opposite her, with two sliced hard-boiled eggs on crispbread. Olivia hesitates—should she tell the others about the stranger at the door?

The shadow lurking outside.

She can't stop thinking about it, why someone was trying to get in in the middle of the night. And who it could have been.

Amir?

William?

Pontus?

She looks at them one by one. Pontus is busy making a cheese-and-cucumber sandwich. William is shoveling down a bowl of fruit yogurt. And Amir is sitting with his head bowed over his porridge.

Was it him?

Who else would it be?

Emil wouldn't have hesitated to call out her name, and neither would William if he wanted to come in and slide into bed with her.

Pontus would never even dare to try.

"A bit," she replies. "It was hard to get to sleep, and then I had terrible nightmares."

"I think we all did," Emil says, sounding as if he too had lain awake half the night. "It's the shock—it's going to take a while to get over what's happened."

Olivia takes a spoonful of porridge; the sharpness of the jelly has a calming effect. It tastes of mountain vacations with the family, when she was little and they used to go to a cottage in Sälen during the February break. Mom would make porridge for the whole family to give them enough energy to ski until lunchtime.

"I just don't understand what went on the day before yesterday." Olivia has already said this several times; she knows she is repeating herself, but she can't help it. She stirs the contents of the bowl until it all turns pink.

"Why would Filippa have gone out into the snow barefoot and with hardly any clothes on when it was so cold?"

No one says anything. No one looks her in the eye.

Olivia gets the strange feeling that she has behaved inappropriately, like talking way too loud during a lecture, or showing her breasts in a slightly-too-revealing dress.

But they have to be able to talk about Filippa and the events that led to her death.

There is no mistaking Amir's disapproval. He gives her a filthy look. They have known each other for a while now, but Olivia has never noticed how narrow his eyes can become, or how cold he can be when that charming smile disappears.

What is he thinking, deep down?

Is he even grieving for Filippa?

She doesn't know where it comes from, but she suddenly feels a compulsion to make him talk. She can't bear him sitting there in silence.

Can she get him to trip himself up?

Olivia is becoming increasingly certain that Amir slept with Filippa the evening before she died. And that he is lying about it.

In which case he could also be lying about her death.

"What do you think, Amir?" she says, so loudly that he cannot avoid answering her question. "What happened to Filippa?"

"How should I know?"

"Don't you have a theory about how she finished up outdoors in the snow? Surely you must have some idea?"

Olivia knows that she is provoking him, but she has no intention of giving up until she gets a reaction.

"What are you doing?" he says. His face has darkened even more.

"I think you know."

For a moment Olivia thinks he isn't going to take the bait, that he is going to ignore her and go back to his breakfast. She can see him struggling with his self-control; his lips are twitching with anger.

Then he opens his mouth. "It almost sounds as if you're saying she was forced out into the cold. To die."

"Can you come up with a better explanation?" Olivia doesn't bother holding back. Right now there are too many unanswered questions. All she wants is to understand what happened to Filippa before she ended up in the snow.

Amir puts down his spoon with some force, slamming it against the bowl.

"I'm sorry, but what you're suggesting is completely bizarre. Do you realize what you're saying?"

Olivia tries to sound innocent. "Please tell me."

"It sounds," Amir says, his voice hoarse and strained, "as if you're accusing one of us of having caused Filippa's death."

William places a calming hand on Olivia's shoulder, but she shakes it off. "And what if that's true?" Her tone is shrill; she probably sounds hysterical by this stage, but so what? The only thing that matters is to get the truth out of Amir. He must be involved somehow. "What if someone in this room is lying about Filippa's final hours?" She turns to Amir. "What if it's you?"

He leaps to his feet, and his chair crashes to the floor. "You're out of your fucking mind!"

Olivia stands up too, challenges him with her gaze. "Am I the one who's out of my mind?" She almost spits out the words. "You were probably the last person to see Filippa before she died, yet you're acting as if you don't know anything." She looks around, stares at each of the boys before fixing her eyes on Amir again. "Someone in here must know what happened. Surely *you* must know?"

38

As soon as Hanna walks into the station, she sees Anton and Daniel in the conference room where they usually meet for briefings via video link with Östersund.

Raffe Herrera, who is based locally and is often brought in for major investigations, is right behind her. He drove into the parking lot just as she walked down from Solbringen.

Hanna sends up a silent prayer that none of her colleagues has visited Expressen's website yet. Going to work usually puts her in a good mood, but it was a shock to see herself exposed in the media like that. She is definitely not ready to discuss her love life with her coworkers yet.

And how will Daniel react when he finds out what is going on between her and Henry? Will he see it as a personal betrayal?

She can hardly explain away her silence concerning a relationship that has gone on for almost nine months by saying that she was trying to get over her strong and altogether inappropriate feelings for Daniel himself.

She should have stayed in Niehku instead of getting stressed out and coming back. Then she wouldn't have been here when the news broke.

Raffe bends down to put his lunchbox in the refrigerator in the kitchenette.

"I believe love is in the air," he says with a smile as he straightens up. "It seems as if you've had a good weekend."

Hanna closes her eyes. A dull headache begins to pound at her temples.

That was quick.

"It's . . . it's all pretty new," she mumbles.

In order to avoid saying any more, she concentrates on the coffee machine. Presses the button for a mug for both herself and Raffe, without even asking if he wants one.

Then again, Raffe doesn't usually need asking. He likes to boast about how much coffee he can drink, a talent he ascribes to his Chilean parents, who fled to Sweden after the military coup in the 1970s.

The machine rattles as it grinds the beans. Hanna stares at it as she tries to gather her thoughts. If Raffe knows the story, it's only a matter of time before everyone else does.

She just hopes her mother won't hear about her relationship with Henry. The very thought makes Hanna feel sick.

To be honest, she has no idea how the press got a hold of the story. Presumably someone must have recognized him at the airport in Kiruna, and secretly taken the pictures.

What is wrong with people these days? Why can't a person's private life stay private?

And how the hell did they find out her name and profession? She isn't a celebrity; she doesn't pop up in the media on a regular basis. She isn't on Instagram, and she has only a deliberately vague profile on Facebook.

She must call Henry after the briefing. She probably ought to speak to Lydia too.

Although the first thing she needs is a painkiller.

A new sound from the machine indicates that the coffee is ready. With a growing knot in her stomach and a well-filled mug in each hand, she heads for the conference room.

"Morning," she says, trying to sound nonchalant as she passes a mug to Raffe.

"What are you doing here?" Anton asks. "I thought you were supposed to be on leave today?" He doesn't seem particularly cheerful; there are dark shadows beneath his eyes. Strange—Anton is nearly always in a good mood.

Maybe it's the seriousness of what has happened.

"Duty calls, as they say," she replies, taking a sip of her coffee.

"Where have you been, by the way?" Daniel asks. He is busy setting up the video link. "You never said." He sounds exactly the same as always. Or maybe he's just pretending.

"North," she says tersely.

Raffe opens his mouth as if he is about to make another comment about Hanna's love life, but she gives him a warning look. Fortunately she is saved by the screen as it flickers into life.

Grip appears, along with two colleagues from Östersund, and Carina Grankvist.

"Hi, Hanna, good to have you back," Grip says with a small smile. "Okay, let's make a start."

Half an hour later Anton and Daniel have gone through the various interviews and background checks on Filippa's five friends. They have also mentioned Emil's conviction for assault, and Anton has taken on the task of checking out the matter with the officer who dealt with the case.

"Umeå have given us priority," Grip reports. "They've promised to carry out the autopsy as soon as possible—I'm hoping it's already underway."

This is critical, Hanna thinks. Everything stands or falls by the forensic examination. If the pathologist concludes that Filippa died of natural causes, then no crime has been committed. However, if it transpires that she was killed, the situation is totally different.

In the meantime she has no intention of sitting around and waiting. She doesn't believe for one moment that it was an accident. Grip seems to feel the same, as she has already decided to launch a preliminary investigation.

"Where are we with Filippa's clothes?" she asks. "Are they still missing?"

"Yes," Carina replies. "We've searched all around the property and in the neighborhood, but nothing has been found. Her friends told us that neither her coat nor boots were in the house—they've been looking for them too."

"How about the house search?" Daniel wants to know.

"I'm hoping we can get started this morning."

The sooner the better, Hanna thinks. She doesn't like the fact that both Filippa's clothes and her boots are missing. As far as Hanna is concerned, this is further evidence that a crime is behind the girl's death.

Why else would they be missing?

"We ought to speak to the neighbors as well," she says. "Check if any of them have seen or heard anything."

"We can do that as soon as we're done here," Daniel suggests. "And have a conversation with Emil about the assault conviction, even if the house search is ongoing." He smiles at Hanna. "You're always good at talking to young people."

Hanna smiles back, grateful for the compliment. That means Daniel can't have seen the article yet—otherwise it would show on his face.

She hopes, completely illogically, that he will never see it.

39

As soon as the dark-blue Volvo parks in front of the house, Åke senses that it's the police, wanting to talk to him.

He is sitting in the wing-back armchair, reading the morning paper on his iPad when there is a knock on the front door. In spite of the poor weather, Peter and the boys have gone skiing, so only Åke and Karin are home.

Åke adjusts his belt before he stands up. He doesn't regret what happened, but he wishes he hadn't lost control. He should have thought about the consequences first.

Although what that girl did was unacceptable.

Indecent.

Karin has opened the door, and a man and woman walk into the living room. They introduce themselves as detectives with the Serious Crimes Unit in Östersund.

"Coffee?" Karin asks, so quickly that she almost speaks over them.

Åke wishes she would calm down. She is circling the two officers like an anxious herring gull, with nervous, flapping movements.

As if they have something to hide.

It is important to maintain their composure. Answer the officers' questions just like any ordinary neighbor. The quicker this is sorted out, the sooner they will be left in peace.

"Not for me, thanks," says the man called Daniel Lindskog.

"I'd love a cup," says the woman—Hanna Ahlander. "With a drop of milk if it's not too much trouble."

Hanna and Daniel.

Åke has always had a good memory for names. Faces too. The two seem to be around the same age, and Åke gets the impression that they are a good team, as if they have worked together for a long time.

They sit down at the dining table, which is parallel with the kitchen island. Karin serves coffee, as black as the granite countertops.

"I expect you've heard what happened next door," Daniel begins. "Unfortunately a young woman was found dead yesterday—she was lying in the yard in front of the house."

"It's so terrible," Karin says.

"It's too early to say whether her death is due to a crime," Daniel goes on, "but we were wondering if you noticed anything unusual at the property during Saturday night or the early hours of Sunday morning?"

Åke sees Karin glance in his direction. She knows how furious he was on Saturday, and that he went over to the Löwengrens' in the evening.

Judging by her anxious expression, it's his late visit she is worried about.

The consequences.

There is no point in hiding the matter. If he denies that part, he will simply arouse suspicions.

"There was a hell of a noise coming from there on Saturday," he says grimly. "The music was so loud it was unbearable. In the end I had to go over and say something."

Hanna Ahlander looks out the window that faces the neighboring property, as if she is trying to estimate the distance to the Löwengrens' ugly house. It looks just as awful as it always does, the big windows shining gray black in the daylight. At this time it is impossible to see in through them, but as soon as the lights are switched on inside, the view is excellent.

You can see exactly what is going on in the huge living room.

"You're pretty close to your neighbors," Hanna says. "I can understand how the music would have disturbed you."

No doubt she thinks he will open up, cooperate, if she shows a little sympathy.

He's not that gullible.

"What time was it when you went over?" her colleague asks.

Åke knows exactly what time it was, but he doesn't answer immediately.

"I think it was just before midnight."

"Do you remember who was there? How many people were in the living room?"

Åke pictures the scene. The glasses and empty bottles, clothes all over the floor, the drunken, blank expressions on their faces.

Some of them could hardly stand up.

"There were six of them. Four boys and two girls, all in their early twenties, I'd say. They were all very obviously drunk; they didn't show any judgment at all. You could almost predict that it would end in disaster."

Hanna makes notes and sips her coffee. "Can you tell us about your visit? How long you were there, what was said? How did they respond when you asked them to turn down the music?"

Once again Åke remembers the surge of rage he felt when the young people made fun of him. The girl who tried to grope him, the music pumping from the speakers.

The feeling of being under attack.

The memory makes him clench his jaw. That half-naked girl provoked him beyond the bounds of decency. There was something very wrong with her judgment; he knew that right away. And she was far from sober.

But that is no excuse.

Now she's dead.

And she deserved it.

"Did anything in particular happen while you were there?" Hanna asks, as if she senses that Åke is holding something back. "Was there an argument?"

Åke picks up an undertone of suspicion in her voice. He needs to explain himself, but would prefer not to go into detail. Whatever he says can be used against him.

"I went over and told them to turn down the music. That was it. Then I came back home."

Daniel frowns. "We have witnesses who claim that there was a physical altercation between you and one of the young women—the one who died."

Åke narrows his eyes. "What exactly are you implying?"

"I just want to understand what happened when you were there."

"I didn't do anything!" Åke can barely control his anger. "However, one of the girls did lose her balance and fall over—probably because she was so drunk she couldn't stand up. But it wasn't my fault—they were all well gone. I'm sure they'd taken drugs as well."

All these unpleasant insinuations. He should have been better prepared, realized they would show up, thought through his answers in advance.

He pushes back his chair to distance himself from the persistent police officer. The movement makes the chair legs screech along the floor.

"And then?" Daniel says.

"I'd had enough, so I left and came back here."

"What did you do when you got home?"

"I went to bed."

Daniel turns to Karin. "This is just routine, but I wonder if you can confirm that your husband came home and went to bed?"

"I often sleep in one of the guest rooms," Åke says before Karin can open her mouth. He is running out of patience, but tries to make an effort. What the hell has their private life got to do with the police? "So I don't disturb Karin," he adds.

"I understand. Is there anyone else who can confirm what you've told us? Your son is visiting—could he help?"

Are they going to drag Peter into all this? Seriously?

Karin glances anxiously at her husband again; he knows she doesn't want him to lose his temper while the police are here.

"My son wasn't awake at that time," he says with an effort.

"Peter and the boys are sleeping downstairs," Karin explains. "They'd gone to bed early because they'd had a long day traveling." She picks up the coffee pot. "Refill, anyone?"

Åke can see how nervous she is; she spills a little coffee when she is topping off his cup. However, she has always been a loyal wife.

"You really do have a good view of the neighboring property," Hanna says, gazing out the window. "Their house is so close you can almost touch it. Neither of you noticed anything else during the night? Or in the morning when you woke up?"

Åke shakes his head, but Karin leans forward as if she is about to say something; then she looks down at her lap again.

It only takes a second, but Hanna notices. "Did you see anything else you can tell us about?"

Karin stirs her coffee. "I don't know if this has anything to do with the young people . . . but I got up in the middle of the night to fetch a glass of water from the kitchen." She pauses, runs a finger around the rim of her cup.

Åke notes that the two police officers are deliberately waiting, rather than filling the silence.

"I thought . . . I thought I saw someone moving around outside the Löwengrens' house."

Åke is taken aback, but tries to hide his surprise. He thought Karin had slept through the night; she hasn't said a word about getting up in the small hours, or seeing someone outside.

She should have mentioned this earlier so that he could have prepared himself. He can't ask her to shut up now, not with the police sitting here—writing down every word that comes out of her mouth.

Hanna leans forward. "Are you sure? What time might that have been?"

"Around two, two thirty, I think."

"Could you tell if it was a man or a woman?" Daniel asks.

Karin looks unhappy, as if she feels guilty about not being able to provide more information. "I'm sorry, I'm not sure . . . It was very dark, and it all happened so fast, my mind was elsewhere. But I got the impression it was . . . a man. In a dark jacket."

Hanna gives her an encouraging smile.

Åke would like to tell her and her colleague to go to hell.

"No problem," Hanna says. "But the smallest detail could be important. Please tell us whatever you can remember."

"I think . . ." Karin hesitates again. "I mean, it was more of a feeling . . . but maybe the person out there was carrying something. As if he had a heavy sack in his arms."

40

William is sitting to the left of Olivia on the Sadelexpressen chairlift, with Pontus on her right. Amir is next to him, leaning back but with his attention focused on where they are going. He still seems angry, and hasn't said a word to Olivia since breakfast. When they were boarding the lift, she did her best not to end up beside him.

Emil hasn't joined them; he said he had a stomachache. Olivia wishes he were here. He has a calming effect on the group. He was the one who interrupted the big argument at breakfast and got her to back down before she said something she might regret.

She is convinced that Amir hates her now.

The two of them will never be friends again.

After breakfast it was William who suggested they should go skiing. Or rather, he insisted on it. They had to do something, he said. They were all so restless and irritable. If they sat around indoors all day, they would only start bickering again.

Olivia allowed herself to be persuaded, even though she didn't want to go skiing at all. But nor did she want to stay in the house all day, driving herself crazy wondering what had happened.

The chairlift is moving slowly between the tall poles. The Plexiglas bubble screen that provides protection from the wind is down, but Olivia's face is still freezing, even though her scarf is wrapped around her mouth.

When she looks out at the slopes, there aren't many people around; no doubt the weather has kept them away. The fog comes and goes, and Åreskutan is barely visible, even though the lifts at the top are allegedly open, according to the app.

"It's good to get out, isn't it?" William says, pushing his goggles up onto his forehead. "I said the fresh air would make us feel better."

"Mmm."

William leans closer; his helmet is almost touching hers. "Why did you go for Amir at breakfast?" he says quietly. "I'm sure he hasn't done anything. You can't seriously think he was behind Filippa's accident?"

The fact that he is calling it an accident makes Olivia uncomfortable. It's a simple explanation, because it means that no one needs to suspect anyone else—but she can't believe they're all buying it.

Is she the only one who doesn't believe Amir's lies?

She can't handle this. She needs to think about something else, clear her mind, if only for a few hours.

"Do we have to talk about this now?" She busies herself adjusting the chin strap of her helmet.

William remains silent for a moment, then turns so that he can see the other two. "I assume we're going up to Skutan?" he says. "We can come back via the Western."

He means the West Ravine. Olivia wonders if this is a good idea, especially if the fog lingers. William wouldn't have any problems; he is the best skier in the group, and he is used to skiing off-piste from his vacations in the Alps. Olivia can usually find her way down without too much difficulty; she is pretty good after many trips to Åre and Sälen, even though she's not as fast as the boys.

But Amir isn't as technically skillful, and Pontus is considerably weaker than the rest of them. He is also the only one with rented skis—Olivia, William, and Amir have brought their own.

The chairlift sways, and Olivia reaches out a hand to steady herself.

"I think we should wait to decide until we see what it looks like up there," she says.

William grins, perfectly relaxed as always.

Olivia thinks she knows why he has suggested the downhill route via the ravine, the off-piste run that is challenging even in good weather. It will give him the opportunity to show off his superiority, how easily he can outclass the rest of the group.

It is as if he can't help it; it's part of his nature.

He simply has to outshine everyone else.

Be the best.

41

The cold makes Daniel draw his jacket more tightly around his body as he leaves the Carlsson house. The Åre valley is enveloped in a gray fog; Åreskutan is barely visible.

"What was your impression of the Carlssons?" he asks Hanna as soon as the front door closes behind them. He is thinking in particular about the way Åke did his best to play down his visit to the neighboring house. When the five friends were interviewed yesterday, several of them said that he had been extremely unpleasant. Olivia even claimed that he had pushed Filippa so hard that she fell over.

He had chosen not to mention that to the police.

"Åke comes across as a bad-tempered old bastard," Hanna replies. "If you'll excuse my language. I actually felt kind of sorry for his wife." She smiles without a trace of regret, but immediately becomes serious again. "But what Karin had to say was very interesting."

Daniel can only agree. Karin could be an important eyewitness.

"If it's true," Hanna goes on, "and providing Filippa's death wasn't due to natural causes, then Karin's information suggests that the perpetrator deliberately carried Filippa's body outside and placed it in the spot where she was found." She shivers and pushes her hands deep in her pockets. "Jesus, it's cold today."

In the background they can hear the sound of the snowplow on Sadelvägen, the road that snakes its way through the area. When Daniel checked the weather forecast earlier, it didn't look good. Gales are on the way, blowing in across Western Jämtland, even though it is misty and there isn't a breath of wind at the moment.

He looks at his watch, nine thirty; the house search is due to start shortly, although there are no police cars outside the Löwengren house. No sign of any activity—maybe no one is up yet.

In which case it's probably best to wake them—it seems more humane than leaving them lying in bed when their colleagues are about to go through the whole place.

"Shall we go over and have a chat with the group? Speak to Emil about the assault conviction before Carina and her team get started?"

"I was just about to suggest the same thing," Hanna says. "Since we're here anyway."

She sets off toward the house. It is so close it's almost attached to the Carlssons' garage.

"At least Karin's statement gives us an idea of the time," Daniel says. "She thought it was around two, two thirty when she got up to fetch a glass of water."

"We ought to speak to the son too," Hanna says. "He might have seen something, even though his parents say he was asleep all night."

They have Peter Carlsson's contact details; he had already left to go skiing when they arrived.

"I can do that this afternoon," Daniel offers. He is about to knock on the Löwengrens' door.

"Do you think the father could have been involved in Filippa's death?" Hanna suddenly asks. "Åke Carlsson?"

Daniel freezes with his hand in midair. Hanna often does this—thinks out loud without taking much notice of the facts. It is one of the major differences between them. He is more circumspect; he prefers to have all the available information at his fingertips before he starts speculating.

"I read the transcripts from yesterday's interviews," Hanna continues. "Maybe he went back later that night and took out his anger on Filippa?"

"There's no point in guessing at this stage," Daniel says firmly. "We still don't know if we're dealing with a crime."

Hanna gives him a skeptical look, as if she is growing tired of his cautious approach. "Most of the evidence points to murder," she says. "Even you have to admit that."

42

Visibility is getting worse and worse, even though it's the middle of the day. It is not yet one o'clock, but Olivia can hardly make anything out when she looks down toward the valley from the top of Åreskutan.

It has taken them about an hour to ski across from Sadeln to the central section of the system. In order to reach Skutan, they then had to take the VM8 lift before continuing with the gondola, the bright-red closed-cabin lift that goes all the way to the top.

They are standing next to the square concrete bunker that houses the end station. To the right they can just see the cables that carry the gondola, to the left the Svartberg trail that leads to Hummelberget.

That's where they will have to turn off if they are heading down to the West Ravine.

"Okay," William calls out. "Everyone in?"

Pontus looks tense. He glances longingly at the gondola, as if he would like to jump on board and turn back.

Olivia feels slightly sorry for him.

So far the skiing has been superb, in spite of the poor weather, and the snow has been fantastic. However, they have skied only on slopes where the snow groomers have done their job, and the ground has been prepared. When they head off-piste, it will be a completely different story. Thick, untouched powder snow takes its toll, even for accomplished skiers. It is particularly taxing on the thigh muscles, and none of them have skis specially adapted for that kind of surface.

Plus Olivia can barely see her hand in front of her face.

The fog is thicker up here, presumably the lifts in the peak zone will close if it gets any worse. The world already feels as if it is wrapped in a gray blanket.

She glances at Pontus. He is going to find the descent hard work, because he always ends up last. Every time they arrive at a new lift, William is first and Pontus last. He is the one they all have to wait for.

Olivia is well aware that it is no fun being the worst in a group. It saps your confidence, and you never get the chance to catch your breath, because those who have been waiting for you have a tendency to take off as soon as the slow coach shows up.

In the long term it almost becomes a form of bullying.

She suddenly has an unwelcome flashback from high school, when she joined a new class. The memory of the cool girls who ignored her is still painful.

She stamps on the snow, sending it whirling up around her skis. Why must there always be a pecking order?

Which means someone is always at the bottom of that pecking order.

Come to think of it, Pontus is the one they always tease; it comes so naturally that she has never even considered it before. But William likes to have his entourage, and presumably that's why he lets Pontus hang out with them. William appears even more cool and worldly when boorish, unconfident Pontus is by his side.

And of course it would never occur to Pontus to question William's authority.

Just like Amir.

He is standing a few yards ahead of Olivia, talking to William, who is adjusting his bindings. There aren't many other skiers up here.

Amir is not going to object to William's suggestion that they should take the West Ravine.

Olivia leans toward Pontus, resting on her poles.

"How are you doing? Do you want to carry on, or shall we call it a day?"

At first he doesn't seem to hear, so she repeats the question, a little louder this time, and adds, "My legs are getting pretty sore. Maybe we should go home instead? Light a fire and make some hot chocolate?"

"I'm fine." Pontus waves away her suggestion. "I'm happy to carry on, but you can go back if you can't cope with the pressure."

Typical. Olivia was trying to be kind, and he simply brushed her aside as usual. Okay, he has only himself to blame. She tried to be sympathetic.

Sometimes she gets so tired of guys and their testosterone.

William waves a pole and calls out to them. "Ready to go?"

Then he simply sets off, without so much as a backward glance.

Olivia has no choice but to follow him, although it infuriates her that William always has to make the decisions, that he never takes the rest of the group into consideration.

He is a fucking egotist.

Amir and Pontus set off too.

William is moving fast, straight down the slope, and Olivia tries to keep up as best she can. She can usually find her way without any difficulty, because she has skied in Åre so often, but it is hard to know where the piste ends in such poor visibility.

The fog distorts all proportions. The slope simply disappears.

She finds herself wishing that at least one of the guys was wearing a brightly colored jacket, like in the eighties. Then she would have had something to focus on. As it is, their black-and-gray ski clothes are swallowed up by the dense fog.

And then she realizes she is completely disorientated.

Where is she?

A second's inattention was all it took. Before she can slow down, she is suddenly off-piste. The solid ground beneath her skis is gone, and she almost falls when her right ski loses its grip. At the last second she manages to swerve with her left ski, lurching backward with her chest in the same direction she came from.

It feels as if her body hovers in the air for an eternity, then she feels solid ground once more, and is able to make a couple of parallel turns to bring her back to safety. The snow is no longer giving way beneath her feet.

That was close.

Her heart is pounding. If she had gone over the edge, she could have been badly injured. Would anyone have found her?

The world is only white and gray, an enormity of mist and fog swirling around in the air.

Olivia looks around for the rest of the group. Her stress levels rise as she slowly slides down the slope.

And there they are; they have stopped a short distance up ahead. Thank God they realized she wasn't with them.

The guys are waiting for her. But this is no fun anymore.

Olivia wants to go home.

43

The door is eventually opened by a tall young man with wavy fair hair. This must be Emil, Hanna realizes; she read up about the five friends and checked out their passport photos before leaving the station.

She explains that they have a few more questions, and asks if they can come in.

"There's only me here," Emil says apologetically. "The others have gone skiing."

So the house is almost empty. That will make the search easier; it's always trickier when people are home.

Carina will be pleased.

They go in and sit down at the dining table, where a couple of dirty coffee cups are left over from breakfast. Two large black metal lamps are suspended from the ceiling, creating a warm glow.

"We might as well get straight to the point," Daniel begins. "We found out that you were convicted of assault in Umeå. Can you tell us what happened?"

Emil's face flushes red. Hanna isn't sure whether it's down to embarrassment or anger, but she sees that he is clenching his fists hard.

"It's a long time ago."

"Four years."

“I was just out of school.” Emil’s voice is quiet and troubled.

“Tell us what happened in your own words.” Hanna’s tone is friendly, she wants Emil to relax.

It takes a few seconds before he speaks. “It was such a stupid thing. I was working part-time in a restaurant, in the kitchen, and one of my friends was in the bar when a customer started arguing with him. After the place closed they carried on quarreling outside. I tried to step in, and in the end I lost my temper too. Then everything got out of hand.”

“You headbutted him,” Daniel says. “And the court felt that this constituted considerably more violence than necessary.”

“Yes. I . . .”

Hanna and Daniel wait for Emil to go on. He runs his fingers through his hair a couple of times. Outside the window the fog is now so thick that it is almost impossible to see the Carlssons’ house.

“I have only vague memories of the incident,” Emil continues apologetically. “It was an instinctive reaction, somehow. As I remember it, the other guy tried to attack me and . . .” He spreads his hands in a gesture of resignation. “I just lost it.”

Hanna thinks he sounds as if he is telling the truth. He seems embarrassed and regretful—but that doesn’t necessarily mean that he is as innocent as he is trying to appear.

Can a single mistake be forgiven? Or is it the start of a pattern, the compulsion to turn to violence in difficult situations?

It could be an unlucky twist of fate that Emil did something dumb when he was a teenager and he is now involved in another criminal investigation.

Or not.

“I’ve never been the kind of person who gets into a fight,” Emil adds. “And after that I was much more careful with alcohol.”

“But you carried on working in hospitality?” Daniel asks.

"For a while. My parents weren't too pleased about it, and I became more and more unhappy. It didn't exactly feel like a long-term career choice. I'd started straight from high school, and eventually I realized I didn't want to spend the rest of my life in a kitchen smelling of fried food. So I sat the Scholastic Aptitude Test and managed to score enough points to get onto the economics course in Uppsala. From the reserve list," he says with a wry smile.

"Why didn't you mention the assault conviction yesterday when my colleague interviewed you?"

Emil rocks back on his chair, so far that Hanna is afraid he is going to topple over. "Because I was embarrassed." He rocks forward again and sighs. "And because I didn't want the others to find out. I haven't told my friends in Uppsala about the court case; I guess I was hoping for a fresh start, in a place where no one had preconceived ideas about me."

"Was that the only reason?" Hanna says.

"The thing is, when Filippa was found yesterday . . . it seemed completely unreal." He searches for the right words. "Not only that she was dead, but that she . . . froze to death, outside in the snow. Just like that. One minute she was in here with us, partying, and then . . . then she was gone." His shoulders slump. "I was scared when you knocked on the door and said you wanted to question us. I thought you might suspect me of being involved if you found out about my conviction. I realize it sticks out like a sore thumb. The rest of them are so . . . decent, I'm the only one who's done something really stupid . . . I haven't even told my parents about Filippa's death yet. It would only scare them. It was bad enough after the conviction, they were embarrassed to face the neighbors. I don't want to worry them even more."

"So you don't think it was an accident?" Daniel says.

"I don't know." Emil suddenly sounds defensive. "I went to bed first, so I have no idea what happened after that."

He is just as vague as his friends. Hanna wishes he could be more precise. Filippa is dead, and he is one of the people who was in the house during the hours before she died.

In general the friends' statements are unclear. They all claim they went to bed without noticing anything in particular on Saturday night.

But the following morning a young woman lay lifeless in the snow.

Hanna refuses to believe that nothing happened during the time leading up to Filippa ending up outside in the cold. In which case surely at least one of them should have reacted.

One of them is lying; she's sure of it.

"You must have an idea of your own?" she says, sharpening her tone. "I mean, you were here."

Emil's jaws are working; then he suddenly gets to his feet. "I want to show you something."

He leads them downstairs to the lower floor. He goes into one of the rooms, where there is a large unmade double bed. Hanna notices that the place is a mess, with clothes everywhere and a suitcase lying open on the floor.

There is a laptop on one of the pillows.

"Is this your room?" Daniel wonders.

"No. It's Pontus's."

44

"Where did you get to?" William shouts.

Olivia has finally caught up, and skis over to the group as quickly as she can. Pontus turns his head and gives her a supercilious grin, as if he is pleased not to be last for once.

Is this the thanks she gets for feeling sorry for him before? That's the last time she tries to be nice to him. There are limits to how much unpleasantness she is prepared to put up with.

"I got disorientated and missed the piste," she admits. "I went too far over to the side and nearly fell down the drop."

The fog is so thick she can barely make out their faces. Not that there is much to see: They are all wearing black helmets and mirrored goggles.

"Did you hurt yourself?" William asks.

He is the only one who seems to care. Amir doesn't even look up, and Pontus yawns.

"I'm fine. I managed . . . to keep my balance . . . so I didn't . . . actually fall."

Olivia is still out of breath, so her words come out in short bursts. She doesn't understand how she could have missed the piste, after all the times she has skied down from Skutan. She drives her poles down into the snow and takes deep breaths through her mouth.

The feeling when the ground disappeared from beneath her right ski and she lost control lingers unpleasantly. Her hands are shaking inside her gloves.

"You mustn't crash on a day like this," William warns her. "The ski patrol would never find you."

Olivia finds this unhelpful, to say the least.

They are halfway down the Tusenmetersbacken, a steep downhill run that leads into the trail to Hummeln.

The West Ravine is on their left—a deep, tree-covered chasm with treacherous terrain. The sharp rocks are concealed by a thin covering of snow, while the Susabäcken stream, which doesn't always freeze over, runs through the middle.

The ravine ends at the Fjällgårdsexpressen lift.

In spite of the poor visibility, Olivia can see that the snow in that direction is untouched. Which means that no one else has taken that route today—presumably because it would be an idiotic thing to do in this weather. If you're not careful, you could get badly hurt.

"Maybe we're pushing too hard for a girl?" Amir suddenly says. "I mean, if Olivia can't stay on her feet even where there's a decent piste?"

He looks at her for the first time since breakfast.

"Maybe you should go home and rest; then we won't have to slow down because of you?"

He hasn't said a word to her since they argued, but now he's really going for it.

Fucking bastard.

Pontus doesn't say anything, but Olivia has the feeling he doesn't object to Amir's attack. Maybe he was offended earlier, when she suggested that the two of them should head home?

She glances at William, hoping for moral support, but he has taken out his phone and is busy reading a message, presumably from his father, who has texted nonstop over the past twenty-four hours.

William seems oblivious to the bad vibes. Either that or he can't be bothered to come to her defense. Maybe he thinks she has only herself to blame after what happened at breakfast.

Under normal circumstances she wouldn't care; she can handle both Amir and Pontus. But today it feels like hard work. The weather is a huge problem, and she doesn't want to be left behind.

They have to stick together.

She really wants to get back to the warmth, to the house in Sadeln. Hang out with Emil, who would never attack her just to win points with someone like William.

But she can't give up—she is not going to give Amir the satisfaction. Besides which, she is as good a skier as he is, probably better.

Amir needs to keep his mouth shut.

Anger makes her throw caution to the wind. Amir is not going to win. *Fuck him.*

"It's cool," she says nonchalantly. "Let's go."

Before William can even open his mouth, she takes the initiative.

"The West Ravine, right?"

45

Daniel is leaning against one of the closet doors in Pontus's room. Hanna is standing at the foot of the bed. She gives Emil an inquiring glance, and he points to the open laptop. It is a silver-colored Mac, the screen is dark and locked, but the characteristic apple can be seen on the back.

"I came in here to borrow a charger just after the others had left," Emil explains. "Pontus has the same laptop as me, and mine had just run out, so I thought I could use his." He sounds uncomfortable, as if he isn't quite sure how to go on. "The computer was still open—the screen hadn't locked, so I happened to notice what Pontus had been looking at."

He falls silent, and a faint flush appears on his pale cheeks.

"And what was that?" Hanna asks.

She sits down in a leather armchair in one corner of the room, next to the window that overlooks the Åre valley. It is in shade now; the sun will go down in just a few hours.

"So . . ." Emil turns away. "Pontus had been googling things I didn't like the look of."

"Such as?"

"He'd typed 'hypothermia as a cause of death' into the search box." Emil makes quotation marks in the air with his fingers, then adds, "That means your body temperature is too low."

Daniel doesn't require an explanation of that particular term. He is well aware of what hypothermia involves. Two years ago he helped save the life of a woman that he and Hanna found in the forest on a dark winter's night. She was suffering from hypothermia, and they got her off to the hospital at the very last minute. It was sheer luck that she survived.

In this case there is a lot to suggest that hypothermia was the cause of Filippa's death. However, as far as Daniel is concerned, the key question is *why* she froze to death outdoors in the middle of the night, with hardly any clothes on.

Did she end up out there of her own free will, or not?

"So what did you think when you saw what Pontus had been doing?"

"I thought it was . . . unpleasant. Given what . . . what happened to Filippa."

"And what did you do?" Hanna asks.

Emil tugs at the sleeve of his top. He is wearing a gray hoodie with the black logo of a well-known sports brand on the chest. It looks well worn, both the sleeves and front are pilled.

"Does Pontus . . . have to know I've told you this?" he wonders, sounding tense.

"We're not going to hang you out to dry right away, if that's what's worrying you," Daniel reassures him. "Go on."

Emil sits down on the edge of the bed. "I thought it was horrible, so I went in and checked out Pontus's search history. And things got even weirder . . ."

"Can you give us some examples?" Hanna prompts him.

Emil points to the laptop. "Unfortunately I don't know the password; otherwise I could have shown you. But what I saw didn't feel okay. There were words like *murder* and *manslaughter* and *causing the death of another person*. He'd also looked up how long it takes for someone to freeze to death in different temperatures. And he'd also . . ." Emil falls silent, as if he is considering how far to go.

"What else had he done?" It is Daniel's turn to push him now; he has already decided to confiscate Pontus's laptop.

"The worst thing was that he'd googled punishments for young adults—penalty discounts because of a person's age, that kind of thing."

"And what did that make you think?" Hanna asks.

"I thought it almost seemed as if he was involved in Filippa's death," Emil admits. "As if Pontus wanted to find out how to get away with it."

46

On the way back from Sadeln, Daniel pulls in at the Efes restaurant on the other side of the E14, in the same building as the ICA supermarket. They have arranged to meet Staffan Berg, the property manager, for lunch; it was the only solution if they were going to find time to eat.

They had still been in the house when the search began, but there was no point in staying. He and Hanna were just in the way when Carina and her team were doing their job.

Each carrying a tray, they sit down at a table on the veranda with a view of Lake Åre. Through the window Daniel can see three snow scooters whizzing across the ice, heading east. In spite of the distance he can see how warmly wrapped up the drivers are, in thick coveralls and with their scarves pulled up over their faces. It must be ice cold, traveling at that speed in such a low temperature. The trees outside are weighed down beneath a thick layer of rime frost, and the cold has drawn fine ice stars on the windowpanes.

And soon the sun will be going down.

He has barely taken his first bite when a middle-aged man approaches their table. He is wearing dungarees, and his woolen hat is pulled well down over his forehead. His face is weatherbeaten, as if he is used to spending time outdoors.

Daniel holds out his hand. "Hi—Staffan Berg?"

The man nods.

"Thanks for meeting us here—please take a seat."

Daniel points to a chair, and Staffan Berg turns it around and straddles it, one leg on either side and his stomach resting on the back.

He looks at Hanna.

"You were in the paper this morning, weren't you?"

Before Daniel can ask what he's talking about, Staffan goes on.

"I presume you've been at Nedre Svedjevägen. Tragic, the death of that girl." He lowers his voice as if he doesn't want anyone else to hear what he is saying. "Do you know what happened, why she died?"

"We can't comment on that at the moment," Hanna replies, putting down her knife and fork with such force that tomato sauce spatters the table.

"So you look after the property for the Löwengren family," Daniel says, attempting to steer the conversation along the right lines.

"I do." Staffan's smile is somehow . . . eager. "I keep an eye on the place, clear the snow from the drive, that kind of thing. You could call me a fixer—I make sure there are no problems with the water supply. I run the taps and flush the toilets, open the blinds when the family are due to arrive, fill up the freezer, and so on."

"So you have a lot to do?"

"I'm very busy at this time of year. In the late spring and summer, it's quieter."

"I understand." Daniel decides to get to the point. "I believe you called in at the house on Saturday."

"That's correct."

"Could you tell us about your visit? What was your impression of the group of friends when you met them?"

Staffan spreads his hands wide. "What can I say . . ."

He glances toward the comfortable seating area at the other end of the room. A couple of fabric Christmas elves are still perched on the coffee table, and a guy in a ski suit is sitting in an armchair with a hot drink.

"Everything seemed okay," he says eventually. "They were having dinner. The table was nicely set, and the food smelled pretty good."

"What was the atmosphere like?"

"They seemed to be having a pleasant evening. Everyone looked as if they were enjoying themselves, as far as I could tell." He pulls off his hat and stuffs it in his pocket. His expression grows serious. "It was a real shock when I heard that one of them had died during the night. It's terrible when a young person is taken too soon."

"You didn't get the feeling that something was in the air when you were there?" Daniel wonders. "A sense that something was wrong?"

"Not at all. They all said hello; they were very pleasant. There did seem to be plenty of booze around. There were several bottles of wine open on the table, and I noticed a case of beer and some bottles of spirits on the kitchen counter."

He gives a wry smile, as if he is speaking from his own experience. According to the electoral register, he has two children in their late teens, a boy and a girl.

"They like to party at that age," he adds. "You know what it's like at this time of year—Åre is full of students who've come here to have a good time."

Daniel knows exactly what he means. The second half of January is actually known as the student weeks. All the prices drop after Christmas. There are few people on the slopes, and it's easy to find cheap accommodation. In addition, hordes of Norwegian teenagers turn up to celebrate their upcoming final exams.

It's tradition.

Hanna is staring down at her plate; she has barely said a word to Staffan Berg since he arrived. Daniel tries to catch her eye, but in vain.

"So how long were you there?"

"Not long, only a few minutes—ten at the most. I was in the area anyway, and just wanted to call by and say hi. William's father had asked me to check on them once they'd settled in."

William's father.

Apparently he has called Birgitta Grip from New York to express his displeasure at the situation. He has made his opinion of the police's attitude very clear—he doesn't see why they are insisting that the group stay on in Åre for the next few days until the forensic examination has been completed.

Daniel is glad to have been spared that conversation. Angry parents always require extra energy. Spending time trying to calm down William's father, when he has already decided that the police are incompetent, is something he is happy to leave to Grip. There are more important matters to deal with right now.

Staffan glances at his watch.

"I really need to go," he says apologetically. "I have a lot of properties to take care of while the owners are away. I'm due to let a plumber into a house on Björnhyllan shortly."

Daniel nods. "One last question. As you look after the house, I assume you have keys to the Löwengrens' place?"

Berg stands up and puts the chair back where it belongs. His smile is smooth, almost feline. "They have a keypad with a code, but yes. I have to be able to get in even if no one is there."

47

After only a few minutes' skiing in the heavy snow, Olivia is regretting her decision. She should never have challenged the boys, never suggested the West Ravine. She could have been on the way home by now, if she'd kept her mouth shut.

Instead she is in the middle of the run, heading straight for the horrific gap where the ravine begins.

Her thigh muscles are screaming as she forces herself down the slope, each turn is more difficult than the last. It is such hard work fighting with the heavy surface beneath her skis, the lactic acid has begun to spread through her legs, sweat is pouring down the back of her neck.

She knows it is important to ski fast on powder snow. If you go too slowly, you become stuck and get nowhere. At the same time, the run is so steep that she has to hold back.

She dare not go as fast as she could, when it feels as if the mountainside is concave rather than convex. Her heart is in her mouth, and she is clutching her poles as tightly as she can. If she falls, things could go really badly. She might break something, and what would happen then?

As William said, the ski patrol probably wouldn't find her.

In addition, a new and terrifying thought has crept into her mind. What if they trigger an avalanche? If the snow comes away from the underlying rock, they are lost. If a cohesive mass comes away and hurtles down the mountain, it would be impossible to escape. Such a mass of snow accelerates much too fast for anyone to be able to ski ahead of it. Avalanches can reach a speed of almost seventy miles per hour, especially in terrain as steep as this.

And none of them have avalanche equipment or a radio transmitter.

Olivia tries to focus on William, who is a few yards ahead of her now. The distance is increasing all the time, even though she is skiing well beyond her ability.

If I fall, I will die.

The thought comes out of nowhere, but she doesn't want to give in to her fear. Instead she grits her teeth, forces herself to increase her speed so that she doesn't lose sight of William.

As usual he appears to be skiing effortlessly, moving forward quickly and efficiently—even elegantly.

While Olivia has to fight for every yard.

Her only consolation is that Amir and Pontus are far behind her. She hopes they are finding it even more difficult than she is, that they are having to make twice as much effort to get down at all.

The fuckers deserve to suffer.

The fog swirling around them muffles every sound. The world is nothing but whiteness, with every contour obliterated.

If she didn't have William ahead of her, she wouldn't be able to find her way. She would really like to call out to him, ask him to stop so they can rest, or preferably turn back, but she knows it's too late. They have already gone too far; it is impossible to turn back.

With this much snow they would never be able to climb back up to the transportation routes and safety.

Right now there is only one way out. And that goes through the sharp black rocks down in the West Ravine.

That is the only way to get home.

48

Another briefing with their colleagues in Östersund has been arranged for two o'clock. That means Hanna has just under half an hour before they gather in the conference room.

She needs time to gather her thoughts.

When Staffan Berg came over to their table and said he'd seen her in the newspaper, she was completely unprepared—so shocked that she could hardly speak.

Daniel was left to conduct the interview while she sat there like an idiot.

Afterward she blamed the time of the month, said she was suffering from stomach cramps. On the way back in the car she sat with her eyes closed, hoping that Daniel had forgotten Staffan's comment. At least he didn't ask her about it; fortunately he had a phone call that took up most of the journey.

She has just sat down at her desk when her cellphone rings. She doesn't recognize the number, but that's not unusual. Maybe it's a relative of one of the friends staying at the Löwengren house? Emil said he hadn't told his family about Filippa's death, but William's father has already been in touch and more or less shouted at Grip over the phone. It wouldn't be surprising if one of the other parents called—Olivia's father, or maybe Pontus's mom or dad.

"Hanna Ahlander."

She switches to speakerphone to keep her hands free, steeling herself in case it's a close relative of Filippa. Those conversations are always the most difficult, because how do you respond to bottomless grief when there is no consolation to be had?

"Hi, Hanna," says a female voice. There is a hint of delight, as if the unknown person is very pleased that she has answered. She certainly doesn't sound like a relative of the deceased. "Can you spare a few minutes?"

Hanna switches on the computer. "What's this about?" She clicks to bring up her password, and the screen lights up.

"My name is Victoria, and I'm calling from *Chat* magazine—I'm sure you've heard of us; we're one of the best-selling weeklies in Sweden."

"Sorry?"

"We think the news about your new boyfriend is so exciting—your romance with Henry Sylvester!"

It takes a second for Hanna to realize that she is speaking to a gossip columnist. This is not police business. She quickly switches off the speaker function and presses her phone to her ear; she doesn't want anyone to overhear.

"Can you tell us how the two of you met? I mean, you're an unusual couple—the policewoman and the financier, it almost sounds like *Lady and the Tramp*, if you know what I mean." She laughs, as if she can already picture the headline. "Did you know what a catch he was when you fell in love? He's very, very wealthy!"

The woman's unabashed curiosity is giving Hanna feelings of panic, as if she is standing naked in front of a fully dressed crowd, all staring greedily at her.

Her palms grow damp, sweat breaks out on her upper lip. She can hardly breathe.

"I'd love to hear more about your romantic trip to Lapland this weekend," says the voice, brimming with enthusiasm.

Hanna tries desperately to regain control. She forces herself to take several deep breaths, grips the edge of the desk with her free hand. She closes her eyes and presses her fingertips against the wood until it hurts.

"Is it true that the hotel opened up exclusively for the two of you?"

How the hell does she know that?

How has she got a hold of Hanna's cellphone number?

Hanna looks around to make sure the door is closed; she can't risk any of her colleagues noticing what is going on.

"Sorry, I have to go," she says breathlessly. It is hard to get the words out. All she wants to do is get rid of the inquisitive journalist. She can't talk to a gossip columnist about Henry, and she has no intention of giving an interview.

She would like to pull a blanket over her head and hide.

"I can call back at another time, if that's better for you? Your choice."

Hanna fights the urge to yell at her that there will never be a suitable time. Instead she manages to say, "Bye," and ends the call.

She is on the verge of tears.

This is not okay.

Somehow she has to put an end to it.

49

At long last William stops with an elegant parallel turn to wait for the rest of the group. Olivia only just spots him in the fog, but she battles her way to where he is standing, with snow up to his knees.

Fear is pecking at her breast. She will never know how she managed to make it down that terrible, steep run. There is snow inside her collar, and the back of her neck and spine are freezing cold.

Right now she never, ever wants to ski again.

"Nice run!" William shouts.

He seems perfectly calm and not in the least bit tired. Olivia can see that he is reveling in his superiority. He can get down any run, and he knows it.

She used to find that absolute self-confidence attractive, but now she just wants to punch him, make that smug smile disappear forever.

But she can't afford to make an enemy of him.

She has enough problems with Amir and Pontus.

Personally, she is completely exhausted. Her muscles are on fire, and last night's lack of sleep and bad dreams are not helping.

What was she thinking when she suggested this route? How stupid was she?

"Was it hard?" William asks, sounding more sympathetic. "You look exhausted. Are you going to be able to cope with the Western?"

Not him as well.

Olivia nods. William is not the type to hold your hand when you feel sad and pathetic; it was her strength and feistiness that he fell for.

This day is not over yet. The worst still lies ahead.

Two dark figures emerge through the milky fog that has taken over the world. First Amir, then Pontus, who is panting audibly when he stops a couple of yards away, his back and shoulders covered in snow.

It looks as if he has fallen over several times.

He pulls off one glove and starts tugging at the chin strap of his helmet. Olivia is relieved to have a brief extra respite. If Pontus needs to rest, then it will give her a chance to recover too.

Her legs feel like jelly, her muscles are beginning to cramp. Her back is soaked in sweat after the exertion of the descent.

Amir doesn't look too good either. He is red in the face, and his chest is heaving.

When he glances toward the ravine, Olivia can see the unease in his eyes.

He knows what is coming.

Before them lies the mouth of hell.

50

When Daniel sits down in the conference room, he is hoping for fresh information from the National Forensic Center in Umeå. In order to move on, they have to know how Filippa died.

He has a cup of coffee in front of him. He made it out of habit, even though he didn't really want it and has already drunk far too many cups today.

Carina has just messaged to say they are finishing off at Nedre Svedjevägen, so she won't be calling in to the meeting. However, she informed him that they haven't found Filippa's clothes or boots in the house—they are still missing.

The door opens and Hanna comes in. She looks pale and somehow defiant. If he had to guess, he would say she is angry rather than suffering from stomach cramps.

When they parted half an hour ago, she sounded as if she was feeling a little better, but now she is positively radiating stress.

"Everything okay?" he asks.

She holds up a dismissive hand. "Fine."

Before Daniel can say any more, Anton and Raffe arrive. In any case, Hanna's gesture makes it clear that she doesn't want additional questions.

Something is wrong, that's obvious.

Daniel quickly runs through the meeting with Staffan Berg, highlighting the fact that he knows the code for the front door, and therefore has access to the house. They might need to check his whereabouts Saturday night through Sunday morning.

Raffe takes over. "I've done a background check on the next-door neighbors."

They can tell from his voice that he has found out something interesting. Raffe is good at digging up information. He has a particular ability to focus on the details, and Daniel can see a glint of satisfaction in his colleague's eyes.

"An incident of sexual harassment involving the son, Peter Carlsson, was reported to the police last year."

"Tell us more."

The ceiling light flickers. It has been doing this for the last few weeks; they need an electrician to come and check it out.

"It happened just over a year ago. Peter Carlsson was in a bar in Gothenburg, where he lives. He was very drunk and was bothering some young girls at a table nearby. According to the woman who made the report, he started behaving inappropriately. She said he touched her thighs a couple of times, then her breasts. When she went to the bathroom, he followed her and tried to kiss her. She later contacted the police."

"Was there a conviction?" Anton asks.

Raffe shakes his head. "It was her word against his, so it wasn't taken any further."

"It's no surprise that that kind of complaint is dismissed," Hanna mutters.

"It cost him his marriage," Raffe goes on. "His wife filed for divorce as soon as she found out."

"Who can blame her?" Hanna says.

Daniel exchanges a glance with Raffe. Hanna really isn't in a good mood.

"Interesting," he says. "Well done. Can you have a chat with Peter Carlsson? With this information it would be useful to meet him face-to-face."

Meanwhile Anton has activated the link with Östersund. The screen flashes and Grip's serious face appears.

"Have Umeå been in touch?" Daniel asks as soon as the microphones are on. "Have they finished the autopsy yet?"

"Yes and no," Grip replies, which isn't like her. The head of the Serious Crimes Unit doesn't usually go for ambiguity; on the contrary, she is known for being clear and direct. A quality that has presumably been a great help during her long career.

Grip is sixty-one, and approaching retirement. Female police chiefs were a rarity for her generation. Daniel is under no illusions about what it took for Birgitta Grip to succeed within the conservative police service.

Hanna looks up.

Daniel can almost see her shaking off whatever has been weighing her down. Admittedly she is the most impulsive member of the team, but at the same time she is phenomenal when it comes to focusing on the job. Nothing gets in the way of police work; she is one hundred percent dedicated.

Daniel admires her ability to concentrate with absolute clarity, which she can switch on in a second.

"Can you explain what that means?" she says, all her attention focused on Grip.

"I've just spoken to Ylva about the case. She was in the car, so it wasn't a long conversation."

Daniel knows Ylva Labba pretty well. They have worked together on a number of major homicide investigations in Åre. She is a conscientious and highly competent forensic pathologist. Her family background is Sámi, and she was born outside Kiruna.

"Ylva started the autopsy today," Grip continues. "But unfortunately she didn't finish it because of a personal matter. She had a call from her son's school, so she had to break off."

Daniel didn't even know that Ylva had a son, which is typical in this profession. Every week he is in contact with colleagues from different parts of the country—but it's always about work; they never get into their private lives. The only person he really discusses that kind of thing with is Hanna, because they often chat in the car on the way to and from Östersund. And even then it took a long time for him to open up to her, even though she told him pretty early on how she had been dumped by her partner in Stockholm.

He found it much harder to talk about his own problems, the difficulties between him and Ida that arose long before the actual separation. He doesn't know if this is because of loyalty to Ida or shame over his own inadequacies as a father and boyfriend.

It was even more challenging to admit that he had started seeing a therapist in order to work through the problems caused by growing up with an absent father. He hadn't told Hanna until last Easter, and he knows that she felt let down because he had kept quiet for so long.

Grip's hoarse voice interrupts his wandering thoughts.

"Ylva promised she would try to finish the autopsy tomorrow. Let's hope nothing gets in her way this time."

"So we still don't know the cause of death," Anton says.

"I'm afraid not."

Hanna sighs heavily, which exactly expresses how Daniel feels.

"But Ylva did pass on one thing that is very interesting, under the circumstances," Grip continues.

"Which is?" Hanna jumps in immediately.

"It seems as if the deceased had sex before she died." Grip pauses briefly. "Ylva found traces of vaginal intercourse that would have taken place not too long before the body was found on Sunday morning."

"Was it rape?" Anton wonders.

"Ylva said she couldn't confirm or deny that at this stage."

"But that changes everything," Hanna says.

She is right. Daniel immediately realizes the implications. None of the boys in the group had breathed a word about being intimate with Filippa during the final hours of her life.

Which means one of them is lying about that.

And maybe that person is also lying about the cause of Filippa's death.

51

Even William is a little more cautious as he pushes off with his poles and heads down into the ravine. Olivia takes care to keep the distance between them as short as possible; if she can stay close, it reduces the risk of losing sight of him or, even worse, crashing straight into a rock or crevasse with no warning.

It has taken them quite a while to get here, and it is becoming harder to see in the growing darkness. It is hard work keeping up with William; as usual he is going much faster than her. She is doing her best to follow his tracks, but she soon becomes disorientated.

William is no more than a dark shadow up ahead.

And then he is gone.

Olivia stares after him so intensely that her eyes fill with tears. She has lilac lenses in her goggles—that's supposed to be the best for seeing in fog—but the visibility is still dire. The tinted glass obliterates all height differences, and destroys any chance of grasping the topography in advance.

The truth is that she is skiing on pure instinct, keeping her knees as flexible as possible in order to deal with any changes of level.

Her attention is focused on the route in front of her, and she doesn't realize that she is too close to a low mountain birch. Suddenly she feels a hard blow to her face, like the lash of a whip. Luckily she manages to bend the rest of her body out of the way just in time, and glides past the tree by a hair's breadth without colliding with the trunk.

She can taste blood at the corner of her mouth.

Olivia clamps her lips together. This is her own fault; she was the one who suggested this route. It is too late to change her mind now.

She has never been so afraid. All at once she knows she can't go on; she stops and drives her poles deep into the ground. She has to find a way to orient herself, regain control.

She leans forward, breathing heavily inside her scarf, which by this time is both cold and damp. The route they came down is no longer visible. It is hidden behind an impenetrable layer of thick, white fog.

How far can it be to Fjällgårdsexpressen, where the ravine ends?

Eight hundred yards? Nine?

It's not far; it must be achievable.

Olivia tries to think clearly. Maybe she could put her skis over her shoulder and walk the last section? Although then she would sink so far down in the snow that she would probably get stuck.

Her goggles have steamed up. Now she can see even less.

"Pull yourself together," Olivia whispers to herself. "You can do this."

Staying put is not an option. It will be pitch dark before long, and then she will be in real danger. But she is reluctant to go on, with all the rocks and sharp outcrops lying in wait. If she runs into one of them, or gets stuck in a drift, she risks not being able to free herself.

If no one comes to help her.

She isn't sure that either Amir or Pontus would do that.

And William has abandoned her. Presumably he has already reached the lift, without worrying about what has happened to Olivia.

Fucking William.

With anger surging through her veins, she glides forward about ten yards. Takes off her goggles, thinks she has reached the point where the ravine forks and the Susabäcken stream appears in the center.

The middle looks like a smooth surface, free from trees and undergrowth, but she knows that the snow cover can be treacherous. The stream should have frozen by now, but sometimes the water continues to flow beneath the insulating layer of snow. A skier can easily fall through if the load-bearing capacity is too low.

If she opts for that route, it could give way with no warning.

Olivia has heard of several accidents where people have underestimated the power of the water course. It is a surefire way of breaking both your legs and your skis.

It is safer to choose one of the sides.

But which one?

She can't remember whether they usually take the left or the right. Her body's exhaustion is making her brain shut down, she can't remember even though she has skied there many times. A swishing sound catches her attention. A diffuse figure, she thinks it's Amir, passes by a few yards away and disappears toward the right side.

Should she follow him, or wait a while longer?

Pontus ought to show up soon; he's slower. Maybe it would be safer to follow him? He would probably be more likely to stop if she falls and shouts for help.

Olivia clutches her poles tightly as she waits for Pontus. She hopes he hasn't already passed by without her seeing him. That would mean she is the only one left out here.

All alone as darkness falls.

52

Time passes, and there is no sign of Pontus. A little while ago Olivia was sweating after the arduous descent, but now the cold, damp layer of clothing next to her skin is chilling her body and making her teeth chatter.

And the temperature is falling.

When they set out this morning, it was minus seventeen, but it must be much lower now. The air is freezing in her nostrils every time she inhales, and the snow has acquired the crispy texture that warns of dangerous cold.

Where the hell is Pontus?

Could he have passed by without her noticing?

Olivia peers in vain into the fog. She can't see any sign of movement in her frozen, lifeless surroundings.

The mountainsides loom above her head. The branches of the trees look as if they are reaching out to grab her. It is unnaturally silent and still.

She has to get out of here.

She shakes her head. She can't wait much longer. Soon it will be completely dark; then the lift system will shut down and she won't be able to get home on Fjällgårdsexpressen.

If she manages to get there.

With stiff fingers she grips her poles. She decides to take the right-hand side, the same narrow route that Amir took. At least she knows he got through.

If he can do it, so can she. She is a much more skillful skier than that idiot.

Little by little she makes her way alongside the dark wall of rock. Visibility is so poor that she can no longer see Amir's tracks.

At first the terrain is relatively flat; it is possible to progress slowly and cautiously; then she is surprised by a steep downhill slope.

It simply appears as the route narrows; suddenly the space is so limited that she can no longer snowplow.

In a panic Olivia tries to reduce her speed by driving her poles into the snow and resisting, but she is moving too fast, she lets out a whimper, and one of the poles is snatched from her hand. She can't do anything about it.

She is moving faster and faster; she loses control.

And comes to an abrupt halt. Both skis are stuck in a large snowdrift, she loses her balance and falls headfirst into the snow.

She feels a sharp pain in one knee; it shoots through her body like an arrow.

And then she tips over onto her side.

She has no idea how she is going to get up again.

53

The digital meeting with Östersund is over. Raffe had to leave, but Hanna, Daniel, and Anton are still in the conference room.

Hanna is doodling on her notepad as she ponders the new information from Ylva.

So Filippa had sex the night before she died. But was it voluntary or not?

And what happened next?

Ylva hadn't found any evidence to prove one or the other, but that isn't necessarily definitive. A woman who is raped rarely behaves the way someone does in a movie or on TV, screaming and fighting. Quite the reverse; the most common reaction is what is known as the freeze response, where the victim enters a state of apathy and becomes paralyzed, simply remaining motionless until the assault is over. This means there may well be no external physical injuries, if the man is merely threatening rather than physically violent.

Hanna has experienced this herself. She still carries the feelings of guilt and regret because she didn't fight back.

In addition, Filippa was very drunk—everyone they have spoken to said the same. She might not even have been aware of what was happening, and certainly not in any state to defend herself.

"So one of the boys is lying about what they did on Saturday," Anton says, leaning back in his chair and linking his hands behind his neck. "Should we conclude that this is because the same person is involved in Filippa's death? And that it wasn't an accident?"

"Sounds reasonable," Daniel says. "Especially bearing in mind what Karin Carlsson saw from her kitchen window: a male figure outside the house next door in the middle of the night."

"What if it was her son?" Hanna wonders. "Peter Carlsson, the guy with the wandering hands?"

It is a spontaneous comment, she hasn't had time to digest Raffe's information yet, nor has she read the original police report.

Daniel has a green elastic band stretched around his thumb and index finger. He pings it in the direction of the wastepaper basket and gives her a skeptical look.

"Wouldn't Karin have recognized her own son, if that were the case? And if she did, do you really think she would have told us?"

Hanna smiles—the pattern is familiar. She is impulsive; Daniel is reflective. It is usually a good combination when they are sitting around and speculating like this.

"Shall we drop Peter Carlsson for the moment and go back to the four boys?" Daniel adds. He goes over to the whiteboard, picks up a blue marker pen, and writes down the names:

Emil
Pontus
William
Amir

"The big question is which of them it could be. We have a choice of four."

He gazes at the list, then adds *A* after Emil's name.

A for assault. Does this mean that Emil is also a rapist?

Hanna finds this hard to believe of the fair-haired young man she met earlier, but it can't be ruled out.

At least not at this stage.

Pontus's online search history has aroused their suspicions. He has googled a series of dubious terms—why would he do that if he isn't involved in some way?

And worried about being caught?

"If Ylva is able to retrieve any sperm from Filippa, we'd be able to identify the male through a DNA test," Anton points out. "All we'd have to do is compare the samples."

"We don't know if there is any sperm to analyze," Hanna says. "They might have used a condom."

"And even if there is, it would take the National Forensic Center months to get back to us," Daniel says gloomily.

He is right—it is no secret that waiting times for the NFC are a major problem. This has been the case for years, even though Sweden's entire police service is aware of how bad things are.

"Let's check it out with Ylva," Hanna says. "What do we do now?"

"I think we should speak to everyone again," Daniel replies. "Push them hard, given the new information."

This is probably the best way forward.

Increase the pressure.

"I'd like to talk to Olivia," Hanna says. "She must have her own opinion of the boys and their relationship with Filippa. It would be interesting to hear what she has to say."

When she read the transcript of the initial interview with Olivia, she found it pretty nondescript. Then again, the girl had been upset and shocked; they had just found Filippa's body in the snow.

That was almost thirty-six hours ago, so hopefully Olivia will be more composed by now.

And nobody had asked targeted questions about Filippa's relationships with the four boys, which is exactly what Hanna wants to do. She also wants to find out more about Olivia's role.

Could she be involved in Filippa's death? Did Filippa do something to make her best friend jealous? Did she sleep with William, for example, who apparently was Olivia's boyfriend? It is possible that the girls fell out over a boy—it wouldn't be the first time something like that had happened.

Hanna glances at the clock—it is almost three. At this time of year, the lifts close around now, so the group should be on their way home.

She would really like to talk to Olivia.

"I think we should go back there."

"Or we bring them into the station," Anton suggests. "That might have more of an impact? First the house search, then a proper interview. It might frighten them into telling the truth."

Hanna considers the idea. If they send a patrol car to bring them in, everything is immediately placed on a more formal footing. However, it could also make them clam up.

If the group shuts down, then it could be even more difficult to find out what actually happened on Saturday—not to mention the risk that one or more of them will demand the presence of a lawyer. That could mean it would take a long time to conduct the interviews; the number of available defense lawyers in Åre is extremely limited.

She turns to Daniel. "What do you think? Should we go up there, or bring them in?"

Daniel's leg jiggles up and down as he considers the pros and cons.

"It's easier to separate them if we interview them here. We have all the facilities." He is right, of course. "But we might get more out of them by speaking to them in an environment where they feel secure. It will be easier to build trust, and the most important thing is for them to be able to open up and tell the truth."

"So we ought to go there," Hanna says.

It is at moments like this that she knows exactly why she enjoys working with Daniel so much. His ability to weigh up the advantages and disadvantages of a course of action, to see both sides of an argument without any hint of self-importance, is invaluable.

"Okay," she goes on, beginning to gather up her things. "Who's coming with me to Sadeln?"

54

The steel construction that is Fjällgårdsexpressen might be the most welcome sight Olivia has ever seen.

When the opening of the ravine finally appears and lets her out, through the narrowest of passageways, she almost collapses with relief. She did it, despite the fact that her knee is throbbing and aching and she has lost one of her poles. Somehow she managed to scramble up out of the snow drift and battle through the last few hundred yards.

A small sense of triumph lifts her heart, even though she is so cold that she can't feel her fingertips. Her toes are like lumps of ice, and the snow has found its way everywhere inside her clothes.

But she made it through the ravine through sheer determination.

The boys can go to hell.

She peers toward the lift, where the waiting area is almost empty. There are no lines at this time of day, all the skiers have gone home.

Have they left without her?

She sets off in the darkness, and eventually she spots William's dark jacket inside the barriers.

Amir is next to him. "At last," he says. He looks completely exhausted. Olivia can't see Pontus—at least she isn't last.

Which also feels good.

"Where did you get to?" William asks.

He doesn't notice that she has lost a pole. Olivia doesn't have the strength to explain. She simply mumbles that she fell and it took a while to catch them up.

After a few minutes they see a weary figure laboriously making its way through the gloom.

"Get a move on, Pontus!" William shouts. "We have to go before they shut down the lift for the day; otherwise we'll have to walk home."

He turns and skis the last few yards to the embarkation point where the chairlifts slow down. Olivia follows in his tracks; the lift operator is standing there shivering. Olivia settles into her seat and rests her shoulder against the armrest. She is trembling with weariness. When the lift rises above the Susabäcken stream, she closes her eyes so she doesn't have to see it.

Would William and Amir have come looking for her if she hadn't made it out of the ravine under her own steam?

She will never know.

And she isn't sure she wants to.

55

Anton has gone into his office and sat down at his desk, where various documents are arranged in neat piles. He likes to have order around him, one of the few things he has in common with his father. Otherwise they have a very fractious relationship.

He hears the odd burst of laughter from a group of uniformed colleagues who are having a snack in the kitchenette.

Anton would have been perfectly happy to go up to Sadeln, but he knows that Daniel and Hanna are probably the best combination. Three is one too many, and Hanna is adept at dealing with young people. She is a good interviewer; she has taken a number of psychology courses at the university, and has also been involved in hostage negotiations.

This is Anton's first major investigation since he formally transferred to the Serious Crimes Unit. He taps on one of the piles of papers with his knuckles. He knows he will have the opportunity to show what he can do; he will just have to be patient.

Although sometimes that can be difficult.

More laughter from the kitchenette. What's so funny? Anton isn't exactly in the mood for hilarity. Thoughts of Carl are lurking in the back of his mind. Should he call him, try to talk through last night?

He takes out his phone, brings up his contacts. Carl's name is at the top, marked as a favorite, easy to access.

At that moment the screen lights up with an incoming call.

It's his father.

Anton's stomach turns over.

He only calls when he wants something. And he never wastes time on small talk, especially not when Anton is at work.

What is it today?

Anton answers on the third ring, even though he would rather let the call go to voicemail.

"Hello?"

"Hello, Anton, it's your father."

The voice is as brusque as always. And as loud.

His father retired from his post as a lieutenant colonel in the army a few years ago, but he still seems to think that every conversation must be conducted in his parade ground voice, as if he needs to be heard by a hundred recruits rather than just his son on the other end of the line.

He probably isn't even aware that he routinely bellows at everyone around him.

In order to spare his hearing, Anton places the phone on the desk and switches on the speaker at the lowest volume. His office door is closed, so there is no risk that his father will disturb his colleagues.

"So I see," he replies, keeping his tone neutral.

"Re Karro's birthday celebration on Sunday," his father barks. "We'll see you then. Fifteen hundred hours."

Also typical—the insistence on giving the time with military precision.

"I know when we're supposed to be there."

Anton has to make a real effort to keep the irritation out of his voice. They look quite similar. He has inherited his father's facial features, and their physique is almost identical, not very tall but muscular, and they both have fair hair. But inside they couldn't be more different.

He has always had a problem with his father's bluntness; he himself is more circumspect, more considerate. His father assumes that he is the center of the universe, while Anton rarely feels the need to dominate a group of people.

The fact that Anton also likes music and plays the saxophone in a jazz band has been a constant source of irritation for his father, who is tone deaf and prefers to spend his time hunting and fishing.

His mother has had to mediate between the two of them on countless occasions.

His father clears his throat.

"Karro's birthday—it's purely a family occasion, as I'm sure you realize. The children will be there too."

Obviously his sister's children will be at their mother's birthday party. Anton tries to work out what his father is getting at.

"And?"

"That's all I wanted to say. That we're keeping it in the family. It's for the best." A strained silence follows. Anton doesn't know what to say. "Goodbye."

His father ends the call.

What the hell was that about?

Anton hasn't dared to introduce Carl to his family yet, but they have been out and about in the village together.

Has his father heard something? Åre is a small community; Duved is even smaller. People might have seen them, and maybe the rumors have started.

Was this his father's clumsy attempt to make it clear that he knows about the relationship but doesn't want it made official?

Was he trying to tell Anton that Carl is not welcome in the family home?

Surely he can't be taking a stand yet, when Anton hasn't even plucked up the courage to talk to his parents about Carl?

He is filled with anger and despair, there are so many emotions that he suddenly wants to express. With a half-muffled scream he slams his hand down hard on the desk.

It hurts a lot, but not as much as the suspicion that his father is not prepared to accept who Anton really is.

56

The sun has gone down by the time Hanna knocks on the sturdy door of the Löwengrens' house. Beyond the reach of the white beams of the external lighting, there is only darkness. Daniel, who is a few steps behind her in a navy-blue jacket, almost melts into the background.

Carina and her team have left.

Once again it is Emil who answers the door. His expression changes when he sees that the two officers from this morning are back.

Hanna can see how much their presence is stressing him out. His eyes become watchful, his jawline tenses. Just like before, he clenches his fists before pushing his hands into his pockets.

Is he worried that they will tell Pontus that the police have taken his laptop because of what Emil told them? Or that they will reveal his assault conviction to his friends?

Or is this about something else?

Maybe it was Emil who had sex with Filippa, but he is afraid to admit it because of the implications.

"We need to speak to you and your friends again."

"They got back a little while ago. They're pretty upset that you searched the house without letting them know in advance."

Hanna doesn't bother to comment. She understands their feelings, but under the circumstances it can't be helped.

"Where's Olivia? I need to speak to her on her own."

They have decided that she will begin with Olivia, while Daniel sits down with Pontus.

"I expect she's in the guest cabin." Emil points to a smaller building not far away. "She went over there as soon as she arrived home."

Hanna turns to Daniel.

"Okay, I'll go and find her, leave you to make a start here."

When Hanna knocks on the door, there is no answer. She tries the handle. It isn't locked, so she steps into the hallway and calls out, "Hello? Olivia?"

The floor is littered with discarded wet ski clothes—a white jacket and a white ski suit—and Hanna can hear the sound of the shower from what must be the bathroom. She calls Olivia's name again, louder this time, and the water is turned off.

The door opens, and a slender girl in a white toweling robe appears. Her black hair is soaking wet, her eyes large and suspicious.

"My name is Hanna, and I'm with the Åre police," Hanna explains quickly, to reassure her. "I'd like to ask you a few more questions about Filippa's death, if that's okay?"

Olivia stares at her, then blurts out, "Was it Amir?"

57

The best place for a private conversation is the study on the lower floor.

Pontus chooses the armchair below the only window, its pane completely covered in snow. He hasn't managed to change out of his skiing clothes yet; he is still wearing his thermals and thick socks.

"When can I have my computer back?" he says aggressively. "You can't just take it like that!"

Daniel sits down at the designer desk. "We'll talk about that later. But actually, we can, given that your friend was found dead outside this house yesterday and your computer could form a significant part of our inquiries."

Pontus gives him a filthy look.

"You're very brave, going skiing on a day like this." Daniel nods in the direction of the window. "When you can hardly see your hand in front of your face."

"It was William who insisted on hitting the slopes. And then Olivia dragged us to that ravine—Western, or whatever it's called."

"You skied the West Ravine today?" Daniel can't hide his surprise. "That sounds like a bad idea."

"Olivia was crazy to suggest it." Pontus practically spits out the words. "If we'd gotten hurt, it would have been her fault. I don't know what she was thinking."

Daniel doesn't ask why Pontus didn't object, but he takes note of the intense dislike in his voice.

So the group isn't as harmonious as it appeared on Sunday.

That isn't necessarily a disadvantage—quite the reverse.

Divide and conquer. Not a bad tactic.

"I have a few questions concerning Filippa's death. On Sunday you said that you fell asleep on the sofa while Filippa was still in the living room. When you woke up, she'd gone." He deliberately pauses. "Is that still true?"

Pontus stiffens as soon as he mentions Filippa's name. Just like Emil did.

Daniel is increasingly convinced that they are both hiding something.

"Yes, it is."

"Where were you sitting when you fell asleep?"

"On the sofa. I already told you."

"I'd like to know exactly where you were sitting. There are two sofas—which one?"

"I . . ." Pontus closes his eyes, as if he is trying to remember. Or maybe he needs a breathing space. "The far one. The one with its back to Åreskutan. In the corner."

"Where was Filippa when you fell asleep?"

"Opposite me, I think."

"And when you woke up, she wasn't there?"

"That's right."

"So what did you think?"

Daniel leans across the desk, where there is a black leather pot containing several pens. Beside it lies an elegant letter opener made of carved reindeer horn.

"Nothing. Well . . . I thought she'd gone to bed like everyone else, because they'd all disappeared."

Pontus fills the armchair. He isn't very tall, but at close quarters Daniel notices how broad-shouldered he is.

Strong.

It wouldn't be difficult for him to carry a body like Filippa's. She must have weighed around 130 pounds. If Daniel remembers correctly she was of medium height, maybe five foot four. Pontus is a few inches taller.

"When was the last time you saw Filippa alive?"

"Before I fell asleep."

"And what time was that?"

"About two o'clock. I don't remember exactly—I was pretty drunk."

His tone is truculent; it is obvious that Pontus doesn't want to talk about this.

Daniel doesn't react. "And who else was in the room, as far as you recall?"

Pontus inhales loudly through his nose. "Olivia had already gone over to the cabin. Emil had gone to bed, and I think William had gone to his room. Amir was still there, he and Filippa were making out on the sofa, like they'd been doing all evening."

Filippa and Amir. No one has mentioned this before. Another piece of the puzzle falls into place.

"I don't remember anything else," Pontus adds. "Except that the living room was empty when I woke up."

"And that was the last time you saw Filippa?"

"Yes."

Pontus bends down and makes a big performance of pulling up his socks, one by one. But Daniel isn't done yet.

"Are you absolutely certain?"

"Yes—I told you!"

Beads of sweat have broken out on Pontus's forehead, by his hairline.

Daniel decides to go for it; there is no point in pussyfooting around with the new information from the autopsy.

"Did you sleep with Filippa on Saturday?"

"What?"

"Did you have sex with Filippa before she died?"

"No, absolutely not! Why would you think that?"

Daniel ignores the question. "Was it you who placed her in the snow where she was found?"

"No!" Pontus shouts the word. Sweat is trickling down his cheeks now, and he wipes it away with the back of his hand.

"And yet you googled things that an innocent person probably wouldn't search for," Daniel says. "Words like *murder*, *manslaughter*, *causing the death of another person*. Which makes me wonder if there might be a crime behind Filippa's death. A crime in which you are involved." Before Pontus can interrupt, he continues: "Please explain why you googled those words if you have nothing to hide?"

Pontus's eyes are darting all over the place, as if he is hunting for a way out, a reasonable explanation so that Daniel will leave him in peace.

"Well?"

"I haven't done anything!"

"Why did you enter those search words if you had nothing to do with Filippa's death?"

Those final words make Pontus slump in the armchair. "I don't know, I just did." His voice is rough. "But it wasn't me who killed Filippa."

58

Hanna and Olivia are sitting on the sofas in the cabin. Olivia is still wearing her toweling robe, and she grimaces when she tucks her legs beneath her.

"Are you hurt?" Hanna asks.

"I twisted my knee in the Western—I fell at the end."

"You skied the West Ravine today? In this weather?"

"It was such a stupid idea—we should never have done it. And it was my suggestion. Well, it was William who came up with it first, because he always has to make the decisions, and then I got mad and . . ."

She breaks off. Hanna gets the impression that some kind of power struggle has been going on within the group. Olivia doesn't seem like the kind of girl who gives in easily, but now she is the only female, along with four boys.

Filippa is gone.

The balance has shifted.

"Do you mind if I take a look?"

Olivia stretches out her leg, and Hanna gently presses the knee-cap and the joint. It doesn't look particularly swollen, so it's probably nothing to worry about.

"I'm sure it'll be fine in a couple of days. If I were you, I'd wrap some ice cubes in a towel and put it on your knee for fifteen minutes or so. If it still hurts tomorrow, you could go down to the medical center and ask them to check it over."

"Thanks." Olivia tucks her leg beneath her body again, then grabs one of the cushions and presses it to her stomach.

"When I arrived, you asked if it was Amir. What did you mean?" Hanna asks gently.

Olivia takes several deep breaths. "Sorry, it just came out."

Her response sounds both apologetic and angry. Hanna wants to know more. She can't ignore those words.

"But you must have said it for a reason?"

Olivia looks down, clutches the cushion with both hands.

"You can tell me anything," Hanna adds. "You don't need to worry about Amir."

Olivia's fingers dig deeper into the fabric. "The thing is . . . I think Amir did something to Filippa on Saturday. It can't have been just an accident, the fact that she died in the snow. She would never have fallen asleep outdoors, with hardly any clothes on. It doesn't make sense."

Hanna gazes at the girl. She sounds convinced, but Hanna has read the transcript of the interview with Amir. What Olivia is saying doesn't match the information he gave; he claimed he went to bed and left Filippa on the sofa.

She might as well tell Olivia about Ylva's observations and see how she reacts.

"We've found out something about Filippa that affects the picture of what happened. It seems she had sex late in the evening—in the hours before she died. We're trying to work out who with."

Olivia's eyes widen. "It must have been Amir! He and Filippa were making out like crazy when we were playing games on Saturday evening."

"But he insists that she was still in the living room when he went to bed. He says he slept alone, not with Filippa."

"In that case he's lying." Olivia's expression is determined now. "Who else could it have been?"

"What about the other boys? Wasn't Filippa interested in any of them?"

"She'd never look at Pontus. She didn't even like him."

"And William?"

Olivia shakes her head. "It can't be him. We've had a thing going on for a while. He'd never go with Filippa. The two of them didn't really get along—he thought she was kind of pathetic."

"How about Emil?"

For the first time Olivia gives a faint smile. "Emil isn't interested in girls. Haven't you worked that out yet?"

Hanna feels kind of dumb. No, she hadn't worked that out. But in some ways it makes matters simpler, provided that what Olivia says is true.

The young woman's face hardens, and her eyes narrow. "It's all Amir's fault. If he hadn't come with us, Filippa would still be alive."

Hanna considers this assertion. Olivia seems utterly convinced, and there is no mistaking her antipathy toward Amir. But it's a big step, accusing a friend of murder.

Even if Amir did have sex with Filippa, it doesn't necessarily mean that he was involved in her death. On the other hand, he might well have been the last person to see her alive.

Or maybe Olivia is right.

Something went wrong between Amir and Filippa on Saturday night, which is why he is lying to the police. Maybe Filippa didn't want to have sex with him, and he forced himself on her. Then he had to hide what he had done.

Suddenly Olivia seems to run out of energy. She buries her head in her hands, panting audibly.

"I can't be here any longer," she whispers between her fingers. "When can we go home?"

Hanna wishes she had a satisfactory answer. In the best-case scenario the autopsy on Filippa will be completed tomorrow, which should give them the cause of death, and they will know if they are dealing with a crime. Until then they need the group of friends to remain together, even though it can't be easy for them to stay in the place where Filippa died.

At the same time, there is a limit to how long they can keep them in Åre. William's father is on their case, and it won't be long before the other parents join in. Which would play havoc with the investigation.

Irate moms and dads are the last thing they need.

"Soon," Hanna says, against her better judgment. "You'll all be able to go home soon."

59

Footsteps on the stairs reveal that William is on his way. Daniel has concluded the interview with Pontus, and is waiting in the study for William to arrive.

The young man closes the door behind him and sinks down in the cognac-colored armchair that Pontus has just vacated. He has showered and changed into jeans and a short-sleeved top. His dark hair is combed back, still damp at the nape of his neck. He leans toward Daniel, his jawline tense.

"My father says you have no right to conduct a house search with no warning."

"Believe me, under the circumstances, we do."

"We weren't even home."

Emil was in the house, but Daniel doesn't bother pointing out that William should be pleased about that, because otherwise the police would have broken down the door.

"I have a few more questions about Saturday evening," he says instead. "Can you tell me who was still in the living room when you went to bed?"

William clamps his lips together so tightly that Daniel wonders if he is going to refuse to cooperate, but eventually he opens his mouth.

"Let's see . . . Pontus, Filippa, and Amir. The others had already gone to their rooms."

"So you decided to do the same? Tell me exactly what happened."

"Nothing special."

"Tell me exactly what you did. Step by step, if you can."

William looks confused, no doubt wondering why he is being asked for such a detailed account. He probably doesn't realize that Daniel is looking for differences in the boys' statements. Those tiny cracks that appear when something isn't right.

However, he does as he is asked.

"So first I went into the bathroom and brushed my teeth. Then I got undressed; then I got into bed and went to sleep."

"Did it take long?"

"Maybe five, ten minutes?"

Daniel tries to visualize the layout of the house.

William's bedroom, the master bedroom, is right next door to the living room, with its own en suite bathroom.

The building is largely made of wood, and Daniel knows from experience how easily sounds can be heard through wooden walls, even though they may look sturdy. If a disagreement had broken out between Filippa and one of the other boys, William should have been aware of it from his bedroom.

"I'm wondering if you might have heard something out of the ordinary from the living room after you'd gone to bed?"

"What do you mean by out of the ordinary?" William asks after a pause that is slightly too long.

Daniel finds it hard to believe that he doesn't understand, but provides an explanation just to be on the safe side. "I'm thinking of loud or angry voices. People arguing, maybe pieces of furniture being knocked over? I wonder if your friends might have gotten into an argument after you'd left the room?"

"I didn't hear anything like that."

"Are you sure?"

"I told you!" William frowns, as if he isn't used to anyone doubting what he says. Daniel senses that this young man is used to others fitting in with him. He expects positive acknowledgment, not pressure or criticism.

Something to bear in mind.

"I'm a heavy sleeper," William goes on. "So I can't swear it didn't happen, but I didn't hear anyone arguing or yelling at each other."

"What was the atmosphere like when you left your friends?"

"Good."

"And you didn't notice anything unusual?"

"No."

Daniel feels as if he is having to drag every single word out of William, and he is growing tired of his attitude. How hard can it be to show a little willingness to cooperate?

"Can you give me a few more details on your perception of how the evening went?"

"We had a good time. Emil had made an excellent dinner—he's a brilliant cook. Then we played Truth or Consequences, and everyone got pretty drunk. Especially Filippa."

"And how was the atmosphere when you went to bed?"

"Okay, but maybe kind of subdued, because everyone was getting sleepy. And it was late, around two in the morning—we had to be up reasonably early to go skiing."

Daniel has no reason to doubt what William says, so he decides to change tack.

"We've found out that Filippa had sex with one of you on the evening before she died. We need to know who that was."

"Wow." Finally a reaction from William. He lifts his chin, grips the arm of the chair.

"Was it you?" Daniel's tone is deliberately brusque.

"What?"

"Did you have sex with Filippa?"

"Of course not!" The answer is immediate.

"Why not?"

"Because . . . because me and Olivia have a thing . . ."

William actually blushes, and Daniel waits to see if he is going to continue. Sometimes silence is better than a series of follow-up questions.

But William says nothing.

"So who do you think it might have been?"

William shifts his position in the armchair, his eyes dart around the room. "I've no idea, but it wasn't me."

60

It is after five when Hanna goes back to the main house to look for Daniel. At least the fog has dispersed; an icy wind stings her cheeks as she knocks on the front door.

She finds Daniel downstairs in the study. He is sitting behind a modern desk made of dark wood, which looks expensive.

"How did it go?" Hanna asks, sinking down in the leather armchair opposite him.

"So-so." He stretches his arms in front of him and twists his head from side to side a few times. "I've spoken to everyone except Amir. They all deny having slept with Filippa on Saturday evening."

He briefly summarizes what Pontus and William said.

"It can't have been Emil," Hanna says. "According to Olivia, he prefers boys."

She can see that this information comes as a surprise to Daniel.

"We'll ask him before we leave," he says. "But if that's the case, I find it strange that neither Pontus nor William said anything."

Hanna agrees to a certain extent, but maybe Emil didn't want to broadcast his orientation? Then again, Olivia passed on the information as if it were something obvious—so surely the other boys must have been aware of his preferences?

Unless Olivia made it up to protect her friend?

Or herself?

Hanna is reluctant to rule anything out at this stage, even though Olivia came across as honest and sincere.

"Olivia is convinced it must have been Amir who had sex with Filippa," she says. "And she also thinks he's involved in her death."

She quickly runs through her conversation with Olivia, highlights the girl's antipathy toward Amir. She also mentions her feeling that the boys don't appear to have behaved particularly well toward Olivia on the slopes today, and that something seems to have happened.

"Well, it's hardly surprising if tensions arise under the circumstances," Daniel says pensively. "But I'd like us to interview Amir together. See what he has to say."

What he has to say in his defense, Hanna thinks.

61

Amir gives Hanna a dirty look when he walks into the study a few minutes later. He stops by the dark-gray built-in bookcase, and Hanna gestures toward the armchair under the window.

She has brought in an extra chair and placed it next to the desk, so the three of them are seated in a triangle. She has her pen and notepad at the ready.

"Good afternoon," Daniel begins. "We have a few more questions about what happened on Saturday, if that's okay?"

Amir makes a small movement with his head as if to show that it is indeed okay, although all three of them know he doesn't have a choice.

"What do you want to know?" His voice is hoarse. Is he coming down with a cold, or is the tension affecting his vocal cords?

"We believe you and Filippa were among the last members of the group to be in the living room on Saturday evening," Hanna says.

"Pontus was there too."

The answer is lightning fast, almost like a reflex. Is Amir trying to hide behind his friend?

Does he need an alibi to prove his innocence?

"Yes, but as we understand it, Pontus had fallen asleep, so he doesn't count."

"But he was there," Amir says stubbornly.

Daniel steps in. "What we're actually wondering is what happened between you and Filippa during the evening?"

"What do you mean?"

"Everyone has told us that the two of you spent the whole time making out," Hanna says. "Did she go with you to your room?"

"No, I went to bed on my own."

Hanna sighs to herself. *Not him as well.*

Are all the boys going to deny that they had sex with Filippa?

If so, they have a problem.

"We know that Filippa had sex with someone in the hours before she died," she continues. "We're assuming it was you, since several witnesses have stated that the two of you were kissing on the sofa."

Amir shakes his head vigorously. "That's not true! Well, okay, we were making out a little bit, but I didn't sleep with her!"

Hanna can see that Daniel is getting irritated too. His fingers are drumming on the desk, and his expression is icy as he looks at Amir.

"In that case please explain why we should believe you. Bearing in mind what your friends have told us."

"Filippa was way too drunk. She was starting to be hard work." He runs a nervous hand through his dark hair. "I mean . . . I know she liked me, and that she wanted to go to bed with me, but she's not really my type. Plus she'd really made a fool of herself when that old guy came over, pulling up her camisole and showing him her breasts." He leans forward, as if he is seeking their approval. "Who does something like that?"

The way Amir is talking about Filippa bothers Hanna. He sounds way too pompous and self-satisfied. Who gave him the right to decide how Filippa ought to behave?

Can you hear yourself? she would like to say to him. *Show some respect. We're talking about a young woman who came to Åre just a couple of days ago, full of optimism and the joy of life. Now she's lying dead in the morgue.*

But it wouldn't help at all if she started lecturing Amir. However, she is beginning to see why Olivia has a problem with him.

"So Filippa didn't accompany you to your room, and the two of you didn't have sex on Saturday?" she says sweetly.

"No, I've told you. I went up to bed in the loft. On my own." He gives her a defiant look. The dislike appears to be mutual.

"And what did Filippa do then?" Daniel asks.

"She stayed on the sofa, with Pontus opposite her."

"Pontus, who didn't see a thing because he'd fallen asleep." Hanna points out.

"No, yes, I guess he had."

"You guess he had?"

Amir sighs. "He was asleep."

Hanna has had enough. "So he can't confirm what you say. That you went up to your room alone, without Filippa, because she stayed in the living room."

"Presumably not."

Silence. They are getting nowhere. Hanna searches for a follow-up question, something that might make Amir contradict himself.

But before she can think of anything, she hears the defiance in his voice:

"It's your problem if you don't believe me, isn't it?"

62

When Daniel turns onto the E14, the road surface is white with snow. To be on the safe side, he slows down; he doesn't want to drive at the permitted fifty miles per hour if it's slippery. He has promised to drop Hanna in Solbringen; then he will pick up Alice from Ida's, because the schedule went wrong over the weekend. How he's going to balance looking after his daughter with the investigation into Filippa's death, he has no idea.

Hanna isn't happy with the interviews they have just conducted; Daniel recognizes the irritated look on her face.

"One of those boys is lying to us," she says, as if she has read his mind. "And if we're to believe Olivia, it's Amir." She breaks off to adjust her seatbelt, which is twisted over her chest. "Most of what we've heard suggests that he was the one who had sex with Filippa. If we can just get him to admit it, then maybe we can crack the big question—why she died a few hours later."

"He wasn't particularly cooperative," Daniel agrees. There was definitely something truculent about Amir. He was on his guard the whole time. However, Daniel isn't prepared to focus on one person right now. "If we assume that Emil is gay, then we're looking at Amir, William, or Pontus. It could be any of them."

"We should start by pushing Amir harder," Hanna says.

Daniel can see the trees along the road already bending in the wind; there is a strong possibility of a storm blowing in overnight.

"Let's leave it until tomorrow. We can't simply rely on Olivia's perceptions. Meanwhile we need to check with the houses nearby, see if anyone else was up during the night, like Karin Carlsson. If we're lucky, other people might have seen something."

"We'll send a patrol up there as soon as possible," Hanna agrees. "If there's anyone available who isn't taking care of students who've had too much to drink."

Daniel gives a wry smile. Yesterday there was a drunken brawl in one of the houses on the square, where lots of student groups often stay. Several young people found themselves sobering up in the cells; the neighbors had complained about the noise.

The exit for Solbringen appears on the right. Daniel turns off and continues up the hill.

"Thanks for the ride," Hanna says when he stops outside her little house. "Time for me to collect Morris."

"Give him a cuddle from me," Daniel says, raising his hand to say goodbye. "See you tomorrow."

He has met Hanna's big, fluffy cat on a number of occasions, and every single time he has left with a considerable amount of cat hair attached to his clothes. Morris makes a point of greeting every visitor by jumping on their lap. He is a sociable cat who loves close contact. He is also convinced that Hanna lives in his house, rather than the reverse.

Daniel watches her as she unlocks the front door. He would love to go in with her. After today he wouldn't have minded sitting down at her kitchen table with a beer, talking through the various witness statements in peace and quiet to get some perspective.

Maybe let Morris have a little sleep on his knee.

Instead he has to hurry over to Ida's place; she is bound to be in a bad mood. Daniel had promised to collect Alice an hour ago, and he knows exactly what Ida will say as soon as he shows up.

His ability to become absorbed in an investigation, to put his work before his personal life, has always been a bone of contention between them. Ida hated it when they were together. He kept promising that things would change, but they never did.

With one final, wistful look at Hanna's kitchen window, he puts the car into gear and drives away.

63

A large glass containing ice cubes and a clear liquid is standing on the coffee table in front of Pontus when Olivia walks into the main house. She can see from his unfocused gaze that he is well on the way to getting drunk. It isn't even seven o'clock.

But it has been a terrible day. Finding out that the police had gone through their possessions while they were out skiing had really shaken her. The thought of someone rummaging around among her clothes . . .

It feels both disrespectful and insulting.

Without warning, the door behind her is flung open, and a strange man is standing there. Olivia gives a start and lets out a little scream; then she recognizes him. It's Staffan, the property manager who called by on Saturday evening shortly after they arrived.

"Sorry—I didn't mean to scare you!" he says.

He is wearing a woolen hat pulled well down over his forehead, and he is carrying a snow shovel.

"I should have knocked first. I'm just so used to coming and going that I didn't think."

Olivia manages a wan smile. She instinctively recoils from the idea that this guy can walk in whenever he likes.

Could he have been the one outside her door last night?

The thought comes from nowhere.

She tries to take a closer look at him discreetly; does he resemble the shadow she saw in the darkness? Was it him, or is her imagination running away with her?

The silence is beginning to feel uncomfortable.

"It's fine," she says. "It's just that the last few days have been a bit much."

"I can understand that." Staffan props the shovel against the wall. "It's terrible, what happened to your friend. Hard to believe it's true."

"Mmm."

Olivia can't talk about it. Especially not with him, a stranger. Someone who might have tried to get into the cabin while she was sleeping.

"Have the police said anything more?" Staffan wonders, with a slightly-too-curious glint in his eyes. "Do they know how your friend died?"

"I have no idea."

Olivia just wants him to leave. She glances at Pontus, half hoping that he will come over and join in the conversation so she doesn't have to be alone with Staffan, but Pontus is ignoring him completely.

"Do they think it was the result of a crime?" Staffan stares at Olivia, as if he is trying to work out how much she actually knows.

"I need to . . ." Olivia points in the direction of the kitchen, hoping he will take the hint and stop asking questions.

It seems to work, because he stamps the snow off his boots on the doormat, then removes them.

"I'm just going to clear the balcony," he explains, picking up the shovel. "It won't take long."

He carries his boots through the living room and opens one of the patio doors.

Olivia remains standing in the hallway, staring at the black handle on the front door.

What's the point of locking up when anyone who knows the code can get in?

64

Hanna's phone rings as she is hanging up her padded jacket in the hallway. She answers without checking to see who it is.

And realizes her mistake as soon as she hears the voice of her mother, Ulla.

It is no coincidence that there are long gaps between their conversations, because almost every single time they speak, Hanna ends up feeling unwanted and like a failure. Her mother has made her feel that way ever since she can remember.

"Hi, Hanna!" Ulla says with unusual enthusiasm.

Hanna is immediately suspicious. What's this about?

"Why didn't you tell me and your father about your new boyfriend? I want to hear every detail! Did you really fly in a private plane?"

Not her as well.

Hanna has barely gotten over the shock from the conversation with the journalist who called earlier. It is only twelve hours since the article was published, but the whole world seems to be interested in her relationship with Henry.

Including her parents, who moved to Spain's Costa del Sol years ago and spend most of their time drinking rosé and enjoying long lunches with other expat Swedes. While bad-mouthing the Swedish tax system and the terrible climate.

"It's all pretty new," Hanna mumbles. "I haven't gotten around to it."

She kicks off her boots, goes into the kitchen, and sinks down at the table. How can she end this conversation? The last thing she wants is to discuss Henry with her mother.

"When do we get to meet him? Surely the two of you can hop on board that private plane and come down for a visit?"

Ulla's voice is positively fizzing with joy. Hanna shouldn't be surprised—no one is as keen on knowing the right people and moving in the right circles. Her mother's greatest talent is name-dropping. For years she has complained about Hanna's choice of profession, constantly comparing her with her successful sister, Lydia, who is a partner in a prestigious law firm and is married to an equally successful man who works for a venture capital company.

Ulla has never approved of Hanna's life choices. And when Christian finished with Hanna, her mother took his side. She also carried on seeing him and his new girlfriend, Valérie, even though he was the one who cheated on Hanna and dumped her in the most brutal way.

Nor did she hesitate to point out to her daughter that she was running out of time to find a new partner, as she was fast approaching forty and—terrible thought—menopause.

Hanna has just turned thirty-seven.

The constant reminders that it will soon be too late to have children hit Hanna right in the solar plexus. Her mother was never there for her, the late arrival who was neither planned nor wanted. She didn't even step up when Hanna was the victim of a sexual assault in Barcelona.

Hanna still remembers sitting on the edge of the bed, shaking, when she called home to tell her parents about the rape. About the hands roaming all over her body, the weight of her boss when he forced himself on her.

She has never felt so alone as she did when she realized that her mom and dad had no intention of coming to help her. Instead it was

Lydia who flew down and brought her home, Lydia who held her when she had terrible nightmares. Lydia who arranged treatment and therapy, and promised that everything would be okay.

While her mother was ashamed and refused to discuss the matter. It was too embarrassing, too stressful.

But today Ulla is thrilled, of course. A well-known financier is joining the family—this will raise her status among her circle of acquaintances!

Hanna stares down at the table and wishes Morris were here. She could do with feeling his soft nose against her cheek.

"I knew you'd sort your life out eventually," Ulla chirrups in her ear. "It's fantastic that you've managed to catch Henry Sylvester. A man like that could have anyone he wants!"

It shouldn't hurt, but it does. The fact that her mother is openly astonished that Hanna, the family's ugly duckling, has somehow snared a man like Henry.

Didn't that journalist say something along the same lines? She said that Hanna and Henry were *an unusual couple*.

Is she really so nondescript that no one can understand why they're together?

"I have to go," she says wearily. "I'll speak to you some other time."

She ends the call before her mother can say another word.

She swallows hard several times, trying to get rid of the lump in her throat. Why does this affect her so much? She has already cried way too often because of things her mother has said over the years.

She can't allow her self-image to stand and fall by her mother's love. She is an adult; she ought to know better. Her mother will never treat her the same as Lydia, who has always been her favorite.

She probably doesn't even realize it herself. Ulla is simply incapable of loving the child she never wanted.

It is what it is.

But the lump in Hanna's throat won't go away.

65

Olivia joins Emil, who is making dinner in the kitchen. Pontus scowls at her when she walks past the sofa, but he doesn't speak. His glass is almost empty; Olivia can smell gin on the air.

There is no sign of Amir or William, thank goodness. After today she would prefer to avoid their company.

"Hi," she says to Emil. "What's on the menu tonight?"

"Pork tenderloin with oven-baked potato wedges and a red wine sauce. It's almost ready."

The smell of rosemary reaches Olivia's nostrils as Emil opens the oven door a fraction to check on the meat. It looks delicious, and in spite of everything, she is hungry; her stomach is rumbling.

The relief that Emil is here makes her feel calmer. Without him she couldn't bear to stay, whatever the police say.

Emil is kind.

Unlike those other idiots.

"You're amazing," she says. "I couldn't have coped with cooking."

Emil reaches for a red-checked kitchen towel and wipes his hands. "We have to eat. Would you like a glass of wine?"

Would she?

Olivia glances over at Pontus. It's so annoying that he's getting drunk again. Maybe she ought to stay sober, to be on the safe side.

She can't really explain why. The worst thing possible has already happened.

Filippa is dead.

While she is pondering, Emil has opened a bottle of red and poured them each a glass. He passes one to Olivia, and she takes a sip.

It is delicious, and she relaxes. Takes another sip. It has been a dreadful day. And then the police showed up with more questions . . . She can't stop thinking about the revelation that Filippa had had sex with one of the boys before she died.

It can only be Amir. Especially if she was both drunk and high.

She turns back to Emil. "Did you speak to the police when they were here? What did they ask you?"

He opens a drawer, takes out two wooden serving spoons.

"I'm not sure," he says over his shoulder. "There were a lot of questions about the atmosphere on Saturday evening. The same things they asked about on Sunday, really. Whether Filippa had argued with any of us, if there had been any kind of falling out within the group."

"And what did you say?"

"I just told the truth—that I was the first to go to bed, and nothing happened while I was still there."

Olivia moves a little closer to Emil. He has begun to slice a head of lettuce and put it in a bowl.

"Did you hear that the police know Filippa had sex on the evening before she died?" she says quietly. "And that they think it's connected to her death?" She glances around to make sure that Pontus isn't eavesdropping. "It must have been Amir, don't you agree? I was right all along, even though no one believed me."

Her words make Emil put down the knife. He looks worried. "That's a very serious accusation, Olivia. Do you really think Amir is involved in Filippa's death?"

Olivia remembers how frightened she was this afternoon. When the darkness came down and she was all alone. When she didn't know if she would be able to get out of the ravine under her own steam.

Amir didn't give a shit about her. She could have frozen to death and he wouldn't have lifted a finger.

Then again, the others didn't bother either. Even William didn't come back to look for her. But he would never have left her there, he would have raised the alarm if she hadn't shown up eventually.

So would Pontus—at least, she would like to think so.

It is only Amir who seems completely ice cold.

He is the only one who cares about no one but himself.

66

It is almost six thirty when Daniel parks outside the apartment block Ida moved to after the separation. It is in Kläppen, between Åre and Tegefjäll.

He hurries up to the second floor, mentally preparing himself to face Ida's displeasure. However, when he rings the bell, it is Gustav who answers. His long hair is loose, the golden curls lying on his shoulders.

As usual he looks ridiculously fresh and fit—a poster boy for the open-air life in the mountains.

"Hi there!" Gustav greets Daniel with a broad smile, which Daniel struggles to return. He can't understand why Gustav thinks they can be best friends. It is childish and undignified to react the way he does, but Daniel can't help it.

"I'm here to pick up Alice," he says, tension in every word.

"Come on in," Gustav says. "Ida is just giving her something to eat."

Daniel takes a few steps into the hallway. There are shoes and boots strewn all over the place in a way that would never have been permitted when Ida and Daniel lived together.

Because he would have tidied up in the evening before they went to bed.

He takes off his shoes and goes into the kitchen, where Alice is sitting in her highchair opposite Ida. More mess—dishes in the sink, dirty glasses on the counter.

Alice has a plate in front of her; Daniel can see the remains of boiled cod with mashed potatoes. Quite a lot of the food has ended up on the table and the floor.

"Daddy!" she shouts gleefully as soon as she spots Daniel. "I eating by myself!"

"Hi, sweetheart." Daniel kisses her forehead before turning to Ida. "Sorry I'm late—I got stuck at work. I came as soon as I could."

Ida is wearing jeans and a turtleneck sweater, with her thick brown braid hanging over one shoulder as usual.

"It's fine," she replies with a shrug. "I read online about that girl who was found dead in Sadeln—I assume that's what you're working on?"

Daniel isn't sure if he has grasped the situation correctly. For once Ida doesn't seem irritated at all—in fact her expression is sympathetic and understanding. She isn't normally so forgiving when it comes to his job, but today she is clearly in a good mood.

His heart rate slows; it's nice to avoid the nagging he had been expecting.

"Alice is almost ready," Ida goes on. "Two more mouthfuls, then it's all gone! I thought it was best to give her dinner before it got too late—otherwise she can get a little cranky, as you know."

Daniel gives Ida a grateful smile. "That was kind of you."

At moments like this their arrangement works really well. *And that's the most important thing,* he thinks. They don't want Alice to suffer because the two of them can't get along. He might have failed to be a good partner, but he is prepared to do whatever it takes to be a good dad.

Which means having a good relationship with Alice's mom.

"I'll try to do better in future," he says, hoping it's a promise he can keep.

"Mmm."

Ida doesn't seem convinced by his aspirations, but she doesn't say anything. Alice finishes eating, and Ida wipes her mouth with a piece of kitchen towel.

"Okay," Daniel says, lifting his daughter out of the chair. "Time to go."

Ida accompanies them into the hallway, where Daniel helps Alice to put on her all-in-one and her little boots. Ida holds out Alice's pink gloves and hat so that he won't forget them. She also hands him a bag containing Alice's soft toys, including Reindeer, who is an essential bedtime companion.

"Exciting news about Hanna," she says when Daniel is almost ready to leave.

"What do you mean?"

Ida gives him a curious look. "Haven't you read the news online? It's everywhere—far more than that poor girl in Sadeln."

Daniel still has no idea what Ida is talking about, but he has a sinking feeling in his stomach.

Didn't Staffan Berg say something about Hanna being in the paper this morning? Daniel had intended to ask her about it after lunch, but it had gone out of his mind when she said she didn't feel well on the way back to the station.

"Hanna's seeing that billionaire from Stockholm," Ida continues. "But I guess you already knew that?"

67

The food is every bit as delicious as Olivia expected, but the conversation is hard work. No one has much to say, everyone seems lost in their own thoughts.

She and Emil have tried to create a cozy atmosphere, with candles burning on the table, but the others are simply staring down at their plates.

Olivia takes a couple of sips of red wine before spearing a potato on her fork. This is her second glass; she should probably take it easy from now on. It's not a good idea for her to get drunk too. She has already taken a painkiller for the tension headache that crept up on her after the conversation with that detective—Hanna.

Emil reaches for the dish of neatly carved pork tenderloin. He holds it out to Pontus, who is sitting diagonally across from him.

"Would you like some more?"

Pontus is the one who has drunk the most this evening. As usual. He started well before dinner. His movements are clumsy, his eyes glazed. This is nothing unusual, but tonight Olivia reads something else in his expression.

Rage. Bitterness.

Hatred?

She doesn't understand what's happening, but she notices that Pontus glares furiously at Emil when he offers him the dish.

What's going on?

Why is Pontus so mad?

Did the boys have an argument this afternoon when she wasn't around?

"There's plenty of meat left," Emil says with a warm smile.

He doesn't seem to be picking up on Pontus's increasing anger; Emil's attention is on the food. It is only Olivia who sees Pontus's face darken.

"Who the fuck do you think you are?" he suddenly yells, slamming his fist down on the table.

Emil jumps and almost drops the serving dish. Some of the meat juices spill onto the pale-colored runner.

"What are you doing?" Olivia snaps, but Pontus ignores her.

"Was it you who told the police about me?"

He is staring at Emil, spitting out the words in a way that Olivia finds chilling. This sounds more like a threat than a question.

"What do you mean?" Emil seems shaken. Olivia doesn't recognize his voice—it is higher than usual, almost shrill.

"The police took my computer. Was it you who'd been poking around? They knew about my search history, knew I'd googled lots of stuff. Murder and manslaughter, that kind of crap."

A shocked silence fills the room. Olivia's mouth drops open. Why on earth had Pontus googled those words?

And why had Emil been looking at his computer?

"They think I'm involved in Filippa's death," Pontus continues. He leans across the table toward Emil. Olivia has never noticed his hands until now. They are big and meaty, with thick, stubby fingers and protruding veins.

"You're the only one who was home during the day. It can't be anyone else!" Pontus sounds even more menacing than before. "Did you look at my computer? What did you say to the police about me?"

Everyone is staring at Emil, whose cheeks are bright red.

"Answer the fucking question!" Pontus bellows. "Are you trying to frame me for Filippa's murder?"

Emil seems unable to move, and not a sound comes out of his mouth.

Then everything happens very fast.

Pontus lurches at Emil. He grabs the collar of his polo top with both hands, and before Emil can react he pulls hard, as if he is trying to force an answer. His elbow hits Emil's plate, which crashes to the floor, with food and shards of porcelain flying everywhere.

"What did you say to them?"

Pontus is still yelling, spraying saliva in Emil's face.

Suddenly Olivia hears her own voice through the chaos. "Stop it!"

Pontus takes no notice of her. His fingers are squeezing Emil's throat now. Emil is taller, but he is sitting down and can't shake him off.

Pontus is stronger, incandescent with rage, and very drunk.

"Stop it!" Olivia shouts again. "He can't breathe!"

Why isn't anyone doing anything?

She is desperate, she tugs at Pontus's clothes, but he doesn't even notice.

"Help him!"

At last William reacts. He races around the table and grabs a hold of Pontus to pull him away. But Pontus refuses to let go, instead his grip tightens.

He seems completely unreachable, lost in his own world of blind fury.

"You fucking homo!"

Emil is beginning to have difficulty breathing. His face is turning purple, and horrible rattling sounds are coming from his throat. His fingers are scrabbling helplessly at Pontus's solid fists.

Soon it will be too late.

"Stop, stop, stop!" she shouts.

William joins in. "For fuck's sake, Pontus! You're killing him!"

Finally Amir comes to life. Together he and William manage to drag Pontus away from the table. Emil slides off his chair and falls to the floor, coughing and clutching his throat, which is covered in angry red marks.

The sound when he tries to inhale is truly terrible.

Olivia drops to her knees beside him to try to help, but Emil simply shakes his head as he struggles for breath. Out of the corner of her eye, Olivia sees that William has bundled Pontus over to the sofa, where both he and Amir are holding on to him.

"We're not letting go until you've calmed down," William says. "Do you understand?"

Pontus struggles for a few seconds, then gives up. Emil is still coughing, but his face is returning to its normal color. Olivia helps him back onto his chair and fetches a glass of water.

"Oh, Emil . . ."

Her entire body is shaking due to the shock. She hardly dares look in Pontus's direction, in case he decides to attack Emil again.

Everything is falling apart.

68

As soon as Alice is in bed and has fallen asleep, Daniel fetches the iPad and sits down in the living room. He has to find out what Ida was talking about.

Hanna is seeing someone.

Ida's words were like a slap across the face. He had to fight to appear unmoved, as if he already knew everything.

Why hasn't Hanna said anything? He thought the two of them could talk about most things.

But he also thought there was plenty of time for him to examine his own feelings for her. He wanted to get the arrangements with Alice and Ida sorted, find his feet in this new life as a father with shared custody of a two-year-old.

The last year has been overwhelming and complicated.

While time was passing by.

It is ten months since he first understood that he felt far more for Hanna than he ought to feel for a colleague. It was during the investigation into the brutal murder at Copperhill last Easter. At the very end, to be precise, when he genuinely feared for her life. The idea that he might never see her again was devastating.

Now it looks as if it's too late.

What an idiot he is.

Another thought strikes him: Of course that was who she spent her birthday with at the weekend. The billionaire, as Ida referred to him. That was why Hanna sounded so vague and evasive when Daniel asked where she'd been.

Why didn't he see what was going on?

He brings up the home page of the largest evening paper and starts to scroll through the flood of news. It isn't long before he finds the headline about the financier and his new girlfriend. There is even a photo of the couple at Kiruna airport.

Only then does he realize the man in question is Henry Sylvester.

He sinks back in his chair.

He has met Sylvester, who was involved in the Copperhill case. That must have been when the two of them got to know each other.

And then the relationship developed.

Daniel disliked Sylvester from the start. The guy is incredibly rich, and incredibly arrogant. Back then he had concealed vital information for far too long. He hadn't even apologized afterward, even though it had affected the whole case.

How can Hanna have fallen for someone like him?

He finds the answer further down in the article, which is about their extravagant trip to Lapland. How the hotel opened just for Sylvester and his new girlfriend.

Who can resist a gesture like that?

But Hanna isn't that kind of person, Daniel tells himself. She doesn't care about money or status. She never has, despite the fact that she grew up in one of Stockholm's more prestigious suburbs.

He knows her well enough to be certain that she isn't in the least impressed by the financial elite or their money.

And yet she is in a relationship with Sylvester.

Daniel doesn't understand.

He stares at the picture of Hanna and her new boyfriend. Sylvester has his arm around her shoulders as they walk toward a waiting helicopter.

The image is intimate, confident. Hanna looks as if she is in love.

Happy.

The air goes out of him. Of course Hanna has chosen a man like Sylvester—who wouldn't? He is in a completely different league. Compared with Daniel, it is like putting the American NHL next to a Swedish junior team.

He leaves the page and searches for Hanna and Henry Sylvester. It turns out that all the newspapers carry the story; the internet is full of articles about the new couple. He really must have been caught up in his work today to have missed it.

Suddenly he can't bear it.

He tosses the iPad aside, and it bounces on the sofa. Fortunately it is saved by the armrest; otherwise it would probably have fallen on the floor and cracked the screen.

For a few minutes he sits there staring blankly at the wall. Then he goes into the kitchen and opens the top cupboard, where he keeps his small stash of wine and spirits. It might be midweek, but he pours himself a large whiskey and knocks back half of it in one gulp.

He can't help imagining Hanna and Henry Sylvester together.

He draws her close. They kiss passionately.

Daniel knocks back the rest of the whiskey.

There is a bitter aftertaste in his mouth that has nothing to do with the alcohol. He knows exactly what has raised its ugly head.

A deep, intense jealousy.

Even though he has absolutely no right to feel that way.

69

Olivia looks down at her hands. However hard she tries, she can't stop them shaking. She is sitting at the table with Emil. He has begun to recover; he is breathing more easily, although he still sounds hoarse. His throat is bright red, and the marks of Pontus's hands are clearly visible on his skin.

"We need to call the police," Olivia says.

Emil shakes his head. He is very pale. "I'm fine."

Olivia glances at the sofa, where William and Amir are with Pontus. He has slumped back, his face hidden in his hands. Right now he doesn't look particularly frightening, but a few minutes ago she thought he was going to kill Emil.

"He tried to strangle you."

"He was drunk—you know what he's like when he's had too much to drink."

Emil doesn't seem to realize how horrible it looked, when Pontus was squeezing his throat and no one intervened. Olivia was convinced that Emil was going to die right there in front of her. That he was about to draw his last breath.

Just like Filippa.

The panic is still there; her heart is pounding; she breaks out in a cold sweat. She can't do this.

"We have to call the police, for fuck's sake!" she almost yells.

Emil sits up a little straighter, although it is obviously an effort.

"No," he says firmly. "I'm not going to report him."

Olivia really wants to understand how he's thinking, but she doesn't get it. Pontus has just tried to strangle him, and now Emil is prepared to forgive Pontus.

How is that possible?

"Why not?"

"It was an accident. Pontus would never have attacked me like that if he was sober."

Olivia doesn't find this remotely reassuring. Pontus has been drunk every single evening since they left Uppsala. What happens if he drinks even more? Would he attack Emil again?

Are any of them safe?

What frightens her the most is how quickly Pontus changed, the fact that he is capable of such rage. It's as if there is another Pontus inside him, a horrible, more ruthless person.

A person who has shown his true face for the first time.

Olivia turns her head and looks over at the group on the sofa. Pontus is sitting in the middle, with William and Amir on either side.

Like two prison guards.

She had been so sure that Amir was guilty, that he was the one behind Filippa's death. Could she have been wrong?

Is Pontus responsible?

What if he had assaulted Filippa when she was alone with him; what if he suddenly lost it? If he could attack Emil, he could have done the same to Filippa.

She turns back to Emil.

"That business with his computer—what did he mean? Had you gone through it?"

Emil sighs heavily.

"I happened to see his search history when you were all out. He'd googled some weird stuff, words that seemed to be connected to Filippa's death."

"And you told the police?"

A faint flush appears on Emil's cheeks. "I did."

"So why haven't they arrested him? Why is he still here?"

"I don't know. Maybe there isn't enough evidence."

Olivia is feeling more stressed by the minute.

"Can't you see how sick this is? Filippa is dead, and Pontus has just attacked you. We have to contact the police, tell them what happened this evening."

Emil shakes his head. "I can't do that to him. He's our friend."

Olivia feels a stab of pain. She would like to remind Emil that Filippa was their friend too. But that didn't make any difference. Filippa is dead.

She makes one last attempt. "Please?"

"Olivia, I've had enough."

She realizes how pale and exhausted Emil is. His face is ashen; the marks on his throat are grotesque.

He will have livid bruises tomorrow.

He needs to get to bed, rest. Although how they are going to sleep after this, she has no idea.

In the absence of something better to do, she crouches down and carefully begins to gather up the shards of the broken plate. Then she fetches a dustpan and brush and clears up the rest before throwing the lot in the trash can.

She hears murmuring from the sofa. William and Amir are talking quietly over Pontus's head. His eyes are closed now, as if he has fallen asleep.

Or simply shut down.

William comes over to the table. He takes a seat next to Emil and places a hand on his shoulder.

"How are you doing?"

Emil gives him a wobbly smile. "That was . . . weird."

William is clearly shaken too. For once he sounds subdued, without his usual energy. His hair is ruffled, and his clothes are still untidy after the fracas.

He looks over at Pontus.

"He's fallen asleep. He probably won't remember anything tomorrow. He's completely out of it."

"We ought to call the police," Olivia says, well aware that she is repeating herself. "What if he'd crushed Emil's windpipe—he could have died!"

William seems to be as unreceptive to her anger as Emil. He glances at Emil, who waves a dismissive hand.

"I've already said I don't want to report him. Just drop it, Olivia."

"Pontus lost control," William says. "He'd drunk way too much, and this entire day has been a disaster. First skiing the West Ravine, then the house search and more interviews. None of us are in a good place right now."

This is the first time William has admitted that the Western was a mistake, which makes Olivia feel a little better. She just wishes he had said it directly to her, actually shown that he realized how hard it had been.

He looks into her eyes, as if he wants to apologize. Then he takes her hand and squeezes it. Olivia doesn't pull away. She appreciates the gesture, the warmth of his fingers against her skin.

"Pontus's computer—what was that all about?" William asks.

Emil gives him the same explanation he gave Olivia, and William looks troubled.

"I wasn't accusing him," Emil says. "But I had to tell the police what I'd seen."

"You did the right thing," Olivia reassures him. "You had no choice."

Emil coughs. "But I'm not going to report him for assault on top of everything else. That kind of thing could destroy his whole life. He'd have a police record forever."

Silence falls.

Olivia doesn't know how to counter Emil's argument; he is right, of course.

But still.

She looks at William. "Do you think Pontus could have attacked Filippa too?"

"I don't know," he answers hesitantly. "But I don't like the sound of his search history."

He starts to gather up the empty plates and carry them over to the sink. Olivia remains at the table. She glances at Amir, who is still keeping an eye on Pontus.

Amir has been vile to her all day. She was convinced it was because he was involved in Filippa's death, but maybe it was simply a reaction to her harsh accusations over breakfast?

Maybe he was angry because he is innocent and felt he was being unfairly targeted?

She told the police it had to be Amir who had done something to Filippa, because who else could it be?

What if she was wrong?

70

Morris has settled himself comfortably on Hanna's chest when Henry calls her cellphone.

After picking up the cat from the neighbors, she had a couple of sandwiches and crawled into bed. She had intended to speak to Henry tomorrow; after such an intense day she simply didn't have the energy to sort everything out. She is also still very shaken after her conversation with that journalist.

During the evening she has been bombarded with messages from both old friends and journalists, all wondering about her relationship with Henry. She has also heard from Karro, Anton's sister, who was her first real friend in Åre. She sent a text full of red hearts and encouraging emojis.

It is as if the whole of Sweden has simultaneously gone online and read about Hanna's new boyfriend, and now everyone wants to know as much as possible. She has already rejected calls from at least half a dozen unknown numbers, which she suspects belong to nosy reporters.

"Hi, darling," Henry says immediately.

As usual his deep voice is comforting; it is full of warmth, and inspires confidence. He has a natural authority that makes Hanna feel safe. But tonight he sounds tired. Maybe he is still in the office on Skeppsbron. He works long days when he is in Stockholm.

Or maybe he is also upset by all the publicity.

"I assume you've seen the headlines?" he says in an apologetic tone.

"Is there anyone who hasn't? I've had countless calls from journalists wanting a comment."

"I'm so sorry you've been exposed to this, Hanna. It was never my intention to put you in such a difficult situation."

"I know that."

There is a brief pause. Hanna rubs her cheek against Morris's soft fur, and ends up with a mouthful of cat hair as a result.

"You're a well-known financier," she says. "It's hardly surprising that the press are interested in your love life."

"I really wish I could have spared you this."

"It's not your fault." Hanna wonders if she is trying to console herself or him. "Of course they're all wondering how you fell for someone like me. It's a nice juicy story."

She regrets the words as soon as they have come out of her mouth. Why must she constantly undermine herself? Her mother does a perfectly good job of that.

"You mean how I was lucky enough to capture a woman like you? I ask myself the same question. All the time."

Hanna can't help smiling. Henry has always been good at making her feel beautiful and attractive.

Desirable.

And today she needs that more than ever.

"I was going to suggest you speak to my media team," he goes on, sounding serious now. "They can help you to handle the situation if it becomes a nuisance. Of course the best response is to say nothing at all."

"Don't worry, I can take care of myself."

Her comment is sharper than she intended, but she can't fight the frustration that has built up during the course of the day. The fact that her mother has also pounced on the news is especially painful.

Henry sighs. "Hanna, I'm not trying to tell you what to do. All I wanted to say is that I'm here if you need me, and that I have resources that are used to dealing with the media. They can protect you. Protect us."

He sounds both sad and resigned, which makes Hanna feel guilty. There is no point in taking her irritation out on him.

It isn't his fault that the press are hounding her.

Or is it? Technically Henry is the cause, but she still can't get mad at him for that.

"Shall I fly up for a few days? Or would you like to come down to Stockholm? We can go overseas at the weekend if you want to get away for a while, avoid the press? London maybe, or Palma? I can send a plane to pick you up from Järpen."

Hanna opens her mouth, then wonders what to say. It's a tempting offer, but she doesn't know where Filippa's case is going. It seems highly likely that her death was the result of a crime, which means that the investigation is going to require her full attention in the immediate future.

What she really wants to do is work, without thinking about her personal life. Focus on what she is really good at: being a police officer.

She's not sure if she can cope with Henry's intense courtship right now.

Plus she wants to be with Morris. She missed her big, fluffy ball of fur while she was away.

If she is seen with Henry, she risks attracting even more unwelcome attention, more pictures, more newspaper articles. If they could take photographs secretly at the airport in Kiruna, it wouldn't be difficult to do the same in Åre.

"It might be better to lie low for a while," she says. "Let things calm down a little."

"Your decision."

There is no mistaking the disappointment in his voice. And she still feels guilty for interrupting their break in the mountains.

"But I miss you, just so you know," he adds.

"I miss you too."

She does, but she can't deny a sense of relief when she and Henry agree not to see each other at the weekend.

She needs breathing space, both from the tabloid press and from him.

And she can't help worrying about what Daniel will think when he finds out about her relationship.

71

Together William and Amir have managed to steer Pontus down the stairs and into bed. Meanwhile Olivia has cleared away after dinner. She is so tired that she sways as she finishes loading the dishwasher, and has to grab hold of the kitchen counter to stop herself from losing her balance.

It is only nine thirty in the evening, but she has never felt so exhausted.

Or despairing.

Emil is resting on the sofa with a blanket over him when William comes back upstairs. There is no sign of Amir.

William joins Olivia, leaning back against the counter.

"Pontus is more or less unconscious. There's no chance of him waking up before tomorrow morning, and when he does, he's going to feel like shit. That's if he even remembers what he's done."

But Olivia remembers. She will never forget how helpless she felt as she tugged at Pontus, trying to pull him away from Emil.

"He isn't usually violent; I've never seen him fight before," William goes on. "It's just that the last few days have been too much." He takes a lemon out of the fruit bowl, examines it for a few seconds, then puts it back. "It won't help matters if the police arrest Pontus for assault, not after everything that's happened."

"He could have killed Emil if you and Amir hadn't intervened. Have you thought about that?"

William might be prepared to gloss over Pontus's behavior, and Emil seems ready to forgive him because he feels guilty about the laptop, but Olivia isn't there yet—not by a long way. However, she doesn't have the energy to keep discussing the matter. It's too late; she's too tired. So she puts a tablet in the dishwasher and switches it on.

When she turns around, William is standing very close. He reaches out and draws her to him.

"Listen," he says quietly. "I'm sorry about . . . today. How things went. I shouldn't have left you like that."

At least that's one thing they agree on.

"So why did you do it?" she mumbles into his chest. "Why didn't you wait for me?"

William pushes her away a fraction.

"I got annoyed when you just . . . took over. I thought if you wanted to be in charge, I'd leave you to it." He plants a kiss on her forehead. "It was stupid. Forgive me."

Another kiss. He smells good; she has always liked his smell.

"The two of us need to stick together," he adds. "Especially when everyone around us has lost the plot."

He nuzzles her ear, and for a second it feels as if nothing has changed.

"Again, I'm sorry. I really mean it."

It would be so nice to melt into his arms, hide there, and yet . . . Where was he when she needed him? Is everything supposed to be okay just because he's whispering sweet nothings?

The way he let her down in the ravine is like a thorn in her heart.

The fear still lingers. The anger.

And why was he so quick to make excuses for Pontus? She is finding that hard to deal with too.

Okay, so William has apologized for today, but Olivia doesn't know if she can trust him anymore. The last few days have been horrific, without any support or consolation on his part. He didn't stick up for her when Amir treated her like shit, or when they were skiing today.

If he's behaved that way once, he can do it again.

"I'm going to bed," she says.

"Wouldn't you rather stay here instead?"

William tries to keep her there, gently caressing her hair, but Olivia pulls away. She can't shake off the idea that this is actually about something else.

That William has a hidden agenda.

72

Tonight not even the music is helping; it is usually Anton's greatest solace. He is sitting in the living room with his soprano saxophone, but he can't lose himself in the chords as he usually can.

Carl is constantly on his mind, over and over again he plays the wrong note. Anton has tried calling him several times during the evening, but it goes straight to voicemail.

He can hardly blame Carl for feeling hurt.

Eventually Anton gives up and puts down the sax. He is too restless, he has to get out of the apartment. He sets off without really knowing where he is going. The temperature is minus twenty-one, the wind is blowing hard, and his breath turns into a cloud of vapor as he walks through the icy darkness.

His footsteps take him toward his parents' house, and after fifteen minutes he finds himself standing outside the place where he grew up. The lights are on downstairs, presumably his mother and father are in the living room, watching the news on TV. That's what they usually do at this time.

A great weariness comes over Anton.

Why does everything have to be so difficult?

All afternoon he has wondered about the strange phone call from his father. Those weird hints about who was welcome at Karro's birthday party.

I can't do this anymore.

He goes up the steps and opens the front door without knocking. They never lock up until bedtime.

"Hello?" his mother, Susanne, calls out inquiringly.

"It's me."

Anton takes off his boots and jacket and goes into the living room. His father is in his favorite armchair; his mother is curled up on the sofa with a cup of chamomile tea. She doesn't like to drink black tea in the evenings, because it keeps her awake.

"Hi, darling," she says. "What a nice surprise. Coffee?"

She is about to get up, but Anton raises his hand and stops her.

"I need to speak to you both."

His father has one eye on the TV and one on Anton.

"Can it wait?" he says. "We're watching the news. It will be finished in quarter of an hour."

Anton bites the inside of his cheeks. This is about his life, so no, it can't wait. He has already waited for far too long.

"I'm afraid not," he says, positioning himself in front of the television so that his parents have no choice but to give him their attention.

"What are you doing? I can't see!"

His father is annoyed, but it doesn't matter. Anton is annoyed too. Furious, in fact. It feels good. His anger gives him energy, the courage to say what should have been said years ago.

His mother gives him an anxious look, as if she realizes that the storm clouds are gathering. That her son is about to challenge his father, and that it will end in conflict as usual.

But this time Anton has no intention of backing down as he has done way too often in the past.

"Turn it off, please," he says to his mother, who is closest to the remote.

"What the hell are you doing?" his father barks. "You can't just come marching in here—you don't get to tell us whether we can watch TV or not!"

"Mom—turn it off."

His mother looks from her son to her husband, then reaches for the remote. One click and the screen goes dark.

"Mats, it sounds as if Anton has something important to tell us. I think we should listen to him. We can catch up with the news later."

Anton takes a deep breath.

He is standing with his legs apart, hands behind his back, just like when he is on duty and needs to show his authority. It's a shame he isn't wearing his uniform; it always makes him feel more secure.

"Your phone call today," he says to his father. "What was it about? Honestly?"

His mother blinks. "You called Anton today? You never mentioned it."

"You kept saying that Karro's birthday party is just for the family. Why was it so important to tell me that?"

At least his father has the decency to look embarrassed, as if he has been caught out doing something he shouldn't.

"We can't have lots of people showing up," his father mumbles in a voice that is nothing like his usual brusque tone.

Anton's mother is starting to look worried. It is obvious that she has no idea what the conversation is about, but she has no difficulty picking up on the tension between the two men in her life.

"Do you know what I think?" Anton says. "I don't think it was anything whatsoever to do with how many people could come, but *which* people. You don't want me to introduce you to the person I'm in love with."

"You want to bring a new girlfriend?"

The pure joy in his mother's voice breaks Anton's heart.

The hopes and expectations.

For years she has nagged Anton about finding a girl; all he has to do is make a little more effort.

His soulmate is out there somewhere.

She really wants him to be happy. Have a family of his own, give her more grandchildren.

That's only going to happen if he can do it his way.

His father hasn't said a word, but Anton can see that he is about to lose his temper. He's not the only one. Anton is making a huge effort not to start yelling.

"Careful," his father warns him. "Do you really want to discuss this in front of your mother?"

There is nothing Anton wants more.

"Of course you can bring her!" Susanne assures him. "She's most welcome!"

Anton wishes there were a way to do this that wouldn't hurt her, but he can't see an alternative. She has to know what the situation is, and he has to be true to himself.

"*His* name is Carl," he says, with a brief pause between words. "We're in love, and we've been together for nine months."

His mother's hand flies to her mouth. She looks as if she has just been struck by lightning.

"If Carl isn't welcome in our family, then you won't be seeing me in the future either."

His father stands up and steps forward so that the two of them are face-to-face. They are the same height; it is only the years that separate them.

And their view of life.

The ability to understand that Anton is different, and will never be able to fulfill their expectations.

"How dare you come here and upset your mother?" his father says stiffly. "Apologize to her immediately!"

Is he really blaming her when he's the homophobe in the family?

"Have you no shame!" his father roars in his military voice, as if Anton is reporting to him like a raw recruit.

Enough.

"The question is which of us has no shame!" Anton yells back. "I've been like this ever since I was born. But you made me deny it, both to myself and everyone else."

"So now it's our fault you're not normal? That's the worst thing I've ever heard! We've only ever tried to protect you, and this is the thanks we get?"

His mother gets to her feet. "Please, Mats. Don't say that."

But there is no stopping him.

"Are you intending to throw your life away on this bizarre idea? It's no more than a whim. What do you think your boss is going to say? Or your colleagues? Don't you realize you'll be booted out of the police if this comes out?"

"At least it will be my decision."

Anton pushes his hands deep into his pockets in an attempt to maintain his self-control. He is seconds away from punching his father, who has put into words all of Anton's own fears, everything that has caused him to avoid coming out and telling his family the truth for so long.

His family and his colleagues.

His mother is on the verge of tears.

"Please, please stop!" she begs, wringing her hands. "I can't bear this!"

His father refuses to back down. His expression is full of something that resembles distaste.

The air goes out of Anton.

What an idiot he was to imagine it would be possible to reason with his parents. That they might accept him with love and understanding if he came out and told them the truth.

His father will never understand.

Because he can't.

Because he doesn't want to.

"The two of us are done," Anton says. He goes into the hallway, puts on his boots and jacket, and walks out. And his parents don't say a word to try to stop him.

73

Olivia crouches down beside Emil, who is lying on the sofa. She isn't sure if he's asleep, and gently touches his shoulder.

He opens his eyes. His gaze is so unfocused that at first she wonders if he recognizes her, but then it's as if his mind clears.

"Hi. I guess I fell asleep."

"How are you feeling?" Olivia whispers, even though they are alone in the living room.

Amir has gone up to bed, and William is in the bathroom. It sounds as if he is brushing his teeth; they can hear him through the wall.

Olivia wonders briefly if he is mad because she refused to spend the night with him, but decides she doesn't have the bandwidth to think about that.

She's had enough for today.

"Better," Emil replies. "But very tired."

His voice is still rough and hoarse. He is noticeably pale and doesn't look good at all, in spite of his claim to the contrary.

"Shouldn't you go to bed instead of staying here?"

"Probably." Emil closes his eyes and makes no attempt to move.

"I'm going back to the cabin," Olivia says. "See you tomorrow."

Then a thought strikes her. She can't get Pontus out of her head. What if he wakes up during the night, still as angry as he was earlier, and attacks Emil again?

What would happen if Emil were asleep, with no chance of defending himself?

It doesn't bear thinking about.

Emil might be prepared to play down what Pontus did, but Olivia is not. If she'd had her way, they would have called the police and asked them to arrest him.

Pontus should be locked up.

"Why don't you come over there with me?" she suggests. "You can sleep in the other room."

Filippa's room, she thinks, and is overwhelmed by a wave of grief.

Emil nods wearily. "Would that be okay?"

"I'd appreciate the company," she says, and realizes it's true. She doesn't want to be alone after this dreadful day. She wants Emil to come with her, as much for her sake as his.

They are in the hallway, putting on their boots, when William emerges from the bathroom, still holding his toothbrush.

"Where are you going?" he asks Emil.

"He's staying in the cabin with me tonight," Olivia informs him. She has no intention of providing any further explanation—William will have to be satisfied with that.

However, he is not happy with her decision. She can see it in his expression; she feels his eyes on her as she walks out through the door with Emil right behind her.

The back of her neck is burning.

William is used to getting what he wants.

TUESDAY

74

Alice's crying wakes Daniel at about two o'clock.

There is nothing unusual in her waking during the night—she has done it ever since she was a baby. However, right now it makes him wish he had left the whiskey bottle alone and not poured himself a couple more glasses before he fell asleep. He is usually careful when Alice is with him, but at the moment he realizes he can't work out whether he is hungover or still drunk. His body feels heavy and slow as he goes into the nursery, and he is ashamed of himself.

He won't make the same mistake again.

Alice grizzles against his chest as he heads for the kitchen to warm up her formula. The clock on the microwave counts down, at long last it pings and she can have her bottle. She holds out her little arms when she sees it, like a drowning person who has just spotted a lifebuoy.

Daniel carries his daughter into the bedroom and settles her beside him. He kept the wide double bed after Ida moved out. It is practical, although it provides a bitter reminder of his failed relationship every time he lies down on what used to be his side.

Alice drinks with her eyes closed, and Daniel listens to the gentle glugging as the bottle slowly empties. He inhales the scent of her warm skin.

She means everything to him, but life often seems inadequate and joyless. It has been hard ever since the separation. Sometimes he wonders if he will ever be able to accept the way things ended between him and Ida.

He spent the whole of last year seeing a therapist in Järpen in order to work through the emotional chaos surrounding his absent father. He was determined to break the pattern, avoid repeating old errors.

And yet in the end Ida didn't want to be with him anymore. And Hanna is seeing the billionaire Henry Sylvester, a man Daniel will never be able to compete with.

Not that he can blame her.

He is the one who has let time run away, who has been too indecisive and slow to act. In his naivety he thought Hanna would still be there while he sorted out his own messed-up life.

He took her for granted, and now it's too late.

He rolls over onto his back and stares up at the ceiling.

Somehow he has to carry on working with Hanna without revealing how he really feels. He must behave like any other good colleague, and carefully conceal his innermost yearning.

And it is entirely his fault.

75

The heat is making Olivia toss and turn.

In her nightmare the room is full of smoke. Her nose is prickling, and she is finding it hard to breathe. She knows she has to get out of the house, but she can't move. It's as if her arms and legs are paralyzed.

The covers are pressing her down against the mattress, while terrifying faces flit back and forth in her mind's eye.

She sees Filippa lying frozen in the snow. Her friend's big, pleading eyes bore into her, asking why she had to die in the winter night.

Why no one came to her rescue.

"Help me," Filippa whispers before she disappears.

Next is William, looming over Olivia. "You should have stayed like I asked you," he says in her ear. "You're going to regret choosing Emil over me."

Amir is standing beside the bed, contempt written all over his face. He laughs scornfully. *You'll never understand how it all hangs together,* his ice-cold gaze tells her. *You're too stupid to work it out.*

Olivia is sweating and crying. *Go away,* she wants to yell, but she can't make a sound.

The faces fade away as the flames grow higher. They are licking the end of the bed, the curtains are ablaze.

Then Pontus's manic face comes into view.

Olivia sees him reaching for Emil, and she can't stop him. Huge tongues of fire surround Emil's throat. His face is on fire, and the smell of burnt flesh fills the room.

She feels as if Pontus is trying to strangle her too. Her throat is constricted; she can't get any air. Her mouth is so dry that her lips are cracking.

The fire is coming closer and closer. The heat is unbearable. She can't breathe; there is a constant beeping sound in her ears.

Olivia knows she's dreaming, but she can't make it stop.

And then she opens her eyes.

Is she awake or not? Is the nightmare over?

Everything is confused and incomprehensible, the darkness impenetrable. Then she realizes that her nostrils actually are prickling. The smell of burning is real. A shrill signal is coming from the hallway, and there is a horrible cracking noise from the seating area.

Olivia switches on the bedside lamp and discovers that the bedroom is full of smoke. There is a grayish-white cloud above her head; she can barely see the ceiling.

The fire alarm is beeping hysterically.

She has to get out of here. Otherwise she is going to die too.

76

In a total panic Olivia hurls herself out of bed and runs to Emil. He is fast asleep, in spite of the fire alarm. She shakes him as hard as she can.

Her eyes are stinging with the smoke.

"Wake up!" she yells. "Fire!"

Emil stares at her in confusion. Then he coughs and realizes the gravity of the situation. "What's going on?"

"I don't know, but we have to get out of here. Now!"

Through the wide window onto the outside seating area, she sees the flames licking at one corner. And at the same moment she realizes they are in a wooden house.

The fire could take off at any second.

And then they are done for.

Out, out, out, screams the voice inside her head.

"Is there a fire extinguisher?" Emil shouts.

Olivia has no idea. That was the last thing on her mind. Where would it be kept, if there is one?

Desperately she flings open the door of the closet in the hallway, searching for something, anything to put out the fire.

There!

Right at the back she sees a red fire extinguisher.

"I've got it, Emil!" She heaves out the heavy cylinder, pushes her feet into her moon boots, and dashes outside with the extinguisher in her arms.

In the distance she can hear the sound of approaching sirens—a neighbor must have called the fire service.

Help is on the way.

Will they get here in time?

The flames are unbelievably large and terrifying. The world is colored in shades of orange and lilac. Everything is burning.

A cloud of powder fills the air as Olivia turns the hose toward the greedy fire and squeezes as hard as she can.

Then she wobbles and almost drops the extinguisher as a thought strikes her. This fire cannot possibly have started by itself.

Someone must have done it deliberately.

Someone wanted her and Emil dead.

77

Hanna is so groggy that she has to force her eyes open when the sound of her phone wakes her. Sleepily she gropes around on the nightstand. She feels as if she has only slept for fifteen minutes, but the clock informs her that it is almost four in the morning.

She sees Daniel's name on the display and is wide awake in a second.

"What's happened?" He would never call at this hour unless it was something important.

"There's been a major fire in Sadeln. Same address where Filippa was found."

"Seriously?"

Hanna swallows. This can't be a coincidence.

"The call just came through," Daniel goes on. "The fire service are on their way, or they might be there already. A patrol car has also been dispatched."

"Anyone hurt?"

"We don't know yet."

Hanna is holding her breath. Another death would be terrible.

Daniel pauses, as if he is reluctant to continue. "Could you go over there?" he says eventually. "I'm on my own with Alice."

Hanna pushes her tousled hair back from her face. She understands his sense of inadequacy, how hard it must be for Daniel to ask for help.

"Of course, don't worry about it," she reassures him. "I've got this."

She reaches for her jeans and yesterday's sweater, her phone pressed to her ear.

"How about Anton? Could he come with me instead of you?"

"I'll call him, ask him to get straight over there."

There is another brief, strained pause. Hanna can hear him breathing on the other end of the line.

"Call me when you're done, whatever the time is," Daniel says in conclusion.

Hanna is almost dressed; she pulls on her padded jacket and heads for the front door.

As soon as she steps outside, the wind grabs her. It is whining around the corners of the house, and the low mountain birch trees are bending toward the ground.

Squally winds—increasing the risk of the fire spreading quickly and getting out of control.

Hanna sets off for Sadeln, driving as fast as she can. She prays that the fire service have made it in time; otherwise more houses could be at risk.

And lives.

78

The flames from the property next door create an eerie glow in Åke Carlsson's dark kitchen.

He is standing by the window, watching as the firefighters hurry toward the flames dragging their hoses. Water sprays, shadowy figures move frenetically back and forth, shouts echo through the night.

He can't make out what they are saying, but there is no mistaking the urgency.

Åke is grateful that the wind is blowing in the opposite direction, away from their home. Otherwise they too could have been in danger, but at the moment there is no risk. The flames are too far away to leap across the boundary, and in any case the cabin is much closer to the main house. He hopes the sparks will rain down on the Löwengrens' revolting property so that he doesn't have to look at it anymore. He would be very pleased to see it disappear from the surface of the earth.

"What's going on?"

Karin's bewildered voice interrupts his train of thought. She emerges from her bedroom, tightening the belt of her robe.

Then she is confronted by the scene outside the window.

"Oh my God, there's a fire at the Löwengrens'!"

Her hand flies to her mouth, and she stares at the blaze as if she is hypnotized by its angry flames casting grotesque shadows on the snow.

"What's happened?"

"I've no idea," Åke replies. "I heard the sirens and got up to take a look. There's a lot of activity."

She doesn't need to know that he was already up.

Karin moves closer to the window and gazes out at the burning cabin, where the firefighters are battling to get the blaze under control.

"What if it comes over here," she whispers. "What if it spreads . . ."

Her face is pale, her eyes huge with fear.

"Thank goodness Peter and the children left today."

"There's no danger; the wind is blowing in the opposite direction," Åke reassures her. "You don't need to worry." He puts his arm around her shoulders, draws her close. "It will soon be over."

Karin is still staring, as if she can't quite believe what is playing out before her. "How can it take hold so quickly?"

Tongues of flame are licking at the walls of the small cabin. The world is a terrifying mixture of colors. The fire and the shouts of the firefighters are tearing the winter night apart.

"I just hope the place was empty," Karin adds with a shudder. "Another death would be terrible."

79

The firefighters are still hard at work when Hanna arrives on Nedre Svedjevägen. A red fire truck is parked in front of the house, and long hoses writhe across the yard like snakes.

When she gets out of the car, she sees to her relief that it's not quite as bad as she feared. The main house appears to be undamaged, the fire seems to be confined to the cabin.

She plods through the deep snow and shows her police ID to the officer in charge, even though she already knows him. His name is Micke.

"So what's the situation?"

He raises a thickly gloved hand in greeting. "We got the fire under control pretty quickly, so now we're focusing on damping down."

He points to the cabin, which is badly charred and has suffered extensive smoke damage. The wooden walls are blackened, and one of the windows has shattered with the heat. The ambient temperature is so low that the water that has run down the undamaged parts has already frozen solid.

The air all around is dense with smoke.

"A little while longer and we wouldn't have been able to save the building," Micke goes on. "And with this wind it could have gotten a lot worse. If the fire had spread, I mean. You can see how close together the houses are, and everything around here is built of dry timber. You can just imagine what could have happened."

Hanna has no problem imagining the terrifying possibility, and she shudders at the thought.

"Was there anyone inside when the fire started?" she asks, stamping her feet to try to keep warm. Her thick socks are fighting a losing battle.

"A girl and a boy. They were asleep—it was the middle of the night. Fortunately the girl woke up. She was very resourceful—she woke up the boy so he could get out; then she got hold of an extinguisher. Her actions gave us a few extra minutes, which were critical."

It can only have been Olivia. Hanna is impressed; not everyone would have been able to keep a cool head in a situation like that. Waking up in the darkness in a house that's on fire would leave most people paralyzed with fear.

And Olivia is still suffering from the shock of losing Filippa.

"Like I said," Micke continues, "if we'd arrived a little later, or if the girl hadn't used the extinguisher, the fire would probably have spread to the main house. Then anything could have happened."

A gust of wind comes tearing along. The trees on the slope bend and sway, the top layer of snow whirls up into the air. Hanna has to turn her face away to protect her nose and mouth.

It wouldn't have taken many sparks to cause a real disaster.

"Was anyone hurt?"

"Not seriously, as far as I'm aware. The girl and the boy are in the main house."

All the lights are on. Most of the neighboring properties have their lights on too; with all this disruption, no doubt everyone is awake.

It must be a terrifying sight.

"So they're okay?"

"They got out in time. A paramedic is checking them over to see if they've suffered from smoke inhalation."

"So they were lucky, in other words."

"Absolutely. It could have ended very badly."

Hanna moves closer to the cabin. The fire may be out, but the damage is extensive, and she can feel the heat. Her lungs hurt with every breath.

It is about five in the morning, so based on Daniel's call, the fire must have started just over an hour ago.

To her untrained eye the facade seems to have suffered the most, which means the fire probably started outside. In other words, it was unlikely to be the result of a forgotten candle on the dining table or a similar careless act.

So how did it happen?

"Any thoughts on the cause?" she asks Micke.

He frowns. "It's too early to say for sure, but looking at the progress of the blaze and the absence of natural causes . . . how quickly it seems to have spread . . ."

"You think it could have been started deliberately?"

"I wouldn't rule it out."

A man in a dark woolen hat comes around the corner of the house and interrupts their conversation. Hanna recognizes Staffan Berg, the property manager.

His jacket is buttoned up incorrectly; he looks as if he got dressed in a hurry.

"What's going on?" he shouts as soon as he sees Hanna and Micke. "Is anyone hurt?"

Hanna shakes her head.

"They got out in time," Micke says.

"Thank God."

Staffan stares at the blackened cabin; he seems to be struggling to process the situation. Gray smoke is still rising into the dark sky.

The snow all around is black and sooty.

"What a mess . . ." He sighs.

Hanna checks her watch again. It's not that long since the emergency services were contacted. She doesn't understand how Staffan heard about the fire and arrived so quickly.

"How did you know there was a fire?" she asks.

Staffan looks puzzled, then points to his phone.

"The app," he explains. "I get a text message if anything is wrong. I came straight over."

"I understand."

Hanna takes a step back, away from the heat, keeping a close eye on him. He sounds genuine, and why would he lie?

Although she does find it a little strange that he comes and goes all the time. That he has an app giving him so much control.

And access to all areas.

80

As Anton parks his Toyota on Nedre Svedjevägen, he sees Hanna plodding around the corner through the deep snow. Most of the firefighters seem to be at the front of the property.

He had had only a few hours' sleep; he is still full of adrenaline following the catastrophic conversation with his parents, and he feels kind of shaky.

Sorrow and disappointment are pounding at his body, making his breathing shallow, but there is no space for that right now. His personal problems will have to wait, be tucked away until he gets home. Instead he needs to prove that he deserves his new role, that he is an asset to the unit who can replace Daniel when he is not available.

He joins Hanna at the front door, beneath the yellow glow of the porch light.

"Thanks for coming so quickly," she says. "I've just been talking to the officer in charge." She gives him a brief summary of the situation—who was in the cabin when the fire started, and how and where it began. She also mentions the fact that Staffan Berg came by and asked about the fire, but has now left.

"Should we take a closer look at him?" Anton asks. He is also a little concerned about Staffan.

Hanna pulls her woolen hat farther down over her ears. Her breath emerges like puffs of white smoke as she considers the suggestion.

"Sounds like a good idea. I find it kind of odd that he keeps coming and going."

One of the firefighters hurries by, dragging a hose behind him.

"So they think the fire could have been started deliberately," Anton says. "In which case we're looking at arson."

First the young woman found dead in the snow on Sunday, and now this. Barely forty-eight hours have passed—they haven't even got the final results of the autopsy from Umeå yet.

A warning bell is ringing loudly in Anton's head.

"I don't like it," Hanna agrees. "Especially bearing in mind everything else that's happened over the past few days."

She drags her foot along the ground, leaving a trail in the snow.

"I just wish I could work out what's going on. See the bigger picture—is there a pattern?"

"We could hardly have foreseen the fire," Anton points out. "Neither of us has a crystal ball."

Hanna gives herself a shake. "I know, but I hate the feeling of not being in control. What if someone had burned to death because we didn't do our job properly?" She reaches for the door handle. "Okay, shall we go in and talk to everyone? See what they have to tell us?"

"Do we think one of them could be behind the fire?" Anton wonders.

Hanna's mouth turns down at the corners. "Who else could it be?"

Staffan Berg, for example, Anton thinks.

81

Emil and Olivia are curled up on one of the sofas when Hanna walks in. She can see immediately that Olivia's entire body is shaking, even though she has a warm blanket around her shoulders.

She is so pale that she is almost transparent.

Micke talked about how resourceful Olivia had been, but it seems as if the shock has caught up with her.

William and Amir are sitting on the opposite sofa in T-shirts and underpants. Both look completely blank; they are clearly as stunned by the events of the night as their friends.

A male paramedic is on his knees, packing away his equipment. When he sees the two police officers, he stands up and takes them to one side.

"How are they?" Hanna asks quietly.

"They'll be fine. They've inhaled a certain amount of smoke, but it's not serious—there's no need for them to go to the hospital. However, they're both very shocked, which is hardly surprising under the circumstances."

He gestures discreetly toward Emil.

"I gather there's been a confrontation between him and one of the others. You might want to check it out."

Hanna thanks him for the information before she and Anton go over to the group.

Both Emil and Olivia are still wearing their nightclothes, presumably because they didn't have time to grab anything else.

As she gets closer she sees that Emil has angry marks on his throat, red that has begun to turn purple.

They look like the result of an attempted strangulation.

Where have they come from?

Hanna has seen marks like that many times before, when she worked for the Domestic Violence Unit in Stockholm. Back then it was almost always down to men who had assaulted their wives or girlfriends.

Although men assault men too, of course.

Something must have gone down before the fire.

"I realize you must both be exhausted," she begins. "But I'm wondering if you could manage a little chat with me and Anton?"

Olivia nods.

"Okay," Emil says. He sounds hoarse.

"What happened to your throat?" Anton asks. "It doesn't look too good."

"It's fine."

"Who attacked you?"

Emil hesitates, and Olivia leans forward.

"Pontus attacked him when we were having dinner last night! He went crazy, tried to strangle him, it was awful. He was furious because Emil had told the police about the search history on his computer."

Hanna recalls that Emil had been worried about that, but she would never have expected something like this.

Emil still doesn't say anything, but William reacts to Olivia's outburst. He opens his mouth, possibly to mitigate her harsh words, then sinks back against the cushions and shakes his head, giving Olivia a resigned glance.

Emil seems uncomfortable too. He changes his position on the sofa, pulls the checked blanket more tightly around his body.

Hanna looks searchingly at him.

"Is this true? Did Pontus physically attack you?"

After a second or two Emil nods.

"He put his hands around your throat?"

"Yes, he did!" Olivia says. "If William and Amir hadn't intervened, you could have died!" Her voice breaks, but she angrily dashes away the tears with her right hand. Her eyes are burning as she continues. "And then the fire started when we were asleep in the cabin." She looks around accusingly. "So who do you think it was? That fire can't have started by itself. It must have been Pontus—who else?"

These are serious accusations, but they could well be justified. A thorough investigation will be required, but the leading fire officer had also expressed doubts that the fire could have started by itself.

She looks at the marks on Emil's throat again. "So where is Pontus?"

The exhausted friends exchange glances, as if each of them is hoping someone else will answer the question.

"I don't know," Olivia admits. "In his room, I guess."

"I expect he's asleep," William adds.

Hanna doubts that very much. Who sleeps through the noise of the sirens and the efforts of the firefighters over the past hour or more? The whole of Sadeln must be awake by now.

"He was so drunk after dinner that Amir and I had to put him to bed," William explains. "He couldn't even walk on his own." He turns to Amir. "That's right, isn't it?"

Amir seems to be in some kind of trance. He doesn't respond to William's question until his friend reaches out and gives him a push.

"Pontus was so drunk he was completely out of it, wasn't he?" William repeats. "You and me had to drag him down to his room."

"Right, yes, he was." Amir lowers his head.

"But not too drunk to attack one of you," Anton observes.

William shuffles uncomfortably. "I'm not trying to excuse what he did to Emil, but he was so drunk I'm not sure he even realized what he was doing."

He gives Emil an apologetic look.

"And he regretted it straight away. He was crying and apologizing when we were taking him downstairs."

As if that alleviates the seriousness of the situation.

Hanna can feel her pulse rate increasing. This is just getting worse and worse—first of all a death under suspicious circumstances, and now a probable case of arson.

All within two days.

"What happened to you is known as grievous bodily harm," Anton says to Emil. "Why are you trying to protect someone who did that to you?"

An embarrassed silence fills the room.

"You should have contacted us yesterday evening when it happened," Hanna says, underlining her colleague's words.

Anton heads for the stairs leading to the lower floor. "Time to wake up Sleeping Beauty," he says over his shoulder to Hanna. "We need to take Pontus to the station."

82

As soon as Anton reappears, Hanna can tell that something is wrong. He moves toward the front door and signals to her to join him, out of earshot of everyone else. He positions himself very close to the coat stand, so that the two of them are hidden by the thick winter clothing.

"There's no one down there," he says quietly.

"You mean Pontus is gone?"

"Looks like it. I've checked every room, and there's no sign of him. He isn't in the house."

"So he was awake," Hanna says, as much to herself as to Anton. "Although according to the others, none of them had seen him since yesterday evening. And then the fire broke out. Surely they should have noticed if he left?"

"He probably used the ski entrance—you can get out that way without attracting attention."

Of course. Lydia's house is the same, with a separate entrance on the lower ground floor so that no one needs to use the main door with their skis and other equipment.

"There's also a patio door that Pontus could have used," Anton adds. He folds his arms. "This doesn't look good for him."

Hanna is too experienced to jump to the conclusion that Pontus is responsible for the fire, but the fact that he isn't here does not bode well. Someone with a clear conscience doesn't disappear in the middle of the night. Especially not in weather like this.

"We need to send out a patrol right now," she decides. "And report him as a missing person of interest."

Anton looks as if he has something else on his mind.

"What are you thinking about?" Hanna asks.

"Given what the others said about Pontus, the fact that he attacked Emil . . . That alone makes him guilty of a serious crime. And if he decided to start the fire as well . . ."

Hanna knows what Anton is about to say. The same troubling thought has occurred to her. Disturbing images of previous suicide victims she has encountered in the line of duty flicker through her mind.

"Do you think he could be suicidal?" she interrupts him.

"We can't rule it out."

"Then we need to find him, as a matter of urgency."

83

If there were a way of absorbing coffee intravenously, Hanna would have willingly paid a fortune to sign up. Exhaustion is clawing at her body when she gets back to the police station at seven thirty in the morning. Just over three hours have passed since she was woken by Daniel's phone call. All patrols are looking for Pontus Englund, and the local cab companies have been informed in case they should come across him. Trains departing from Åre will be monitored, as will buses going to the airport on the island of Frösön.

The team are about to have a meeting via video link with Östersund to report on the latest developments, and to decide on their next moves. Hanna spoke briefly to Birgitta Grip in the car on the way back to let her know about the fire.

Daniel and Raffe are in the conference room when Anton and Hanna arrive. No doubt they only need to glance at her to realize how worn out she is. Anton doesn't look great either—the result of being on the go long before dawn.

Raffe is the only one who seems to have had plenty of sleep. His coal-black ponytail is gleaming with hair oil, and he is bright and alert.

Hanna would like to borrow some of his energy.

"You've had a tough start to the day," Daniel says, his voice betraying a guilty conscience. "I'm sorry I couldn't come out when we got the call."

"No problem," Hanna lies. "Is Alice okay?"

Daniel looks even more guilty.

"She's fine. I've just dropped her at preschool, so she's in good hands."

Changing the subject, he pulls the keyboard closer and begins to set up the link with Östersund.

"Try these," Raffe says, pushing over a plate of chocolate cookies. No doubt they are from his girlfriend, Nilla, who loves baking and regularly supplies the station with delicious treats. Hanna reaches out and takes two. Maybe the sugar will help.

"By the way, I've double-checked the information about Emil Sandström being gay," Raffe continues as Hanna chews. "He referred me to his parents, and I've spoken to his mom, who confirmed what Olivia told you. There's also an ex-boyfriend if we want to speak to him."

"Did she say anything else?" Hanna mumbles with her mouth full.

"She was worried, of course. Emil hadn't told his parents about Filippa, so they had no idea what had gone on over the last few days. His mother asked if they should come up, but I advised them against it and said Emil would be able to leave very soon."

"Good morning," Grip says from the screen on the wall. "This case seems to be getting more and more complicated."

You could say that, Hanna thinks as she munches her way through yet another cookie.

Today Grip is in uniform. That usually means she will be holding a press conference later in the day. Otherwise she prefers practical clothing like jeans and a sweater, occasionally a black jacket.

She turns her attention to Hanna.

"Can we start with a summary from you? I believe it's been a dramatic night."

Hanna washes down the last few crumbs with a swig of her coffee. She begins by describing the fire, and the chief officer's suspicions that it was started deliberately. Then she reports on Pontus's involvement in the confrontation the previous evening. She also mentions that Staffan Berg showed up.

"Arson is a serious matter," Grip says. "Any theories about how it happened?"

"Not yet, but Carina is going over there this morning to investigate."

Carina has barely had time to report on the house search carried out yesterday, and now she has a fresh crime scene to examine.

What is going on?

"If the fire really was started deliberately, I'd expect some form of accelerant to have been used," Daniel points out. "Like T-Gul lighter fluid. It shouldn't be hard to find out."

Hanna reflects that T-Gul is sold in every gas station. If traces are found, it would prove only that the fire had been started deliberately—not by whom.

But it's a start. If it is arson, then they have another serious crime to investigate. They need to start door-to-door inquiries in Sadeln to see if they can track down any eyewitnesses.

Hanna finds it difficult to believe that it was an accident. First Filippa's tragic death, then a potentially lethal fire two days later.

It was sheer luck that no one was seriously hurt.

Not to mention Pontus's violent attack on Emil.

There is something unhealthy going on at the house on Nedre Svedjevägen. Something damaging and ominous that is making her increasingly ill at ease.

She doesn't believe in all these coincidences.

"How convinced are we that Pontus Englund was responsible for the fire?" Grip asks.

Hanna closes her eyes, tries to think. Before she can speak, Anton takes over.

"The rest of the group told us that he physically attacked Emil Sandström during dinner yesterday evening. Both Hanna and I have seen the strangulation marks on Emil's throat. It doesn't look good."

"I've asked Emil to call in at the medical center during the day so we can document his injuries," Hanna adds.

"So there are witnesses to the attack?" Raffe wonders. He is the only one who hasn't met the friends yet.

"Four of them," Anton confirms. "They were all at the dining table when Pontus went for Emil."

Although the victim did his best to play down the incident, Hanna thinks to herself, *just like the other boys.* She brushes a few crumbs from her fingers. Could it be because Emil knows what it means to be convicted of assault? He is well aware of the consequences of legal action.

That is probably why he hadn't told his parents about Filippa; he didn't want to worry them even more.

"The boys kept stressing the fact that Pontus was very drunk," Hanna says. "They believe the incident was spontaneous and unplanned, that he didn't know what he was doing when he attacked Emil."

She finds it difficult to understand why William kept defending Pontus, but presumably it's a case of misplaced loyalty.

"Well, he was sober enough to leave the scene of the crime," Raffe notes with skepticism in his voice.

"Exactly," Hanna agrees.

"Any other suspects?" Grip asks.

"What about the property manager?" Anton suggests.

Hanna has also been thinking about Staffan Berg and whether he might be involved. She reports briefly on her conversation with him outside the cabin.

"He had a legitimate explanation for his presence, but he does keep showing up."

"But what motive would he have had for killing Filippa?" Daniel says. "If we think he could be a suspect."

Exactly. Hanna has asked herself the same question.

"As far as we're aware they didn't know each other before she came to Åre," she says. "But that doesn't necessarily rule him out."

Raffe has been twiddling a piece of string between his fingers. He puts it down on the table, and it curls up like a little snake. "A neighbor actually phoned to say that a man was standing outside the door of the cabin late on Sunday evening," he says. "The description matches Staffan Berg."

Staffan hadn't mentioned that when Hanna spoke to him earlier at the property. She tries to remember exactly how the conversation went. Shouldn't he have said something, if he's completely innocent?

Grip scratches the back of her neck. "I think we should make finding Pontus our priority. We also need to contact his family." She looks at Hanna. "Can you deal with that?"

Then she turns to Raffe. "We're not dismissing Staffan Berg—I'd like you to take a closer look at him."

"No problem." Raffe makes a note.

"By the way, how did it go with Peter Carlsson, Åke's son?" Hanna asks. "Did you manage to speak to him?"

Raffe nods. "I did. I met up with him briefly yesterday afternoon, before he went back to Gothenburg. He said he was asleep in bed on Saturday night and Sunday morning, and didn't notice anything unusual. He woke up when his youngest son came into his room at about two o'clock, but went back to sleep as soon as the little boy had crawled in under the covers."

"What did he have to say about the accusations in the police report?" Daniel says.

Inappropriate touching, Hanna wants to say. *Sexual harassment. He touched a woman's body without her permission.*

Call it by its proper name.

Raffe flicks through his notebook and opens a page sporting pale-brown coffee stains. "He claimed it was an isolated incident, and that he was having problems in his marriage at the time. On that particular Friday he'd gone to a bar and had too much to drink. If I can quote Peter Carlsson, he said it was an evening he has regretted deeply every single day since then."

"So now we know," Grip says. "We'll set him aside for now; there are more important individuals to focus on at the moment."

Daniel raises a hand.

"What are the implications of the fire when it comes to Filippa's death? Do we think Pontus is involved there too?"

Hanna finds the thought depressing. That would mean Pontus is not only an arsonist, but also a murderer.

Anton, who isn't usually quick to judge people, lets out a snort.

"What are the odds of it being two different perpetrators? Seriously?"

"We can't tie ourselves down to any conclusions yet," Grip says firmly. "First I want to hear what Ylva has to say."

Hanna had almost forgotten that the autopsy on Filippa's body was scheduled to continue today. The last few hours are catching up with her; she is starting to have difficulty concentrating. She would really like to lie down and close her eyes, if only for half an hour.

"Like I said, the most important thing right now is to locate Pontus Englund," Grip continues. "Before he can do any more damage."

84

After a few hours' sleep in the spare guest room on the lower ground floor, Olivia wakes up, disorientated and still tired. It is almost eleven o'clock in the morning when she sits up in bed.

It takes only one breath before the events of last night come crowding in. She can still smell smoke inside the house, and through a gap between the roller blind and the wall, she can see the blackened cabin.

A man and a woman are walking around in the snow; it looks as if they are examining the remains of the fire.

She feels a sudden pressure in her chest.

She will never forget the fear she felt when she woke up in the night. They nearly burned to death, she and Emil.

Olivia can't understand how someone could set fire to a building where people were sleeping. How someone could hate her and Emil so much.

But Pontus obviously could. She knows that now. And it leads to the next terrifying thought: If he is capable of doing such a dreadful thing, then he is presumably the person responsible for Filippa's death.

He is clearly ice cold and ruthless.

Of course that was why he lost it completely when he realized Emil had helped the police to catch him by telling them about the search history on his computer. Pontus knew he was about to be exposed. When the other boys prevented him from strangling Emil, he decided to take his revenge during the night.

Olivia could never have imagined that someone could be so evil.

And on top of everything, Pontus has disappeared to avoid facing up to what he has done. He isn't just an arsonist and a murderer; he is also a coward.

She curls up in bed, whimpers into the pillow. As soon as she closes her eyes, she can see the fire, feel the heat from the terrifying purple-and-orange flames reaching for her and Emil.

If only she could go home to the safety of Västerås.

Suddenly she is overcome with longing for her dad, their little house, and her old room.

Surely the police have to let them leave Åre now they know who is to blame?

Most of all Olivia would love to feel her mother's arms around her, hear her promise that everything is going to be okay.

Although that wouldn't be true. Olivia lets out a sob. Nothing will ever be okay again. Mom is gone, Filippa has died, and Olivia almost lost her life too.

The recollection of all the time she has spent with Pontus makes her loathe both him and herself. The evenings when they partied together, post-assignment celebrations in various bars, all the dinners they've shared.

How could she be so blind that she didn't see his true self?

Who he really was?

She doesn't know how she is ever going to be able to believe in anyone again, not after what Pontus has done. Not only did he almost kill her, he has also shattered her trust.

She licks her dry, flaky lips, wishes she hadn't had a go at Amir at the breakfast table yesterday morning. She should never have accused him of being responsible for Filippa's death in front of all the others.

But at the time she was convinced of his guilt. She couldn't imagine it was anyone else. Especially not Pontus—she would never have thought he was capable of what had happened.

It's all so confusing.

It's not just that Pontus has proved himself to be totally false. This is also about her own ability to read people. She was absolutely certain that Amir was involved in Filippa's death.

And then it turned out that she was wrong.

He was innocent, while Pontus was hiding in the shadows.

How can she trust her intuition in the future when she got it so wrong this time?

Nothing is as it seems.

Olivia gets up, wraps a blanket around her shoulders, and leaves the bedroom. She is thirsty and ought to eat something. Maybe a sandwich and cup of tea will go some way toward dispersing her dark thoughts?

As she goes up the stairs she hears voices from the living room. It sounds as if William and Amir are chatting on the sofas. They are speaking quietly, but she can make out parts of the conversation.

One of them seems to be trying to persuade the other. The insistent tone comes across, but she isn't sure if the voice belongs to William or Amir.

"You have to talk to the police."

The words make Olivia freeze on the spot. She dare not move for fear they will discover that she is eavesdropping.

Who needs to talk to the police?

"They'll never understand," the other one replies.

"It's better if it comes from you rather than someone else."

"I'll just be getting myself into a whole lot of trouble."

Was it William or Amir who made that final comment?

Olivia tries her hardest to work out who is saying what, but their voices are fainter now, dropping to a murmur that is impossible to understand.

She moves quietly up a few more steps, as far as she thinks she can risk it without being seen.

"If they catch up with Pontus and he talks, you'll really be in the shit."

"Pontus will keep his mouth shut."

The latter speaker sounds very sure of himself—and annoyed.

But which is which?

The words that follow make Olivia feel so dizzy that she has to sit down. There is no misinterpreting the softly spoken threat.

"Not one word to the police about me and Filippa."

85

The morning has been eaten up by what feels like a thousand tasks, all related to the fire in Sadeln. The first time Daniel looks at the clock it is gone twelve. No wonder his stomach is complaining.

He goes along to Hanna's office. She is on the phone, but mouths "Nearly done" when she sees him in the doorway.

"That was Pontus's father," she explains when the call is over. "I've been trying to get a hold of the parents all morning, but I've only just managed it."

"Not an easy conversation, I'm guessing."

Hanna nods and pushes back a few strands of hair that have fallen over her eyes. "First of all he was shocked, but then he insisted that they must come up here to help with the search. He had no idea what had been going on over the last few days—Pontus hadn't told them about Filippa's death."

Daniel frowns. "Another one . . . I find it very strange. Surely you call your parents right away when such a tragedy happens?"

"Unless you're involved in some way . . ." Hanna grimaces. "Then you probably decide to keep quiet."

Is this further proof of Pontus's guilt?

Daniel can't rule it out.

"It's not exactly going to make our job easier if the parents start interfering," he says. "They'll make our lives more difficult. Plus we don't even know if Pontus is still in Åre."

He has experienced this kind of thing many times in the past, parents who refuse to believe that their child could possibly be guilty of the crime of which they are accused. Moms and dads who swear that it must all be a misunderstanding, only to fall apart when it becomes clear that they were wrong. They hadn't had a clue about what their offspring were capable of, even though they had thought they were so close.

He doesn't want to be cynical, but he has seen the same course of events play out over and over again.

"What if it were Alice?" Hanna says. "Wouldn't you do the same? Start searching, yourself?"

She is right, of course. If Alice were accused of a crime, he would move heaven and earth to defend her.

It is one thing to act as a police officer, and another to be a parent.

"Probably."

Hanna pulls a face, and Daniel can see that she is trying to suppress a yawn.

"Shall we go and get something to eat?" he suggests. "You look exhausted. We could try the restaurant on the ground floor."

A new food outlet has opened in the same building as the police station. Close and practical.

"Sounds like a good idea." Hanna gives in to the yawn and picks up her purse. "Look," she says, holding out her right hand. "I'm almost shaking. I need calories before I collapse."

While Hanna pays a quick visit to the bathroom, Daniel heads for Anton's office to see if he wants to join them, but he isn't there. Presumably he has already gone to lunch. Raffe isn't around either, so maybe they're together.

A few minutes later Daniel and Hanna go downstairs to the pleasant and welcoming restaurant. Daniel chooses chicken casserole, while Hanna goes for a veggie burger and a Coca-Cola.

As if by silent agreement they take their trays to a quiet corner.

Daniel observes Hanna discreetly as she eats quickly and with concentration. The morning has been so intense that he has barely had time to think, but now the newspaper articles come back to him. The photograph from the airport of Hanna smiling lovingly at Henry Sylvester.

Her new boyfriend, the billionaire.

Should he say something? Defuse the issue by a neutral comment that shows he's obviously heard about what's going on, but doesn't care.

They're just work colleagues, after all.

Daniel spears a piece of potato as he wonders what to do. Maybe it would be better to ignore it? This is Hanna's private life; who she's seeing has nothing to do with him. If he mentions the articles, it might look as if he's been snooping.

The chicken tastes of lemon and thyme.

Hanna must have seen the articles; she can't be unaware of the media interest. Maybe that was why she seemed so shaken up yesterday. If he knows her as well as he thinks he does, she would have found all that intrusive speculation very difficult to handle.

But he still doesn't understand why she hadn't told him about her relationship with Henry. That would have been the natural thing to do, given how much time they spend together. He has been open with her about his emotions following the separation from Ida, the shock when she reconnected with Gustav and told him she wanted to split up.

Maybe he talked about it too much? Maybe Hanna didn't want to tell him about her newfound happiness when he was drowning in his own personal problems?

Before she left him, Ida made it very clear that he's not particularly good at reading women. However, Daniel would still like to think that Hanna trusts him, that they are closer than ordinary colleagues.

He could be wrong, of course.

"Hello?" Hanna says. "You haven't said a word since we sat down. What's going on?"

Daniel realizes he can't talk about Henry Sylvester. It's impossible. He would give himself away immediately; Hanna would pick up on how difficult it is for him to see her with another man.

He can't face the humiliation.

"Sorry," he says, searching for an excuse. "This whole weird story is going around and around in my head. There are too many loose ends, nothing really hangs together."

"I feel exactly the same." Hanna opens her can of cola with a hiss, and half fills her glass. "It's so frustrating."

Daniel agrees. Uniformed officers have started door-to-door inquiries, but so far there hasn't been a single report of any resident having seen anything of note.

Hanna takes a couple of sips of her drink. "Not to mention Filippa's death, and the fact that we still don't know if she died of natural causes."

"Hopefully we'll hear more about that this afternoon."

"I want to know right now!"

Hanna brings her hand down on the table and Daniel can't help smiling. It's typical of her to express her impatience that way. She always wants to make rapid progress in every case.

She is beautiful in the light coming in through the window, even though she's wearing no makeup and has been on the go since four o'clock this morning.

He would love to reach out and touch her cheek, let his fingertips linger on her soft skin.

The sound of someone calling his name makes Daniel turn his head. Raffe is coming toward them.

Hanna puts down her knife and fork, as if she suspects that the brief respite is over.

"You need to come up to the conference room," Raffe informs them. "Ylva has finished the autopsy, and Grip wants us to link up right away."

Daniel quickly shovels down one more forkful.

"One more thing," Raffe goes on. "I've just spoken to Staffan Berg about Sunday evening. You remember the neighbor who said there was a man standing outside the Löwengrens' cabin around midnight? Berg confirms that it was him."

Daniel picks up his phone and slips it into his pocket. "And what was his explanation?"

"He says he received a text from an app, indicating that the intruder alarm in the cabin had been triggered. He drove over, but when he got there everything seemed to be in order. He said he was practically reaching out for the door handle, but because everyone seemed to be asleep he didn't go in—he didn't want to disturb them. He left and went home."

"Do you think it's just a coincidence that Staffan Berg was there the night after Filippa was found dead in the snow?" Hanna asks, picking up her tray.

Raffe leans against the white wall while he considers her question.

"It sounds like a reasonable explanation to me. Berg said he has an app that enables him to monitor all the houses he's responsible for."

"I still find it odd that he keeps showing up," Hanna mutters.

They head for the exit. Daniel holds the door open for Hanna, but she doesn't seem to notice. He turns to Raffe.

"Take another look at Staffan Berg, and ask for a screen dump from his phone. I'd like to see proof that he really did get an alarm call on Sunday."

86

Anton is driving toward Sadeln. He can't stop thinking about where Pontus might have gone. The fact that he was able to sneak out of the house last night without being seen feels like a failure on the part of the police, so in the end Anton decided to skip lunch and take a look around.

It would be good if he could track down Pontus by himself, prove that he deserves his place with the Serious Crimes Unit.

There aren't many vehicles on the E14, but he sticks to the speed limit. His phone rings as he is passing the exit for Holiday Club. As he answers he realizes it's his mom. She's the last person Anton wants to talk to right now, but he can't bring himself to end the call.

"What do you want?"

His tone is brusque, but rather that than let her know how empty and sad he feels. He has no intention of breaking down again in her company.

Yesterday evening was enough.

"Anton," she says, and starts crying.

He can't deal with her emotions as well as his own. It's too much. He tried calling Carl this morning, and once again it went straight to voicemail. The fact that he has broken off relations with his parents for Carl's sake doesn't help if he can't actually tell Carl what has happened.

It feels hard, being rejected by everyone.

"Anton." Another sob.

It's not his mother he's angry with; she can't help it if her husband is an asshole.

"What is it?" he says more gently.

It sounds as if she is trying to pull herself together; he hears her take several deep breaths.

"I had no idea . . . Why have you never said anything about your . . . inclination?"

The accusatory note in her voice immediately puts Anton on the defensive again.

Why does she think?

Obviously he has wanted to come out to his parents for a very long time, but the scene yesterday confirmed what he has always feared—that there would be no understanding whatsoever at home.

His father is stuck in his outdated way of thinking. An old soldier who always believes he knows best, and is not prepared to change his point of view.

Not even for the sake of his own son.

He behaves as if he were born in the nineteenth century.

However, Anton doesn't get how his mother could have been so blind. Isn't a mother supposed to be the first one to understand her child? How could she *not* realize how things stood?

If feels as if she too has denied him.

"Anton?" She takes a jagged breath. "Are you there?"

He has reached the exit road for Sadeln, and signals left. He stops at the junction, waiting for a gap in the oncoming traffic.

"How can you even ask why I've never said anything until now?" he says. "Wasn't it obvious yesterday, given Dad's reaction?"

"You know what he's like. He overreacted, he can't help it."

Anton has grown up with his father "overreacting." And with his mother doing her best to smooth things over, explain it away.

She has always acted as the buffer within the family, the one who tried to pour oil on troubled waters. Sometimes she has jokingly referred to herself as Switzerland, a small neutral country caught between two superpowers in conflict.

The difference is that Anton doesn't want to be part of it anymore.

You can't choose your family, but you can choose to remove them from your life.

"You have to give him time to digest all this," his mother begs. "Can't you talk to him?"

Anton grips the wheel tightly. Then he speaks from the heart, without mincing his words.

"I never want to see him again. Nor you, if you're taking his side."

He hears a sharp intake of breath on the other end of the line.

"You can't ask that of me—you can't expect me to choose between my husband and my son," his mother whispers.

She sounds devastated, but it is what it is. Anton can't help her; it's out of his hands.

"I'm not asking anything of you."

He changes to a lower gear as he drives up the steep hill leading to Sadeln.

Then he corrects himself.

"Actually, I am. I want the two of you to accept me as I am. Otherwise we're done."

87

Hanna hurries up the stairs to the police station on the second floor. Ylva might have completed the autopsy quickly, but it has still felt as if they've been waiting for the results for an eternity.

Hanna knows what her intuition is telling her.

Filippa was murdered.

On the way to the conference room, she stops in at her office and grabs a pen and her notepad.

"The moment of truth," Raffe says, arriving at the same time as Hanna.

"Where's Anton?"

"I don't know. I tried calling him, but the line was busy, so I sent him a text."

Daniel joins them and sits down on the opposite side of the table. Within a very short time Grip appears in one box on the screen, Ylva in another. Carina Grankvist isn't there—maybe she's still in Sadeln, examining the scene of the fire. As soon as the fire service have completed their work, the forensic team takes over—those are the rules.

Hanna is itching to find out the result of that examination too.

"It's good that we could all get together at such short notice, and that the autopsy has been completed," Grip begins. "Ylva, over to you."

Ylva's face fills the screen. Today she is wearing a white lab coat over her dark turtleneck sweater, and her tight ponytail accentuates her high cheekbones.

"I just finished. It might take a little while before you receive a copy of my report, but I thought I'd give you a verbal summary because I know it's urgent."

Hanna listens intently as Ylva starts with the usual basic observations. Then she becomes more specific.

"The deceased had a significant blood alcohol ratio at the time of death. Over 2.0 mil—2.35 to be exact. Not high enough to be fatal, but certainly enough to significantly reduce her cognitive ability. There were also traces of cocaine in the body."

Hanna makes a quick note. Ylva's comments fit with the information given by Filippa's friends, apart from the presence of cocaine. Then again it's probably not surprising that they didn't want to mention the use of illegal substances.

"There were no obvious signs of external violence or other injuries that could explain her death," Ylva continues.

They already know this. *Get to the point,* Hanna wants to say, but she knows that wouldn't go down well. There is no point in annoying the forensic pathologist.

Ylva doesn't respond to being hurried along.

The screen freezes for a few seconds, then Ylva is back.

"As I've already said, the victim had had vaginal intercourse not very long before her death. However, once again there was no sign of violence or anything else to indicate that this was a sexual assault. There is no evidence of rough treatment or physical coercion. Nor did I find any sperm, so presumably a condom was used, which again indicates consensual sex."

Hanna makes another note. That still leaves the question of which of the boys Filippa was with. Not Emil, given his sexual orientation.

Hanna had wondered whether Pontus might have forced himself on Filippa, based on Olivia's contention that Filippa would never have chosen to go to bed with him.

But if it was consensual, then that leaves only Amir and William.

Hanna pictures the two boys. Both have been questioned several times, and both have denied that they had sex with Filippa shortly before she died.

One of them is lying; there is no other explanation.

She focuses on the screen again, keen not to miss anything Ylva has to say.

"In other words, at first sight it looked as if the victim had died due to hypothermia. That she simply fell asleep in the snow without realizing that she was putting herself in mortal danger."

Ylva pauses to consult her notes.

"The high level of intoxication means that she was not accountable for her actions. She might not even have been aware of the low temperature outside. In that case my conclusion would have been that she froze to death as a result of excessive drug and alcohol consumption, to put it in layman's terms."

Hanna can tell that there is a *but* coming.

"However, there is something that doesn't fit. I found very faint traces of petechiae—tiny spots of bleeding on the mucous membrane inside the eyelids."

Hanna purses her lips. She knows exactly what that means. Tiny spots of bleeding indicate that a person was suffocated to death.

She knew it.

Filippa was murdered.

"I have to stress that this result is not unambiguous," Ylva adds, as if she is keen not to tie herself to a conclusion. Maybe she is just being professionally cautious, as most forensic pathologists are.

But Hanna can't contain herself.

"It sounds as if you think Filippa was suffocated to death. Are we looking at murder?"

"Victims of suffocation present a particular challenge to forensic pathologists," Ylva replies. "If the deceased didn't fight back, it is almost impossible to determine the cause of death. Sometimes we can find the impression of fingernails if the perpetrator covered the person's mouth, or fibers on the palate if he or she used a pillow or cushion, for example, but if the victim was unconscious, or highly intoxicated as in this case, then it's very difficult to determine if a murder has taken place."

That wasn't a proper answer either.

Hanna is growing increasingly impatient.

"It does seem as if you're leaning toward the conclusion that a crime lies behind Filippa's death," Daniel says. "If I've understood you correctly?"

Ylva seems indecisive; she clicks her ballpoint pen several times as if she is torn between her gut instinct and the scientific data.

"It's not within my remit to speculate," she says eventually. "I can only report back on the results of my investigation."

"Oh, come on, Ylva," Grip says. She too seems to be losing patience. "We're not going to report our informal discussions to the National Board of Forensic Medicine. You've worked on cases like this for a long time. Just tell us what you think, and I promise we'll leave you in peace."

Ylva considers for a few seconds, then gives in and leans forward.

"Okay. I have a feeling that something might have been pressed against the victim's face. There are tiny, almost microscopic scratches on the cheeks that I can't explain either. We are talking about minimal impressions, but I can't find a reasonable explanation for how they could have occurred. And combined with the traces of petechiae . . ."

Hanna glances over at the notice board, where photographs of Filippa's body have been put up. She was lying on her side, with her face half-buried in the snow.

A thought comes to her out of nowhere, and she has to speak up.

"Is it possible . . . that Filippa was suffocated with the help of the snow?"

Now she's said it out loud, it sounds slightly ridiculous, but she wanted to ask the question.

"How do you mean?" Ylva asks.

Hanna hasn't worked it out yet, she tries to clarify her ideas as she is speaking.

"If the murderer pushed Filippa's face down into the snow on the ground so that she couldn't breathe, couldn't that constitute the cause of death? If she was too drunk to fight back . . . then there would be no imprints of fingers or nails, no fibers, but she would still have been suffocated to death. And the snow against her skin could explain the microscopic scratches."

No one says a word when she has finished, which immediately makes Hanna wonder if her theory is completely unrealistic. Maybe she should have kept quiet.

This isn't the first time she has opened her mouth without thinking.

But Ylva gives her an appreciative nod.

"I can't exclude the possibility that it could have happened that way," she says slowly. "Such a scenario definitely provides a plausible explanation for my own observations."

Hanna is grateful for Ylva's support.

Daniel also seems impressed; he too gives her a nod.

"Murder, in other words," Grip says firmly. "So now we know what we're working with."

88

Anton turns into Nedre Svedjevägen so fast that the car almost skids and ends up in the ditch. With a silent curse he slows down and manages to stay on the road.

He is still upset following the conversation with his mother; he is so tired of being the one who always has to explain himself and apologize.

He has sent yet another text message to Carl, asking—almost begging—to meet up with him this evening.

But now he must focus on the job. He will soon be level with the Löwengrens' house, but that's not where he's heading this time.

Anton has another idea.

There have been no reports of Pontus, even though every cab firm and bus company has been contacted and given his description. And he can hardly have sneaked on board a train, but the station is under close surveillance. However, bearing in mind how cold and windy it was overnight, Anton wonders whether Pontus would have strayed very far from the house. He has no car, no other form of transport. His skis were still in the storage rack—they checked.

Maybe he's still somewhere nearby?

If Anton's theory is correct, then Pontus acted in a panic. Nothing of which he stands accused seems to have been premeditated; everything seems to have happened spontaneously rather than as the result of a carefully thought-out plan.

So if Pontus disappeared in the middle of the night, then maybe he didn't get very far. It's possible that he's hiding somewhere, scared and desperate, not knowing where to go.

Anton would love to be the one who finds him.

He parks the Toyota by the side of the road and gets out. It is still breezy this high up, but the wind has dropped considerably over the past few hours. It is still very cold, though, probably around minus fifteen or sixteen degrees.

Which is another reason for suspecting that Pontus hasn't left the area, especially if he was on foot.

When Anton looks around, he sees several empty driveways in front of houses where there is no sign of life. January is low season, and most students prefer to rent accommodation down in the village, within walking distance of bars and restaurants.

Admittedly officers were sent out this morning to conduct door-to-door inquiries, but Anton wonders about the properties where no one is home?

It can't hurt to check them out.

The snow on the road has been churned up by passing cars, but it doesn't look as if the snowplow has gotten here yet.

Which is exactly what he was hoping for, because that means the snow on the driveways of the empty houses is untouched. Therefore, it will be possible to see footprints left by anyone who shouldn't be there.

Like Pontus, if he tried to get inside somewhere.

89

After the meeting Daniel, Hanna, and Raffe remain in the conference room. Daniel feels the need to discuss the situation with his colleagues. He is slightly taken aback by Ylva's conclusions, and by Hanna's subsequent theory as to how Filippa's murder could have happened.

If she's right, she has once again proved what a fantastic instinct for police work she has.

His cellphone rings—it's an internal number.

Carina Grankvist.

"I'm putting you on speaker," he says, placing the phone on the table so everyone can hear.

"We spent the morning on Nedre Svedjevägen with the fire service, examining the site of the blaze," Carina begins.

"Did you find anything interesting?" Hanna asks.

"Indeed we did." They can all hear the smile in Carina's voice. "There is no doubt that the fire was started deliberately—there are clear traces of lighter fluid. That also explains the rapid spread that Olivia and Emil witnessed."

Daniel sighs. He is pleased to have confirmation, but it is undeniably a depressing explanation. It means they are facing two taxing investigations, while the suspected perpetrator has disappeared.

"Any traces of the perpetrator?" he wonders.

"I'm afraid not."

There is a distinct buzz on the line, and Carina's voice fades in and out. It sounds to Daniel as if she is outside; presumably the wind is affecting her phone. Maybe she's still at the cabin.

"You can imagine what the ground looks like after the firefighters were there with their hoses," she continues. "There's no possibility of identifying individual shoe prints or other details."

"How did yesterday's house search go?" Hanna asks, leaning closer to the phone. "Have you had time to complete the report?"

"It's ongoing." Carina's voice is stressed, her vowels clipped. "We can't do everything at the same time. We're working as fast as we can. However, as you know we didn't find the victim's outdoor clothes or boots in the house—they're still missing."

Daniel extracts the promise of a written summary as soon as she can manage it before she ends the call.

"So, murder and arson," Raffe says. "That's a lot to take in."

"I'm wondering about something else," Hanna says. "Do we think the four friends are safe?"

Raffe drums his fingers on the table.

"Do you think they could be in danger? Because of Pontus?"

"I don't know." Hanna chews her pen. "But I don't like it. Maybe we should have officers there overnight, just to be on the safe side?"

Daniel had considered the idea, but decided they didn't have sufficient resources. Given the direction the case has taken, they are going to need to work even more overtime.

"Pontus is unlikely to return," he says. "And we've got patrols everywhere searching for him."

Hanna concedes defeat. She draws a circle on her pad before putting down her pen. "There's something wrong with William's and Amir's statements."

"You mean the fact that Filippa had what appears to be consensual sex before she died, and that it's hardly likely to have been with Pontus?"

Hanna gives Daniel a grateful smile, pleased that they are thinking along the same lines. "One of them is lying to us. But which one, and why?"

Raffe puts his elbows on the table, rests his chin on his hands.

"They're young, maybe they're embarrassed? Who wants to admit they had casual sex with a girl who was then found murdered?"

"That's not a good enough reason," Hanna insists. "We've questioned them several times. Lying to the police is a big deal."

Not to everyone, Daniel thinks.

He remembers the years in Gothenburg when he worked on gang crime. Not telling the truth was virtually a reflex action. In Bergsjö, suspects lied constantly when the police asked questions; there was no appetite for cooperation.

"We should bring the boys in for formal interviews," he suggests. "See if we can get more out of them at the station. And it might be a good idea to separate them too."

Hanna gets to her feet.

"I agree. Come on, let's go and bring them in."

90

The tiredness catches up with Hanna again when she gets into the unmarked police car. Lunch chased it away temporarily, and the adrenaline rush following Ylva's report helped too. But the warmth in the car is making her sleepy, even though she needs to stay sharp.

They will soon be seeing the four friends again—she has to be focused.

Daniel is driving toward Sadeln, silent and concentrating on the road. There are few cars on the E14, and for once no trucks en route to Norway. A group of young men with skis over their shoulders are walking in the opposite direction, even though the vehicles are passing dangerously close.

Student weeks, Hanna reminds herself. The other day there was a girl who, following après-ski and several shots, zoomed straight onto Årevägen on a sled. It was sheer luck that no cars were passing at the time—they would have had no chance of stopping.

"Filippa's clothes," she says in an attempt to wake herself up. "They have to be somewhere. Surely the murderer must have taken them—who else could it be?"

"Seems logical."

Daniel sounds more brusque than usual. He's been that way all day; he hardly said a word when they sat down for lunch. She had to work hard to get anything out of him before Raffe showed up.

She studies him discreetly, wondering for the umpteenth time if he has seen those awful articles. Is it the gossip columns that are making him so taciturn?

They are approaching the exit for Sadeln.

The clouds are so low that they are hiding the mountain known as Renfjället on the other side of the lake. They are like a lid on top of the whole valley, and odd flakes of snow drift down through the air.

It is sleeping-cat weather.

Hanna has started calling it that, because Morris likes to curl up with one paw covering his nose and sleep through this kind of weather. He is a clever cat, probably smarter than his owner.

"How are things with Alice when you have to be at work so much?" she asks, mainly to try to bring Daniel out of his shell.

His weary expression gives her the answer. "You mean how are things with Ida now we have another murder to investigate?"

"That too."

"So far she's been very understanding. I hope it lasts, but there's always a risk that it won't, especially if the case drags on."

"You need a nanny who could jump in at short notice; then you wouldn't have to call your ex every time there's a problem."

"Elisabeth usually helps out."

"Isn't that the same thing? If you call Ida's mom, then Ida will find out."

Hanna can't see why Daniel doesn't get it. If Ida is annoyed because he isn't doing his share, then it won't exactly improve things if he asks her mom to step in when he has to work.

Being a police officer can entail unreasonable working hours when a case is hotting up. Because Daniel is a single dad to a small child, it's hardly surprising if he is finding it hard to make things fit. But that means finding a practical solution. In Hanna's world that means a neighbor or a childminder who can be there, not an ex-mother-in-law with a direct line to an already critical Ida.

"I'm sure you're right. I ought to get to grips with that. I just haven't gotten around to it yet."

He sounds tired, almost defeated. As if life is on the point of overwhelming him, which isn't like Daniel at all.

Hanna wants to lean over and squeeze his hand, give him a supportive hug, but she keeps her hands on her lap.

"Can I help you find someone?" she says instead. "I could ask Karro if she knows anyone who'd like to earn a little extra as a childminder. She's friends with just about everyone in Åre and Duved, and the surrounding area. Or you could put a query on the Facebook group—that reaches most people around here."

Daniel knows Anton's sister, Karro, and he nods gratefully.

"I'd be happy for you to contact her—if you have time?"

"No problem. How about Facebook?"

Daniel frowns. "Let's leave that for now. I'm not sure I want to advertise my situation on social media."

Hanna can certainly sympathize with that.

More than Daniel can imagine.

"I'll give her a call this evening." She allows herself a brief touch, an encouraging pat on his arm. "We'll sort something out, I promise."

91

Slowly and methodically Anton has scanned every driveway on Nedre Svedjevägen. By the time he reaches the turning area at the end of the road, he is just about ready to give up.

Maybe this was a stupid idea. Pontus could easily have gone in the opposite direction, toward the highway, and hidden somewhere else. There are hundreds of houses and apartments in the area. Even if he hasn't left Sadeln, he could be anywhere.

Anton looks around again.

To the left is a patch of common land that is so full of low-growing mountain birch and undergrowth that it forms a kind of barrier. The trees are weighed down with snow; the lowest branches are almost sweeping the ground. Here and there the wind has formed irregular drifts, like small hillocks in the white landscape.

It looks like hard work to get through, especially if it's dark. However, Pontus could have blundered off that way out of sheer desperation. It's not impossible, anyway.

Then something catches Anton's attention.

The last house on the street is set high above the turning area. By the roadside is a large stone with the inscription **VILLA SYNNÖVE**. Both the name and the turfed roof suggest Norwegian owners. This is not unusual; Åre is crawling with Norwegians who like to exploit the weak Swedish krona in order to purchase property, food, and alcohol.

Halfway up the drive is a freestanding garage—with a set of footprints leading to it.

Anton's heart rate increases. There is no sign of prints leading away, and the house itself looks empty. The curtains are closed—often a sign that no one is there.

Unless an uninvited guest has sought refuge in the garage.

Anton approaches cautiously, stooping to avoid being seen from the rectangular window set high in the side wall. The snow muffles every sound. The light is gray, thanks to the clouds covering the valley.

Tall evergreens tower up behind the property, forming an impenetrable wall.

Anton is only yards from the garage now. Apart from the main entrance there is also a side door, which looks as if it has been opened recently. At the bottom the snow has been pushed aside and trampled on.

As if someone has opened the door, then closed it again.

And that's where the footprints end.

Anton crouches down. There are no other traces leading to or from the garage.

There can only be one person hiding in there.

92

Hanna recognizes Anton's red Toyota as they approach the Löwengrens' house. What is he doing in Sadeln?

"Did you know Anton was coming here?" she asks Daniel.

"No. He didn't mention it to me."

At least that explains why Anton missed the briefing with Ylva, but Hanna thinks he should have told someone where he was going; it's not like him to sneak off like that. Then she smiles to herself—who is she to judge? Taking off to check something out on her own is something she often does.

Daniel parks, and they get out of the car.

When Hanna looks up at Åreskutan, the mountain is hidden by a massive wall of gray fog.

She points to the Carlsson property.

"I'm wondering whether we ought to speak to them again. Check out what they might have seen last night."

She knows that officers will call on them as part of the door-to-door inquiries, but reading someone else's report isn't the same as speaking to the person.

Or asking a key question.

Karin Carlsson turned out to be an important witness in the investigation into Filippa's death. Maybe she was also up when the fire broke out?

It might be worth a visit.

"Later," Daniel decides, setting off toward the front door. "First we need to pick up these boys—that's why we came here."

Hanna follows without protesting.

This time it is Emil who answers the door. His eyes are tired and his complexion sallow, apart from the angry red marks still clearly visible on his throat.

The events of the last few days have taken their toll. However, he doesn't seem surprised to see the two detectives again.

"Hi," Daniel says. "We'd like to see William and Amir—there's something we need to talk to them about."

"They're in bed, but I can wake them."

"And how are you doing?" Hanna asks as they step inside.

"Not bad."

Emil runs his fingers through his hair, which needs washing. Hanna can almost smell the lingering odor of the fire in those greasy curls.

"Have you found Pontus?"

"Not yet."

Hanna peers into the living room, but there is no sign of Anton or anyone else. "Where's Olivia?"

"I think she went for a lie-down too. I'll go down and tell the others you're here."

Hanna and Daniel wait in the hallway. There are shoes scattered everywhere, but the jackets are neatly hung up beneath the hat shelf. Hanna suddenly notices a white alarm keypad on the wall, just below the hooks. She didn't notice it the last time she was here, presumably because it was hidden behind a coat or jacket, but today there is only an empty hanger.

She recognizes the layout; there is an almost identical one in Lydia's house. When you open the front door, you have thirty seconds to enter a code, otherwise the alarm goes off.

She remembers that Lydia has something else linked to her alarm system.

Outdoor cameras attached to the house facade.

Lydia has an app that means she can see who is at the front door or any of the other entrances, even when she is in Stockholm.

Hanna nudges Daniel and points. “Look. I wonder if they’ve got cameras linked to the alarm. My sister has. If so, the cameras should have registered anyone moving around outside,” she explains.

“Do you think we could be that lucky?” Daniel sounds skeptical, as if he dare not believe in that kind of scenario.

“It’s certainly worth checking out,” Hanna replies. “Imagine if we can find footage from the night Filippa died. Or when the fire started.”

“How long is the footage stored?” Daniel asks. “Doesn’t it only exist in the moment?”

Hanna has no idea. She has never owned a house where an alarm was needed. She doesn’t have anything that valuable.

But she knows who to ask.

“I’ll call Lydia as soon as we’re done here. She’s bound to know.”

93

Anton flaps his arms to try to get warm. He feels as if he has been standing outside the garage waiting for backup forever. He is running out of patience. He is worried that Pontus might spot him and make a run for it, plus his feet feel like lumps of ice.

Approximately nine hours have passed since Pontus disappeared. If he really is hiding in there, he must be both hungry and thirsty by now.

And desperate.

Someone who can start a fire in a house where his friends lie sleeping is presumably capable of anything. Emil and Olivia could have died, if she hadn't woken up and gotten them out in time.

Pontus is ruthless, that much is clear.

Anton doesn't know how cunning he might be. Maybe he intends to stay put until he believes the danger is over, then make an attempt to leave Åre.

Or launch a fresh attack on his friends.

Anton checks his watch yet again and makes a decision. He can't wait any longer. He places a tentative hand on the door handle. There is no sign of a break-in; maybe the owner forgot to lock it.

Slowly, with the utmost care, he pushes down the handle. He doesn't want to give himself away in case Pontus is lurking inside, waiting for him. He opens the door very slowly and draws his gun.

He has no intention of taking any risks; he could be dealing with a murderer and arsonist.

He peers into the garage, which seems pretty large. A red Jeep is parked next to a snow scooter, and rows of skis are hung on racks beneath the ceiling. The walls are lined with shelving, providing storage for ski suits and other equipment.

Then Anton spots something worrying. At the far end is a wooden workbench, with a collection of tools displayed above it: hammers, axes, and saws of different sizes.

But there is an empty space in the middle. He stares at it.

Has Pontus armed himself?

Anton tightens his grip on his gun. He must be prepared; he can't risk letting himself be taken by surprise.

Should he change his mind, wait until backup arrives?

He stands still, decides to hang on a little longer, but time passes, and there is still no sign of anyone down the road.

He feels sweat break out on the back of his neck. What should he do? He mustn't miss the chance of catching Pontus, not now he's so close.

An almost imperceptible sound from inside the garage settles the matter.

And Anton steps into the darkness.

94

"I'll take a look outside, see if there are any cameras," Hanna says.

She is still in the hallway with Daniel, waiting for William and Amir to show up. To be fair, it is only a few minutes since Emil went downstairs; if they were asleep, it could be a while before they are up and dressed.

Daniel gives a brief nod. "I'll stay here until the boys are ready."

Hanna inspects the facade carefully. It's hard to see properly in the gray light; she has to screw up her eyes to make out the details. The lights are mounted at regular intervals along the entire front of the building, modern LEDs with beams pointing both upward and downward to create atmosphere.

And then she spots small black cameras, cleverly concealed.

She walks slowly around the house to see how many there are. With each step she sinks deeper into the snow; she has to lift her feet high up to get anywhere at all. She discovers that there are cameras at every access point—above the front door, the ski entrance, and the patio door on the lower level.

She stops outside the sauna, craning her neck to try to work out the camera angle. It's doubtful if it covers the place where Filippa was found, but it's not impossible.

If the footage still exists, this would mean a real breakthrough in the investigation. It would help them to identify the person Karin Carlsson saw.

The next question is whether whoever started the fire was caught on camera.

Hanna heads toward the blackened cabin. The snow all around has been churned up by countless feet and fire hoses, and the entire west-facing side of the building is damaged. It's doubtful if the place is salvageable. The charred smell still lingers in the air, making her nostrils prickle. She has a feeling that it might be dangerous to inhale the combination of wood and other material that burned.

It could have been the smell of death, if Olivia hadn't woken in time.

A chilling thought.

Hanna looks up at the gable end. That was probably where the fire started, according to the forensic examination. Someone poured lighter fluid at the western corner, then lit it with a match.

She goes over to the ski entrance to try to work out whether the closest camera might reach the cabin. It depends on what direction it is pointing in. The black lens shines down at her as she stands on tiptoe to check the angle.

Yes! The camera should have picked up anyone moving around the building.

She has prayed to higher powers for a little luck.

And it seems as if her prayer has been answered.

95

Hanna is about to rejoin Daniel when the door to the patio opens and Olivia appears, dressed in gray sweatpants and a fleecy top.

"Hi, Olivia, how are you? Emil said you were resting when we arrived."

"Not great."

Olivia is very pale. Her coal-black hair against her white skin creates an almost ghostly impression. Only two red patches burning on her cheeks give her face any color.

"I realize it's tough," Hanna says. "But you did an amazing thing last night—you probably saved both your own life and Emil's. It's not surprising that you're tired; you need time to recover."

Olivia glances over her shoulder; she seems anxious in case someone sees her talking to Hanna. Is she still scared? Maybe they should send a uniformed officer over to keep an eye on things for the next day or so?

But Hanna reminds herself that Daniel was against the idea, and so was Raffe. Neither of them thought that Pontus would be dumb enough to return to the house, and it can only be a matter of time before they track him down.

"I have to tell you something."

The girl's voice is weak and uncertain, nothing like her usual self. However, she has gone through a great deal in the past twenty-four hours, which is bound to take its toll. Maybe she has a fever? What has happened to her could make anyone ill.

Hanna moves closer. "I'm listening."

"It was this morning. I happened to overhear William and Amir talking in the living room."

Then Olivia tells Hanna about the conversation, how one of the boys was trying to persuade the other to admit what he had done to Filippa, but Olivia couldn't tell which of them it was.

Which of them was the guilty party.

"You should have called and told me this right away," Hanna snaps. She regrets her tone immediately; there is no point in chastising Olivia when she is already so upset.

"I know." Olivia bites her lip and looks away. "But I was shocked and confused; it was like I couldn't think clearly. So I went back to bed."

Hanna places a hand on Olivia's shoulder, gives her a gentle squeeze. "It's good that you've told me now."

The pieces of the puzzle are falling into place, one by one. If they can interview the boys at the station and get the truth out of them, they will be able to solve the case—she's sure of it.

Then Hanna realizes something else. Pontus isn't necessarily responsible for both Filippa's death and the fire.

These are two separate crimes.

They could be looking at two separate perpetrators.

96

Slowly, slowly Anton edges into the dark garage.

When he stepped inside he felt around in vain for a light switch, but maybe it's over by the main entrance, and not the side door he has used.

He moves cautiously in the gloom, with the help of the small amount of daylight seeping in through the partly open door.

"Pontus?" he calls out. "My name is Anton, and I'm a police officer. Come into the light with both hands in the air."

Silence.

"Pontus? I know you're in here. There's no point in hiding."

He crouches down and peers under the Jeep to see if Pontus might be on the other side. It's hard to tell, could someone be lurking behind the red car? He has a strong feeling that he is not alone.

Someone else is breathing in here.

"Pontus. Come out with your hands raised above your head."

He doesn't move, listens hard. He thinks he hears a faint scraping sound, right by the main door.

Out of the corner of his eye, he sees a moving shadow.

Then the garage door squeaks loudly and Anton realizes it is being opened. As he stands up, an object comes flying through the air. He just manages to turn his head so that it strikes him above one eyebrow rather than full in the face.

His head is burning, the pain is intense. There is a loud crash as whatever was thrown at him lands on the floor.

Somehow his gun drops from his hand and slides across the floor, beneath the Jeep's engine. Meanwhile the roller door has continued to open, leaving a gap of about three feet.

As Anton scrabbles for his weapon he sees a figure hurl itself forward and roll beneath the door.

Something warm is trickling down his face, only now does he realize it's blood. At long last his fingers find the butt of his gun. He grabs it, stumbles to the entrance, and follows Pontus.

He can see the boy running down the hill, heading toward the main road. He has a start of around twenty yards.

Anton goes after him, but the blood running over his eyes makes it hard to see. He is beginning to feel dizzy and nauseous. The distance between him and Pontus is increasing; there is nothing he can do about it.

He is running out of steam.

At that moment the front door of the Löwengrens' house opens, and Daniel and Hanna emerge with two of the other boys.

"Daniel!" Anton yells with the last of his strength. "Stop him! Stop Pontus!"

97

Anton's voice makes Daniel react instantly.

He has just come out of the house with William and Amir when he sees Pontus racing away from the turning area. Anton is following him, but something is wrong, he staggers in the middle of the road, his face is covered in blood.

Anton drops to his knees, and Daniel breaks into a run to stop Pontus, who has just passed the end of the drive. He is about ten yards ahead and refuses to stop, even though Daniel is yelling at him.

Daniel has no choice but to draw his service weapon.

Pontus cannot be allowed to get away.

Raising the gun, Daniel bellows as loudly as he can, "Stop or I'll shoot!"

Pontus ignores him, and increases his speed as Daniel removes the safety catch and fires a warning shot into the air.

The loud report echoes among the houses, and Pontus casts a terrified glance over his shoulder. Daniel can see the desperation in his eyes, but still Pontus refuses to give up. He carries on down the hill, despite slipping and almost losing his balance.

Hanna comes racing up behind Daniel.

"Take care of Anton," Daniel calls out, forcing himself to run faster. "I've got this."

He has no intention of letting Pontus escape, not when he's so close.

They have almost reached the crossroads. Pontus is about to continue over to the other side when a large snowplow appears around the bend. The noise of the engine drowns out every other sound, and the driver's attention is focused on the route ahead.

He doesn't notice the boy who comes flying from the left.

Daniel sees Pontus hesitate for a microsecond as he tries to weigh up the odds; is he going to be able to make it across the road before the enormous machine gets there? It is way too close to be able to brake. If the huge steel scoop hits Pontus, he has no chance.

But Pontus looks as if he isn't going to stop. He is too desperate; he is incapable of thinking clearly.

"No!" Daniel roars as he hurls himself forward.

It is like a slow-motion sequence. He reaches for Pontus's jacket, fumbles in thin air, then manages to grab a piece of fabric and pulls as hard as he can. Through sheer force of will, Daniel manages to drag the boy out of the way as the snowplow thunders past with only inches to spare.

Its vibrations can be felt through the ground. It was so close that Daniel felt the draft against his cheek.

They both fall to the ground and roll into the ditch, with Daniel on top.

"Are you out of your mind?" he pants, shaking Pontus. "You could have killed both of us!"

He has to fight to hold back his anger, but somehow he manages to regain control. He quickly takes out a pair of handcuffs and secures Pontus's wrists behind his back.

This time Pontus offers no resistance, but simply lies motionless on the ground. Daniel drags him to his feet, keeping a firm hold on his elbow.

Pontus's face is smeared with snow and gravel.

"You have a lot of explaining to do," Daniel says. "Murder, arson, assault, and resisting arrest."

Pontus is breathing laboriously.

"I haven't done anything," he says without looking up.

Daniel contemplates him wearily.

Filippa is dead and Emil's throat still bears the clear marks from Pontus's fingers. Last night the cabin was in flames.

It is not Pontus who is the victim in this story.

98

When she found out that the police were taking William and Amir to the station, Olivia felt nothing but relief. She doesn't want to see them anymore. She is afraid of giving herself away, revealing that she was eavesdropping on the stairs when they had their mysterious conversation about Filippa.

Just being in the same room as them makes her shudder.

She had hoped that the police would hold William and Amir for a long time, but then all that business with Pontus kicked off. The two detectives changed their plans, because they had to deal with him and take care of their injured colleague.

So William and Amir remained in the house.

Now they are sitting on the sofa, gaming, while Olivia is in the kitchen making tea. Emil is resting in his room; he still seems to be in shock following the fire and Pontus's attack.

Twilight is falling, but the beautiful view is hidden by thick cloud. Olivia is so tense that her shoulders are aching. She hopes neither of the boys saw her talking to Hanna outside the sauna. They already seem suspicious, they've hardly said a word to her all afternoon.

Through the window she can see the blackened remains of the cabin, a chilling reminder of what happened last night.

Olivia will never forget the sight of Pontus in handcuffs. Or the injured officer with his face covered in blood. She can't get her head around the idea that Pontus almost killed another person. She had simply stared after him as Daniel, the bearded detective, led him toward a patrol car.

As the water heats up she takes a mug out of the cupboard and drops a tea bag into it. She adds a drop of milk and is about to replace the carton in the refrigerator when she realizes that William is standing by the door.

"How are you doing?" he asks.

She can barely look him in the eye. "Not great. It's hard."

He gives her a searching look. "I saw you over by the sauna. What were you talking to that cop about?"

Shit. So he did see her. "Nothing special."

In order to avoid looking at him, she moves a few things around in the refrigerator—butter, cheese . . . She moves the cucumber onto a different shelf.

William steps forward and closes the door. She has to step back to avoid getting her hand caught. "You must have been talking about something."

"She was just asking how I was feeling." Olivia tries to keep her tone light, but she can feel her cheeks beginning to burn. "I told her the truth—it's really difficult at the moment. What did you think we were talking about?"

Suddenly William is very close. He grabs her arm and tightens his grip. "You wouldn't accuse me of being responsible for Filippa's death, would you?" he says quietly. "Like when you went for Amir? Spread lies about me, even though there isn't a shred of truth in any of them?"

Olivia tries to pull away, but he keeps hold of her forearm. If he doesn't let go soon, she is going to have a bruise.

His eyes are ice cold without a trace of sympathy as he continues: "You can't just come out with serious accusations. I hope you understand that."

His grip tightens even more. He is frightening her, but Olivia can't escape and dare not protest.

Her arm is hurting.

"I do understand," she manages eventually. "I won't, I promise."

William keeps his eyes fixed on her.

"I know you haven't done anything," Olivia whispers.

Suddenly he lets go and is back to his normal self.

"Good." He smiles and points to the kettle. "I'd love a cup of tea if there's enough hot water."

99

The activity in the neighborhood this afternoon has not escaped Åke Carlsson. He followed the whole drama from the kitchen window, watched the dramatic chase after one of the young people from next door, noted the number of police cars that gathered immediately afterward.

It looked as if one officer was badly hurt. His face was covered in blood; he could barely stand as the female detective who was around the other day helped him to a car.

So they've caught a suspected perpetrator.

Åke smiles contentedly.

When the front door opens and he hears Karin stamping the snow off her boots, he calls her into the kitchen. She has been in Storlien all day, buying the week's groceries at the new mall that has become a magnet for everyone.

"What's going on?" she asks. "I only just managed to get the car through."

She is carrying two enormous bags, and presumably there are twice as many in the hallway. The prices in Storlien are unbeatable, so it's no surprise that eager Norwegians make regular pilgrimages over the border.

"It looks as if the police have solved the murder of that girl," Åke explains. "They've arrested one of the boys; I saw them take him away in handcuffs."

Karin puts down the bags so abruptly that one falls over, and several apples and oranges roll across the floor. Her hand flies to her mouth.

"But that's terrible! They're only children! They've got their whole lives ahead of them!"

"What's that got to do with anything?" Åke is pleased with the outcome, pleased that the police have discovered that one of the group is the guilty party.

"If you commit a crime like that, you have to take the consequences," he goes on. "They've definitely reached the age of criminal responsibility."

"I'm sure you're right, but the thought of one of them being locked up is terrible." Karin sounds upset. She sinks down onto the nearest chair. "Do you know which one the police arrested?"

Åke shakes his head. He can't tell the difference between those young boys.

"It wasn't the Löwengren boy—he's the only one I recognize."

He finds it impossible to feel sorry for anyone in that family. He turns to the window and looks out at the hated neighboring property. He still wishes that the flames had swallowed up the main building as well, not just the cabin.

But maybe things will turn out for the best? This might make the Löwengrens decide to sell up. In which case he would love to buy the eyesore and pull it down, or at least paint the facade a decent color before selling it on.

He folds his arms and smiles. He doesn't feel the slightest pang of conscience.

Karin has started to gather up the fruit from the floor.

"I still think it's terrible that they've arrested one of the boys," she says quietly. "But I'm sure you're right—we all have to take the consequences of our actions."

Åke knows exactly what he thinks. "The main thing is for the crime to be cleared up quickly, so we can sleep easy in our beds again."

Karin sighs. "I just want it to be over. The whole thing is so awful."

100

Back at the station Daniel is trying to sort out some kind of order of priority for the rest of the day. He is at his desk and has just finished updating Grip over the phone.

The news about Anton was particularly hard to pass on to their boss. He keeps seeing Anton dropping to his knees in the middle of the road, deathly pale and with blood pouring from a gash in his forehead. When a colleague is injured in the line of duty, it upsets everyone. Being a police officer inevitably involves risk, but that doesn't mean you become immune to incidents like this.

Quite the reverse—you become more cautious.

Pontus has been arrested, and is now in custody waiting for a formal interview.

Hanna has gone with Anton to the medical center so they can carry out an initial assessment. It is likely that he will be transferred to the hospital in Östersund.

They also need to question William and Amir, especially in view of Olivia's revelations, but at the moment Pontus is their main focus.

He hears Raffe's rapid footsteps in the corridor; then his colleague appears in the doorway, holding his phone. He looks relieved.

"I've just spoken to Hanna. It seems things aren't quite as bad as we feared, thank God."

"What did she say?"

"The doctor has examined Anton: He has a concussion and will need stitches in his forehead. They're sending him to Östersund where he'll be kept in for observation, but it could have been much worse."

Daniel relaxes a little. A weight he didn't even realize he was carrying is lifted from his shoulders.

"That's good to hear. It was horrible, seeing him like that."

"I can imagine," Raffe replies. "According to Hanna, the doctor said the angels must have been on his side. If the hammer had struck him half an inch lower down, he could have lost the sight in his right eye."

In spite of his relief, Daniel can't help wondering why Anton took off on his own like that. He ought to know better than to go looking for a suspect without backup. It was pure luck that Daniel and Hanna happened to be on the scene; otherwise Pontus would have gotten away again.

But that is a discussion for another day.

"Pontus has a great deal to answer for," he says.

"It's a tragedy to have something like this on his conscience at such a young age," Raffe observes. "How old is he—nineteen?"

"That's right."

Raffe slips his phone into the back pocket of his jeans and leans against the doorframe, looking pensive.

"Hanna asked me to tell you she'd be back soon—in case you want to wait for her before interviewing Pontus?"

"Thanks for letting me know—in that case I will wait."

No one is better in situations like this. If anyone can get the truth out of Pontus, it's Hanna.

101

As she leaves the medical center, Hanna decides to go for a short walk. A few minutes in the fresh air would be good. Seeing Anton in such a state was horrible. As they drove away from Sadeln, she was half expecting him to faint right there in the car.

He is in good hands now, but she needs a little break before returning to the police station. She needs to be on the top of her game for the interview with Pontus, not feeling shaken as she does now.

She heads north along Kurortsvägen, then walks quickly toward the Tott Hotel, drawing the cold air deep into her lungs. The snow squeaks beneath her boots. In the distance she can see the Tott lift up at the top. It has shut down for the day; it is after three o'clock, and the sun will be going down in half an hour. At this time of day there are no T-bar lifts or skiers on the piste; the slopes are deserted.

Hanna has to admit that this case is having a profound effect on her. There is something particularly disturbing about young people being mixed up in serious crime, and she finds it difficult to maintain her distance as she should. Only a few days ago they were a group of friends traveling to the mountains for a week of skiing and partying. Now their lives will never be the same again. Pontus could be facing many years in jail, Olivia has lost her best friend, and she and Emil almost died in a fire.

How can life change so fast?

Hanna buries her chin in her scarf and tries to calm the anxiety fizzing through her body. At the moment the indications are that Pontus is guilty, but they can't rule out the possibility that others might be involved. The information Olivia passed on is still in the back of her mind; William and Amir must be questioned as a matter of urgency.

She has almost reached the hotel, and realizes it is time to go back. Daniel is waiting for her.

The working day is far from over.

Maybe she should call Lydia? Ask her sister if she knows anything about the cameras that are presumably linked to the house alarm at Nedre Svedjevägen 7.

Lydia should still be at work. Hanna takes out her phone and makes the call. Lydia answers right away, and Hanna quickly explains the situation. She is keen to avoid unnecessary small talk.

"Yes, our cameras are positioned to film all the different access points to the house," Lydia confirms.

"Do they run all the time?"

"No, I think they're motion sensor, but you can choose for yourself."

"What do you mean?"

"Our cameras start filming only if something or someone moves within their range, but there are different kinds that run nonstop."

That was exactly what Hanna had hoped to hear.

"Do you have any idea whether the footage is stored for a specific period?"

"I've never thought about it," Lydia replies. "You need to contact the security company—they might store the footage in the cloud, or on their server."

Hanna is grateful for any information she can get.

"Thanks, I'll call them right away."

"Which company is it?"

Hanna tries to picture the white panel in her mind's eye.

"Nordic Security, I think."

"That's the company we use. They're very professional, and they cover the whole country. I'm sure they'll be able to tell you what you need to know."

Hanna is about to thank her sister for her help and end the call, when Lydia jumps in with a completely different question.

"So why didn't you call me back yesterday?" There is no mistaking the reproachful note in her voice. "I'm dying of curiosity here, with all those online articles . . ." The pause is brief but meaningful. "What's going on with you and Henry Sylvester?"

Not Lydia too.

Hanna loves her big sister, but the last thing she has time for right now is a discussion about her tangled love life. The investigation has to take precedence.

"Another time," she says.

"Mom is absolutely thrilled," Lydia continues. "She called me yesterday, couldn't stop talking about your new boyfriend. You do realize she's already started planning your wedding? How do you feel about that?"

"Lydia, please!"

"Okay, okay." Now she sounds offended. "I thought we could talk to each other about this kind of thing."

Hanna really doesn't want to upset her sister. Lydia has stepped up for her many times over the years. But she doesn't have time for this at the moment.

"It's . . . complicated. I'll call you later and tell you more. I need to speak to the security company before they close for the day."

"Promise you'll call me back?"

"I promise. Scout's honor."

They end the call, and Hanna wishes she could split herself in two—one person to take care of her private life, and one to focus on the job.

Time to hurry back to the station and get to grips with Pontus. Nothing is more important.

102

The walls of the interview room are as white as the rest of the police station.

Daniel glances at his watch; it is almost four o'clock. Time has flown since the fire this morning.

They are about to conduct the first formal interview with Pontus. Hanna is sitting beside him, reading a message on her phone. Her eyes are hidden by strands of hair that have escaped from her ponytail, but her complexion is gray with tiredness.

"What a day," she sighs, putting her phone away.

Daniel can only agree. He is still shaken by the attack on Anton, and wants nothing more than a little peace and quiet. However, that will have to wait. Right now he has to find fresh energy.

The working day is not yet over.

There is a knock on the door, and Pontus is brought in by a uniformed officer. Since his arrest he has been given something to eat and the opportunity to have a wash. His face is clean but chalk white, with dark shadows beneath his eyes.

Daniel points to the chair opposite. Pontus sits down slowly. He almost seems out of it, as if he can't quite grasp the difficult position in which he finds himself.

Hanna gives him an encouraging smile.

They have discussed their tactics in advance, and decided on the tried-and-tested good cop–bad cop scenario. It is Daniel's task to play hard, while Hanna will provide consolation and establish contact.

It feels kind of old fashioned to opt for what some may see as outdated gender stereotypes, but it works surprisingly often.

Hanna reads out the usual introductory information for the benefit of the tape recorder. Pontus's full name and ID number, names of other persons present, and finally the crimes of which he is suspected.

"Things aren't looking good for you," Daniel begins. "I hope for your sake that you're prepared to cooperate; otherwise you really will be in a mess."

"What you have done means that you risk many years in jail," Hanna adds, but in a much kinder tone of voice. Her face shows nothing but sympathy, conveying the impression that she has Pontus's best interests at heart, and understands the gravity of his situation.

Pontus closes his eyes.

From a purely formal point of view, he has the right to remain silent and to have a lawyer present, but Daniel is hoping they will be able to carry out the interview without Pontus demanding legal representation. Otherwise they won't be able to proceed until tomorrow, and they would probably have to transfer him to Östersund; there is unlikely to be anyone locally who could step in.

Which would make everything more difficult.

Pontus opens his mouth, but nothing comes out. His lips are pale, and it looks as if he has been chewing them. A strangled sound emerges from his throat, something between a low groan and a sob.

Is he about to break down, after everything that has happened?

This wouldn't necessarily be a disadvantage. Daniel just wants to get to the truth, find out what has gone on at the house on Nedre

Svedjevägen over the past few days. It is hard to take in the remarkable series of events, let alone understand it.

"Would you like some water?" Hanna asks.

Pontus nods, and she pours him a glass, pushes it across the table. He takes several gulps, clutching the glass so tightly that his fingertips turn white. The stress seems to be eating him up from inside.

And maybe a guilty conscience?

"Shall we begin with Filippa's death?" Hanna says. "Can you tell me about your involvement?"

Daniel can hear that she is making a huge effort to sound compassionate, building up trust so that Pontus will relax and start talking. It is often a relief for a person to admit their part in a serious crime. Guilt plays on the mind of most people. There are very few—even among the most hardened criminals—who can live with what they have done in the long term.

In Pontus's case it will be even harder. He is young, and hasn't been in trouble before.

Meanwhile Daniel sits with his arms folded, a threatening reminder that he is going nowhere, while Hanna leads the questioning in a gentler tone.

Daniel is convinced that this is the best tactic to elicit a confession.

Pontus draws a ragged breath.

Then he opens his mouth.

103

"I had nothing to do with Filippa's death," Pontus says hoarsely. "I swear I didn't touch her, not then."

His words strike Hanna as odd. *Not then?*

"So did you try it on with Filippa on another occasion?" She adjusts the tape recorder so that it is right in front of Pontus.

His cheeks flush red.

"It was on the train to Åre."

"And what happened?"

"I'd had way too much to drink, and during the night, when Filippa had gone to bed in her bunk, I . . ."

"Go on," Daniel prompts him sharply.

"I . . . I climbed up, and I . . . touched her. It was nothing serious; I was lying on top of the covers. I just wanted to . . . have a feel."

"Was Filippa happy to go along with that?" Hanna wonders.

"Not exactly." Pontus looks even more embarrassed. "I mean, she was asleep, I don't think she woke up."

"So you lay down next to a sleeping woman and started touching her body without her consent?" Daniel says.

He doesn't try to hide his contempt, and Hanna is equally disgusted. But she doesn't want to destroy the role-play, to risk the delicate balance they are attempting to build up.

What the hell is wrong with some young men, she thinks, striving to hide her anger. *Their view of women's bodies, the liberties they believe they can take.*

It is completely bizarre.

"It was only for a minute or two," Pontus says in his defense. "Filippa had her clothes on the whole time."

"And what happened next?" Hanna keeps her tone neutral.

"Someone woke up, I think it was Emil, and I didn't dare stay there. So I climbed down to my own bunk and went to sleep. The following day it was as if it had never happened. That's how it felt, anyway."

Daniel has had enough. "Did Filippa bring it up? Didn't she ask you what the hell you thought you were doing?"

"No. She never mentioned it. I don't know if she was aware of what was happening—like I said, she was asleep."

Hanna can't let this go. "Did you at least apologize?"

"No." Pontus looks down at the table. "I was too ashamed once I sobered up. I realized it wasn't okay. And then I started to panic and I was horrible to her. It was all so difficult."

"Okay," Hanna says. They need to move on, find out what happened on the night when Filippa died. "We'll leave that for now. Tell me about Saturday night. And Filippa."

104

The side room at the medical center is empty when Anton opens his eyes. It is dark outside the window; he must have slept for a while after the doctor had examined him.

He is exhausted and feels nauseous, but the doctor explained that this is to be expected following a concussion. His forehead is throbbing where it has been stitched, but it could have been so much worse. If the hammer had struck him slightly lower down, he could have lost the sight in his right eye.

The doctor has told him to take it easy for a few days; he can't go back to work until next week. Anton's instinct was to protest, but then he realized the doctor was right—as soon as he sat up, his field of vision contracted.

He looks for his phone, sees his jacket on the end of the bed, and removes the phone from his pocket with slow, careful movements.

The display shows that his sister, Karro, has tried to reach him several times. Presumably Mom has contacted her, and no doubt she has told her about yesterday's big argument.

Is Karro going to be dragged into this mess too?

Anton sighs, he can't deal with this now, not the way he's feeling. He will talk to his sister later.

He checks his messages, half hoping for a text from Hanna, an update on the case. He wants to know how it's gone, whether Pontus has broken down and confessed, but she hasn't been in touch.

Nor has Daniel.

Most of all he would have loved for Carl to have answered his message about meeting up this evening, but there is nothing. Anton's pride prevents him from asking again. It is how it is between them, he just has to accept that.

There is a knock on the door, and a gray-haired nurse comes in. His name badge reveals that he is Dario.

"How are you doing?"

"I'm starting to feel a little better," Anton replies with a forced smile, even though he really doesn't feel too good.

"I've just spoken to the doctor," Dario says. "We're sending you to the hospital in Östersund, where you'll be kept in for observation for twenty-four hours. We're just organizing the transfer by ambulance."

Anton would much rather go home, but there is no point in arguing. After all, it's not as if Carl is waiting for him in Duved.

"Do you have a friend or relative who can bring in a toothbrush and other bits and pieces before you go?"

Anton can't contemplate calling his parents and asking them to fetch his toilet bag. He doesn't want to speak to Karro either. And contacting Carl is out of the question. He refuses to beg and ask for his help just because he's been injured; at least he can spare himself that humiliation.

"Maybe I can borrow what I need at the hospital," he says, closing his eyes and sinking back on the pillow.

He never thought he would feel this lonely again.

105

Pontus presses his chin down toward his chest. His cheeks are puffy and sallow.

"Enough," Daniel says in a tone that makes it clear it's time to be honest. "Was it you who had sex with Filippa before she died?"

A shake of the head.

"But you know who it was?" Hanna says.

"I . . . I *think* so. Or maybe not . . ."

His voice dies away. The evasive answer tests Daniel's already dwindling patience. *Give us a proper answer!* he wants to yell, but he knows there is a limit to how unpleasant he can be.

The most important thing is to get the truth out of Pontus.

Hanna, with her gentler approach, has a better chance of succeeding. He lets her take over.

"In that case I think you should tell us, once and for all," she says.

Pontus looks troubled. He tucks his hands beneath his thighs, like some kind of buffer between his body and the chair.

"Pontus? Talk to us."

"On Saturday, Emil and Olivia went to bed soon after midnight. William too; there was only Amir, Filippa, and me left in the living room." His voice is little more than a whisper as he continues: "Filippa was in love with Amir, everyone knew that. But Amir didn't seem particularly interested, even though she was offering herself to him on a plate. She was drunk and high; she could barely stand up. They sat next to each other on the sofa, making out during the evening, but in the end it was as if Amir had had enough. He said good night and went off to his room."

Pontus glances at the window. Darkness has fallen during the interview, and large snowflakes are falling. Snow has landed on the windowsill, forming a white, irregular pattern.

"Filippa was devastated. It was obvious she'd been hoping Amir would ask her to go up to the loft with him, and that they'd spend the night together. But Amir didn't care; he just left. Filippa was really upset; I could see her fighting to hold back the tears."

"So what did you do then?"

"Not much. I was nearly as drunk as she was; I could hardly speak. But then the door of William's room opened, and he came out wearing his robe. And he . . . he put his arms around Filippa, and then . . ."

"And then?"

"Then he slept with her."

Daniel is taken by surprise. He can see that Hanna is surprised too; she drops her pen.

If Pontus is telling the truth, then it was William who had sex with Filippa on Saturday. In which case it must have been his voice Olivia heard from the stairs, when one of the boys told the other to keep quiet about him and Filippa.

Pontus seems genuine; he doesn't look as if he's lying.

"Are you sure about that?" Daniel asks anyway.

"The walls between the rooms are very thin. I could hear . . . what they were doing."

"Why didn't you tell us this from the start?" Hanna says.

"Because . . . because William told me to keep my mouth shut. When Filippa's body was found in the snow the next day."

Pontus alters his position on the chair. He frees one hand, scratches his neck beneath his ear.

His eyes are darting all over the place.

"William was afraid you'd suspect him of being involved if you found out what he'd done. It wouldn't look good, and William isn't the kind of guy who wants to be dragged into a problem like that. It could affect his future, his entire career. He's already got it all planned. He's going to start working as a management consultant when he graduates."

Daniel shakes his head. William is only twenty; it's crazy to have your whole life mapped out at that age. And who the hell wants to do a job like that?

He feels a stab of pain in his heart as he remembers the article about Hanna and Henry Sylvester. The well-known financier also started out as a management consultant back in the day. Now he is richer than most people in Sweden.

And he is with Hanna.

"William needs a perfect résumé," Pontus explains.

"What do you think?" Hanna asks. "Is he so perfect that he couldn't possibly have anything to do with Filippa's death?"

"No idea." Pontus shrugs. "I fell asleep before she came out of his room. When I woke up a bit later, there was no one around." He gives them a pleading look. "It's true. I don't know what happened, maybe they started arguing and it all went wrong."

Daniel doesn't give much for his assurances. It remains to be seen whether Pontus is a credible witness, but if it is true, then at least they know who was with Filippa before she died.

It's a small step forward.

If William had been honest from the start, they would have saved a great deal of time.

"Was that why you carried out those online searches?" Hanna says.

"I was scared you'd come for me if you found out what I'd done. That I'd lied for William's sake."

"Are you afraid of him?"

"It's hard to explain." Pontus's head droops. "It's like . . . you do whatever he tells you. Everyone does, it's not just me."

His tone gives away how powerless he feels. There is no doubt that Pontus realizes he gave in when he should have stood up for himself.

Hanna has been making notes even though they are recording the interview. Now she gives him a searching look.

"If we move on and accept that you didn't have anything to do with Filippa's death . . . what made you start the fire at the cabin when Olivia and Emil were sleeping in there?"

"But I didn't."

Daniel can't keep quiet any longer. "Do you seriously expect us to believe that you attacked Emil and tried to strangle him in front of everyone, but that it wasn't you who started the fire later that same night?"

"It wasn't me!" Desperation makes Pontus almost scream the words. "I'm not a murderer!"

"So who was it?"

"I don't know, but I had nothing to do with it!"

"Why did you take off if you were innocent?" Hanna asks. "You must see that it's a cause for concern."

"Because I realized how it would look." Pontus sounds resigned. "You'd seen the search history on my laptop, and you were suspicious. It's true that I attacked Emil, but I wasn't myself at the time. I'd drunk way too much, and I was angry; I never would have done it otherwise. And then I was woken up in the middle of the night by the flames and the firefighters. I knew you'd accuse me, and I panicked. All I could think of was getting away."

"And you thought it was a good idea to break into a neighbor's garage?" Daniel says.

"It wasn't locked," Pontus counters.

Daniel has no intention of arguing over semantics. They passed that stage long ago. If Pontus thinks this is a grammar lesson, he is very wrong.

"Call it what you like. You entered someone else's property without permission."

"I just needed a place to hide. I didn't have time to think; there was no plan."

Pontus scratches the back of one hand, so hard that long white marks appear.

Daniel glances at the clock. They have been going for over an hour, and he is starting to feel stressed. He needs to collect Alice from preschool very soon. The truth is he's already late and ought to message Ida or her mom and ask if they can step in at short notice.

No doubt Ida will make the most of the opportunity to score points off him yet again, but he has no choice. Discreetly he takes out his phone and sends her a quick text.

"What did you think when our colleague tracked you down?" Hanna asks.

"I was terrified. And when I saw that he had a gun in his hand, I thought he was going to shoot me. My brain kind of froze."

"So you decided to attack him with a hammer." Daniel slips his phone back into his pocket. "You do realize you could have killed him?"

"I didn't mean to hurt him."

"You didn't mean to hurt him? Seriously?"

Daniel has no time for Pontus's excuses. He might be young, but surely he has to take some responsibility for his actions.

Hanna gives Daniel a warning look, as if she realizes that he is about to explode. She has seen him lose his temper on other occasions, and it has rarely had a positive outcome.

Learning to control himself is one of the things he has focused on during those expensive therapy sessions.

"Please explain," Hanna says to Pontus.

"All I wanted was to get away. I was terrified when he came into the garage. I never meant for the hammer to hit him on the head—I was trying to knock the gun out of his hand so he couldn't shoot me."

"You assaulted a police officer," Daniel says coldly. "The hammer struck his forehead. It's pure luck that he hasn't ended up blind in one eye."

"I'm sorry," Pontus whispers.

Daniel leans back on his chair. He can't fit the pieces together. Pontus has told them that William was the one who had sex with Filippa, but he is denying everything else. If he wasn't responsible for Filippa's death or the fire, then it must be someone else.

One thing is clear, in any case.

They need to bring in William right away. If he lied about having slept with Filippa, then he isn't as innocent as he would like to appear.

106

A patrol car has been sent to Sadeln to bring William in, and in the meantime Hanna has ordered pizzas from Werséns. There was an extra-long waiting time, presumably because of all the students in the village.

She is sitting in the kitchenette at the station with Daniel, hoping to find fresh energy by loading up on carbs. The harsh fluorescent lighting gives her quattro stagioni an almost artificial appearance.

Raffe has joined them for an update while they eat.

Hanna shovels down two-thirds of her pizza while Daniel summarizes the interview with Pontus, who has now been placed on remand following a decision by the prosecutor in Östersund. They have ninety-six hours before he must be arrested or released.

"So what do you think?" she asks Daniel when he's finished. "Do we believe him, or not?"

Daniel is carefully cutting up his pizza into small pieces and eating it with a knife and fork. Enjoying his food instead of shoveling it down. Perhaps his Italian heritage on his mother's side is showing through.

Hanna is using her hands as cutlery.

"If he's innocent," she adds before Daniel can speak, "who's responsible for Filippa's death and the fire? Or could we be looking at two different perpetrators?" She breaks off a piece of the crust with her fingers. "What if we're wrong, and it wasn't the same person?"

She had already been thinking along those lines, but then it seemed as if Pontus was both the killer and the arsonist. However, after the interview she has her doubts. Pontus claims that William was the one who had sex with Filippa, and that Pontus had nothing to do with either the murder or the fire.

Which makes Hanna uncertain.

Could it be that William is involved in the murder, while Pontus was behind the fire? Or is Pontus actually telling the truth, which might mean that William is responsible for both crimes?

Nothing is clear.

"We need better forensic evidence," Raffe points out. "At the moment there's nothing to link anyone to either incident."

"Let's see what Carina finds," Daniel says.

She has just messaged to say that the report on the house search is ready, but as she didn't contact them earlier, Hanna doubts that it will contain any new information. And if they have to wait for the results of DNA testing or other biological traces, it will take months.

She wipes her mouth with a napkin and realizes that she hasn't told Raffe about the external security cameras. She contacted the company earlier and left a message saying that the police need to know as a matter of urgency if any of the footage is saved.

She quickly fills Raffe in on her hopes that the company might be able to help them move forward. "With a bit of luck we should hear from them tomorrow," she concludes.

"It would be fantastic if someone or something has been captured on camera," Raffe says.

"Absolutely," Daniel says with a nod. "I don't think I've ever been involved in a case where we've had so little to go on."

"Any more information on Staffan Berg?" Hanna asks Raffe.

The indoor fan is humming faintly in the background, and the smell of detergent lingers in the air following the janitor's visit at about five o'clock.

"I've seen screenshots from his phone. They show that he got an alarm call about the cabin late on Sunday evening, so that's true. I've also checked out his background, and he's clean. He doesn't have any kind of record, and he pays his taxes. No complaints against his company."

"So everything seems to be in order?"

"Looks that way. The company provides for him and his wife, who takes care of the admin and bookkeeping. Sometimes she helps out with cleaning jobs." Raffe checks his watch, then picks up his jacket from the back of the chair. "Sorry, but I have to make a move—I'm already late. We're going to Nilla's parents' for dinner."

Hanna considers this new information. Maybe Staffan Berg is an exemplary citizen who just happens to have an alarm app and the key code for a property where serious crimes have been committed.

But it's still too early to rule him out altogether.

"I think we should bring him in for another interview," she says with her mouth full. "As soon as possible."

Raffe is on his way out. "I can do that tomorrow. Sorry, but I really do have to go now."

The door closes behind him. Hanna finishes off her pizza as her thoughts return to the house on Nedre Svedjevägen.

"I can't understand how none of the five friends have seen anything that can help us. Two such serious crimes, and not a single eyewitness. It's as if they're all blind and deaf."

"That's not entirely true," Daniel points out. "We still have Karin Carlsson, who was up on Saturday night."

"That's not enough." Hanna's frustration is clear in her voice. "She didn't see the perpetrator's face clearly enough to be able to make an identification."

"That's true, but at least we've cut down the number of suspects. This case seems to center on two people: Pontus and William." Daniel puts his knife and fork down neatly on his plate. "Things should make more sense once we've questioned William."

Hanna thinks they ought to question Amir as well. Push him on what he knows. But they have to prioritize William. There are only twenty-four hours in a day, and with Anton in hospital they just don't have the resources.

"Even if William is behind the murder, we still have to be able to prove who started the fire," Hanna says. She finishes off her Coca-Cola, grimacing at its tepid sweetness. "Pontus definitely had a motive, given the attack on Emil. But he categorically denies it. William has lied about having sex with Filippa, and insists that he had nothing to do with her death. And Amir seems prepared to do anything in order to protect William."

She closes her eyes for a few seconds, tries to suppress the sense of hopelessness, the feeling of treading water.

For three long days they have searched for connections and patterns that might not even exist. Every time they think they understand how it all hangs together, something doesn't quite fit.

She pushes her plate away with such force that it knocks over the empty Coke can. She gives Daniel a resigned look.

"How are we going to get those kids to confess when they all just keep denying everything?"

107

They don't start interviewing William until seven o'clock.

Daniel thinks he looks furious more than anything when he is led into the room by a colleague. Unlike Pontus, who resembled a dog that was terrified of being beaten when he was brought in.

William is of a completely different caliber—a young man who has grown up on the sunny side of society, with everything that brings with it in terms of privilege, security, and confidence. In his world the police do not automatically evoke distrust. Quite the reverse: he and his ilk expect positive discrimination and special treatment because they pay high taxes and therefore, in principle, are paying police officers' wages. His parents are currently on a flight home from New York, heading straight to Åre so they can inform Birgitta Grip what the police may and may not do with their son.

Let's see how that goes, Daniel thinks.

William sits down with a mulish look on his face while Hanna switches on the tape and records the relevant details.

"Where's my phone?" he demands as soon as she's finished. "You can't just take it."

Hanna pushes a glass toward him without commenting on his assertion. "Would you like some water?" she asks with her hand on the carafe.

"I want to speak to my father. I'm entitled to a phone call. You can't deny me that."

"You've been watching too much TV," Daniel says. "That's not how the law works in Sweden. There is no automatic right to call anybody. However, we can contact your family when we're done here to tell them we're holding you on remand. If *we* feel that is appropriate."

His directness makes William lose a little of his self-assured attitude.

"I haven't done anything."

"You lied to the police," Hanna points out. "We've spoken to you and questioned you on several occasions, and not once did you tell us that it was you who had sex with Filippa on the night before she died." She doesn't raise her voice, but what she says clearly hits home. William stares down at the table.

"I know I have the right to a lawyer," he says.

"That's correct," Daniel replies. "And if you want legal representation, a lawyer will be appointed for you. In which case we will have to end the interview now and wait until we can find someone who is available. Let's hope we can do that by tomorrow or the next day. In the meantime you will be held in custody. There's a well-used plastic mattress on the floor that you're welcome to sleep on. It might smell of vomit and urine, but I'm told you get used to it . . ."

Daniel doesn't take his eyes off William. If he thinks he's going to get away with his unpleasant attitude, he is very wrong.

Everyone is equal before the law.

"Or you could start by answering our questions," Hanna suggests. "Then we can make a decision about what happens next—whether you need to stay here overnight or not."

William pushes back his hair from his forehead, considerably less bumptious than when he walked in.

"What do you want to know?" he mutters.

108

And then there were three.

The quotation from Agatha Christie is going around and around in Olivia's head. She is sitting at the table with Amir and Emil, poking at her food, goulash from a couple of cans that they heated up in a pan.

Not even Emil had the energy to cook after the latest events.

In a way Olivia is relieved that William isn't here, but at the same time it feels surreal. The whole day has been like a bad dream.

Emil picks up his bowl and carries it over to the sink.

"I'm going to bed," he says, and disappears down the stairs.

Olivia glances at Amir. They haven't been alone in the same room since she hurled all those accusations at him during that terrible breakfast. It feels as if half a lifetime has passed since then.

She ought to apologize. Since the police came for William, it's obvious who was who in the unpleasant conversation she happened to overhear. Amir must have been trying to persuade William to admit to the police what he'd done.

She swallows nervously. "Listen, I'm sorry for what I said to you the other day."

Amir seems to have been lost in his own thoughts, because he gives such a start that some of his soup spills onto the table.

"What did you say?"

"I'm sorry for accusing you of being involved in Filippa's death. I was wrong, I should never have said that to you."

For the first time since this all began, Amir's expression softens a little when he looks at Olivia. He gives her a look that is not full of distaste.

"It was horrible," he says. "I couldn't believe it when you went for me like that—and in front of everyone else."

Olivia doesn't know what she can say to fix things. She really does regret her outburst, but she has been shocked and confused ever since Filippa was found dead in the snow, she has had so many weird thoughts about different people.

"Why didn't you stick up for yourself?" she asks eventually. "Why didn't you just tell me I was wrong?"

"It's not that simple . . ."

Amir looks away, and gradually Olivia begins to make sense of it all.

This is about William.

Of course.

"Because you knew what William had done to her," she says slowly. "And you were trying to protect him." It is a statement, not a question. "You knew all along that he was the one who had slept with Filippa."

Her voice is stronger now. She hears her own words, but she still doesn't get it. Why would her best friend have slept with Olivia's boyfriend?

She reminds herself that Filippa was drunk and high. She probably didn't even know what she was doing. Maybe she was so mad at Amir because he'd dumped her in the middle of the night that she tried to get back at him by having sex with William?

Olivia will never know the answer.

Amir interrupts her train of thought.

"It wasn't just that," he says in a toneless voice. "I saw them together in the snow too. Afterward."

He wipes up the spilled soup with his paper napkin. Rubs away at the surface of the table as if he dare not look at Olivia.

She tries to understand, but she is too exhausted.

"What do you mean?" she says after a long silence. "Saw them doing what?"

Amir puts down the napkin, but continues to avoid making eye contact.

"I heard them having sex; you know how thin the walls are. Then later, during the night, I woke up when Filippa was leaving. She was arguing with William, and I heard her yell at him before she took off."

He falls silent, swallows hard. Olivia is afraid of what is coming next.

"I couldn't get back to sleep. For some reason I got up and went over to the window. My room faces the front, and . . ."

"And?" Olivia prompts him.

"And I saw Filippa lying there in the snow. William was kneeling beside her, I could see the back of his head, his dark hoodie." Amir's face crumples. "She was still there the next morning. Dead."

Olivia reaches out and places her hand on his.

"You have to tell the police."

"I can't," Amir whispers.

"We'll call them. Right now. William is at the station being interviewed."

"I can't betray my best friend." Amir lets out a strangled sob. "You can't say anything to anyone. Promise!"

Olivia starts to shiver; her fingers are ice cold. The truth is worse than she could possibly have imagined. William is not only a liar and an asshole, he is a murderer too. He slept with Filippa even though he was Olivia's boyfriend. More or less.

First he exploited Filippa; then he killed her.

Olivia has to swallow several times to stop herself from vomiting up the soup.

"You have to tell the police what you saw," she says, trying to sound calm and convincing even though her head is all over the place.

"I can't."

"If you don't tell them, I will."

"No!"

Amir grabs Olivia by the shoulders, shakes her hard. She sees sheer desperation in his wide-open eyes.

"If you do that I'll kill myself."

109

They have been interviewing William for over an hour and have gotten precisely nowhere. Daniel is dangerously close to losing his temper when William insists yet again that he had nothing to do with either Filippa's death or the fire.

"You had sex with Filippa late on Saturday night," Daniel says in an accusatory tone. "You were the last person to see her alive. And yet you want us to believe that you didn't kill her. Do you think we're completely stupid?"

"It wasn't me," William repeats.

He looks tired, but the stubborn expression remains unchanged.

"You lied about the fact that the two of you slept together, in spite of being questioned on more than one occasion. Why should we believe you now?" Daniel says.

"Wouldn't it be nice to tell the truth?" Hanna says gently. "I promise you'll feel better as soon as you get it off your chest."

William clamps his lips together. He is angry and on the defensive.

"You're simply prolonging the agony by not admitting what you did," Daniel points out. "We can sit here all night if you want, but it would be better if you told us how it happened; then we can call a halt for the evening and let you rest."

"We already know you followed Filippa and pressed her face down into the snow until she stopped breathing," Hanna adds.

William gives a start. "I'm not a murderer!"

"But, William," Hanna says quietly. "If it wasn't you, then who was it?"

"I've explained what happened." William raises his chin. "We had sex, and then I asked her to leave. She got mad and stormed out of my bedroom, and that was the last time I saw her alive. I heard the front door slam, and I assumed she'd gone back to the cabin. Then there she was the next morning, just lying in the snow."

"Can't you see how bad this looks?" Daniel pauses for a moment. "Why did you do it?"

"What is it you don't get?" William hisses. "I didn't kill Filippa!"

He waves his hand with such force that he knocks over the glass, and water goes all over the table. Daniel grabs a few paper napkins and mops up the worst of it.

William stares at the wall, making no attempt to help. He doesn't seem to be softening under pressure. Quite the reverse—his expression is belligerent, and he keeps repeating the same answers like a parrot.

It is almost nine o'clock. Daniel glances at Hanna. They have tried every possible angle to try to get William to admit the truth. Are they going to get much further tonight?

The air in the interview room is warm and stuffy. Daniel's eyes feel like sandpaper. Maybe it would be better to stop now, make a fresh attempt tomorrow?

Somehow they have to find a way of breaking William's resistance, but right now he has no idea how they are going to do that.

110

Fifteen pounds of pure love comes barreling toward Hanna when she steps over the threshold of her little gingerbread house.

It is almost like having a dog, given the enthusiasm with which Morris is rubbing against her legs. He is purring like a tractor.

"Hello, sweetheart." She makes a fuss of him before heading for the kitchen, her clothes covered in cat hair.

It has been an incredibly long day. And deeply unsatisfying. She longs for Henry; she would love to sink into his warm embrace and simply shut out the rest of the world for a while, but he is almost four hundred miles away in Stockholm.

Because she interrupted their vacation in order to throw herself into the new investigation.

Her body is throbbing with exhaustion. She has worked for almost seventeen hours nonstop, and she can barely stay on her feet. And still they are getting nowhere.

It has proved impossible to break William, at least not this evening. Both he and Pontus are spending the night at the station, but without more evidence they will have to release William tomorrow. They have no forensics to connect him to the murder, and no witnesses who can place him at the scene of the crime.

Karin Carlsson's statement is not enough.

They will have to try again in the morning.

Hanna takes out milk, cocoa, and sugar. She mixes a mug of chocolate, and while it is heating up in the microwave, she puts fresh food and water in Morris's bowls.

She is tired and shivery, but still buzzing. It is going to be hard to get to sleep, even though she has to get up at six thirty and needs to be rested.

She must get a few hours' sleep tonight; otherwise she is going to collapse.

She takes her drink into the bedroom and crawls beneath the covers. It is twenty to ten; she ought to call Lydia. She really doesn't want to, but a promise is a promise.

She picks up her phone and reads through the texts that have arrived during the day. A sweet message from Henry warms her heart. Karro has also been in touch, saying that she knows it must have been difficult with all the online articles, and telling Hanna to call if she needs to talk. Hanna types a quick reply thanking her for her kindness. She also asks if Karro knows anyone who might be able to help Daniel with childcare.

Then there are way too many messages from nosey gossip columnists. There are even inquiries from overseas, wanting a comment about her and the well-known financier.

Hanna finds the contrast with the ongoing investigation upsetting. Filippa, who was only nineteen years old, has lost her life, but these people couldn't care less. In a way it's good that the media haven't shown a prurient interest in the case as they have with other homicides, but at the same time the obsession with Hanna's relationship with Henry feels inappropriate.

She sips her hot chocolate; it calms her and makes everything seem a little better. It is a reminder of another life, skiing in the early spring sunshine, waffles in a café by the slopes, relaxing days on the piste, far away from brutal murders and troublesome journalists.

A heavy thud at the foot of the bed tells her that Morris has followed her from the kitchen. Full and contented, he picks his way across the covers and settles himself on Hanna's stomach. She tries to shuffle him to one side, and after some compromising he ends up right next to her ribs. This means they have physical contact, but without her internal organs being squashed.

Morris is purring loudly and happily. Maybe she should stick with him as her life partner? She scratches him beneath his chin, and he stretches his neck so that she can reach the perfect spot.

Hanna has never had a successful long-term relationship. They have always ended in tears and disaster. Christian's betrayal still hurts; she has never felt as worthless as she did on the day when she found out he had been seeing Valérie behind her back for months.

The odds on her relationship with Henry going wrong are also overwhelming. He just doesn't know it yet. Or maybe he is so used to getting what he wants that he hasn't considered an alternative outcome.

While she is too afraid, too damaged to give him a decent chance.

Will she ever be able to love for real again?

Morris bumps her nose with his head, as if he wants to distract her from such upsetting thoughts. True love and devotion shine from his eyes, and this is a love she can definitely return.

Time to call Lydia.

Hanna finishes her chocolate and clicks on her sister's number, secretly hoping that Lydia has switched off her phone and gone to bed.

"At last!" Lydia says, as if she has been sitting there waiting for Hanna to call. "I want to hear all about your new boyfriend!"

Hanna closes her eyes. "There isn't much to tell."

"Nonsense. Start talking."

Hanna does her best to explain when she and Henry first met, and how the relationship has developed since last spring. Why she tried to keep a low profile initially, and above all why she hasn't said a single word about him to anyone, including Lydia.

She does not, however, mention Daniel or how her feelings toward him have affected the situation. Lydia doesn't know anything about that part.

It's too embarrassing. Hanna hasn't revealed to anyone that she has had forbidden feelings for her colleague for a long time.

"He sounds fantastic," Lydia says. "Almost too good to be true—a financier with a conscience."

"That's because of his previous career," Hanna clarifies. "He says he needs to make up for a number of things."

They haven't talked about it in detail, but Henry has hinted that he probably pushed the boundaries in certain situations when he was building up his fortune. Now he is trying to do better, and among other things has set up a foundation that works to keep the Baltic Sea clean. The foundation takes up a great deal of his time these days. Henry is putting both his energy and his money into various initiatives aimed at improving the water quality of the sea on which Sweden is so dependent.

"I like the fact that he's intending to leave the majority of his fortune to a climate organization when he dies," Lydia says. "Instead of the whole lot going to his sons so they can live it up on the French Riviera."

"Have you been checking him out?" Hanna asks with a smile. Her eyelids are getting heavy, she needs to end the call and get a few hours' sleep.

"Of course I have."

Of course you have, Hanna thinks, unable to suppress a yawn. Lydia never leaves anything to chance; it's not in her nature. Especially not when it comes to her troublesome little sister.

"Is this the real thing?" Lydia asks.

Hanna is taken aback.

"Are you in love with him?" her sister goes on before Hanna has the chance to speak.

Is she?

Hanna doesn't know what she is most afraid of—asking herself that question, or giving the answer out loud.

"He asked if I want to move in with him," she offers instead. "When we were in Niehku at the weekend."

Lydia inhales sharply. "Wow—so it's serious, in other words?"

"Yes. Yes, I guess it is."

Hanna sees Henry's handsome face in her mind's eye, the tenderness in his voice when he brought up the subject. She thinks about his carefully chosen birthday present, which is in its box on the nightstand because she doesn't want to wear the bracelet to work.

She really, really likes him.

And yet something is holding her back.

Is it because she is afraid of being hurt again? Because she can't forget Christian's deception?

Or is it still all about Daniel?

WEDNESDAY

111

For the first time in several days, the sky is clear above the Åre valley as Hanna sets off for work on Wednesday morning.

All the storm clouds have disappeared, and instead a glowing white half-moon hangs above the mountain known as Renfjället, lighting her way as she heads down the steep hill in the direction of Kurortsvägen and the police station. The thermometer was showing minus twenty-three Celsius when she opened the front door, but the cold is dry and fresh. The short walk clears her head. She slept for eight hours, and her strength has returned after the challenges of yesterday.

A small forest hare skitters across the road when she has only a few hundred yards to go.

Daniel turns into the parking lot as she arrives. He doesn't live far away and can easily walk to work, but today he is driving. His face is grim when he opens the car door, and the sight of Hanna plodding toward him through the snow doesn't seem to improve his mood.

Her first thought is that he must have seen the articles about her and Henry. Her stomach contracts. She should have said something to him a long time ago, explained the situation.

"Good morning," she calls out, raising a hand in an uncertain greeting.

Daniel gives a start, and his expression softens when he sees Hanna—she assumes he hadn't actually noticed her before. It is still dark, and the street lighting is sparse; the sun won't rise for a few hours.

"Hi." Hanna can't bring herself to ask how he is. "Everything okay?"

Daniel presses the key, and the doors lock with a click.

"Could be better." He gives himself a shake. "Ida was furious yesterday. She had to take care of Alice even though it was my turn to pick her up—you know how late it was when we finished interviewing William. I'm not exactly in her good books."

He kicks out at a pile of snow, sending crystals whirling through the air as he holds up his phone.

"She messaged this morning to say that Alice was upset because she was the last one left at preschool, so they probably don't think much of me either."

"I get it," Hanna says.

So it's not about her and Henry at all. She is ashamed of her selfish reaction, but at the same time she can't help feeling relieved.

"Ida will get over it," she says. "Shared custody isn't easy—there are often problems."

As if Hanna would know—she only has a big, fluffy cat to take care of.

"By the way, I texted Karro yesterday and asked if she knows anyone who can help out with Alice."

"Thanks." This doesn't seem to cheer Daniel up very much.

"Anyway, I'm really grateful that you stayed for the interviews last night," she says, hoping to boost his mood. "It wouldn't have worked without you. Just so you know."

This time he barely reacts. Hanna does understand how difficult it is for him, being torn between work and his responsibility for Alice. He has told her about the hours of therapy, how he is fighting to be a better father. And yet he still blames himself for everything that goes wrong.

It's typical of Daniel—he is always ready to accept responsibility, and never blames anyone else.

Hanna would like to tell Ida to pull herself together. They are in the middle of a homicide investigation, and Daniel's input is indispensable. Sometimes a murder victim has to take precedence over the task of dropping off and picking up a child from preschool.

But it is not Hanna's place to lecture Daniel's ex.

They set off toward the entrance in silence, with Daniel a few steps ahead. Their breath forms white clouds in the air with each step.

Hanna would love to take Daniel's hand in hers and give it a consoling squeeze.

But how would that look?

112

Daniel is seething with anger as he returns to his office after the morning briefing with Grip and their colleagues in Östersund.

The prosecutor, a new guy that Daniel hasn't met before, refused to let them hold William any longer. His view was that they couldn't arrest him, because there was insufficient evidence. The fact that William had sex with Filippa and then lied about it wasn't enough for the arrogant little shit. *It's not illegal to sleep with someone,* as he put it.

When Daniel tried to put forward his standpoint, he was told that it was the police's task to obtain sufficient evidence.

"Don't blame me if you're not happy," the prosecutor said. "It's your job to prove that your suspicions are well founded."

Just as Daniel was about to launch into another argument, Grip had given him a warning look. *Enough,* it said. *Go and do your job.*

It's easy to sit in your ivory tower at the prosecutors' office and spend your time on legal niceties. *Welcome to reality,* Daniel wanted to yell.

Instead he didn't speak for the rest of the meeting.

Back in his office he slams the door so hard that the frame shakes. He knows he's overreacting, but he can't help it.

The thought of Hanna and her new boyfriend has haunted him all night, and Ida's whining text this morning was the last thing he needed.

He already feels guilty enough because he had to prioritize work over Alice yesterday.

And now they have to deal with that idiot prosecutor who has probably never won a single case.

If he were alone in the station, he would open the door and slam it again, but instead he has to content himself with sinking down in front of the computer and gritting his teeth.

There is a knock. A very tentative knock. Then Hanna opens the door a fraction and peers through the gap.

"Is it safe to come in, or do I need protective clothing? Your poor door will probably never be the same again . . ."

"Sorry. I was just so fucking furious with that prosecutor splitting hairs."

Hanna takes the chair opposite him. "To be fair, he's right. We don't have enough to hold William. There's nothing substantial, not a shred of forensic evidence linking him to either the murder or the fire."

Daniel tugs at his hair. "I know!"

Then he stops himself. He shouldn't be taking his bad temper out on Hanna. It's not her fault that the prosecutor is useless.

Or that Ida's text message ruined his morning.

He can't even blame her for her relationship with Henry Sylvester, and he has promised himself that he will treat that particular matter with the utmost professionalism. He has to; otherwise they won't be able to work together any longer.

"Sorry, I didn't mean to get so angry. It's just been a really shitty day, even though it's barely started."

In Hanna's eyes he sees sympathy and understanding. She has already forgiven him. She is fantastic in so many ways, and he can't even tell her that.

"Well, I might have some good news," she says, waving her phone at him. "I've just spoken to a guy at the security company. He called while we were in the meeting. They've tracked down the footage that's saved on their server from Nedre Svedjevägen 7."

Daniel's irritation is gone in a second. Could this be the breakthrough they've been waiting for?

"Footage from the nights in question?"

"Exactly. They're sending it over right away."

Hanna glances down the corridor.

"How about interviewing Pontus again in the meantime? I'd really like to push him on the fire. I mean, it has to be him—who else could it be?"

113

Pontus is pale and drawn when he is brought into the interview room. He doesn't look as if he slept particularly well on the plastic mattress in the custody suite. He is wearing the same clothes as yesterday and gives off an acrid smell of sweat as he pulls out the chair opposite the two police officers.

He looks like a complete wreck.

Good, Hanna thinks. It might make him more inclined to tell the truth about the fire. She is growing heartily sick of all the denials and lies coming out of both William's and Pontus's mouths. After the previous day's interviews, she is leaning increasingly toward the theory of two different perpetrators, with William being behind Filippa's death, and Pontus responsible for setting fire to the cabin. Two different crimes, two different motives, but the one triggered the other, hence the connection.

Something tells her that Pontus is lying about the fire. He had both motive and opportunity, and has shown his violent tendencies.

Plus he ran away.

It doesn't matter if he continues to deny everything—Hanna simply doesn't believe him. They just need to find enough evidence to make him confess.

"So how are you today?" she asks once the tape is running.

"Not great." Pontus picks at a cuticle, avoids meeting her gaze.

"I know it's not easy," she says with more sympathy in her voice than he deserves.

"We'd like to talk a little more about the arson attack on the cabin," Daniel says. "We had an interesting conversation with William. He denies any involvement in the fire, which leaves only you in the frame."

He is pushing the boundaries, but his assertion has the desired effect.

Pontus's face loses all its color, and he seems to be fighting back tears.

"Olivia and Emil were asleep in the cabin when the fire started," Hanna reminds him. "Do you realize what could have happened if Olivia hadn't woken up in time? They could both have died. A terrible, agonizing death in the flames."

"Two more homicide victims," Daniel adds. "That means a life sentence in jail."

"It wasn't me."

Pontus's words are barely audible, but Daniel doesn't let that stop him.

"There are three troubling facts as I see it. One, you were there on the night in question, which your friends will confirm in court. Two, you had a motive to harm Emil, whom you attacked earlier and tried to strangle with your bare hands. Three, you ran away from the scene of the crime immediately afterward and tried to hide." He holds up one finger at a time as he goes through the key points. Pontus recoils with each statement. "In my eyes you're in a real mess. And we haven't even started to discuss the fact that you are going to be charged with assaulting a police officer. Or the small matter of entering the neighbor's garage illegally."

Pontus is breathing with his mouth open.

"And you lied to us about William and Filippa," Hanna adds.

She can see that he is on the verge of breaking down. His face crumples; his lips are twitching. A night in custody often has a real impact.

Come on, Pontus. Time to tell the truth.

"Seriously—why should we believe you just because you claim you're innocent?" Daniel leans across the table. "Who else would have started the fire?" His harsh tone is gone. He sounds almost gentle as he places a hand on Pontus's arm. "Who else, if it wasn't you?"

"Talk to us, Pontus," Hanna says. "Trust me, you'll feel better. This must be very difficult for you to cope with all on your own. We do understand."

Pontus buries his face in his hands. "I didn't mean it," he mumbles through his fingers.

At last.

Hanna holds her breath as she hears the words, thick with tears. She signals to Daniel to give him some breathing space; it's better to allow Pontus to compose himself before they continue. She has no doubt that he is going to tell them everything now he has taken the first step.

"What happened that night?" she says after a pause. "What were you thinking?"

"I was so angry," Pontus snivels. "And drunk. I didn't know what I was doing. After the row with Emil, I just collapsed on my bed, but then I woke up and needed a piss. When I went past the laundry room on the way to the bathroom, I saw a bottle of lighter fluid on the bench by the sink . . ." His eyes are huge and full of fear as he continues: "I felt like I had to show them that they couldn't just ignore me. And somehow it felt good to see the cabin burning. I thought they'd all feel sorry for what they'd done, especially William; he treats me like shit. But then I heard Olivia screaming inside . . ."

"Two people were sleeping in the cabin," Daniel reiterates. "They could both have died in the flames."

"I know." Pontus's face contorts. "I didn't know that Olivia and Emil were in there. I swear on my mother's honor, on God, on my grandfather's grave. Emil had the room next to mine, and I thought Olivia was sleeping in the main house after everything that had happened. I would never have tried to kill them, never."

"Was that why you ran away?" Hanna asks.

Pontus sighs heavily. "The fire took hold so fast. I still don't understand how it spread so quickly. And then, when Olivia came running out with the extinguisher . . . I thought I'd die of shame, what if she saw me and realized what I'd done . . . So I just . . . ran. All I wanted to do was hide."

"That's why our colleague found you in the garage?"

When Pontus looks up, his expression is one of utter hopelessness. "I'm so ashamed of what I did to him. I never meant to hurt him so badly." He puts his elbows on the table and lowers his head. He is sobbing so hard that his entire body is shaking. Between the sobs comes a low groan: "What's going to happen to me now?"

114

Half an hour later Hanna is sitting in the conference room with Daniel and Raffe. At least they now know what lay behind the fire. It was a relief when Pontus finally broke down and confessed. Admittedly he is still denying any involvement in the murder, but on the other hand he also denied arson for a long time.

Hanna is counting on the footage from the security cameras to help them to make progress in the case. They need to find out who took Filippa's life.

Whether it was Pontus who attacked her.

Or William.

She has linked her computer to the big screen so that they won't miss any details. It transpired that the Löwengrens had cameras that both livestreamed and recorded when the motion sensors were activated, and could distinguish between human and animal activity. Thanks to a 135-degree field of vision, they have a range of up to fifteen feet.

The cameras are also adapted for night vision, so Hanna has high hopes as she clicks on the files she has received.

She opens the first one and a surprisingly sharp image fills the screen. It is from the camera above the patio door by the sauna. It seems as if the lens is slightly crooked. It doesn't cover the whole of the doorway, but it does show part of the yard in front of the house.

Is it enough?

Hanna tries to remember exactly where Filippa's body was found in relation to the position of the camera, but it's difficult.

Her eyes ache with concentration as the film continues. At first there is only darkness and snow, but then Filippa appears.

Hanna holds her breath.

She is clearly visible, staggering along on unsteady legs before sinking down in the snow in front of the house.

"Freeze it there," Daniel says.

Filippa is lying on the ground with her arms and legs outstretched, almost as if she is making a snow angel. It seems like her anger at William has passed; she looks happily drunk more than anything, as if she is enchanted by the beauty of the winter night.

Hanna doesn't understand.

"Look," Raffe says. "She's wearing her jacket and boots. And her jeans."

He is right. Filippa is fully dressed, not half-naked as she was when her body was found.

"Okay, let's see the rest." There is tension in Daniel's voice.

Hanna clicks on the trackpad and the film resumes.

A shadow pops up out of nowhere. A dark figure approaches Filippa and kneels down by her left-hand side.

"Who's that?" Raffe wonders.

It's impossible to tell. The figure is wearing a dark jacket with the hood pulled up. They can't make out the facial features, but Hanna thinks she sees a hint of a smile on Filippa's face, rather than anger.

That might suggest it's Pontus, because she had just had an argument with William. But it could also be Amir, or even Emil.

Unless William followed her outside in order to apologize, and Filippa was smiling because she was going to forgive him.

It's hopeless. Hanna feels like hurling her laptop at the wall. There is no way of telling who is concealed beneath the hood.

Suddenly the person leans forward, hiding Filippa from the camera. It looks as if he is lying on top of her, pressing her down into the snow, but they can't see exactly what is going on.

The shadows blend together, their outlines melting into one.

But Hanna knows that this is the moment when it happens.

The murder is being carried out right in front of them, and they can't intervene or lift a finger.

It is too late. Filippa is already dead.

After a few minutes the shadow moves back and stands up. Filippa is motionless now, with one cheek buried in the snow. The figure pulls off Filippa's jeans, jacket, top, and boots, leaving her half-naked.

He disappears from the screen, taking the items of clothing with him.

All that is left is Filippa's lifeless body.

The camera continues to film for a short while, then everything goes black.

Raffe is the first to speak.

"At least we know how she died." He takes a deep breath, almost fumbling for the right words. He is as deeply affected as Hanna by those terrible images. "She was definitely murdered."

Hanna doesn't know which is worse, the sense of impotence or disappointment. She had anticipated so much from the footage, thought it would give them the solution to the mystery.

The perpetrator's head on a plate.

Instead they have barely made any progress in the hunt for Filippa's murderer. All they have is an intangible shadow, an unidentifiable figure of darkness.

The frustration is like a dead weight in her chest.

How are they going to find him now?

115

A short while later they have watched all the footage twice more, including the material from above the patio door in slow motion. Daniel is determined that they will not miss a single detail; he has hardly blinked.

The film from the night of the fire shows a brief glimpse of Pontus, so they have the forensic evidence to confirm his guilt. But the fact remains that Filippa's murderer cannot be identified from the footage.

Daniel can see his own disappointment reflected in Hanna's eyes across the table.

"What about the IT guys in Östersund?" Raffe suggests. "Sometimes they can work miracles with this kind of material—pick out details that the human eye can't see."

"Good idea—we'll send everything over to them," Daniel agrees. "And ask them to work as fast as they can."

Hanna runs the footage of Filippa one more time. When they reach the frame where the perpetrator is most clearly visible, she freezes the image.

A dark jacket.

"Raffe, do you think the IT guys might be able to identify the jacket? If we knew what brand it was we could check it against William's and Pontus's outdoor clothing."

Daniel is staring at the screen, with the distinct feeling that something isn't right.

It looks like a perfectly ordinary padded jacket, but there are hundreds of dark-blue or black padded jackets in Åre. And even if they could see a label, that doesn't mean its owner is guilty of Filippa's murder.

They have to be able to prove that the perpetrator was wearing that particular jacket at the time of Filippa's death. It would be very easy for a defense lawyer to claim that someone else had borrowed it late at night. It doesn't necessarily have to be the same person.

He narrows his eyes, hoping to sharpen his focus.

The proportions are distorted; it's hard to tell how tall or short he is. Although he doesn't look as if he's as tall as Emil. Daniel is tending more toward Pontus, who is around five eight.

But they can't rule out William, even though he is taller. It is quite simply impossible to work out who it is from the footage.

Something is still bothering Daniel, but he can't quite get a hold of it. He stands up, moves closer to the screen, but it doesn't help.

"Run it again," he says to Hanna. "From the moment when Filippa appears."

By this time he knows the sequence by heart. Filippa staggers into view and sinks down onto the snow with a smile on her face. She spreads her arms and legs in a snow angel. Then a dark figure comes in from the left and kneels down by her side.

Suddenly he knows what doesn't fit.

Karin Carlsson's eyewitness statement.

"Freeze the image where the perpetrator appears."

Hanna does as he asks, and Daniel points to the screen.

"Look. Didn't Karin Carlsson say that the person she saw through the window seemed to be carrying something heavy?"

Hanna nods. "From what she said, it sounded as though the perpetrator was carrying Filippa's body. At least that was my interpretation."

"But that's not what the footage is showing." Daniel points to the image again. "Filippa was already lying in the snow. She got there under her own steam."

Hanna frowns.

"She was probably mistaken," Raffe says. "It was the middle of the night, and she'd only just woken up. She went to the kitchen to fetch a glass of water, if I remember correctly."

"It's still strange," Hanna says thoughtfully. "She expressed herself exactly like Daniel said."

"I think we should go and talk to her, just to be on the safe side," Daniel says. "We could take a look at William's and Pontus's jackets while we're there. See if either of them owns a black or dark-blue ski jacket."

116

Anton's head feels better when he is woken from his morning nap by a nurse coming into his room. She introduces herself as Marie-Louise before taking his blood pressure. She tells him it's looking pretty good, although it's still slightly low.

"We're planning on discharging you today," she says, rolling up the blood pressure cuff. "As soon as the doctor has time to see you."

"Are you very busy?"

"We're a little understaffed, and a bad skiing accident has just come in. A knee fracture."

Anton broke his arm near the elbow on the slopes when he was a teenager, competing in Duved. The pain was among the worst he has ever felt—indescribable. When the skeleton is damaged, the body goes into shock and thinks it is going to die.

He never wants to experience that again.

Marie-Louise sticks a digital thermometer in his ear. It beeps, and she informs him that his temperature is normal; then she checks the stitches in his forehead.

He shuffles a little farther up the bed.

"What time do you think I'll be discharged?"

"Like I said, as soon as the doctor has time to come and see you."

Good. He is feeling considerably better than yesterday, and really wants to get home to Duved. He has a great deal to think about.

The nurse gathers up her things. "By the way, your sister is waiting in the corridor, if you can cope with a visitor?"

Karro is here? In Östersund?

Anton can't work out how that has happened. He hasn't contacted his parents or her. But he can hardly turn Karro away if she has gone to the trouble of coming all the way here.

"That's fine," he says. "You can let her in."

A few moments later the door opens, and there stands his sister, who is two years younger than him, with her blond hair in a messy ponytail. As soon as their eyes meet, she bursts into tears.

"Hey, take it easy," Anton warns her as Karro hurls herself at him and flings her arms around him. She holds him tightly, and in the end he has to push her away so he can breathe.

"It's not so bad. I'm okay. I had a concussion and I needed a couple of stitches, that's all."

"You could have died."

"But I didn't. And I'm allowed to go home soon, when the doctor gets around to discharging me."

Karro dries her tears and takes off her jacket. She perches on the side of the bed, and Anton realizes she is going nowhere.

"I'll drive you."

"It could take a while."

"That's fine, I can wait."

Anton smiles at his stubborn sister. He's so glad to see her.

"How did you know I was here?"

"Hanna called me."

Of course she did. Karro and Hanna have been friends ever since Hanna moved to Åre—before her job was confirmed and she started working with Anton.

"Has that woman never heard of confidentiality?" he mutters. "Or loyalty to a colleague?"

"Don't be ridiculous."

Karro swipes him on the arm, and suddenly everything is back to normal. He much prefers this version of his sister to the crying, anxious one.

"Maybe you're not quite as badly hurt as I first thought," she goes on. "In which case can we talk about the elephant in the room?"

Anton considers playing dumb, pretending he has no idea what she's talking about.

But he is long past that stage.

"What do you want to know? You can ask me anything you want."

"Tell me about Carl."

117

The sunbeams make the frost-covered trees on the bend sparkle as Hanna turns off the E14 and drives up toward Sadeln. The ice shimmers in the frozen waterfalls on the hillside; the snow on the ground sparkles in the bright sunlight.

The Åre valley is shining.

However, today Hanna doesn't have the energy to care about the beauty of nature. She is still filled with disappointment over the footage from the security company. Maybe it was naive of her to believe that the case would be solved just like that, but she had really thought there would be a breakthrough.

The footage has been sent over to the IT department in Östersund, and all they can do is wait. With a bit of luck the team might be able to work their magic; otherwise she will have to accept that it's a dead end.

Daniel is sitting beside her, absorbed in reading a message on his phone. Probably just as well, given his attitude earlier. It's been a long time since he was in such a bad mood.

Although Hanna has to admit that she's glad she isn't the reason.

The road winds its way up the steep slope; she has to engage a lower gear for the last section as her mind continues to work overtime.

There is something about the Carlsson family that bothers her. Karin's statement doesn't hold up, and her son was reported to the police for sexual harassment. Hanna has read the original documentation, and the event played out exactly as Raffe had said.

Could this mean that Peter Carlsson was involved in Filippa's death? And if so, is his mother trying to protect him?

At the same time, it is a big step from sexual harassment to murder. Presumably Peter Carlsson is just a pathetic, grubby little man who can't keep his hands to himself when he's had too much to drink.

Hanna can't see how the pieces fit together, and her impatience makes her put her foot down a little too hard. She accelerates and takes the next bend so sharply that Daniel drops his phone. It lands by his feet with a clunk.

"What the hell are you doing?" he says, fumbling under the seat.

"Sorry, I was thinking about something else."

Hanna slows down and gives him an apologetic smile. She crawls through the center of Björnen and past the long-distance-skiing arena on the right. The parking lot is full—the fine weather has inspired lots of people to go skiing today.

"Where shall we start?" she says. "With the Carlssons to ask Karin about her witness statement, or at the Löwengren house to check the color of William's and Pontus's jackets?"

"If the Carlssons are home, let's go there first."

They have reached the turning for Sadeln, where two huge wall-like signs covered in slate rise up on either side of the road. *Sadeln* is printed in tall copper lettering with a welcoming gleam, but it doesn't make Hanna feel any better.

She drives into the area with a heavy heart and a thousand questions in her head.

How are they ever going to solve this case when they're getting nowhere?

118

A white car is parked outside the Carlssons' garage, which suggests that Åke and Karin are home.

Good, Daniel thinks. At least they ought to be able to get this cleared up before lunch. He follows Hanna to the front door and waits while she knocks.

"You again," Åke says when he answers. He is wearing pale-gray thermals and looks as if he has just come back from skiing.

Hanna manages a smile. "Can we come in? We have one or two more questions."

Åke steps back to let them in. Karin is standing at the kitchen island, making coffee. She is in ski clothes too, and her hair is tousled. The close-fitting thermal top reveals that she is in good shape, despite her age.

She looks surprised, but points to the coffee machine. "Can I offer you a cup?"

"Not for me, thanks." Daniel has already drunk too much coffee today, and this morning's bad temper has given him an acid stomach, which he probably deserves several times over.

Hanna also declines, and they sit down at the table while they wait for Karin to join them.

"What a performance yesterday!" Åke says. "Almost like a TV show. But I'll tell you one thing: I've distrusted those Löwengrens ever since they built that terrible house. I wish they'd sell up and leave Åre."

Daniel notes that neighborliness seems to be in short supply.

"You can't say that," Karin objects. "Why should we have anything against that particular family?" She gives her husband a reproachful look, as if he is embarrassing her in front of the two police officers.

"Those people have caused trouble ever since the first day they moved here," Åke replies. "You know that perfectly well—how often have we talked about it?"

"You're exaggerating."

"What's wrong with you today?" There is no mistaking the indignation in Åke's voice. He lifts his cup to his mouth and drinks, ends up with coffee at the corner of his lip but doesn't seem to notice. Then he turns his irritation on Daniel and Hanna.

"What is it this time? You've caught the murderer, haven't you? I saw one of the boys being led away in handcuffs. I assume he started the fire as well? Hoodlums, the lot of them."

"The thing is," Hanna begins, "we have a couple of questions about Karin's statement." She turns so that she is facing Karin. Daniel assumes she is hoping to avoid further comments from Karin's husband. She flicks through her notebook and opens it at a page covered in writing.

"So when we spoke to you the other day, you said you'd seen someone moving around during the night close to where Filippa's body was found the next day. You told us that this person was wearing dark clothing that blended in with the surroundings, and you also said that you assumed it was a man, even though you didn't see his face."

Karin listens attentively without interrupting. She seems much more inclined to be helpful than her husband.

"That's correct. And it was the posture that made me think it wasn't a woman—I can't explain it any better."

Hanna gives her an encouraging smile, but Daniel wonders where she is going with her questions. Why hasn't she mentioned the footage from the security cameras? Is she intending to go through Karin's statement line by line before she gets to the point? That could take forever, and they have other things to do today. He tries to catch her eye, but she ignores him.

"You also said it looked as if the person in question was carrying something heavy?"

"That's right."

"Could it possibly have been the body of the young woman who died?" Hanna gives Karin a few extra seconds, then adds, "It's important that you try to remember exactly what you saw. Every detail could be crucial. All that matters is that we get it right."

Karin closes her eyes, then nods thoughtfully. "It was very dark, but I'm sure that's what happened. Obviously I can't swear to everything, but the more I think about it, the more clearly I can picture it." She wraps her hands around her coffee cup, frowns as she concentrates hard. "The person I saw was probably carrying the girl when he appeared. I'm almost sure of it."

"And what did he do then?"

Daniel hears a hint of tension in Hanna's voice.

"Can you try to remember?" she goes on.

Karin rubs her forehead with her fingertips, as if she is trying to conjure up the image in her mind's eye.

"I think . . . he laid her down in the snow in front of the house."

"And then?"

"And then he walked away."

"So he just left her there? Do you remember if he did anything else to her body or her clothing?"

"No." Karin pauses briefly, gives the matter more thought. "It all happened so fast. He just put her down in the snow and left her there."

Daniel is beginning to understand what Hanna is doing. She is allowing Karin to entangle herself, enticing her to add more and more details about something that never happened.

Because Karin did not see a man placing Filippa's body in the snow in front of the house. It didn't happen, and the camera footage provides solid evidence of that.

Karin is lying to them.

119

When Karin reproached her husband for criticizing the neighbors in front of the police, it struck a false note to Hanna's ears. She noticed how surprised Åke was, as if he suddenly didn't recognize his wife.

That was when she decided to ask some control questions.

By this stage Karin has tied herself in knots.

"Are you sure you wouldn't like a freshly brewed cup of coffee? Or maybe a glass of water?" she offers.

"I'm fine, thanks."

Hanna pretends to study her notes to give herself some extra time. She needs to think. Choose her route.

Karin is lying, that's obvious. But why? Is this about protecting her son?

Or maybe her husband?

Could one of the men in the family be involved in Filippa's murder, since Karin has come up with this story?

But then surely Åke wouldn't openly show his contempt for the neighbors in front of the two detectives. Nobody can be that dumb. It would be tantamount to self-harm.

Unless he's doing it for that very reason.

To make it appear even more unlikely that he could be guilty.

Or maybe it's about Peter, their son.

There are more and more question marks. Hanna would like to speak to Daniel alone. She can't make sense of Karin's statement.

Åke is growing impatient. He has finished his coffee and pushes the cup away.

"Was there anything else, or are we done here? I don't want to be rude, but I need a shower after skiing."

Hanna isn't usually unsure of which way to go in an interview situation, but today she is finding it hard to make up her mind.

How should they deal with Karin's lies?

Is it better to put their cards on the table, tell her they know her story is pure invention, or should they continue to let her fantasize even more?

Suddenly she knows exactly what to do. This can't be resolved in the Carlsson family kitchen.

They need to carry out a formal interview at the police station.

120

Daniel waits for Hanna to continue her questioning. He can see that she is unsure of how to proceed with Karin.

He too is taken aback by the woman's lies. The more she talks, the stranger it gets.

Hanna closes her notebook.

"I'd like you to accompany us to the station," she says to Karin. "There are a number of points in your statement that we need to check."

Karin's expression changes from friendly and cooperative to strained.

"I'm sure we can clear this up right now." She licks her lips nervously. "What do you want to know?"

"It would be better to go through it at the station," Hanna says firmly.

"I've told you everything I saw that night." Karin turns to her husband with a pleading look.

"I don't understand," he says. "Why do you want to take my wife to the station?"

"It's just routine," Hanna assures him. She does her best to sound calming, but it has the opposite effect. Åke flares up.

"You have no right to treat us this way! We're not criminals, like those kids next door! Who do you think we are?"

"We absolutely can ask you to accompany us to the station," Daniel says quickly to back up Hanna.

She seems to appreciate his support, but Daniel has had enough of this nonsense too. They have to find out what is behind Karin's peculiar story.

"My colleague is absolutely right. We need to clarify a few details in Karin's statement, which is why it would be better for your wife to come with us."

Karin leaps to her feet and accidentally knocks over her coffee. It trickles across the table and drips onto the floor. "I haven't done anything!"

"We're not saying you have," Hanna reassures her. "We just want to continue this interview at the station."

"What are you accusing my wife of? How dare you!" Åke is shouting now.

The atmosphere has changed in seconds. Daniel realizes they are in danger of losing control of the situation.

"You can't force me!" Karin's voice is loud and shrill.

Åke is on his feet now. He is a powerful man with broad shoulders; his flushed cheeks are quivering with agitation as he grips the edge of the table.

He dominates the room.

"You are not taking my wife!"

Daniel stands up too. "Don't do anything stupid, Åke."

"I'm warning you—my wife stays here!"

"We just need to talk to Karin at the station," Hanna says calmly. "That's all it is."

Daniel's mouth has gone dry. He takes out his phone in case they have to call for backup. Hanna has also stood up. She is standing with her feet apart, ready, as if she thinks Åke might attack them.

His fists are clenched, and Daniel can see that he is close to losing it. He is so tense that his muscles are trembling, and it looks as if a blood vessel in one cheek might burst at any moment.

The adrenaline is pumping through Daniel's body too. All he can focus on is the fierce expression on Åke's face, the unexpected and out-of-control aggression coming from the older man.

The rage.

He switched with no warning. How could it happen so fast?

Daniel places a hand on his gun. Why didn't he foresee the risk? If Åke attacks, anything could happen.

They stare at each other as the seconds tick by. Daniel can hear his pulse pounding in his ears, louder and louder.

And then it as if Åke pulls himself together. He sinks down on his chair and takes several deep breaths. Gives Hanna and Daniel a shaky smile.

"Sorry," he says. "I didn't mean any harm. I didn't intend to lose my temper." He blinks a few times. The clenched fists are gone, his hands are resting loosely on his lap. He sounds a lot more composed, and Daniel is relieved that the explosive atmosphere has disappeared.

"It's fine," he says. "You were caught unawares. These things happen."

He tries to read Åke's expression, work out what he's thinking and feeling. Was his reaction a reasonable reflexive response to his wife's plea for help, or is he involved in Filippa's murder?

Karin's irrational behavior suggests that this might be the case—why else would she have given a false statement?

And Åke's aggression just now shocked Daniel; suddenly the seventy-year-old showed a frightening dark side that hadn't been in evidence before. Daniel is painfully aware that Filippa wouldn't have had a chance against Åke if he had confronted her in the same angry state of mind.

He gazes at the man for a moment, then decides it would be best to take both husband and wife to the station. After this unpleasant scene they need the chance to question them in peace and quiet, separately, without worrying about their reaction to each other's testimony.

He looks around for Karin, and realizes she is no longer in the room. "Where's your wife gone?"

At that moment Hanna yells, "She's out there!"

Through the kitchen window Daniel sees that Karin is behind the wheel of the family's white Volvo. Before their very eyes she floors the gas pedal, and the car shoots toward the road, traveling way too fast.

Shit. They have made a serious error of judgment.

"She's leaving!" he shouts, and runs toward the front door.

121

Hanna screeches away from the drive as fast as she dares. She continues along Sadelvägen, which leads out of the area. Karin can't have taken any other route. The big question is which way she went after that—south toward the E14 or north along Fröåvägen toward Kallsjön.

They are approaching the junction and have to make a decision.

"Fröåvägen or the E14?" she asks Daniel.

He is on the phone, mobilizing patrol cars to look for Karin Carlsson, providing the registration number and her description.

When he doesn't answer, Hanna opts for left. Fröåvägen it is. She is taking a chance on the idea that Karin didn't dare risk the E14, where it is easier to put up roadblocks. She might have thought that if she went in the other direction, it would be possible to get away using minor roads.

Hanna is driving on hard-packed snow. The surface isn't slippery, but the route is narrow and winding. In some places it is only wide enough for one car. Hanna isn't too bothered about the forty-five-mile-per-hour speed limit, but she doesn't want to lose control and end up in the ditch or in a snowdrift.

They drive past Fröå mine without seeing any sign of the white Volvo. At each side road they pass, Hanna tries to spot if there are any fresh tire tracks, which might indicate that Karin has left the main road. But there is nothing, only depressing whiteness.

The landscape swishes by, the snow-clad fir trees almost blending into one another. The bright sunshine from earlier in the day has been replaced by gray afternoon clouds, giving the light a misty quality and making Hanna screw up her eyes to see properly.

Daniel has finished making his calls and is leaning forward, looking out for the Volvo with intense concentration.

"Do you think we've lost her?" he asks after a couple of miles.

"I don't know."

Soon they will reach the lake—Kallsjön—and the bay known as Grundviken. At that point they will come to another crossroads, a crucial choice if they are going to have any chance of catching up with Karin. It is impossible to guess where she has gone. There are countless different ways she could have chosen.

Maybe she is trying to flee to Norway?

"I can't believe she got away right in front of our eyes," Daniel mutters.

Hanna has no time for that kind of self-reproach. She has her hands full keeping the car steady. A couple of years ago she was involved in a serious car accident, when she was run off the road between Järpen and Åre, and almost died. The fear when the car's wheels left the carriageway still haunts her nightmares.

The last thing she wants is for something like that to happen again.

A few drops of sweat trickle down her forehead; she is getting more stressed by the minute. She is clutching the steering wheel tightly with both hands.

A large tractor appears up ahead, and Hanna tries to assess the possibility of overtaking it without finishing up in the ditch.

The road is terribly narrow.

"Blue lights and siren," she says to Daniel. "Hopefully this guy will realize he needs to get out of the way."

Daniel clamps the equipment to the roof, and the noise fills the air above their heads.

But the tractor driver, surrounded by the throbbing of his engine, ignores them completely.

Get out of the fucking way!

Hanna grinds her teeth. She is going to have to slow down, or she will crash into the back of him.

Why isn't he reacting?

She is about to brake when the driver suddenly realizes he has a police car behind him. At last he pulls over to the right, and they are able to pass with inches to spare.

Hanna sends up a silent prayer that Karin will also have been held up by the tractor. If so, they might not be as far behind her as Hanna had feared, and they might still have a chance to pick her up before it's too late.

If she took this route. It was a fifty-fifty choice, and they might easily have made a mistake.

They are only a hundred yards or so from the lake when Daniel suddenly yells, "There she is!"

The white Volvo has just reached the junction. They see the rear lights disappear as Karin turns onto Husåvägen, heading west, possibly making for the Norwegian border.

"Try to catch up with her—we can't lose her!"

Hanna increases her speed as much as she dares; she screeches up to the T-junction and follows the Volvo, both hands gripping the steering wheel.

And then she sees the car again, but with its nose in the ditch. Karin must have skidded, driven too fast when she put her foot down after turning. The rear wheels are up in the air.

"We've got her!" Daniel shouts.

Hanna slows down, fighting not to lose control and suffer the same fate. She manages to pull up right behind the other vehicle. The driver's seat is empty, but the airbag has deployed. The engine is still running.

"Where is she?" Hanna wonders.

"She can't have gotten very far," Daniel replies.

Hanna jumps out and looks around. Where can Karin have gone?

"Over there," Daniel calls out, breaking into a run.

Ahead of them Karin is tottering out onto the ice.

122

The figure out on the frozen lake has a head start of a few hundred yards, but Daniel follows as fast as he dares on the uneven, snow-covered terrain.

Time slows down. All he can hear is his own ragged breathing. The air is incredibly cold, and it is hard to get enough oxygen when his lungs are screaming with the exertion.

Hanna is a short distance behind. She is fit, but not as fast as Daniel.

He is catching up with Karin.

She looked in good shape when he saw her in the kitchen, but there must be thirty years between them. She is also afraid and panic stricken, and probably dazed after the accident, given that the airbag had deployed.

It must have been a hell of an impact, and now it looks as if she is stumbling rather than running.

They are in one of the narrowest sections of the lake. Kallsjön is long, but not wide. Over on the other side, to the west, lies the village of Kall, where Raffe lives.

Maybe Karin is hoping to pick up another car there.

Suddenly she stops, as if she has realized that she is being followed. Then she changes direction and heads to the east.

This is not good. She is on her way to the small island of Storholmen, where the ice is notoriously unpredictable. Kallsjön is treacherous by nature; it may be one of Sweden's deepest lakes, but it has strong currents. It is also regulated. The water level is controlled by limiting the outflow, which affects the formation of the ice and its reliability. Daniel is well aware that the thickness can vary significantly, even when it looks fine.

Only a few years ago two snow scooters carrying four people went through the ice, in spite of low temperatures.

Karin is dangerously close to Storholmen now.

Daniel continues his pursuit while trying to keep an eye open for wet patches. This is a warning sign, an indication that the ice is thin just there. Going through is no joke, especially when it is this cold.

There are no more than a hundred yards between them at this stage.

Karin turns her head as she limps along. She keeps glancing over her shoulder, even though it slows her down.

The distance shrinks even more.

And then she is no longer there.

It happens so fast that Daniel doesn't even see it. One minute she is right there in front of him; the next she is gone.

He knows exactly what has happened.

The ice has broken beneath Karin's feet. She is in the water, and if they don't get her out very quickly, she will drown.

Daniel has never run faster.

He covers another fifty yards, then stops dead. Ahead of him the ice is wet and mushy instead of dry and hard.

It would be lethal to continue.

Karin must have been so busy looking back that she didn't see the danger until it was too late.

Daniel stares at the gaping hole. The water is dark and opaque, with broken shards of ice floating around.

Then something breaks the surface.

Karin, gasping for air and waving her arms in the air, desperately trying to grab onto the sharp edge of the ice.

"Help me!" her voice echoes out across the lake.

But the ice breaks under her scrabbling fingers.

123

How long do they have to get Karin out of the hole?

Minutes. If she suffers cold shock, even less time.

Daniel pulls off his belt and pushes it into his pocket to use as a rescue line. Then he lies down on his stomach and begins to wriggle closer, with the utmost caution.

Hanna has caught up and realizes what he is doing. She lies down too.

This is the only way to save Karin from certain death. The emergency services won't get here until it is too late.

The ice creaks beneath them, an unpleasant, ominous sound that makes Daniel shudder.

"Be careful," Hanna calls out from behind him. "You can't risk falling in too."

Daniel shuffles forward, a few inches at a time. Karin's cries are growing fainter. She is trying to heave her upper body onto the ice, but keeps slipping back as it breaks.

Daniel can hear distant voices from the shore, other people have seen the drama playing out on the lake. But it will be over before they can help.

They don't have many minutes left if Karin is to survive.

"Take my belt," Hanna shouts. She throws it forward and he catches it. Supporting himself on his elbows, he ties the two belts together to form one longer line. It still measures no more than just over six feet.

It's not enough.

Daniel shrugs off his jacket and ties one sleeve around a belt buckle. That gives him an extra four to five feet.

Please let that be enough.

The cold snatches his breath away as he resumes his crawl, with only a sweater between his skin and the ice and snow.

He is so close that he can see the muscles twitching in Karin's terrified face.

Only ten yards to go.

"Keep fighting," he shouts. "We're nearly there!"

"I can't," she gasps, her voice weak and failing.

"You have to!"

The ice creaks again, and Daniel stiffens. He daren't move.

How far away is he now?

Will the improvised rescue line reach?

Another creak. Waiting is not an option. He hurls the line in Karin's direction. She holds herself up with her left hand and tries to catch it, but it is too short and lands several feet away from her.

She looks as if she is on the point of giving up. Her strength is fading; her lips are blue.

If she sinks back beneath the surface, she will die.

"Take my jacket," Hanna gasps.

Daniel ties it to the sleeve of his own jacket. His fingers are clumsy with the cold, but at last he manages it, and their makeshift rope is a few feet longer.

He edges forward a few inches. *Please let it work this time.*

It has to.

"Here goes!" he shouts.

"Karin!" Hanna yells. "Throw yourself forward as far as you can, and you'll catch it."

It flies through the air. Daniel hardly dares look in case it is still too short, but as it comes toward her, Karin manages to heave herself over the edge just a tiny bit.

She stretches her arm, her fingers reach out, and against all odds she manages to grab the belt that forms the first section of the line.

She's got it!

"Hold on as tightly as you can!" Daniel encourages her.

"I'll crawl backward; then you can follow me," Hanna says.

"Just be careful." All Daniel's attention is focused on Karin's ashen face. "We can't lose her again."

Hanna grabs onto his legs as she begins to shuffle away from the hole. At the same time Daniel pulls on the line to haul Karin out.

Slowly, slowly her chest appears as she tries to help. For a second it looks as if the ice is going to break, but then Karin manages to heave herself a little farther. She kicks out with her legs—at last she is out of the water.

"No violent movements," Daniel says to Hanna over his shoulder. "We have to get away from the thin part before we're safe."

He is so cold his whole body is shaking, but there is nothing to be done about that.

They wriggle back ten yards from the hole, then twenty, at a snail's pace. Daniel's arms are aching with the strain. It is hard work both crawling and taking Karin along with him, especially as her strength is almost gone. She can barely move; he is virtually dragging her across the ice.

It is harder moving backward than forward, but at least the ice isn't creaking anymore.

Soon they will be safe.

Out of the corner of his eye, he sees several scooters speeding across the ice from Kall.

Help is on the way.

124

It is six o'clock in the evening before Daniel and Hanna can begin questioning Karin Carlsson.

Daniel has just sat down in the interview room. The entire afternoon was spent getting Karin examined by a doctor, and dealing with the formalities. At last they are able to hold an initial interrogation before Karin is taken to Östersund.

Daniel has no doubt that the idiotic prosecutor will agree to Karin's arrest. The Carlsson family house was searched a few hours ago, and they found Filippa's clothes, which Karin had hidden in a shed in the yard.

The evidence speaks for itself.

Karin looks exhausted and haggard as she enters the room, wearing sweatpants and a pullover that is too big for her.

"We need to talk to you about the murder of Filippa Smedsås," Hanna begins once the tape is running.

Karin's eyes are filled with despair.

"Tell us about the night Filippa died. You lied when you said you'd seen someone outside the Löwengrens' house, didn't you?"

Karin lets out a little gasp. "Yes, I did."

"What is your involvement in Filippa's death?" Daniel asks.

"It's all my fault." Karin hides her head in her hands, rocks back and forth on her chair. In the background the heater is humming away as usual. "But I didn't mean to kill her. It just . . . it all went wrong." Her voice is shaky.

Daniel is taken aback. Did he hear correctly? Has Karin just confessed to murdering Filippa?

Maybe it's the shock after almost drowning that has made her blurt out the truth. Or maybe she feels a strong need to ease her conscience.

"So in other words it was you who killed her?" he says, to avoid any misunderstandings. He looks at her closely, and suddenly realizes why they mistook her for Pontus or William on the security camera footage. She is tall and slim, she must be around five foot eight. In a black, bulky jacket it wouldn't be hard to mix her up with one of the boys.

Karin nods.

"You need to answer out loud for the tape," Hanna says.

"Yes."

"Why did you do that?" Daniel asks.

"I wanted to . . . teach her a lesson."

Something sad yet defiant flits across her face. She keeps chewing at a finger, so intensely that it begins to bleed. Daniel can see that the cuticle is ragged and torn. When they were sitting in her kitchen she seemed calm and composed, but now they have a different person in front of them, a woman at breaking point.

"I saw the whole performance on Saturday," she continues in a shrill tone. "When Åke went over to ask them to turn down the music. The panorama window in their living room faces our kitchen. I saw him go in and try to talk some sense into them, but instead of listening, they behaved arrogantly, disrespectfully. That girl flaunted her naked breasts at him! She even tried to touch him between his legs, for God's sake!" Karin's eyes are burning, as if the scene is playing out in her mind. "She humiliated my husband in front of her friends. They were all laughing at him!"

Daniel is still having difficulty understanding what went on. "So what happened later that night? When Filippa died?"

It looks as if Karin can barely hold up her head; her chin is drooping toward her chest. Maybe the shame is catching up with her.

She is a murderer, whether she is prepared to admit it or not.

"Karin?" Hanna prompts her.

Reluctantly Karin continues her story.

"When I woke up during the night and went into the kitchen to get a glass of water, I saw someone lying in the snow in front of the house next door. I was worried because it was so cold; I pulled on a jacket and went out to see if they were okay."

"What happened then?"

Karin wraps both arms around her upper body. She suddenly looks very small, perched on the edge of the hard wooden chair.

"When I got closer I could see it was the same girl who had behaved so indecently toward Åke earlier on. I was furious, I lost control."

"You killed her?"

"It happened so fast, I barely knew what I was doing . . ." Karin rubs her forehead, her breathing is shallow. "I just bent over. I kind of covered her body and pressed her face down into the snow. I never intended for her to die; I just wanted to teach her a lesson. I pressed harder. But then . . ." Her expression is agonized. "Then she wasn't breathing anymore."

Hanna gazes at her in silence. "So what did you do next?"

"I panicked. When I realized she was dead, I mean. That was why I took off her clothes. I thought it would look as if she'd woken up in the middle of the night and staggered out into the snow and died by accident. Because she was drunk . . ." She breaks off, looks pleadingly at the two detectives. "No one else is involved, especially not my husband. Åke doesn't know anything about this; he has no idea what I've done."

Daniel finds this difficult to believe.

He still remembers Åke's angry outburst, the unexpected aggression. Åke is currently being questioned by Raffe and another colleague who has been brought in, but right now he must focus on Karin's account.

"Why did you lie to us about the events of Saturday night? You made up a whole tale about what you'd witnessed."

Karin's eyes are darting all over the place. "I thought it would divert any possible suspicions. If I said I'd seen someone carrying something heavy during the night, you'd think one of her friends was to blame for everything." She presses her palms to her cheeks, shakes her head. "I'm so sorry. I've felt really guilty about that, letting you accuse an innocent person. But I was desperate by that stage . . ." Her voice cracks; she is drowning in self-reproach. "It was a terrible thing to do, I know that."

Her eyes fill with tears, and they spill over, run down her cheeks, and drip from her chin, but she makes no attempt to wipe them away.

Her age shows clearly now in her lined, ashen face. Her sorrow and regret fill the room. She looks down at the table.

"I wish I was the one who died instead of that poor girl," she whispers.

THURSDAY

125

When Grip's face appears on the screen, Hanna, Daniel, and Raffe are gathered in the conference room. Anton has been given strict orders to stay at home for a week, or at least until after the weekend.

"Well done, you two." Grip is smiling at Hanna and Daniel. "Excellent work yesterday, both in solving the case and rescuing that woman when she fell through the ice."

Hanna finds it hard to return her boss's smile. It was a great relief when they managed to save Karin Carlsson, but the last few days have taken their toll. The tragic truth is hard to deal with, even for experienced officers.

"Who wants to start?" Grip asks, taking off her glasses.

Daniel waves a hand at Hanna. She looks at him. Then they start talking at the same time, and Hanna bursts out laughing, in spite of how low she was feeling a moment ago. Sometimes you have to laugh, even if you're at work and in the middle of a serious investigation.

It makes the weight on her chest ease a little.

"We have a confession from Karin Carlsson," Hanna begins. For such a complex case it became almost unbelievably simple once they understood who the perpetrator was.

Something of an anticlimax, really.

Hanna is still slightly bewildered by the speedy resolution. She had thought the investigation might drag on for months, and that they might never identify the killer. Who could have imagined that a woman of almost seventy was capable of murder?

"So why did she do it?" Grip asks. On the screen they can see that she is sitting in a conference room in Östersund, along with Carina and two other colleagues. "What was her motive for killing Filippa? They'd never even met, had they?"

"She describes it as a moment of madness," Daniel replies. "She wanted to punish Filippa for her behavior toward Karin's husband earlier that evening."

"What a tragic explanation," Grip says. "A young woman is dead just because she treated an older man disrespectfully."

Carina clears her throat. She is sitting opposite Grip, wearing a traditional Norwegian sweater that Hanna has seen before. It must be a favorite.

"Her defense lawyer is bound to claim that she wasn't in her right mind when she committed this crime," Carina says. "We're looking at a psychiatric assessment, if you ask me."

She is probably right, but Hanna is not in a position to judge whether that will be enough to explain away Karin's extraordinary actions. This case is already verging on the incomprehensible.

"And the husband?" Grip says.

Raffe dealt with Åke while Daniel and Hanna were interviewing Karin. Åke denies all knowledge of what had gone on, and Karin backs him up.

"He insists he had no idea what Karin had done. He says he was asleep all night and didn't notice when she left the house," Raffe reports back.

"And Karin is adamant that her husband knew nothing," Daniel adds. "She is taking all the blame."

Even when they pushed her, Karin kept repeating that Åke didn't know about her involvement in Filippa's death. She was the sole perpetrator.

It is impossible to ascertain whether she is lying for his sake, or telling the truth. For the moment they have to accept her version, especially as they have no forensic evidence linking Åke to the crime.

"Anyway, I'm very pleased that the case can be regarded as cleared up from our point of view—even though there's still a lot of work to do before our dear prosecutor will be satisfied." Grip winks at Daniel, and Hanna gets the feeling that she too was annoyed the other day when the two men clashed.

Although she gave nothing away at the time.

No doubt their boss is experienced enough not to show her displeasure openly in a situation like that, but Hanna appreciates the fact that she too dislikes callow prosecutors who try to teach the police how to do their job.

Grip pushes up the sleeves of her dark-blue sweater, which she is wearing over a smart white shirt. "So how are the young people doing?"

"They're going home this evening," Hanna replies. "Apart from Pontus—he's still in custody."

"The prosecutor is going to approve his arrest," Grip tells them. "I spoke to him just before this meeting."

This is hardly a surprise. Arson is a serious crime, and of course they have forensic evidence because Pontus was captured by the security cameras. And obviously he will be charged with assaulting a police officer.

Not to mention the attack on Emil.

"How is Anton, by the way?" Carina asks. "Has anyone spoken to him today?"

Hanna is thinking of going to see him this afternoon. She wants to know how he's feeling, and no doubt he will be interested to hear how the case has been resolved.

But first she is heading for Sadeln. The four friends need to know that Filippa's murderer has been found.

126

Daniel picks up his phone from the desk. He has agreed with Hanna that they will leave for Sadeln in fifteen minutes, but first he has to make a call.

To Ida.

Her waspish text message got right under his skin, but they can't keep quarreling about Alice and her schedule. Their daughter will soon be old enough to notice when they are mad at each other. Plus Ida really has stepped up this week, in a way that he probably has no right to expect after their separation. He can't blame her for the fact that his work sometimes takes up all of his time and energy.

He clicks on her number, unsure whether he hopes she will pick up or not.

She does. On the second ring.

"Hello?"

Her tone is wary—of course she can see it's him from the display.

"Hi." Daniel takes a deep breath. He has prepared a little speech, and he needs to get it off his chest.

"I just wanted to thank you for being so understanding this week," he begins quickly so that she can't interrupt. "It means a lot to me. I know you don't like it when the job takes over, but sometimes it's hard to avoid. And this case was really intense."

His words seem to take Ida by surprise; for a while all he can hear is her breathing.

"Hello?" he says when the silence goes on for too long.

"Sorry, I was just a bit . . . surprised."

"I meant what I said. Thank you for stepping up. You're a fantastic mom to our daughter. I'm so glad she has you when I . . . when things get crazy at work."

They chat for a little while, and the tone is a lot more friendly than in Ida's last message.

Someone in the background calls out to her. Daniel can't make out the words, but Ida giggles and says, "Sure, darling."

Gustav.

Daniel can't help feeling a stab of pain in his chest. Ida sounds so happy.

In love.

He shouldn't be resentful. It's great that Ida is in a good place in her life—she deserves it. It's better for Alice if her mom is happy and contented.

But it makes Daniel feel even more alone. He is a failure when it comes to love.

Ida has Gustav, and Hanna has Henry.

He should probably upload a profile on Tinder, like everyone else does these days, but to tell the truth he has no desire to start dating new women.

There is only one person he would want to be with.

And she is already taken.

127

Olivia has just finished packing the suitcase on the double bed in her room when there is a knock on the front door. She didn't have much to pack—most of her clothes were damaged by the fire and the smoke. She listens, hoping one of the boys will answer, but there is another knock, so she goes up the stairs and opens the door.

The two police officers—Hanna and Daniel—are standing there. Olivia immediately feels nervous. She doesn't trust them anymore. She couldn't believe it when William came back from the police station—how could they let him go after what had happened?

She tried several times to persuade Amir to contact the police and tell them what he had seen on Saturday, but Amir refused to betray William—as he saw it.

And then William simply showed up, as if everything were normal.

Olivia is counting the minutes until she can get out of here.

"Hi, Olivia," Hanna says. "Do you have time for a chat?"

Olivia steps back to let them in.

"Could you ask your friends to join us?" Daniel says. "We'd like to update you on where we are in our investigation. Quite a lot has happened over the past twenty-four hours."

Before long they are all sitting around the dining table: Olivia, Amir, William, and Emil.

Hanna begins by summarizing the events of the last couple of days. She informs the four friends that they have arrested a perpetrator who has confessed to murdering Filippa, and that it was Pontus who started the fire in the cabin. Daniel fills in the details and explains how the two crimes took place.

"So who killed Filippa?" Olivia asks.

"Unfortunately we can't tell you that at this stage," Daniel replies. "That information remains confidential until the prosecutor agrees that it can be released."

Olivia has never heard of such a thing. "But we have to know who it is! You can't do this to us! You can't tell us you've caught the murderer without giving us his name!"

Daniel holds up both hands. "It's a person who is outside your circle. Nothing to do with any of you, or anyone we think you've met."

"So why did he kill Filippa?"

"I'm afraid we can't answer that either."

Olivia feels dizzy. The last few days have been a nightmare. She has accused virtually everyone in the house of being responsible for Filippa's death. And Amir finally admitted what he thought he'd seen—William kneeling by her lifeless body.

And now it turns out they were both wrong. It was a completely different person, someone whose name they can't even be told.

She can't bear it.

"When the person in question is prosecuted, you'll find out who it is," Hanna explains. "Until then I'm afraid we can't reveal their identity."

William glares at them. He hasn't forgiven the police for the hours he spent in custody. Olivia knows he has spoken to his father several times since then; apparently herr Löwengren is intending to make a formal complaint about the way the police treated his son.

Although he deserved it, Olivia thinks. He lied about sleeping with Filippa.

She looks at him with distaste; she feels like spitting on him. She doesn't understand how he could do that to her, or to Filippa, who was presumably so drunk and high that she didn't know what she was doing.

William ought to be locked up too.

"What's going to happen to Pontus?" Emil asks.

Hanna's expression is grave. "He will be charged with arson and assaulting a police officer. He could have seriously injured our colleague, and you and Olivia could have died in the fire. There is also his attack on you."

Emil's hand flies up to his throat. He has wound a scarf around his neck, but it doesn't hide all the livid purple marks.

"What kind of punishment will he get?" Amir wonders. "Will he go to jail?"

This time it is Daniel who answers.

"More than likely. The minimum penalty for arson is two years, and assaulting a police officer can result in a fine or a maximum of two years in jail. Then, as we said, there's the violence against Emil. The court will probably take Pontus's age into account, and the fact that this is his first offense, but it doesn't look good."

Pontus is finished, Olivia thinks. He won't be able to complete his studies, and his life will never be the same again.

How is he going to move forward after this?

How are any of them going to do that?

Tears spring to her eyes. Emil puts his arm around her shoulders and draws her close, as if he understands what she is thinking. She can feel the warmth of his body through her top; she rests her head on his shoulder and closes her eyes.

Hanna pushes back her chair. "We'll leave you in peace. We just wanted to bring you up to date."

"You will all be called as witnesses when the cases come to trial, but it could take a while," Daniel says. "The law isn't known for its speed."

Emil gets to his feet too. "Thank you for coming. It feels better now we know . . ." He looks away and swallows. "Now we know you've caught Filippa's murderer."

Olivia couldn't agree more, and she is glad Emil has expressed their gratitude when no one else was able to. He is the one who behaves most like an adult; he has handled the situation better than the rest of them over the past few days.

Right now she just wants the two officers to leave so that she can be in peace with her grief over Filippa.

On the way out Hanna turns around. Her eyes meet Olivia's, and she jerks her head a fraction, as if she wants Olivia to go with her.

Olivia follows her into the hallway, and Hanna takes her aside.

"You've been very brave. I just want you to know that. This must have been a terrible experience. I hope you will find the support you need from your father and your friends—you can get through this."

"I'm just so sad," Olivia whispers.

"I know." Hanna's expression is full of sympathy. "You should really go and talk to a therapist when you're back home. Get some professional help."

She gently strokes Olivia's hair, almost as if she were her big sister. Hanna sounds calm and reassuring, which provides solace and makes Olivia feel a little better.

"Believe me," Hanna goes on. "I've seen girls in similar situations who have been exposed to dreadful, traumatic things. It's too much to carry on your own. No one should have to go through what has happened to you this week. You need help to process it all, and that will take time."

Olivia nods and manages a shaky smile. She tries to put into words the question that has been burning in her mind.

"What's going to happen to William? Shouldn't he be charged too? He exploited Filippa when she was drunk."

Hanna has just put on her jacket. The look she gives Olivia is filled with both frustration and empathy.

"You're absolutely right, and if it were my call, he would be charged. But it's never going to happen. There is no forensic evidence to prove it was an assault, and William insists it was consensual." She bends down and pulls on her boots. "It's not even one person's word against another's, because Filippa can't dispute William's version. From a legal point of view, he's untouchable."

Olivia thought that might be the case, but it still hurts to hear it.

Hanna reaches for the door handle, then turns back and gives Olivia a brief hug.

"You've got my phone number. Call me anytime. I mean it."

Olivia stays where she is after Hanna has gone. The detective's warmth and thoughtfulness bring tears to her eyes once more. She has tried to keep it together, but she misses Filippa so much. She is too tired to stay awake, but she can't sleep because of all the bad dreams.

She is also dreading the thought of returning to Uppsala, where Filippa's room will be empty.

She can't even bear to look at William.

All she wants is to go home.

To her dad.

128

The sound of the doorbell wakes Anton from his afternoon nap. He is more tired than he thought, and has had to reluctantly accept that he needs to take it easy for a few days.

It is almost five o'clock; he has slept longer than he'd intended.

He pads over to the door without bothering to put anything on his feet. Hanna is standing outside, clutching a bunch of gas station tulips. Admittedly they are wilting slightly, but Anton is touched by the gesture and the fact that she has taken the time to call by.

"Come in," he says, waving her into the hallway.

"How are you?" The warmth in Hanna's voice cheers him up.

"Let's go into the kitchen—would you like a coffee?"

"A quick cup. I won't stay long—I just wanted to check how you are, and let you know that we've arrested Filippa's killer."

While Anton arranges the flowers and makes coffee, Hanna fills him in on the latest events. The frantic chase after Karin Carlsson, the motive behind the murder, and Pontus's eventual confession to arson. When she has finished, she gazes searchingly at Anton.

"You look tired. Was this too much for you?"

He actually feels a little dizzy; he should probably go back to bed.

"I'm fine," he lies. "No problem."

Hanna clearly doesn't believe him. "It's time for me to leave anyway. Go and get some rest—I can see myself out."

Anton returns to the bedroom and sinks down onto the pillows. The doorbell rings again, before Hanna has left.

"I'll get it," she calls out from the hallway.

Then silence.

Hanna reappears, pokes her head around the door.

"I think your boyfriend is here," she says with a smile.

"My . . . boyfriend?" Anton sits up, resting his back against the headboard.

"Well, that was how he introduced himself." She gives him a conspiratorial wink. "He's pretty cute. You can tell me more when you're feeling better."

She disappears, and a second later Carl is standing in the doorway. Anton can't hide his surprise, he searches for something to say. But Carl simply walks over to the bed and perches on the edge.

He takes Anton's hand in his.

"I'm so sorry," he says, his voice thick with emotion. "I've been an idiot, behaved like a spoiled child."

Anton manages a weary smile. "I could say the same. About myself, I mean."

"It wasn't your fault, Anton. I was just so hurt on Saturday. It felt as if you couldn't stand up for me. Or us."

Anton shakes his head. That is true, unfortunately. He is about to tell Carl about the argument with his parents when Carl points to the dressing on his forehead.

"Is it very painful?"

"Not too bad."

Carl strokes Anton's cheek. "When your sister called and told me what had happened, I was so scared. The thought that I could have lost you was terrifying."

Anton is about to reassure Carl, play down his injury, when the full impact of his words hits home.

"Did you say my sister contacted you?"

"That's right—Karro."

Yesterday at the hospital he had told her about Carl. In a way it was a relief to be honest at last, to talk about his love for Carl to at least one member of the family. Karro had listened attentively, asked to see a photo, and said with a smile that Carl was very attractive. Anton had good taste. She hadn't uttered a single reproachful word about Anton's silence over all the years.

Or revealed that she'd already had her suspicions.

For once his chatty, slightly flaky sister had simply listened with empathy, provided loving support when he needed it the most.

But he could never have imagined that she would go so far as to get in touch with Carl.

"She was really nice," Carl continues. "She said we're very welcome to go along to her birthday party on Sunday."

Carl winks at him, and Anton remembers how their original quarrel began. The discussion about the birthday party and the fact that Anton wanted to go alone, so that he didn't have to open up to the family about his relationship with Carl.

Anton would love to carry on talking, but the tiredness is overwhelming, he can hardly keep his eyes open.

"I'm sorry, I think I need to sleep."

Carl walks around the bed and lies down on top of the covers. He shuffles closer to Anton and nuzzles the nape of his neck.

"Can I stay with you tonight?" he asks quietly.

There is nothing Anton would like more. "You don't even need to ask," he murmurs, and realizes that he is smiling.

Then he reaches for Carl's hand. Next time they walk through the town, he won't let it go.

129

"Daddy!"

Alice's cry of pure joy when she spots Daniel in the doorway at preschool sweeps away all the dark thoughts that have haunted him over the past few days.

She comes running toward him as fast as her little legs will carry her, and he scoops her up in his arms and whirls her around. Hugs her warm body tightly to his chest, inhales the smell of his beloved child.

One of the teachers smiles at him.

"She's been asking for you all day. Good to see you here."

Daniel isn't sure whether she's being straightforward or having a little dig at him. He's been invisible virtually all week, but to be honest he doesn't care. All he wants is to be with Alice, go home and have something to eat together, then put her to bed with a story. She will be with Ida this weekend, so he has her only until tomorrow afternoon. The fact that Ida took care of Alice while he was working doesn't mean that the schedule changes—she wants the weekend with her daughter.

And Daniel certainly isn't going to criticize her for that.

"What do you want for tea?" he asks Alice as he helps her into her pink snowsuit and her cute boots.

"Pizza!"

That means a margarita, her favorite. He usually saves that for Fridays, but this evening can be an exception.

He would have liked to go with Hanna to visit Anton, but then he wouldn't have made it to the preschool before it closed.

He's pleased he managed to sort things out with Ida. He is going to have to learn to live with the pain of having Alice for only half of the time, and he has to make the best of the situation. After today's conversation it feels as if he and Ida have cleared the air. And Karro has sent him the names of possible childminders; he will contact them this weekend. That will help too.

"Ready, sweetheart?"

He takes her hand in his. Reindeer is firmly clutched in her other hand. They set off toward the car. He just needs to swing by the ICA store to pick up a few bits and pieces before they go home.

He settles Alice in her child car seat and plants a kiss on her forehead.

At least tonight they are a little family, even if it consists of only two people and a cuddly toy.

130

On the way back from Anton's apartment, Hanna gets stuck in a line of traffic that begins by the VM8 lift. She is stuck there for quite some time before it eases, and it occurs to her that she might as well swing by the ICA store while she is on the road.

Both she and Morris are running out of food.

She turns off after the Q8 gas station and continues toward the parking garage at the train station. She can leave the car there and buy what she needs.

Anton and Carl! She can't help smiling.

She recognized Carl as soon as she opened the door. He was an important witness in a homicide investigation a couple of years ago. And now he and Anton are an item.

Hanna is pleased for her colleague. She has sometimes wondered why he never mentions a partner during their coffee breaks, why he has seemed so lonely when he's such a great person.

But Carl's appearance explains everything.

Good for you, Anton. He needs some love in his life.

Who doesn't?

As if by magic, her phone rings. Henry. Hanna feels an unexpected burst of happiness when she sees his name on the display. She has been so focused on the investigation recently, and now she longs to talk about anything but terrible crimes.

The stress over the media reports has eased—it faded away when the job took over. Suddenly the gossipy articles seemed so pathetic compared to what had happened to Filippa and the other young students in Sadeln.

She answers as she drives into the underground parking garage, looking for a space.

"Hi there!"

"Hi, darling."

Henry's voice is warm. They chat as she pays for her parking and takes the stairs up to ground level. A train from Stockholm has just arrived—probably the same one the four friends will catch to travel back to Uppsala.

Poor kids.

Hanna hopes that Olivia has a good network around her. She is going to need a great deal of support to work through the experiences of this week.

The boys too, especially Emil.

"Where are you, by the way?" Henry asks.

Hanna is heading for the ICA store with her phone pressed to her ear. The station is very busy; she has to dodge between tourists arriving for a skiing vacation and people taking the train back to the capital.

"I'm at the train station. I need to buy cat food for Morris and something for my dinner."

"What a coincidence."

"Sorry?"

"Turn around."

And there he is, holding a large bag from one of Stockholm's finest fish shops in the Östermalm food hall.

Hanna can't believe her eyes.

"What are you doing here?"

Henry looks mischievous. And very pleased with himself.

"I wanted to surprise you. As we had to interrupt our vacation. And maybe make up for you being hounded by all those annoying journalists. I read online that you'd caught the perpetrator and solved the case, so I thought you might have some time to spare for me at long last."

He opens his arms wide, and Hanna runs straight into them.

And spots Daniel approaching from the opposite direction, holding Alice by the hand.

For a couple of seconds they look straight at each other. In his eyes she sees the same yearning she has carried in her heart for so long. Then he turns his head away and picks up his daughter, as if he hasn't even noticed Hanna.

They disappear into the food store among the crowd of shoppers. Henry caresses her back; Daniel and Alice are gone before she has time to react.

She must have imagined that look.

Or did she?

ACKNOWLEDGMENTS

The fact that *Hidden in Lies* was written at all is something of a miracle. Or the result of blood, sweat, and tears. I had just made a start on the book when I broke my leg in what felt like a thousand places up on Åreskutan, and it turned into a very different winter, to say the least. At first I couldn't write at all, and then when I came home after weeks in hospital and was able to come off my strong painkillers, writing became a lifeline. The fact that I could still use my creative side—when so many other abilities had been taken from me—was a huge consolation and a way of coping with a long and difficult healing process.

As usual this book wouldn't have been nearly as good without help from many fantastic individuals who generously gave of their time and knowledge.

I would especially like to thank Dan Lang, a mountain guide and rescue worker in Åre, and my dear "youth readers": my son, Leo Sten, and Anna Lyrvall, who is like a second daughter to us. They both helped out with the concepts surrounding young people's partying, how they express themselves, and how they act when they are alone and within a group.

Many thanks to Detective Inspector Rolf Hansson, who has helped me with my manuscripts for many years, and to my dear friends Anette

Brifalk, Helen Duphorn, Madeleine Lyrvall, and Gunilla Petersson, all of whom read the text and commented during the writing process.

I am also deeply grateful to the following people whose time and expertise ensured that the finished novel is as good, correct, and true as possible:

- Eva Rudd, forensic pathologist, Swedish National Board of Forensic Medicine
- Detective Inspector Andreas Zehlander, squad commander Åre/Krokom
- Alf Lerner, former chief medical officer at Åre medical center
- Robin at Niehku Mountain Villa

If anyone thinks I have exaggerated the danger of skiing in the West Ravine, or the thinness of the ice on Kallsjön, I have done so for dramatic reasons. And I confess that the Årelagat restaurant (the one in the same building as the police station) didn't open until 2023, but I have included it anyway.

I accept full responsibility for any other errors.

As always, every new book is the result of teamwork. I would therefore like to thank my wonderful publisher, Ebba Östberg, and my development editor, John Häggblom, who also acted as editor when I really got stuck! John—you rescued me when I needed you most! Warm thanks also to the fantastic Yrsa Winbergh, who stepped in as editor during the final stages.

It is a constant privilege to work with the super-professional Sofia Heurlin and everyone else at Bokförlaget Forum, along with Elin Olsson and the brilliant PR gang at Micael Bindefeld AB.

Anna Frankl, you are a super-agent and wonderful in every way! Big thanks also to Joakim Hansson, Sara Tiala, and everyone else at Nordin Agency.

And finally—*Hidden in Lies* would never have been written without my beloved husband, Lennart, who was there for me 24-7 after my skiing accident. For many months he took on the role of nurse, head chef, chief shopper, cat litter tray emptier, and, not least, housekeeper, while I was confined to bed and barely able to get myself to the bathroom.

"For better or worse, darling," was the first thing he said to me when I was taken to the medical center in Åre by ambulance. "We can do this."

And we have, in spite of the trials and tribulations of last winter. After thirty-three years of marriage, I have never been more grateful that I share my life with him.

Lennart—this book is for you!

Åre, August 2023
Viveca Sten

ABOUT THE AUTHOR

Photo © 2023 Peter Knutson

Viveca Sten is the author of *Hidden in Snow*, *Hidden in Shadows*, *Hidden in Memories*, and *Hidden in Lies* in the Åre Murders series—which has been adapted into a runaway #1 hit series on Netflix—and *Buried in Secret*, *In Bad Company*, *In the Name of Truth*, *In the Shadow of Power*, *In Harm's Way*, *In the Heat of the Moment*, *Tonight You're Dead*, *Guiltless*, *Closed Circles*, and *Still Waters* in the #1 internationally bestselling Sandhamn Murders series. Her books have sold more than ten million copies, and the Sandhamn Murders series has been adapted into a Swedish-language TV series seen by an estimated one hundred million viewers around the world, in close to a hundred countries. Today, Viveca divides her time between Stockholm, Sandhamn, and Åre. For more information, visit www.vivecasten.com.

ABOUT THE TRANSLATOR

Marlaine Delargy lives in Shropshire in the United Kingdom. She studied Swedish and German at the University of Wales, Aberystwyth, and she taught German for almost twenty years. She has translated many novelists, including Kristina Ohlsson, Helene Tursten, John Ajvide Lindqvist, Therese Bohman, Theodor Kallifatides, Johan Theorin, with whom she won the Crime Writers' Association International Dagger in 2010, and Henning Mankell, with whom she won the Crime Writers' Association International Dagger in 2018. Marlaine has also translated nine books in Viveca Sten's Sandhamn Murders series, and *Hidden in Snow*, *Hidden in Shadows*, *Hidden in Memories*, and *Hidden in Lies* in Sten's Åre Murders series.